"It's one of the best I've read all year! I can't recommend it highly enough!"

"Murder, blackmail, and racial tension electrify the story."

"Holcombe has clearly done his research and it shows . . . a fun and classic murder mystery . . . a good story, full stop!"

"Excellent characters and plotting. Vivid scene descriptions transport you back to the roaring 20's."

"I read it in a matter of days. Even with the pauses to let scenes simmer."

"I could easily see this story turned into a Netflix miniseries. It has all the elements for amazing television."

"The grittiness, the ambience, the characters for that time. What a great read. I can't wait for *The Blind Tiger*!!

THE BLIND TIGER

THE 2ND HIDDEN GOTHAM NOVEL

CHRIS HOLCOMBE

BOOKS
LIKE US

Published by Books Like Us, LLC

90 State Street, Suite 700, Office 40, Albany, New York, 12207

"Molly Malone," Irish Traditional.

"Cecilia," words by Herman Ruby, music by Dave Dreyer, © 1925 Published by Irving Berlin Music. Public domain.

"Don't Wake Me Up [Let Me Dream]," words by L. Wolfe Gilbert, music by Mable Wayne and Abel Baer, © 1925 Published by Leo Feist, Inc. Public domain.

"Just A Little Drink," words and music by Byron Gay, © 1925 Published by Villa Moret. Public domain.

Published in the United States of America

ISBN: 978-1736445808

ALSO BY CHRIS HOLCOMBE

THE HIDDEN GOTHAM SERIES:

The Double Vice (2021)
The Blind Tiger (2022)
Untitled Book 3 (coming 2023)

For the badass women who never cease to amaze me:

Claire, April, and Sonoko

One simply didn't wear his day suit after the sun went down, but a man waving a gun would change the plans of even the most stubborn stylish gent.

"He can just ask to see me, you know," Dash Parker said. "No need for the entourage and the private chauffeur."

The motorcar bounced across the intersection, rattling his trim, six-foot frame against the ceiling. He rubbed the top of his head, simultaneously patting down his misbehaving brown hair.

The corpulent shape beside him rasped, "Where is the fun in that?"

In the darkness of the backseat, Dash saw the giant bald man smile.

He would be amused. This is the part of the job he enjoys.

He certainly enjoyed the first time Nicholas Fife sent for Dash. A faceless man lunging out of the shadows in front of Dash's building. The car sliding up behind him, the door opening seemingly by itself. The polite, but firm, request to get inside. When Dash did, shaking as he went, he saw Lowell Henley, Fife's lead torpedo, in the backseat with that same closed-mouth grin, that same raspy breath.

Now here they were again, sitting in a five-passenger luxury sedan while a nameless driver roared through the grid of Manhattan. The streetlights whipped by, their balls of yellow blurring and stretching into comet streaks.

If only Fife would come around once every hundred years.

"I'm not a toy he can toss around for his amusement," Dash said.

Lowell turned his head, his eyes glassy and black. "You'll be whatever he wants you to be." He faced the front again. "He'll like that suit though. You'll have to make another just for him."

Dash looked down at the Banff-blue pinstripe fabric that set his hazel eyes aflame. The crisp white shirt underneath allowed the bright red tie to flare like a firework. The topper, the gray felt Homburg, he held between his hands. He mentally accepted the compliment, but he longed for his usual tuxedo. After all, it was 1926, and the city was popping like a champagne cork at an Astor wedding. Even if he'd just bathed and shaved, at least then it would *feel* like he was going to a party instead of to . . . wherever he was actually going. Which, he sincerely hoped, wasn't to his death.

We had to know. Fife has to understand that, doesn't he?

Dash said, "You know I don't make suits, Lowell."

It was the honest-to-God truth. Though Dash owned Hartford & Sons Tailor, he was not gifted with needle and thread. Quite the opposite. But that wasn't why the Greenwich Village men visited his shop on West Fourth Street. It was the secret club called Pinstripes, hidden behind the changing room mirror, that brought them in droves.

Lowell kept his face forward. "You took his measurements."

"That's the one part of the job I *can* do. My club's doorman did the rest."

"I'm told you took great care with his measurements. In fact, he said his trousers were fitted down to the last inch. In all the right places."

The driver of the car flashed a look over his shoulder and smirked.

Dash read his mind.

Well, Dash had been called worse, especially by the anti-vice nannies clucking around the city. They were starting to work with the police, of all things, engineering stings and traps to catch men like Dash. And for what? They couldn't stop so-called "degenerates" from seeking each other out any more than they'd been able to stop men from seeking out a drink.

"Turn here," Lowell said to the driver.

The motorcar squealed around a corner, tossing Dash against Lowell. The bald man growled and shoved him back across the seat. The car shuddered with a large bounce as it began climbing upward. Dash looked out the window and saw they were on the Queensboro Bridge.

Just as he suspected.

He was being driven to Fife's Queens warehouse, where there were crates stacked upon crates of re-distilled liquor to be sold to the thousands of illegal speaks and clubs throughout the city. Even Pinstripes received a few.

Dash adjusted his tie. "Does Fife want to talk about her?"

Lowell took a raspy breath. "He didn't say, and I don't ask."

"I'm sure he appreciates your discretion."

Lowell didn't take the bait on that one, so Dash sat back and looked out the side window. The bright lights of Manhattan had been replaced by the inky void of the East River.

How many secrets does this river hold? Dash wondered.

And then, a terrifying thought: *Will I be one of them tonight?*

It wasn't outside the realm of possibility, given what he and Fife shared. Cold sweat flashed across his palms. Fife's world thrived on secrecy, as did his. Yet his impetuous decision in the dead of night had blown that secrecy sky-high with big, bold newspaper headlines and column after column of newshawks ruminating, insinuating, and, in some cases, flat-out lying. Given who she was, though, how could they have possibly avoided the press frenzy? It was inevitable! And as much as Fife would dislike it, both he and Dash needed her to know what really happened. Their customers' lives depended on it.

The motorcar landed on the other side of the bridge with a thud. The driver careened around the sharp curves. Dash braced himself by placing his hand on the ceiling. Soon they pulled up to a nondescript riverfront warehouse.

Lowell exited the luxury car, assuming Dash would follow. As he stepped outside, placing the Homburg on his head, Dash's nose was overtaken by the smell of pungent salt and sour decay. The East River in all her glory. He looked up at the warehouse expecting to see the familiar sign of Fife's cover business, which said: QUEENS FURNITURE, PIECES FIT FOR ROYALTY!

Or at least it had.

Now it said DANZIGER PAPER.

Dash looked to the fleet of delivery trucks surrounding them with the new moniker and a new tagline to go along with it: *THE CLASSIEST OF SALUTATIONS WITH THE BEST OF REGARDS*. Even the trucks themselves had been repainted, a pale blue with the new text in a rosy pink.

Dash pointed to the fleet. "New business?" His voice was only slightly shaking.

"New business," Lowell echoed.

Dash arched an eyebrow, trying to be nonchalant. "Gotta stay up on the latest trends."

The driver said with a proud smile, "Danziger's the name of a girl I go with. She's thrilled."

"I bet."

"Sal," Lowell said, "keep your trap shut."

Sal, properly chastened, replied "Yes, sir."

"Stay here. You," Lowell pointed at Dash, "come with me."

Dash nodded. "Right."

He looked to Sal. The driver's face gave no indication whatsoever as to what was in store for him.

"Mr. Parker!"

Dash looked up to see Lowell halfway to the warehouse. The large man beckoned with his hand.

Even if you're scared out of your wits, his older brother Maximillian used to say, *never, ever let the other man see it.*

One of the few bits of familial advice Dash held onto years after the family abandoned him completely.

He took a deep breath, put on his bravest face, and hurried after Lowell.

They walked past the warehouse's main loading dock to a small side door embedded in the fading brick. A narrow hallway with jaundiced lighting welcomed them. Exposed pipes ran just above their heads, the joints emitting little droplets of water that tinkled into the puddles polka-dotting the concrete floor below. Damp mold filled the claustrophobic air, and Dash fought off a shudder as they walked down to the other end.

When they reached it, Lowell turned and knocked on a closed door. A muffled voice responded on the other side. Lowell nodded to himself once, then turned the knob and entered.

Dash hesitated for a moment, thinking: *Should I run? Give myself a fighting chance?*

A Dumb Dora idea. He was in the middle of nowhere. Where could he go for safety? And no matter how fast he ran, Lowell's bullets were undoubtedly faster.

The bald head peeked out from the room he just entered. "You coming?"

Dash saw in his eyes that the torpedo was hoping Dash would be resistant, be difficult, so he could engage in his well-practiced violence.

You're not getting that satisfaction tonight, you big lug.

Dash forced a smile. "On my way."

2

Dash followed Lowell into a small, lavishly decorated room that was more stylish than anything his own wealthy family had designed. A bright red Persian rug sprawled across the floor. Against the far wall to his left was a brown leather sofa bookended by round side tables with intricate ivory inlays. Bronze peacock lamps sat on top. The lamps were unlike anything Dash had ever seen. The base was the body of the bird, and the light bulbs illuminated the glass of the feathers. An appropriate choice since Fife was a man who liked to "peacock" in front of others.

"I see you are impressed," a voice said to Dash's right.

He turned.

Nicholas Fife—the man himself, the one the newspapers nicknamed "Slick Nick" for his ability to remain uncharged with any crime—was leaned back in a padded barber's chair. A white bib was tied around his neck while his jawline was being painted with white foam by a man Dash's age, twenty-six, maybe a little older. The barber had long, narrow dimples carved into his cheeks, short black hair, dark brows, and lips that always smiled, even when at rest.

The barber finished with the white foam, then went to a side table holding all of his shaving accoutrements. The barber traded the brush for the sharp metal razor, the blade glinting in the light provided by the peacocks.

In front of Dash and Lowell, the man gently leaned Fife's head back and with smooth short strokes, shaved the notorious gangster. The two men locked eyes as the blade carefully slid down both sides of the jawline. When the young man lifted Fife's chin to shave the neck, both of their lips parted, their breathing soft, like the moment before a kiss. An unspoken thought passed between the two men, and they chuckled in unison.

The barber was finishing off the last of Fife's neck when he paused near the chin. He said, "Should I?"

Fife twitched his lips. "Do it."

"Are you sure?"

"Oh, yes. Yes, I am."

The barber, with a flourish, flicked the blade upward, catching the last of the chin's whiskers. Fife cried out, causing Lowell to tense and step forward.

"Sir!"

The barber and Fife laughed. A joke from the twosome, as Dash saw no blood on Fife's chin. The barber went to the side table and grabbed a towel. He wiped away the last remnants of white foam and tossed the towel to the side. He removed the bib from around Fife's neck, and, with his bare hands, cupped Fife's face. His fingers slowly ran over the gangster's cheeks, chin, and neck. Not once did they break eye contact.

"You are silky smooth, sir," the barber said.

Fife reached up and grabbed the barber's right hand. He caressed the fingers one by one. "Thank you, Wim."

"Any time, sir," Wim replied.

Fife's mouth relaxed into a lazy grin. "I shall hold you to that."

"I should hope so."

A moment passed before Fife released Wim's hand. Wim disengaged the barber's chair by pulling a lever on the side, and Fife surged forward into an upright sitting position. Dash irrationally envied his black trousers, white silk shirt, and white waistcoat, thinking *at least he's dressed for the evening.*

He then mentally shook his head at himself.

Keep your wits about you so you can make it out of here alive.

Wim busied himself cleaning the blade.

The spell broken, Fife finally addressed Dash. "Mr. Parker! How good of you to come."

"Mr. Fife," Dash replied, taking off his Homburg and holding it with both hands. His voice was still shaky. He cleared his throat, hoping to steady the next words out of his mouth. "To what do I owe the pleasure?" That was better. More confident.

Fife put on a fake frown. "Why all business? Can't two distinguished gentlemen have an evening together? It is nighttime, after all. A time for pleasurable company."

He reached back and pinched Wim on the backside. Wim jumped once, then peered over his shoulder with a wolfish grin. The man's eyes flicked down, then up, taking in Fife with embarrassing detail, and the gangster, for his part, returned the scrutiny. The air hummed along with the electrical wires in the room. Even the hairs on the back of Dash's neck stood on end. What was going on here?

Wim went back to his chores, now drying the razor against the towel.

"They can," Dash belatedly answered. "It is rather late, and I should be returning to my club."

Fife, keeping his eyes on Wim, said, "Ah, yes, your club. The tiny room behind a tailor shop. Pinstripes, is it called?"

"Yes, sir."

"A clever name. Don't you find it clever, Wim?"

Wim turned his gaze to Dash. The young man had grey eyes, calm and still like the ocean just before dawn.

"Sounds ritzy," he said.

"Like the owner," Fife replied. "And I do so admire a well-put-together man, don't I, Wim?"

The dimpled smile again as he returned his gaze to Fife. "That you do, sir."

"Indeed," Fife purred. "Indeed, indeed, indeed. Thank you, Wim."

Wim nodded at the gangster. With the barber supplies in hand, he was about to walk out of the room when Fife touched his arm.

"Leave them."

A curious request, but Wim did as Fife asked. He then left the room with a bemused air, Fife's eyes following his every move.

With Wim gone, Fife finally turned his attention to Dash, showing off his, admittedly, very attractive features. Short brown hair in a slight wave. Gentle brows arching over warm brown eyes. A narrow nose leading down to full, pink lips. The skin of his face was impossibly smooth, like a baby's, yet he didn't appear young. Dash supposed Fife had seen and done too much to hold onto his youth.

Fife stood up from the chair, revealing his substantial height and presence. "Mr. Parker, you look a little haggard, if I may say so." He placed his hands on his hips. "What can we offer to revive you?"

Dash shrugged, trying to look unbothered by the situation. "A good drink, perhaps?"

"Ah. That is an excellent idea. Mr. Henley?"

Lowell snapped to attention. "Yes, sir?"

"Would you be so kind as to bring us some cocktails. And use—oh, what was your favorite liquor again? Oh yes, now I remember—use some gin, if you please."

Annoyance flashed across Lowell's face. He wasn't used to being the errand boy. Dash supposed men like Wim did these menial tasks.

The bald man nodded once. "Yes, sir." He gave Dash a menacing look and then also left the room.

Now Dash was alone with Fife—alone with no witnesses.

Fife sauntered towards him. "I hope the journey over was satisfactory?"

"It was fine, sir."

"And what did you think of the car? The Stutz? I myself find it *very* impressive."

"From what I could see in the dark, it is quite the creation."

Fife now stood directly in front of him. He placed his hands on Dash's shoulders, the palms wide and heavy. "The Vertical Eight engine has a nice roar to it, didn't you find? Such power vibrating the steering wheel. I'm envious of my drivers whose fingers get tickled by it."

Dash's mouth dried out. "It certainly moved fast." His voice was back to sounding cracked, dammit.

"But it isn't just powerful," Fife said. "I'd never be as coarse as that. It's also quite beautiful. That regal royal blue on the outside, the sophisticated pale-blue interior, and those teak-outlined windows? A genius touch." Fife's eyes flashed. "And my, my, my, look at *this!* Your suit complemented its color scheme perfectly!" A cheek-stretching grin. "Must be destiny."

He suddenly raised his hands to Dash's face, causing Dash to flinch, then stiffen. Fife cupped his cheeks as Wim had cupped Fife's a moment ago. Those opaque brown eyes stared into his and Dash didn't dare look away. Soft exhales brushed against his lips, breathy kisses of bourbon and cigarettes.

Fife shook his head. "No. No, no, no. That, Mr. Parker, will not do." He released Dash's face, turned, and walked towards the barber's chair.

"What won't do? The press coverage of the girl? I can explain—"

Fife raised a hand to cut him off. "It's that shadow. It must go." He gestured to the barber's chair. "Please. Sit."

Dash didn't comprehend the order. "I'm . . . sorry?"

Fife turned to face him again. "The shadow on your face. Whiskers. Can't have you looking like a roustabout, now, can we?"

Dash automatically rubbed his chin. Fife wasn't wrong; he was in dire need of some cleanup. But why should that matter now? "Unfortunately, your man intercepted me before I could have my bath and shave," Dash replied, then inanely added, "I usually go after I close up the shop, but tonight . . . well, you know why I never . . ."—he swallowed the lump in his throat—". . . why I never got to have them." He could kick himself. He needed to stop babbling and pull himself together.

Fife said, "Not to worry, my good man." He patted the cushion of the chair with a quick *whomp whomp.* "Sit. We shall get rid of them."

"Oh, that's not necessary."

Fife smiled. "Please."

"Truly. I wouldn't want to be a burden."

"Then consider it a gift from me to you."

Dash pointed to the door. "Perhaps we should wait—"

"*I* am waiting, and I don't mind telling you, Mr. Parker, I am *not* a patient man."

Dash looked from Fife's face to the side table holding the barber supplies. The bowls, the towel, the brush.

The razor.

Run! You have to run, Dash!

His voice shaky, he said, "Perhaps I should go—"

"Go where? The East River? There is nowhere to go, my dear boy. We have water to the west of us, unmanned factories to the east, and not a cab in sight for miles. You can continue to stall . . . or you can accept your gift like a gentleman."

Dash was trapped and both men knew it. If Dash tried to escape, he'd be caught, and the punishment would be far worse than whatever Fife had planned for him now. And he undoubtedly planned this. *Leave them,* he'd said to Wim, meaning the shaving instruments.

He's a peacock, Dash told himself. *This is nothing more than a show. It's all for show.*

But the razor!

It's a trick to scare you. It has *to be. It has to—*

"Mr. Parker? . . . Tick tock . . . "

Dash's legs shook as he took uncertain steps towards the barber's chair. Once there, he turned around. Fife grabbed the Homburg and tossed it to the leather sofa across from them. His powerful hands gripped Dash's lapels and he slipped off the coat. With a flick of the wrist, the coat joined the hat on the sofa. Then his hands found Dash's shoulders again and pushed them downward, forcing Dash into the barber's chair.

"There you go," Fife said, his voice jovial.

With a wrench of the lever, Dash felt himself go flying backward. His feet were now up high, his head down low. All he could see was the ceiling of the room, a mishmash of gray metal tubes going to places unknown.

Panicked, he glanced to the side. He saw Fife dipping the brush into a bowl of foam and turned towards him. Dash fought for control of his escalating breathing and lost. The gangster noticed Dash's rapidly rising and falling chest and smirked. He leaned Dash's head back, running the brush along the neck, jawline, chin, and cheeks. The foam was cool, causing a slight shiver.

Fife arched an eyebrow. "Don't you find one man shaving another to be one of the more gentlemanly things in the world?"

"I—I suppose."

Dash's eyes moved wildly from side to side, trying to see if Lowell, Wim, anyone else was there. Anyone who could help him.

Ah, but would they?

Fife finished painting with the foam and paused to admire his handiwork. "Good."

He dropped the bowl of foam onto the side table with a jolting *crack!* He picked up a towel and tucked it into the waistband of his trousers. Up came the razor. Like before, the blade caught the light from the peacock lamps, creating a blinding white flash.

Dash winced.

Fife leaned down. "This won't hurt . . . unless you want it to."

Dash watched warily as Fife gently pulled the skin of

his right cheek taunt and the blade went down his jawline in short, fast strokes. The room was unnervingly quiet, save for the buzz of the electrical wires and the scrapes of the blade. Fife's concentration on the task was absolute. There was a rhythm to his movements. A couple of slides of the razor. A wipe of the blade on the towel. Repeat.

Once the right cheek was done, he stepped around the chair to Dash's left and began the same process on the other cheek. Fingers pulling the skin taunt. The rapid-fire slides of the blade. Wipe. Repeat.

When Fife spoke, his voice was so soft, Dash almost didn't hear him. "I want you to know that what we have, Mr. Parker, is a partnership. And, considering recent events, a very accommodating one. Do you know how a partnership flourishes?"

The blade stopped. Fife wanted a response.

Dash guessed, "Trust?"

A shake of the gangster's head. "My dear, sweet, naive Dash. Trust is bought and sold with the capricious whims of emotions and dollars! A partnership built on trust is bound for disappointment and failure."

"If not trust, then what?"

"Balance," was the reply. "Yes, a successful partnership is a constant motion of give and take, an ebb and flow, if you will. Sometimes one partner gives; sometimes he receives. It's only when things become imbalanced do partnerships fail. Do you see?"

Dash nodded.

"Good! Now. You've been receiving my bottles of gin and beer. Oh, and whiskey. Can't forget your bartender's favorite sip." Fife leaned forward. "Mr. O'Shaughnessy is quite the specimen, isn't he?"

Joe.

He would be panicked right about now, frantically searching for Dash. And unfortunately for them both, Dash could never get a handle on the exact location of Fife's warehouse. It was always dark, the cars always fast, the routes never the same twice.

I'm sorry, Joe. I'm sorry—

Fife turned Dash's head to the side to get the hairs in that difficult crease behind the ear lobe and the abrupt end of the jaw. All Dash saw was the spotted brick of the wall.

"You've been receiving a lot from me, Mr. Parker," Fife said into Dash's ear. "And you haven't been giving lately. I'm not one of those men who only likes things one way. Sometimes, dearest Dash, I like to take as much as I receive." He turned Dash's head forward again and moved away from the chair. "So I'm afraid, Dash, we'll need to revisit the terms of our . . . agreement." Fife wiped the blade clean and stepped towards the chair, the razor held horizontally this time. "Raise your chin, please."

Dash gasped and tried to move away, to no avail. His feet couldn't get purchase on the metal rungs of the chair and his back, covered in sweat, stuck to the leather cushions.

"Mr. Parker."

I'm sorry, Joe.

"Mr. Parker!"

Dash's breathing was so shallow, he wondered if he was getting any air at all. The room seemed to pulsate in time with Dash's own rapid heartbeat. Was this it? Was Fife truly going to kill him? He looked up and locked eyes with the gangster, hoping Fife saw the pleading for forgiveness, for another chance.

Fife stared back, his eyes no longer their usual warm chocolate, but black coals seething with fire. "You've been taking so very much from me, and I'm starting to feel a little taken advantage of."

"W—w—what did I take?"

"Do you honestly not know? My power, of course. When you told my men to disobey my orders. *My* men, not yours."

Dash's mouth was so dry, he struggled to form his next words. "I—I only wanted—"

"My men already explained everything to me."

"It—it—it's just that one of your men had said—"

"At first, I was a little, oh what's the word? *Hurt* at your lack of faith. But then again, you are young, and you have much to learn about this world." Fife bent forward, his face now less than an inch away from Dash's. "I didn't want her face plastered all over the papers," he hissed. "Her name spoken across all the radios. You made her famous, Mr. Parker."

"She was already famous with the tabloids," Dash replied, his voice small and thin. "It wouldn't have mattered."

"It wouldn't have *mattered*?"

"At least this way, we have some answers."

Fife backed away. "How shall we solve this problem? Hmm? How shall we make this situation more—what was the word you used with my men that night?—*amenable?*"

Dash's eyes kept watch of the razor, still poised in Fife's steady hand. There weren't any good answers. Hell, there weren't any good lies. How the devil did he get into this position?

His sentimental nature, that's how.

Damn you, Rosalie. Of all the speaks in Manhattan you had to die in . . .

THREE DAYS EARLIER

3

EARLY MON MORNING, SEPT 13, 1926

Before Rosalie Frazier entered their lives, Dash and his club partners were going about their business as usual.

Or, in the case of Dash, trying to.

Sunday night had been a decent one. By Dash's calculations, Pinstripes had been roughly three-quarters full, with the bar buzzing but not overbearing, the dance floor energetic without being intimidating, and the band, in the words of Dash's friend, El Train, one of Harlem's famous nightclub performers, "kept it easy."

The remaining patrons, a group of bell bottoms on shore leave, remained mildly flirtatious in Monday's early morning hours, engaging in easy gossip rather than the lust-filled aggression of a Friday or Saturday night. Nothing about the evening suggested any danger was imminent.

Dash was sitting at the bar, dressed in his tuxedo, his foot tapping in time with the music. He sipped his usual Gin Rickey while chatting with Joe about the biggest headline of the day: the latest assassination attempt of Italy's Premier Benito Mussolini.

"Imagine seeing Mussolini's limousine coming down

the road," Dash said, pointing to the front page of the newspaper laid out on the bar in front of him. "Everyone is applauding and cheering the man—"

"As he's trained them to do," Joe quipped from behind the bar.

"—He's waving to his admirers through the glass. Suddenly a young man runs up to the motor car and throws a bomb at the window. The glass breaks but doesn't shatter. Instead of going inside the car, the bomb bounces back onto the street. The limousine driver surges forward *seconds* before it explodes." Dash shook his head. "Luck was not on the assassin's side."

Joe, clad in his usual open-collared white shirt with the sleeves rolled up, leaned forward with his elbows on the bar. "Lassie, yer the only man I know who brings a newspaper into a club."

Dash shrugged. "This is the first chance I've had to read it all day. Besides, I was too hungover this afternoon to function."

"Yer own fault. Ya never could handle whiskey like a good Irishman."

"At least I can handle the good Irishman." Dash wiggled his brows, earning a flash of Joe's emerald eyes.

"Not last night, ya couldn't."

The remark was made without malice, but regardless, Dash felt a flash of heat on his face. Embarrassed, he remembered throwing back several whiskeys and then trying, and failing spectacularly, to be intimate with Joe. It had been happening increasingly often ever since the harrowing events of a few weeks ago, when he found a dead body and then witnessed the shooting of a vicious blackmailer named Walter Müller. Both bullets destroyed the heads of the victims. The blood, the brain splatter, the bone fragments. No matter how hard Dash tried, he could still see those grotesque images in his mind's eye.

Will they ever go away?

Dash cleared his throat. "At any rate, I've only just now begun to feel jake again."

"Aye." Joe nodded towards the front page. "How many times have Mussolini's own people tried to kill him now?"

Grateful for the change of topic, Dash glanced down at the article. "This is the third attempt in the last year, fifth in total."

Joe scoffed, "If he were any more beloved, he'd have to ride around in an armored car."

"I'm surprised he doesn't already."

A voice called to them from the other end of the bar. Both Dash and Joe looked up. The group of bell bottoms wanted another round. Joe left to tend to them.

Dash watched as Joe listened to the giggling bunch, his hands on his hips squeezed into brown trousers, before he started mixing various liquors with limes, lemons, and sugar into two shakers. The light from the surrounding lamps caught his fiery red hair, which was tangled and long. Meaty arms bulged as he lifted the metal cylinders up to his square shoulders and shook, the ice rattling in double time to the rhythm of the music. Freckled fingers then deftly arranged the teacups on the bar and once the concoctions were poured, his wide hands passed them on to the sailors. He had to lean forward to collect their money, which, despite his brown suspenders, caused his shirt to gape open, revealing a hairy, freckled chest glistening with sweat.

Heat ignited at the base of Dash's spine and worked its way towards his core. He took a long sip of his Gin Rickey to cool himself down, thankful that not *all* of him was broken.

Now just hold onto that feeling for a little while longer.

Joe returned to Dash's place at the bar and tapped the newspaper. "Mussolini isn't just Italy's problem." He nodded to the other front-page story. "See this car that was bombed in Harlem's Little Italy yesterday? Betcha it's related to that mess over there."

"Retaliation for Benito?"

"What else could it be?"

Another voice cut in. "What on *earth* are you two hens cackling on about?"

Dash turned to see their roommate and the club's only waiter, Finn Francis. Tonight, his oval-shaped face sported pencil-thin eyebrows and turquoise painted eyelids that accentuated the wide blue eyes underneath. Orange rouge sunsetted on his cheeks, and an impish, upturned nose perched over a red-lipped mouth. He wore black pinstripe pants, matching suspenders, and no shirt, his narrow, hairless chest exposed for all the patrons to see.

The white flower he had pinned to his dark, short hair grazed Dash's shoulder as he walked up to the bar. He set a collection of teacups down in a heap of tinkles. Two of them rolled towards the edge, threatening to fall to the floor. Joe reached out quickly and grabbed them, shooting Finn an exasperated look.

Dash replied, "The latest assassination attempt on Mussolini. I'm wondering, Joe, if that man worked alone, or with some secret underground group—"

Finn interrupted him. "Who cares about that Italian thug when there are other events of the utmost importance."

Joe gathered up his patience as he placed Finn's discarded teacups into the soapy bin underneath the bar. "And those are . . . ?"

Finn smacked the top of the bar with his palm. "Mardi

Gras, you brute! It started tonight, and, by the grace of the goddesses, the Coney Island shore saw the sun for the first time in *weeks*."

"Finney, why do ya want to go all the way out to Coney to act a fool?"

Finn glanced at Dash. "How can you stand him? All work and no play."

Dash replied, "I'll allow the question."

Finn gasped. "Not you too! I didn't peg you for a flat tire."

"I'm not, but it's *Coney*. Takes half a day to get there and half a day to get back, and all for cheap carnival tricks and crowded beaches."

"And parades and confetti and bands. Then there's the amusements, the funhouses, the roller coasters, the shoot-the-*chutes*! I'll bet the shoreline is half a million strong tonight and I'm stuck here—" Finn gestured to the emptying club behind him. "—cleaning up after Sunday night drunks." He turned to Dash. "Can I have one night off this week? Just to experience one night of it. Pretty, pretty please?"

Joe shook his head. "Ya'd get yerself into too much trouble, Finney, me boy. It's best if ya stay right here so we can keep an eye on ya."

"Oh, stop acting like a Father Time."

"*Some*one's gotta be yer father ever since yers threw ya out."

Dash took a sip of his Rickey. "You know, I never did hear the full story on that one."

Now it was Finn's turn to exercise a little patience. "Because, dearie, it's dreadfully common and I—"

Dash and Joe joined Finn in saying, "—am anything but common."

"And anyway, it was *your* fault, dearest Joe."

Joe was incredulous. "How was it *my* fault ya ended up living with me for all of eternity?"

"If you hadn't had been so full of whiskey and called out '*Finney, what the hell is tha' bloody bell bottom doin' in yer bedroom window?*' my father would've *never* discovered my steady diet of seafood." Finn looked over to the bell bottoms at the other end of the bar and winked at one. "Speaking of which, hello, boys."

Joe sighed.

Dash replied, "Alright, Finn, you can have one night off this week. But not a Friday or Saturday," he amended quickly. "We need all the help we can get in here on those nights."

Finn reached up and gave Dash a wet, sloppy kiss on the cheek. "Praise be to Athena! Thank you, thank you." He then gave Joe a baleful glare. "At least *one* of you cares about me."

Joe rolled his eyes, but Dash knew that, despite the barbed words, Joe and Finn really were inseparable . . . in their own way.

Finn glanced around the room, taking stock. "Are we ready to close, you think, Bossman? There's no one left at my tables."

"I suppose," Dash replied. "We haven't had anyone wander in for the last hour or so."

"Just that stumbling girl in pink."

Joe grunted. "She was pretty far gone. Atty shouldn't have let her in." He meant Pinstripes's doorman, Atty Delucci, a short, balding Italian with the muscles of a boxer who sat out front in Hartford & Sons. He spent every evening doing the alterations from Dash's daytime measurements while also listening for the secret knock on the front door. Those who knew the syncopated rhythm were let inside. Those who didn't were told, *"We're closed."*

Finn's eyes narrowed. "Huh. I don't see her now. Come to think of it, I don't think I took her order."

"She went through me," Joe said. "Ordered two high-balls at once."

"In my defense, I had the most *demanding* little priss at table three wanting every little thing to be just so, or she'd kick up the biggest fuss. My word. She was lucky she was cute; otherwise, I'd have strangled the boy." He scanned the room again. "Well, Miss Pink isn't underneath any of the tables." A deep sigh. "Let me check the WC. If the goddesses would grant me one wish tonight, please let her not be pulling Boones in there. Last thing I need is to be scrubbing up vomit that went all over the place. Excuse me, dearies."

Finn walked to the back of the club. Dash watched as he knocked on the water closet door, which stood to the right of the three-man house band. Finn knocked again, pressed his ear to the door, then pushed it open and disappeared.

Dash turned his attention to the main room of the club. A narrow but comfortable space. The roughhewn bar stood near the secret entrance and was the first thing patrons saw upon entering. Stretching forward, the blue–painted walls surrounded six round tables and chairs, a set of three on each side to make room for the dance floor in the middle. A jazz trio played against the far wall, and for that, Dash defied convention—and city laws—by employing two black men and one white man. Scandalous and *extremely* illegal. So much so, he ended up paying a driver named Boris to have the mixed-race band picked up from East and West Harlem, respectively, and driven down to his club. It was an added expense, one that Joe balked at initially, but the music the threesome played was so good, Dash didn't care how many grains of sugar he had to spill to get them here.

Good jazz. Good gin. And good men. Dash had so much to be thankful for, so much worth living for. That alone should erase August's memories . . . shouldn't it?

The WC door opened again, and Finn stood in the doorway with a queer expression on his face. He gestured for Dash to come over. Dash sighed. Guess the goddesses didn't answer Finn's prayer.

Dash took one more sip of his drink, and then crossed the empty dance floor, pausing to give an appreciative nod to the band. Once he was standing in front of Finn, he said, "Yes?"

"Bossman, we have a problem." Finn's voice was decidedly serious.

Dash hadn't yet picked up on the change in tone and body language. "And that is?"

"Take a look."

Dash meant to humor his friend, so he stepped inside the cramped space, which held a tiny sink and the toilet. The pale light from the overhead bulb cast more shadows than illumination. Yet despite the poor lighting, details emerged in flashes, like when the tabloid photographers snapped their cameras at night.

Golden curls coiled in perfect ringlets.

Delicate rouge and ruby lips frozen in a grimace.

China-blue eyes wide and open, like a doll's, and just as unblinking.

A coldness settled in Dash's chest.

"Oh hell," he breathed.

4

The girl was seated on the toilet.

Her upper body was slumped over the sink, her face turned towards them in expectation. Her left arm had fallen into the sink's bowl, as if trying to brace herself, while her right arm hung lifelessly at her side, palm upturned, fingers slightly splayed.

The dress she wore was a pale pink, the pattern smooth and flawless save for one dollop of crimson on the collar that had dribbled from the corner of her mouth. It was then that Dash noticed the foul smell of vomit permeating the air. He tried to find evidence of the girl's sickness. Nothing. She must've managed to find the toilet.

You poor dear, he thought.

What struck him most about the room was the stillness, the silence. An indefinite pause. An unfinished thought. A word never to be said, not even "goodbye."

Why is Death following me?

Dash nodded to the girl's body. "Is she . . . ?" He knew the answer, but he was struggling to comprehend.

Finn closed the door, locking them in the cramped room. "I believe so. I felt for a pulse and didn't find one."

"How did she . . . ?"

"I don't know."

Dash looked around. There was no evidence as to how this presumably young, healthy girl died. And not to be uncaring or uncouth about it, he didn't much care. He had a corpse sitting in his highly illegal club with patrons still inside of it.

Finn, his voice soft, said, "I don't suppose we can call the police."

"Indeed not."

"What shall we do?"

Dash's eyes took in the slumped body of the young girl. She must've been seventeen or eighteen, nineteen at the most. A sorrow bubbled up inside of him. She was somebody's daughter, sister, friend. They'd discover her missing before too long, and then the excuses would come. She was probably out on a lark with friends, and she simply lost track of time. An impulsive trip upstate. A secret lover. Perhaps arrested in a raid. Inconsiderate and irritating, but as long as she returned, as long as she was safe and sound, then all would be forgiven. Their worst fears hadn't yet been confirmed . . . but they soon would be.

He shook his head. Now was not the time for being sentimental. Now was the time to act. And quickly. "Lock the door after I leave so nobody else comes in here."

Finn grabbed Dash's arm. "You're going to *leave* me with her?!"

"Just for a quick moment, Finn. I'll close out the club as fast as I can and send the band on their way."

Finn flicked concerned eyes back to the girl. "What happens after that?"

Excellent question.

Dash remembered a card he was given almost a month ago that had a telephone number he could "call at any time." He was told this by the only person in Manhattan who wouldn't lock them up for selling liquor, engaging in degeneracy, and possessing a corpse.

He extracted Finn's hand from his arm. "I need to find a telephone."

"Bloody hell," Joe muttered for the third time since he'd been told about their situation.

The three of them were inside Pinstripes, perched on barstools nursing drinks. They'd managed to clear out the club without incident. Dash then ran down to the Greenwich Village Inn just before it closed and talked his way into using their telephone for a private call. He first called the band's driver to take them home, thankful Boris wasn't out and about. The second call was to Nicholas Fife.

Joe swallowed a large mouthful of whiskey and licked his lips. "We're lucky none of our boys needed a piss. Otherwise they'd have found her before we did."

"Perhaps the goddesses were looking out for us after all," Dash mused, his finger tracing the lip of his gin-filled teacup.

A sad sigh from Finn. "That poor girl. Such a young thing. How could the gods have taken her?"

"Use yer head, Finney," Joe replied. "The gods take people all the time."

"Yes, but . . . it's all so *senseless*. I mean, what's the point of creating all of us if they're just going to snuff us out like candle flames?"

No one had an answer for that existential question. Heaven knew Dash asked it enough times when his younger sister Sarah died from the so-called "Spanish Flu." She would've been around the same age as this dead girl, had she lived. The blond hair in ringlets certainly was reminiscent of Sarah's golden curls. Would Sarah have become a flapper? Dash half-smiled at the thought, at the scandal it would've caused the Parker family. Then he remembered something odd about the girl in their water closet.

He frowned. "I don't like the blood coming from her mouth."

Finn shuddered. "It is grotesque."

"That and it points to her ingesting something poisonous."

Joe looked over at Dash with worried eyes. "Lassie, you think she drank something here that was bad? How can that be? Fife's supposed to test all his liquor with that chemist fella, what's-his-name?"

"Angelo Avogadro. Yes, I'm aware."

Joe's accent got thicker the more agitated he became. "Well, what's the bloody point of buyin' from Fife when we're rollin' the same dice as the rest o' the bleedin' city?"

Finn turned to Dash. "How could it have happened? You said his operation looked so careful and airtight."

"It is," Dash replied, defensiveness creeping into his voice. "Maybe something slipped through by accident. One of Fife's men picked up an untested crate by mistake and put it on the truck."

Joe's brow furrowed in panic. "And we just poisoned the entire neighborhood?! Mary Mother of Christ!"

Finn placed his hands over his ears. "I'm not hearing this."

Dash spoke with a calm he didn't feel. "Look, gents, we

don't know what happened. I don't even know how fast bad liquor works. She could have drunk it somewhere else and died here, but that's another problem for another day." He nodded his head towards the WC. "The first problem is, how do we get her out of here?"

Joe grunted. "Hopefully this Fife character has some ideas."

Finn pursed his lips. "This should be right up Slick Nick's alley. Rumor has it the man has made many a person disappear without a trace." He reached to take a large swig of his martini, eyed it with suspicion, and then pushed it away. "Did ol' Saint Nick say when he'd be arriving?"

Dash shook his head. "He won't be. One of his men is on his way. Oh god, I hope it's not Lowell. In any event, I told Atty what I was told: watch for a man who will stand on the sidewalk, hands clasped in front, not saying a word or knocking on our door."

"How will Atty know he ain't a cop?" Joe asked.

"He'll know."

"Just like he knew that girl was a dyin' drunk?"

"He says she got here by taxi, could do the secret knock, and could stumble through the mirror. We've had more zozzled men do less to get in here." Dash paused. "Atty did tell me one odd thing about her. As soon as he let her in the tailor shop, she tried to give him a small folded piece of paper and asked to see a hat."

Now it was Finn's turn to furrow his brow. "A hat? What on earth for?"

Dash shrugged. "Atty had no idea."

Joe asked, "What was on the paper?"

"He didn't open it, just handed it back to her."

"I'm seriously concerned about Atty's lack of curiosity," Finn said. "It's only slightly worse than his aim with that hideous pistol of his. Did we find out her name? I couldn't bear to look through her things, much less look at her."

Dash said he had. After closing the club, he returned to the WC and found her pink fringed purse lying at her feet. He opened it to find a red satin–lined interior filled with a round powder case, a tube of lipstick, a wad of dollar bills, an empty flask, and an identification card.

"Rosalie Frazier," he said. "Name doesn't mean anything to me. Joe, have you heard her name before? Around the neighborhood?"

Joe shook his head.

Finn sighed. "Once again, your ignorance astounds me. You two seriously have no idea who the Fraziers are?"

They earned yet another massive eye roll from the small man.

"Athena preserve me. The *Fra-ziers* are the most famous family in Manhattan right now."

A pit opened up in Dash's stomach. "Famous?"

This was the last thing they needed: a high-profile disappearance.

"Yes," Finn replied. "Their daughter is . . . was . . . a wild child. A woman after my own heart."

"I'm surprised you didn't recognize her."

"As I said, I couldn't bear to look at her. And anyhow, the ink on our papers doesn't produce the best photographs. Now that I've seen her in the flesh, those grainy pictures don't do any justice to her beauty."

Joe asked, "Why is she so famous, Finney?"

"Her father tried to get her to stop her flapper ways. Rosalie would not acquiesce. She said she wouldn't live the Victorian life and her father couldn't force her to. Then he took his own daughter to court. Can you imagine? The child you supposedly love unconditionally is dragged into

an open courtroom under the threat of being institu-
tionalized."

"Whatever fer?" Joe asked.

"She hung out with the 'Broadway crowd,' as the papers
put it. Her father Leonard Frazier was beside himself. *'My
daughter has been blinded by the white lights of Broadway
and led astray by the immorality that flourishes there.'* That's
a direct quote, dearies. It seems Miss Rosalie was staying
out until four or five in the morning every night, coming
home smelling of booze and men's cologne. Which, quite
frankly, sounds like a good time to me."

Joe was incensed. "Her father took her to court over
tha'?"

"It's surprising, really. From what the papers also
reported, Leonard was almost . . . *modern.* He had
supported the suffragists, champions artistic works from
Harlem, continues to debunk conspiracies about the Jewish
set. But then, he's so old-fashioned when it comes to drink."

Dash tapped the sides of his teacup with his fingernails.
"People are complicated, Finn."

"Her father and her aunt—Beverly S-something—tried
everything to persuade her. Increased her allowance, then
cut it. Demanded she stay home, then ordered her out of the
house. Once, Mr. Frazier tried to lock Rosalie inside their
mansion; supposedly Rosalie just climbed out the window
and escaped. Another time, Mr. Frazier tried locking
Rosalie *out*, thinking she'd learn her lesson if she spent a
cold night on the front stoop after stumbling home." Finn
shook his head. "It didn't work. Rosalie, with the strength of
the goddesses before her, simply smashed the glass window
of the front door, reached in, and unlocked it from the
inside." He clasped his hands over his heart. "What a
woman! Refusing to bend as her father tried to break her."

"How old is . . . was she?" Dash asked.

"By the time her father took her to court, Rosalie was nineteen years of age. An adult. And look at how they treated her! As if she had no mind of her own."

"That's how we've always treated women, unfortunately. And the court case? How did that come about?"

"Desperation. Her father and his attorney found some bluenose judge to take up the matter. They ordered Rosalie into court, threatening to institutionalize her for her irrational and so-called dangerous behavior. They would not stop unless she publicly recanted her way of life."

"What was her defense?"

"That she was nineteen and could do as she pleased."

Joe scoffed. "Bet that went over well with the judge."

"He was furious. He was reported as saying, *'young lady, you come from one of the best families in the city. Your mother, if she were alive today, would be ashamed of your foolish behavior.'*"

Dash smirked. It was similar language his father used when he found out about Dash's midnight activities. Were all men of a certain generation cut from the same cloth?

"What was her response to that?" he asked, knowing Finn knew the dialogue by heart after countless readings and re-readings of the trial proceedings.

"*'My behavior is my own as is my body—and my money.'*"

"Ah, now we get to the crux of the matter."

Joe grumbled, "Say again?"

"The wealthy always have a trust somewhere for their children. I'd wager Rosalie receives hers soon?"

Finn clicked his tongue in appreciation. "Nicely done. She was due to get a sizable sum, which her father worried she'd waste on liquor and men and whatever else her puckish heart desired."

"How much was the trust?"

"Ten million dollars."

Dash snapped his head to Finn. Though he had grown up with money, his jaw still dropped. There had been a trust for him, but it wasn't *that* much.

Joe swore under his breath. "That's a lot of bloody money."

"Enough to risk public embarrassment with a big trial," Dash said.

"Wha' th hell do the Fraziers do for a livin'?"

"Manufacture railroad cars, I believe," Finn replied. "And despite that sizable sum, Rosalie defied the judge and her father. She claimed he started this, so she would see it through."

"And did she?"

Finn's smile fell into a flat line. "No. As you may have already guessed, she folded. At first, she maintained she didn't care about her trust; she cared more about her freedom. She wasn't living at home during the trial, but with her Broadway friends. However, her father shrewdly closed her accounts, so Rosalie didn't have access to her usual supply of sugar. Rumor has it, she was forced to get a job selling hats, and we all know how well they pay women. She could barely afford that rat-infested Times Square hidey-hole she shared. Eventually, she went into court and renounced her ways. The old guard wins again."

Joe sent his friend a well-meaning smile. "Finney, me lad, rich men always win. The poor lass didn't have a prayer."

"She could've made a stand. After all, dearest Dash, *you* did."

Dash nodded. "Yes, well, I do not have my family trust. That was lost in the 'Great Defection.'"

"Ya were smart enough to sock some away," Joe said.

Dash held up a pointer finger. "That is true. Unlike poor Rosalie, I knew what would happen if my parents ever caught wind of . . . my night life. I simply planned ahead." He glanced back again at the WC. "Although my plan didn't include dealing with situations such as this." He paused a moment. "Finn, when was all this? The court case, the settlement?"

"Rosalie recanted just one week ago."

Damn. She would be fresh in the press's memory, and they would surely pounce upon the timing between her recanting and her death.

The secret door by the bar opened. The three men turned to see Atty standing in the doorway bathed in shadow.

"Boss, he's here."

5

The man didn't remove his hat.

The wide brim cast a shadow across his eyes. A set of irises glowing like pinpoints stared directly at Dash. The face of the man was slightly wrinkled but otherwise unweathered. He wore a black tuxedo as slick as a freshly shined limousine with a white waistcoat, shirt, and bow tie as bright as tire rims, encasing a body built for speed. The only hint of wreckage was the start of a scar, red and angry, at the center of his throat, where the shirt collar dipped down just low enough to expose it.

Those glowing pinpoint eyes never wavered as he spoke. "Mr. Dashiell Parker?" The voice was deep, no nonsense, the accent neutral.

"Yes?"

"You called about a shipment to pick up?"

Dash looked to Joe and Finn. "I believe we did."

"Did you or did you *not*?"

No nonsense, indeed.

Dash cleared his throat. "We did."

"Good. And where is the package?"

Dash nodded towards the WC. "This way."

He stood up from his barstool and walked across the club, aware of the hollow thuds their shoes made on the abandoned dance floor. He opened the door to the WC and gestured towards the inside.

"In there," he said.

Those glowing irises pierced Dash's skin again. "Nothing else in there but the package?"

"Just the toilet and sink. Your typical state-of-the-art water closet."

"I am not a man who likes to be amused, Mr. Parker."

"I can see that. No, sir. Just the package is in the room."

One more long look, then the man stepped into the WC. Standing behind him, Dash could make out dark hair underneath the black hat. The back of his neck was slightly pink, as if fresh from a barber's shave.

The man, whom Dash mentally named Pinpoint Eyes, asked, "Do you know her?"

Dash shook his head, then realized Pinpoint Eyes had his back to him and couldn't see the gesture. "We do not."

They stood still for a moment.

Afterwards, Pinpoint Eyes muttered to himself, "Another one."

Dash leaned forward with interest. "Excuse me?"

Pinpoint Eyes didn't answer him.

Dash tried again. "You mentioned *another one*. Has this happened before in one of Fife's speaks?"

The man turned to face him, those pinpoint eyes flaring in response. "I'm not here to bump my gums, mister, I'm here to get rid of your problem." He snapped his fingers.

Suddenly Dash became aware of another man who had entered his club. Now when the hell did *he* walk in? He, like Pinpoint Eyes, was also dressed in a slick black suit and kept his hat on. His eyes were black.

The second man pushed Dash out of the way and entered the WC along with Pinpoint Eyes. The two men lifted Rosalie's body, getting her upright, and began to maneuver her out of the cramped room.

Dash backed away, watching as the second man hooked his hands underneath Rosalie's arms and walked backward. As soon as Rosalie cleared the doorway, her body began to dip downward. Pinpoint Eyes then grabbed her feet and lifted. Now it looked like the two men were ambulance workers carrying a stretcher—only the stretcher, in this case, was a corpse.

Dash felt his mouth set in a line of distaste.

As they carried her through the main room of Pinstripes and towards the secret door, Dash saw a piece of paper flutter to the floor. Dash waited until the two men and Rosalie passed him before reaching down and palming it. It was folded, the edges torn, the paper cheap. He opened it, expecting a scrawled note, a reminder, a request, an address even.

A crude drawing of a teacup.

Just the outline of it in black ink. Dash's brow furrowed in confusion. What the devil was this? Was this what she tried to give Atty? But why say something about seeing a hat with a picture of a teacup? Poor girl. She truly was zozzled out of her mind.

He heard Pinpoint Eyes call to Atty to hold the secret door open. He refolded and pocketed the drawing and caught up with them.

They had to stand Rosalie upright again, what with the turn from the bar to the secret door too tight an angle to keep her horizontal. Much like they had in the water closet, they "walked" her through the doorway before flattening her out again.

She cleared the secret door held open dutifully by Atty, whose square face was pinched with worry. As Dash stepped through the doorway, he gave Atty a reassuring nod before entering the tailor shop. Atty had turned off all the lights, turning Fife's men and Rosalie into darkened shadows. They were almost at the front door when he called out to them. "You can't carry her like that."

Pinpoint Eyes dropped Rosalie's heels and stared at him. "What did you say?"

Dash cleared his nervous throat and repeated, "You can't carry her like that. Our neighbors are a curious bunch. They'll want to know tomorrow what happened to the poor girl that was carried out like a corpse."

"Tell them it's none of their business."

"Easy for youse to say," Atty said. "Youse don't have to keep up appearances; we do."

Dash nodded in agreement. "Our livelihood as well as our lives depend on it."

Pinpoint Eyes was clearly unimpressed with their plea.

"Alright then," Dash said, "how about Fife won't be able to get a cut of his money if the four of us are in jail for murder. Will that make you more amenable to our point of view?"

Pinpoint Eyes pursed his lips. "Then we'll carry her like she's passed out drunk, one of us on each side under her arms. If anyone sees, they'll think we're helping her home." He leered at Dash. "Will that be more *amenable?*"

"I—I think that should suffice, yes."

Pinpoint Eyes glared a moment longer at Dash before turning around. He and the second man arranged Rosalie as he described, one man under each of her arms. Her head lolled to the side, her joints loose and uncooperative in death.

Once they had her in position, Pinpoint Eyes growled, "One of you get the door!"

Dash hopped to and did as requested. He held up a finger. "One moment while I check the street."

He stepped around the grotesque threesome and out onto the sidewalk. The night air embraced him, causing a slight shiver. The days were still warm, carrying a few remnants of summer tempered by autumn's cool breezes, but at night, winter's promised chill slipped through the widening cracks between seasons. He glanced up and down West Fourth, checking the corners of Cornelia and Barrow. Empty. The silence was absolute. Not a car horn, a truck motor, a dropped garbage can lid, not even a yelling match between two neighbors to be heard. It was strange. Otherworldly. Manhattan was never this quiet. Certainly not the Village and all its rowdy bohemians.

Dash looked up. The sky was pitch-black, as were the windows of the surrounding buildings. He watched for signs of an insomniac: the orange glow of a cigarette end, the thin line of smoke lazily rising upwards, the shadow on a fire escape.

"Mr. Parker!" hissed Pinpoint Eyes.

Dash turned and nodded. "Coast is clear."

Stepping sideways, the second man walked out first, then Rosalie, then Pinpoint Eyes. Their movements were awkward and slow, reminding Dash of all the times he had helped drunks stumble out of here before. (When one was a speak owner, it came with the territory.) Fife's men clenched their jaws from the awkwardness of Rosalie's literal dead weight as they stumbled her forward.

"Where are you carrying her?" Dash asked.

Pinpoint Eyes, breathing heavily from the strain, said, "To Barrow. The truck is waiting there."

He and the second man began "walking" Rosalie westward. Dash watched after them. Two upright shadows holding up a sagging, bowing figure in between. The toes of Rosalie's shoes scraped against the sidewalk, sounding like chalk against a blackboard. Despite the difficulty of Rosalie's body, Fife's men were covering quite a bit of distance in a short time. They were almost at the corner of West Fourth and Barrow.

Atty came to the tailor shop door. "Boss? What about her family? You're not gonna let them toss her in the river like trash, are youse? Her family needs to know what happened to her, so they can grieve and honor her memory. Give her a proper burial."

The very thought had occurred to Dash as well, which complicated the situation immensely.

Dash replied, "I will do all that I can to ensure her family gets that chance."

He went after them.

Once he was in ear shot, he said, "Excuse me, sirs? One moment."

"We're not stopping!" whispered Pinpoint Eyes.

They were now crossing the street towards Barrow.

"May I ask where you're taking her?"

"The Waldorf Astoria. Where do you think?"

Dash looked up and saw one of Fife's trucks, the motor off, sitting in the dark next to his usual lunch and dinner spot, the place where he had also telephoned Fife, the Greenwich Village Inn. It was dark and locked up tight. They passed the cab of the truck, in which Dash saw the silhouette of another man in the driver's seat. The lookout.

"Keep moving," muttered Pinpoint Eyes, whether to the second man or to Dash was unclear.

"Please," Dash said. "Her family will never be at peace until they know what happened to her."

They carried Rosalie to the truck's rear. They set her down, Pinpoint Eyes holding onto her while the second man opened the back doors.

Pinpoint Eyes regarded Dash with irritation. "Excuse me, Mr. Parker, but we are trying to help you. The last thing *you* need is attention. A dead girl, doesn't matter who, is going to get attention. Tell me, do you want coppers sniffing around your club? Your partners? Your clientele?"

"No, but I—"

"Then you're going to let me do my *fucking* job. And you're going to keep your *fucking* mouth shut while I do my *fucking* job. Do you *fucking* understand me, you nosy, fairy *fuck*?"

The second man stepped up inside the hull of the truck and held out his hands. Pinpoint Eyes maneuvered Rosalie so the second man could grab her wrists. Pinpoint Eyes then stooped down and picked up her ankles. While the second man pulled, Pinpoint Eyes lifted. Rosalie rose upwards and slid inside.

Dash looked up and was surprised by what he saw. "I'll be damned," he breathed.

The truck's hull held furniture. Actual furniture. And a cursory glance told him the quality was of a higher grade than Pinstripes's own table and chairs.

Dash was absurdly enamored with it all. "Are these for sale? Because I desperately need some new tables. Mine are too wobbly for words."

Nerves, he thought, *it's gotta be the nerves.*

"Shut up, ya clown," Pinpoint Eyes replied.

Rosalie now inside the hull, the second man dragged her across the truck bed and nestled her in between a chest of drawers and a bed's detached headboard.

Pinpoint Eyes stepped away while the second man exited the hull. They both shut the doors, secured the latch, and went to the cab.

Dash trailed after them. "Don't you want to know what happened to her?"

"No."

All three were beside the truck's cab now.

Dash spoke fast. "It's happened before, right? You said so yourself. Wouldn't Fife like to know what's happening in his speaks?"

The second man opened the passenger door and climbed inside the cab, sliding across the seat and sitting next to the driver.

Pinpoint Eyes said, "You worry less about Fife and worry more about you if you don't shut your mouth."

"Speaking of mouths, there was blood in hers."

"I care?"

"She ingested something poisonous."

"A lot of that in the city. So what?"

Pinpoint Eyes pulled himself up into the cab, slamming the door in the process.

The driver cranked the ignition until the engine caught. Dash felt the vibration in his chest, despite the fact he wasn't inside the vehicle.

"So *what?*" Dash said, his voice and temper rising. "If Fife is serving up bad booze, then *this* nosy, fairy fuck would like to know. Because if he is, then he and I have a big *fucking* problem, because I pay him too much *fucking* money to put up with girls *fucking* dying in my club. You *fucking* understand me, you two-bit hoodlum *fuck?*"

The conversation stopped cold.

The rattle and hum of the truck's engine filled the silence.

Dash and Pinpoint locked eyes, Dash not once looking away. The obscenities felt strange in his mouth—he never had much use for them before—but he had to admit he loved the surge of adrenaline when they bounced off his lips.

The second man kept this head and eyes forward.

The driver, who also kept facing forward, said, "We leaving yet?"

Pinpoint Eyes continued to stare at Dash.

The driver said, "Yo, we gotta go soon. You ladies finish bickering or what?"

Pinpoint Eyes said, "Alright, Mr. Parker, what shall we do with her? Drop her on her mother's doorstep? Display her in Times Square?"

"That isn't what I meant."

"You're the big shot now, Mr. Parker, you tell me. Come on. You're so tough. You. Tell. Me."

The second man sighed, speaking for the first time since Dash saw him. "Jesus Christ, we'll take her to Bellevue."

Pinpoint Eyes turned to face the second man. "Excuse me?"

"We'll take her to Bellevue. Guy there cuts 'em open and figures out what killed them. What's his name? Norris."

"Are you crazy?" Pinpoint Eyes hissed. "Norris works for the police."

"Yeah, but he also works against them too. Contradicts a lot of their so-called investigations. Shows them up in court. Plus, he hates the mayor and the governor. Haven't you seen his letters in the papers?"

"We are not—"

Dash cut in. "You said this Norris gentleman can discover how she died?"

The driver replied, "Sure can."

Dash did a quick mental calculation. Rosalie Frazier was famous. Whether she disappeared or died, she was sure to be a news sensation. That was neither here nor there. What Dash needed to know was if Fife's booze supply had been contaminated. Forget the business implications, Dash didn't want the men coming to Pinstripes looking for a safe space to mingle, flirt, dance, perhaps even fall in love, only to be poisoned and maimed or worse. It sounded like this Norris fellow could determine that.

Dash nodded. "I'm amenable to that as a solution."

Pinpoint Eyes mimicked a lisp. "*I'm amenable to that as a solution.*" He glared hard at Dash, his voice back to normal. "Fife wanted her gone. You want her found and—what's the word—autopsied? You want to go against Fife, be my guest, but I wouldn't recommend it."

"As I see it, I'm doing Fife a favor."

Pinpoint Eyes scoffed. "I doubt that."

The driver said, "Ladies, enough chitchat. We going to Bellevue or not?"

Pinpoint Eyes cocked his head to the side. "You must have a death wish, Mr. Parker." He gave Dash one last long look and then faced forward. "Bellevue. Go."

The driver shifted a gear and the truck surged forward. They took a left and rattled down West Fourth, crossing over Seventh Avenue and disappearing from view.

The enormity of what Dash had done suddenly hit him. What had gotten *into* him? Going toe-to-toe with a man like Pinpoint Eyes? Joe would be apoplectic if he saw Dash risking his life over a strange girl. A strange *dead* girl who could cause immense problems for them and for Pinstripes.

"Stop bein' so soft-hearted!" he could hear Joe say. "The way she was livin', she was bound to meet a bad end. This has nothin' to do with us."

And the Joe in Dash's head was most likely right. However, Dash remembered meeting a young man a few weeks earlier who was later strangled and thrown into the weeds of Central Park like he was trash. The very thought of it even now depressed him. It was so . . . oh what was the word for it? . . . *inhuman.* Dash couldn't give that same disregard to Rosalie and live with himself.

"Rosalie," he said aloud. "I hope you get buried with *some* dignity and that your family will soon find peace." He glanced to the side where the truck used to be. "As for me, I sincerely hope Fife understands . . ."

6

It took just one day for the city to discover the fate of Rosalie Frazier.

That following Tuesday morning started with several door slams and raised voices. Dash sat straight up in bed, heart pounding, eyes darting this way and that. Ever since the removal of her body, he'd been on edge, wondering when and where Fife would make his displeasure known. Joe kept by his side at all times, acting as a security guard of sorts, but it did little to quell the anxiety that relentlessly clawed at his skin. Dash didn't sleep well at night and during the day, he uneasily eyed the streets and alleyways of the Village, expecting at any moment for Lowell Henley, or some other nasty torpedo, to appear.

The bedroom was still dark. Bright light peeked out from the edges of the shades drawn across their only window. Cool air wrapped around his naked chest, and a chill pressed itself against his shoulder blades.

He glanced around the bedroom. Nothing unusual here, just the flourishes of a typical Greenwich Village apartment. Cracked baseboards, crumbling plaster molding, uneven floorboards at a slight slant. A water-stained ceiling that one could argue was a cubist-inspired fresco. A chest of drawers overstuffed with clothes leaned on one wall; a narrow wardrobe full of suits braced itself on the other. An empty wooden chair sat next to the window with a teacup perched behind it on the sill, filled to the brim with cigarette ash.

No shadowy figure standing in the corners.

No pistol pointing at his chest.

Dash squinted. An argument, soft at first, was growing in intensity and seemed to be right behind his head. Ah, it was coming through the wall next to their headboard.

A murmured voice tried to utter reassurances.

A raised voice, female, high-pitched, and full of theatrical vibrato replied, "Reggie, you think I'm some kind of sap? I *saw* you with her!"

The murmured voice raised in volume, proving itself to be male. Dash could now decipher his words.

"You're screwy, you know that?! I can't sit next to any skirt without you getting the screaming meemies?"

The bedroom door suddenly opened and Finn barged into the bedroom. He was dressed in his Chinese silk pajamas complete with a tan mandarin-style collar, wide vertical blue stripes, and silver frog clasps. His dimpled grin was at its widest.

"Athena be praised, they're at it again!"

Joe groaned next to Dash from underneath the bed covers. Dash turned. All that was visible was the tangled red of his hair splayed out against the pillow.

"Finney," Joe murmured, the blanket muffling his voice, "why are you in here?"

"Because your room backs up to the dressing rooms, and I can't miss another episode in our little melodrama."

Another groan from Joe earned a "Shh!" from Finn, who pulled up the wooden chair from the window to the shared wall.

The joys of living above a playhouse. The Cherry Lane Playhouse on Commerce Street, to be exact. Home to the three men—and, apparently, more noise than the rattle and squeal of Seventh Avenue. Though Dash had to admit, he was curious to see where this morning's drama would lead. At the very least, it was a momentary distraction from Fife and Rosalie.

He turned back to Finn, whose wide blue eyes were now narrowed in concentration. His oval face, scrubbed clean of makeup, stared at the wall, as if he could see the principals in this impromptu performance.

Dash couldn't hear what the male voice said next, but the female voice—and her response—was loud and clear: "Oh baloney! You had your *arm* around her!"

"A fella can't be friendly?"

"Not *that* friendly."

Finn said, "Ooo, you tell him, lady!"

Tell him, she did. "And listen here, bub, if you think I haven't seen how she's been making eyes at you, you must think I'm blind. Batting her fake lashes, painting her eyes and lips like she's my age instead of—of—however old she is, that goddamn face-stretcher."

Finn gasped. "An older woman! Now that's a twist I didn't see coming."

Dash couldn't help but smile at his friend.

Joe, however, was not amused. He tossed and turned, saying, "Saints preserve me. How can ya care about this nonsense?"

Finn waved Joe off. "Stop being an old sour puss. We need *some* entertainment since we put Pinstripes on hiatus, and frankly, this is better than radio! Especially since we don't have one, de*spite* my pleas."

"I swear to the All-Holy Mother—"

Dash cut in before the two men started an argument to rival the one they were eavesdropping. "Boys, enough."

The male voice from the wall tried, in vain, to defend himself. "I can't help what she does."

"But ya don't have to encourage it!"

"Aww, but that's half the fun," Finn purred.

Joe muttered something from underneath the covers. It sounded to Dash like "Christ bleedin' on the cross," but he couldn't be sure. He looked at Finn who mouthed the words "Mrs. Grundy." Dash suppressed a laugh bubbling up.

The male voice softened his tone. An excuse was coming. "Listen, doll, if you wanna know the truth, I was trying to cozy up to her so she can put in a good word for you. Get you out of the chorus."

"Oh please," said both Finn and the woman.

"Please, nothing," the male voice replied. "Didn't you tell me you wanted to be more than just a hoofer for the rest of your life? Well, how do you think it's done? It's *who* you know. She puts in a good word for ya, you've got an *in*. You understand me?"

Finn whispered, "Don't fall for it, don't fall for it . . ."

A tense pause, then the female voice became more contrite. "I guess so. I just don't like seeing ya that friendly."

Finn gave a disappointed sigh. Surprisingly, Dash was disappointed as well.

"It's an act, doll," the male voice said. "That's what we actors do."

The voices calmed down and blurred back into indistinguishable murmurs.

"Talk about acting," Finn replied. He looked up at

Dash. "That's the biggest bunk I ever heard. No lead actress is going to stick her neck out for a chorus girl."

"Yes, but he told her what she wanted to hear. In my experience, that's what mollifies most people. I do it once or twice a week myself."

Finn stood up and put his hands on his hips. "Does that mean you—what's the word you used?—mollify me by telling *me,* your friend in goddess, deceitful lies?"

Dash smiled. "Never. I always tell you the pure truth."

"That's what I tho—wait a minute!" The blue eyes widened. "You just did that molly-act to me, didn't you?"

Dash laughed. To his surprise, he heard snuffles of laughter next to him from underneath the bed covers. He pulled them away from the tangled red hair. "I see someone's finally awake."

Joe replied, "How can I sleep with the two of ya gumbeaters?"

He pushed the covers down and sat up in bed next to Dash. The bed itself was too small for the two men, especially when one of them was the size of Joe. His bare, wide shoulder pressed against Dash's smaller, narrower one. Like Dash, Joe also slept in the nude.

This caused Finn to shake his head at them as he returned the chair to the window. "Look at you two, sleeping without pajamas like philistines."

"Says the lass who poses naked at least once a week," Joe shot back.

"That's different! That's art."

"Then how came ya come home with flecks of paint in yer hair?"

"Don't be such a simpleton. Don't you know that good art is supposed to touch you?" Finn stared at the shared wall with the Playhouse dressing room. No more voices echoed from the other side. "I suppose today's show is over. Any idea of when we'll open again?" He meant Pinstripes.

"Finney, it's been only one night!" Joe said.

"Which is an *eternity* when you're dependent on it for money and men."

"We will reopen when we know what killed her and confirm it wasn't our booze," Dash replied.

Finn sighed. "This Mr. Norris is certainly taking his time."

"Look at it this way, Finn. You get to have a second night of Mari Gras."

The little man grinned. "I did enjoy it thoroughly last night. Had my palm read—long life line, thank you—almost lost my cap on the shoot-the-chutes. Even treated myself to Nathaniel's famous frankfurter."

"You mean Nathan's."

"Who?" Finn returned to the bedroom door and grabbed the doorknob. "Alright, philistines, I'm *finally* off to bed. Ciao!"

And with that, Finn swung out of the bedroom, shutting the door behind him.

Joe sighed and looked at Dash. "Why do we put up with him?"

Dash reached over and picked up his watch. Eight in the morning. He'd just gone to sleep a little past seven.

He sighed. "We need help with the rent to pay for our extravagant apartment." A one bedroom with a narrow hallway, where Finn slept, that somehow was classified as a second bedroom.

Joe rubbed his eyes and shook his head. "Goddamn greedy landlords."

"Amen."

They buried themselves under the covers, but Dash

couldn't fall back to sleep, despite Joe's gentle coaxing. An hour later, they were both dressed—Dash in a gray plaid suit, bright blue shirt, and navy blue and red striped tie; Joe in his usual white open-collared work shirt, brown suspenders, and matching brown trousers. Joe would have still been asleep at this time, but, as promised, he wasn't letting Dash out of his sight.

They left the Playhouse and walked up Commerce, which was relatively quiet, before coming upon the bells and whistles of Seventh Avenue. Motorcars filled the road, their engines growling, gears squealing, horns blaring. Trolleys clanged away as they threaded themselves in between Ford's and Chrysler's inventions. How they missed each other, Dash couldn't figure.

Joe placed his hands over his ears. "Christ, lassie, how do ya stand it first thing in the morning?"

"You get used to it," Dash called in return.

A cop was blowing his whistle at ear-splitting volumes, trying to direct the sea of vehicles across the asymmetrical crosshairs of Seventh, Commerce, Bleecker, and Jones. As they waited for their cue to cross, Dash saw three men across the street shouting unsuccessfully for taxis. No amount of arm-raising and hand-waving had any effect for the three men in suits trying to get downtown. A woman suddenly appeared on the curb next to them, still dressed in her evening wear, though the midnight magic was rapidly fading. Makeup slightly smeared. Pale green dress slipping off her shoulders. Stockings with runs like tear-stains sliding down to unbuckled shoes. She placed her fingers between her lips and let loose a whistle so loud and so piercing that it caused the three men to wince. A cab immediately pulled to the curb, and before the three men who'd been shouting and waving could get a word in edgewise, she jumped into the back and the cabbie drove off.

The cop, whose cheeks were cherub red from all the whistling, put his hand up to stop the downtown traffic and directed Dash and Joe, as well as a few others, to cross the tangle of streets.

They made it through the mayhem and turned onto Barrow. The baby-blue sky above them was streaked with thin, wispy clouds, like torn cotton. A welcomed respite from the rain that had owned much of late August and early September. The crisp, cool air brought with it the smells of woodsmoke, the sweet hickory mixing with the mouthwatering aroma of cured meats. Dash tried to revel in the smells of autumn, to ignore his nerves crackling like water droplets in hot oil. But once they arrived at the other end of the street, he couldn't help warily eyeing the spot where Fife's men had carried the lifeless Rosalie.

"Yer alright," Joe murmured. "No one's gonna get ya."

Dash nodded and the two of them headed towards the Greenwich Village Inn.

The inside of the Inn was typical of cafés and restaurants in the Village: warped floors, splintered wood tables covered in etchings, and dusty brick walls dropping crumbs of mortar onto the baseboards. Cigarette smoke and sawdust mixed with the sweetness of spilled liquor and the spice of body odor. A far cry from the crystal chandeliers of Dash's youth, and yet, he found comfort in the dirt and the grime. There was a gruff honesty in this place whereas in finer rooms with finer manners, there was always a sense of charade, of staged superiority. Dash found the act exhausting.

The Inn clientele was a boisterous mix of bohemians: artists, musicians, socialists, old-time suffragists, and pro—

labor union supporters. Dash expected them to still be discussing Mussolini's assassination attempt. After all, it seemed like every morning paper's edition brought about new information regarding the unsuccessful bombing. Half of the bohemians believed the assassin to be working alone, whereas the other half believed he was part of a larger conspiracy. Dash, himself, was in the former camp, Joe in the latter.

But one second inside the Inn showed that Mussolini was already yesterday's news. For everyone in the dingy, smoky room was talking about Rosalie Frazier.

7

The two men slid sideways glances at one another.

Dash murmured, "It sounds like the proverbial cat is out of the bag."

Joe gave a curt nod. "Act natural and no one will ever know what happened two nights ago."

As they wound their way through the tables full of gossiping patrons, the Rosalie discussions echoed around them.

"That Frazier family is cursed," lamented a gruff male voice. "First the mother dies a few years back, now the daughter."

"I *knew* she was lyin' to the judge," another man rasped. "A girl like that was never going to fully repent."

"Volstead Cancer strikes again," boomed a large female voice. "The Drys are gonna make sure we all die horrible deaths for their so-called purity!"

The gruff male voice said, "Not to sound uncaring, but is anyone surprised?"

A younger woman's voice replied, "I think the bigger

question is *who* dropped her off at Bellevue? And why? Doesn't it strike anyone as *odd* . . . ?"

The only ones who didn't join in on the gossip were the three former Wall Street traders who sat in the back, silently sipping their coffee cups filled with enough octane to start an automobile. They were called The Ex-Pats. Nobody knew what happened to them on the trading floor and, after one glance at their bloodshot eyes and trembling lips, nobody asked.

Dash and Joe found two free barstools. Emmett, the owner of the Inn, stood on the other side of the bar. The tall, thin man with snowy white hair and thick white eyebrows had the *Times* sprawled open in front of him. He glanced up as Dash and Joe settled themselves.

"You're up early," he said, gruffly.

Dash replied, "I couldn't sleep."

"Looks like it. If the bags under your eyes got any bigger, you'd need a bellhop to carry 'em."

"You always know how to make a man feel welcome." Dash pointed to the paper. "Mind if we take a look? Just the front page."

Emmett frowned. "Joining in on gawking at a dead rich girl?"

Dash forced a smile. "Got to keep up with the latest news."

"Ha! Nothing newsworthy about it. She went where she wasn't supposed to go and paid the price for it."

"What's eating you, Emmett? You usually love a good scandal."

Emmett sighed and grabbed a carafe of coffee. "Lost another waiter to that damn fool place The Pirate's Den." He set two mugs in front of Dash and Joe, and filled each one to the brim.

Joe couldn't believe it. "That *ridiculous* restaurant on Christopher?"

A rueful smile. "Ridiculous as it may be," Emmett said, "it's taking away customers and staff. I can't believe someone would willingly dress up as a damn pirate and parade around a fake ship's interior, saying *Arr ye maties* and *dead men tell no tales* while serving goddamn sandwiches. Whatever happened to just sitting and eating, for chrissakes?"

Joe raised his coffee cup in a faux toast. "Hear! Hear!"

Emmett nodded in appreciation but still scowled. "But damn it all. I don't know how I'm supposed to compete with three floors looking like the inside of a ship."

"Not everyone wants a show with dinner," Dash offered, trying to be helpful.

It didn't work. Emmett made an angry gesture. "Bah. Pirates and dead flappers. What the hell is this country coming to?"

Despite his frustrated words, Emmett still turned over the paper and pushed the front section across to Dash and Joe. They looked down and saw:

`Society Girl Gags on Giggle Water`
`Coroner Says Methyl Alcohol to Blame`

`Rosalie Frazier meets her deadly destiny`
`Railroad baron and father devastated`
`"Bright lights of Broadway killed my girl!"`

Ice trickled down Dash's spine. He looked over and saw Joe's face had paled. Neither one was surprised by the news coverage, but expecting it and experiencing it were two different things.

"Oh lassie," Joe muttered. "What have we done?"

"We did the right thing for her family," Dash muttered back. Was he trying to convince Joe or himself? Perhaps both of them. "And quite possibly, the right thing for us. Now let's see what caused her . . . demise, and whether or not we need to be worried about our supply."

Dash skimmed the paragraphs dedicated to the mysterious appearance of Rosalie at Bellevue Hospital and her eventual identification by her father, who had been out of the city for the weekend and, upon finding her missing, contacted all the city hospitals. It took the urging of his sister for him to reach out to the city morgues.

The last half of the story, continued on page three, were the autopsy results by Charles Norris, the coroner at Bellevue Hospital.

"Here we go," Dash said.

Joe snapped to attention and the two of them read through Norris's analysis:

According to city coroner Charles Norris, Miss Frazier ingested methyl alcohol, also known as "wood alcohol." Mr. Norris told reporters last night that unlike ethyl alcohol, which was in America's liquor supply before Prohibition and can easily be broken down by the human body, the liver enzymes struggle to break down the compounds of methyl alcohol.

"The result of this slow metabolism is that the poison lingers longer in the body, simmering in the body's vital organs," Mr. Norris said. "The by-products of methyl alcohol are formaldehyde and formic acid, both equally destructive compounds."

Reporters were told that formaldehyde is a well-known irritant while formic acid is an essential component in the venom in bee stings.

Joe pinched his brows. "Good Lord. Is that what we've been drinkin' all this time?"

Dash shook his head. "If we were, we'd be like Rosalie here." As well as the rest of their customers. Dash hoped that there weren't illnesses or deaths he didn't know about.

He continued reading.

"Methyl alcohol will not cause death right away," Mr. Norris continued. "In fact, after the initial ingestion of the poison, Miss Frazier would feel the effects similar to a bad hangover and then recover. This is due to the slow metabolism of the compounds. However, after thirty or so hours, the by-products would break down and the human body would begin to be poisoned."

Mr. Norris went on to describe, in lurid detail, the effects of this process. The toxic by-products would attack a person's eyesight. The vision would blur, as the optic nerve tissue becomes swollen, bloody, and spongy. Damage also occurs in the

> parietal cortex, a region of the brain
> essential for processing vision. Limb
> coordination would be affected as well.
> Headache and vomiting could occur.
> Eventually, the by-products of the poison
> accumulate in the lungs, breaking down the
> pulmonary tissue and causing death.

They sat in silence for a moment. There it was. Confirmation that Rosalie died from poisonous liquor. The poisonous liquor from which Nicholas Fife was supposed to protect them.

"Christ Almighty." Joe's hand left his brow and began tapping a nervous rhythm on the surface of the bar.

"What a horrible way to go." Dash re-read the analysis, remarking to Joe that, to the outsider, the person would appear drunk.

"Aye, no one would be the wiser." He looked at Dash. "That's why nobody had a clue she was dyin'. Probably not even her."

The dull ache of guilt pressed itself against Dash's chest. "Could we have saved her?"

Joe's eyes were gentle. "No, me bonnie boy. Based on what this Norris chap was sayin', she was too far gone."

Dash nodded, the aching guilt subsiding somewhat, and went over Norris's words again. A new set of implications took shape.

He pointed to a paragraph. "Joe, look at this. Charles Norris said it would take up to thirty hours before the toxins would begin affecting the human body."

"Ya? And?"

Dash's voice became excited. "That means that—"

Joe put a quick finger to his lips.

Dash lowered his voice. "—that means she couldn't have possibly been poisoned at our club. It was somewhere else."

Joe began nodding his head. "Yer right. By God, yer right. It wasn't our booze."

"It wasn't our booze."

The two briefly smiled at one another.

"Ya think we can reopen now?" Joe asked.

Despite the good news, Dash waffled his head from side to side. "I don't know. In this one instance, we're in the clear, but . . . now I'm having some doubts."

Joe grunted. "Might be time to have a chat with this Fife fella."

"If he's not too angry about this," Dash replied, pointing to the news coverage.

"All we can do is pray, me boy."

"May the Lord be on our side for once."

As it turned out, the Lord wasn't.

Tuesday came and went without incident. Dash took measurements at Hartford & Sons while Joe watched, perched on a stool in the corner, his arms crossed over his broad chest. A few customers eyed him uneasily. Every once in a while, a man would eye Joe hungrily. That's when Dash told the customer about Pinstripes and gave him the secret knock. At six o'clock, they closed up shop, unwound at the Carmine Baths, and returned to their apartment.

Wednesday was more of the same, but it was Wednesday night when things went awry.

They were at the Carmine Baths, a red-bricked, three-story trapezoid with rounded archways on the ground floor, tall rectangular windows on the second floor, and short, squatty square windows on the top.

Inside, Dash and Joe joined the line of men— a mix of suits and coveralls—looking to clean up before night fall. They continued moving forward, eventually coming to a bored olive-skinned man in shirt sleeves sitting behind a counter. The man handed them a pen and pointed to a large, leather-bound ledger filled with illegible signatures. They added theirs to the long list of scribbles and paid a dollar each. Without a word—or even a change of expression—the man handed Dash and Joe two keys, two towels, and two robes.

Past the check-in desk, they walked up to the second floor, the size and scale still taking Dash's breath away. Warehouse-high ceilings. Expansive stone floors. Row after row of intersecting private rooms. The noises of the place were just as loud as the streets outside. Thundering water against porcelain tubs, heavy rain on shower floors. Steam pipes hissed and spat, and echoing voices were interrupted by sudden sharp bursts of laughter.

In the changing rooms, they both undressed, Dash trying hard not to openly stare at Joe's big body. Meaty arms, wide chest, thick thighs, and a slight belly Joe found irksome but that Dash found endearing. A soft contrast to that strong, intimidating frame.

They placed their clothes in a locker, securing it with the keys they'd been given. Fully robed with towels draped over their arms, they returned to the main room with the bathing booths.

Joe murmured, "Want to share one, lassie?"

Dash turned and saw the twinkle in Joe's eye. He felt himself blush. Joe had often made the same offer back when they first got together. Before Pinstripes, before Cherry

Lane. When every place they went, the air seemed to crackle with electricity, like the spark between two filaments in Edison's lightbulbs. Sizzling, buzzing, constant.

At least, it *had* been.

Now, ever since the events of the previous August—when Dash saw Walter Müller shot to death in front of him—he hadn't been able to tap into that electrical current for very long. Indeed, the lust he felt in the locker room had given way to caution. Joe's flirtation suddenly seemed trivial, even ridiculous. And in this moment, it felt dangerous.

"It's against the rules for two men to be in one booth," Dash said.

"It's against the rules to be doin' what we're doin' in our apartment."

"But it's safe there." He saw Joe's expression, which was a mix of disappointment and concern. "I'm sorry. I can't seem to . . . " A heavy sigh. ". . . can't seem to get into the mood."

Joe laid a comforting palm on Dash's shoulder. "It's alright." He saw a vacant booth and nodded towards it. "Take that one."

Dash shook his head. "No, you go. I'll wait for the next one."

Joe gave him one last look, then walked slowly into the booth, closing the door behind him.

Dash breathed in the steam and the heat, berating himself with every exhale. What good was living life as a so-called degenerate bohemian if he didn't partake in its indulgences every once in a while? As the War and the Flu taught him, life was pitilessly, mercilessly short. He survived those global catastrophes as well as his family's rejection. He even survived Walter Müller, an insidious blackmailer who was going to kill him.

You're stronger than you know, he told himself. *Which means you're stronger than this.*

A group of three men walked by in their robes chatting in their native language—Russian, by the sounds of it. Two men followed after them. They complained in English about their boss, who was a *"tight-fisted son of a bitch who can't even write his own name, much less spell it."* An Irish voice in the distance began braying a song about Molly Malone. It brought a smile to Dash's lips. It was Joe.

In a voice full of gusto (but lacking in pitch), Joe sang above the sounds of the baths:

> *In Dublin's fair city*
> *Where the girls are so pretty*
> *I first set my eyes on sweet Molly Malone*
> *As she wheeled her wheelbarrow*
> *Through streets broad and narrow*
> *Crying, "Cockles and mussels, alive, alive, oh!"*

A few more voices from the locked booths joined in on the refrain:

> *Alive, alive, oh*
> *Alive, alive, oh*
> *Crying, "Cockles and mussels, alive, alive, oh!"*

Dash laughed out loud and decided *to hell with it* and began walking towards Joe's bathing booth.

It happened quickly.

A voice behind him murmured, "Get dressed and come with me, Mr. Parker."

Something pressed against his back.

"Make any sudden moves or loud noises, and this goes off. Understand?"

More men shouted:

Alive, alive, oh!
Alive, alive, oh!

The smile vanished from Dash's face. "W—w—who are you?"

"Don't concern yourself with that."

Dash looked around the cavernous room to see if anyone could help him. The two businessmen had disappeared into the steamy fog. So had the three Russians. No one else appeared in the humid haze. It was just Dash and this armed stranger.

"What do you want?" he asked.

The voice of the unseen man moved closer, his lips right next to Dash's ear.

"Mr. Fife wants to see you."

BACK AT FIFE'S WAREHOUSE

8

Dash's body felt glued to the barber's chair, his eyes still locked on the razor held in Fife's steady hand.

"Hmm?" Fife said, then repeated his question. "How shall we make this situation more *amenable*, Mr. Parker?"

Dash couldn't think of an answer, so he kept silent.

"What's the matter? Cat got your tongue?" Fife smirked. "Give and take, Mr. Parker. That's what a partnership consists of. Do we have a partnership?"

His jaw tight, Dash replied, "Yes."

"Well, then. You've been taking quite a lot from me these days. My liquor. My men. My *power*. And now, now you must give."

"Please," Dash murmured.

"Raise your chin."

Dash shook his head.

"I said, raise your chin, Mr. Parker."

Teeth chattering, he slowly did as Fife asked. He breathed in sharp when Fife swiftly brought the blade to the front his throat and held it there. The razor was just below his Adam's apple. The edges of his vision blurred with tears. All Dash could see was Fife's face. All he could hear was the pounding of his heart. All he could feel was the blade lightly touching his throat.

I'm sorry, Joe.

If only he had responded to Joe's flirtation at the Baths. If only he hadn't hesitated—

"Will you give tonight?" Fife said. "Answer me!"

There was only one answer. It took three tries before he said, "Y-y-yes."

Silence.

Stillness.

Then the cool blade more forcefully touched Dash's skin. His whole body jolted and his neck jerked back. The blade paused, then returned to the skin of his neck and . . . slowly moved upward to his chin in those short, fast, incremental strokes.

Fife had gone back to shaving him.

The slide of the razor. The wipe against the towel tucked in Fife's waistband.

"I want you to know," he said, "that what happened to that girl is completely and thoroughly unacceptable. And according to that body cutter Charles Norris, she couldn't have drank the stuff at your club. That should be a comfort to you and that burly bartender of yours."

Fife kept shaving. The whiskers were rapidly disappearing from Dash's neck and the underside of his jaw.

Almost there. Keep it together now.

"Any idea where she went?" Fife idly asked. "Before she so rudely stumbled into your place and died?"

Dash waited for the razor to leave his skin before shaking his head. "She arrived in a taxi, so she could've been coming from anywhere in the city."

"No matchbooks in her purse? Monogrammed napkins? Addresses on scraps of paper?"

Dash's eyes widened. "She did say something odd to my doorman. She asked to see a hat and tried to give him a small piece of paper with a teacup drawn on it."

"A teacup?"

"Does that sound like the codes to a speak of yours?"

Fife considered the question. "No place comes to mind, but I'll look into it. Do you still have that drawing? You do? Good. A word of advice: keep it with you at all times. You never know when—what is it the coppers call it?—a piece of evidence will come in handy."

"I'm not sure it *is* evidence, Mr. Fife—"

"She was murdered, my dear boy. Either through negligence or sabotage, but the result is still the same." One more slide of the razor, then a pause followed by a satisfied grunt from Fife. "Much better. Now we can discuss this as gentlemen."

Fife reached down and with a wrench of the lever on the side of the chair, Dash was pushed forward into an upright position. His body was covered in sweat, his shirt soaked through, hair damp, armpits ripe. He couldn't fathom just how close he had been to certain death. His hands immediately went to his neck, his fingers gingerly touching his throat, as if trying to convince himself that he had been spared the blade.

The door to the room opened and Lowell Henley entered, balancing a silver tray holding two glasses of yellow liquid.

"Excellent timing!" Fife said.

Was he waiting in the wings, like an actor for his cue? Dash thought.

Fife went over to the corpulent bald man and picked up

the two glasses. He returned to the barber's chair and handed Dash a cocktail filled to the brim.

As soon as Dash gripped the glass's stem, Fife clinked their rims together. "To partnership," he said. He took a big swig of the cocktail, humming to himself. "Lord, that's delicious. Lowell, what is this called again?"

The bald torpedo glanced at the ceiling, keeping his anger in check. "The Bee's Knees."

Fife gave a chef's kiss. "Wonderfully done. Perhaps you can tend bar for Mr. Parker to give his Irishman a night off." He looked at Dash. "What say you? Your thoughts?"

Dash looked at the liquid in his glass.

Could this be poisoned?

He slowly raised the glass to his lips. Cool juniper. Sweet honey. Sour bite of lemon. Heat of fermentation warming his throat and chest.

He looked at Fife and nodded.

Fife grinned at Lowell. "Mr. Parker approves!" He took another sip, humming to himself. "Yes, quite delicious. You may leave us again, Lowell."

Lowell's dark, beady eyes slid from Fife to Dash. "Are you sure, sir?"

"Positive. Carry on with your normal duties."

Lowell glared at Dash for a moment longer, then left.

He sincerely does not care for me, Dash thought.

Lowell closed the door behind him with a click.

Fife strode over to it and turned the deadbolt. He said to Dash's questioning expression, "Privacy."

He then sat on the leather sofa across from Dash, crossing his legs at the knee, cocktail in hand, and looking quite pleased with himself. And why shouldn't he be? He was about to get what he wanted from Dash.

"As you have so adroitly deduced the night you had my

men disobey my orders," Fife said, "I am having to remove way too many corpses from my speaks. And my customers are threatening to buy from another source. They claim I'm trying to kill them."

"The . . . corpses . . . did they all die from drinking methyl alcohol?"

"We don't know for certain. Only you, dearest Dash, had the brains to send her to Bellevue. But the circumstances surrounding the bodies seem to fit with what happened to poor Rosalie. All were seen arriving at the clubs on their own, or with help. They appeared incredibly drunk—trouble seeing, walking, talking. Some had hallucinations. Others were easily confused. They blended right in with a group of imbibers at a bar, so no one suspected a thing. Until, poof! Deader than doornails. Blood in the mouth. Vomit nearby. Skin an odd color, which my men said indicated suffocation."

I'm not going to ask how they knew that.

"How horrible." Dash took another sip of his cocktail for courage. "And you're certain your liquor supply is safe."

Fife sighed. "I used to be certain, but now, now my dear boy, I'm having doubts. Strange. I don't have doubts often. It's an uncomfortable feeling and I don't much care for it."

"These speaks, did they serve the same type of customers? Perhaps special clientele . . . ?"

"You mean, were they all pansy and bulldagger joints? No, they were normal speaks. Only yours, dear Dash, hosted what the nannies call 'degenerates.'"

"What about others? Race-filled? Mixed-race filled?"

"A few Italian speaks here and there. Same with Spanish. None in Black Harlem, though I don't have much reach up there, much as I would like to."

That ruled out specific targets. "The speaks themselves appear to be randomly chosen then?"

"It appears that way. The only common denominator is me."

Dash searched his memory for gangster terminology, the words and phrases repeated by newshawk after newshawk. "Are other syndicates having the same problems?"

"Not that I've heard. And they're gleefully snapping up the customers I'm losing. '*Why buy Slick Nick's snake oil when you can buy the Real McCoy?*'"

Dash took another sip of his cocktail. The strong gin was doing its part to relax him, and he could almost believe he was having a tete-a-tete with a friend, not with someone who, just moments ago, threatened to slit his throat.

"I guess the next logical question to ask would be whether you think this is an inside or outside job?"

Fife sat forward. "Now that, my boy, is an excellent question. Who among my men, my top men, would want to see me fail?"

"You have any ideas?"

"A few. In this position, no one is ever truly your friend. My lead man Mr. Henley loves to yield power, as you've undoubtedly noticed. There's Mr. Makowski who may want a taste of something more."

"Who's Mr. Makowski?"

"He's the one who's been moving all the bodies. You've met him; an angry scar across his neck. He wanted to kill you, by the way, for bossing him around. I told him not to." Fife sat back on the couch and sipped more of his cocktail. "You're welcome, by the way."

Alarmed, Dash muttered a thanks and nearly drained his glass. He wiped his wet lips. "Anyone else?"

"There's my chemist Angelo. Much as it pains me to

say, he has the most direct access to my supply and the most control over it. In fact, I suspected him first because Mr. Henley and Mr. Makowski can't spell denaturing, much less perform it. They know violence; they don't know chemistry."

"Could it be a mistake? An error?"

Fife gave Dash a flat look. "You've seen Angelo work firsthand. How would you describe it?"

Dash recalled the first time he met the chemist. His concentration on his tasks were absolute. Nothing could shake his concentration, not even Fife's pontificating and Dash's fear. His ever-watchful eyes never left the test tubes once until the task was complete.

"Meticulous and unshakeable," Dash replied.

Fife nodded. "Agreed, so we can assume that no errors are being made." He held up a pointer finger. "But I can't for the life of me figure out Angelo's motive, if he indeed is doing it. Angelo has no ambition beyond science. If he were to take over, what could my role offer him in that regard? He'd be trapped in the world of business, which he despises, and handling the politics of the trade, which he also despises."

"Could he have been hired by a competitor?"

A throaty chuckle and an approving smile. "Clever boy. Yes, I have thought of that, and I've checked into his bank accounts. Unless he's been stuffing cash into his mattress, there isn't any more in there than what I've been paying him. Which, I don't mind saying, is beyond generous."

"I see." Dash considered Fife's explanations. "The Why is obvious: take you down. The Who is pretty well cloaked at this point. The How is our only remaining question: how your supply is being contaminated. I see two possibilities, either inside or outside of your warehouse."

Fife grinned. "I told you you're clever, Mr. Parker. And now we come to you giving something to me."

Dash did not like where this conversation was going. "Oh?"

"I want you to find out if a switch is being made and how it's being done. And most importantly, *who* is doing it."

"Mr. Fife," Dash said, massaging the back of his tightening neck, "I am willing to help you, but I am *not* a detective. I wouldn't even know where to begin!"

"Oh, I think you're far more skilled than you realize. You've demonstrated how clever you are, just now." Fife gestured towards him with his cocktail glass. "And I do believe you solved a murder last month, did you not? Don't bother to deny it. I watched you, remember? I *saw* with my own eyes."

Damn him.

"Why can't you have one of your own men help you with this?"

"*Who* could I trust? If I tell one man, word might get around to those co-conspirators. Hell, that one man may even be in on it himself. A tricky situation, isn't it?"

Dash's hand left his tight neck and went to his forehead, squeezing the brows together to try to relieve the pressure building behind them. "How am I supposed to go about this? Watch the speaks?"

"No, dearest Dash, watch the trucks. I want you to follow deliveries. I've identified several routes of suspicion, you might say."

"I can't, Mr. Fife. I—I don't have a motorcar of my own. And even if I did, I don't know how to drive." His older brother was supposed to teach him, but Max never did. Perhaps his brother knew even then Dash wouldn't be staying long with the family.

"Not to worry," Fife said. "When I lamented about who to trust, I was overstating a bit, I confess. I do have one man I trust implicitly, and he can drive you. He also knows all the routes and normal activities, so if anything queer happens, he'll let you know."

"And what am *I* doing in this situation? Seems to me this driver is better suited to notice anything odd or strange."

"Because as trustworthy as this man is, he's not the cleverest. *You,* Mr. Parker, you see things other men don't. That's what I need you for, to observe the mechanics of the mystery most people stare at and still overlook." Fife finished off his drink. "My driver will be by your apartment tomorrow at eleven o'clock in the morning. You'll spend all day and night watching and observing, then you'll report back to me. Are my instructions clear?"

Dash finished his drink as well, reluctantly nodding. He set the empty glass down on the side table next to the barber's chair. "That takes care of the outside, but what about the inside? The warehouse? What if the sabotage is occurring in there?"

"I will investigate that angle. Too many of my people know who you are. The Man Who Went Against Makowksi. No, my dear boy, you just worry about the trucks."

Dash stood up from the barber's chair with a loud crackling noise. The dried sweat of his back had created an adhesive with the leather cushions of the chair. "I'll do this, Mr. Fife, but I have one thing I would to ask of you."

Fife stood as well. "Oh? I'm not so sure you're in a position to ask *any*thing of me."

"Perhaps. However, since you've had multiple poisonings, if I'm to reopen Pinstripes, I would like my supply retested."

The two men stared at one another.

A tense silence passed.

"You've got stones, I'll give you that," Fife said. Then he nodded. "Deal." He reached out his hand.

Dash hesitated, then shook it. "Deal."

Fife grinned, keeping hold of Dash's hand. "How exciting! Dearest Dash, *we* are going to make the most wondrous team."

9

"Tha' little shite! I'll fuckin' put a bullet in him myself!"

Joe was furious—not at Dash, but at Nicholas Fife. When he came out of the bathing booth and couldn't find Dash, he was frantic. He practically turned the bathhouse upside down. Then the apartment. Then the club. He was about to start in on the neighborhood when Fife's driver dropped Dash off, shaken but unharmed. He seethed at what Fife did and at what Fife asked Dash to do. Alone in their bedroom, he paced the floor, his hands making angry gestures, spittle flying from his lips.

"And so he's gonna have ya follow his men, playin' detective? Day and night?"

"That's what he said."

Joe shook his head. "I swear on the All Holy Mother— I'm comin' wit ya."

"He won't like that."

"I don't bloody *care* what he likes! He can' jus' kidnap ya, threaten ya, and then make ya his—his—" An incomprehensible string of words followed, his Irish brogue in full force.

Once Joe's sputtering profanities waned, Dash said, "Never a dull moment with me, is there?"

That seemed to deflate the big, ruddy man. "It's not you, me bonny boy," Joe replied, his voice sounding tired. "It's this bloody city." A thoughtful pause. "Maybe we should leave it. Go to the country. I hear plenty of blokes are doin' it. No coppers to bribe, no gangsters to pay. They live . . ." He searched for the word. ". . . true."

It was a beautiful thought.

"I'm not exactly the country type," Dash replied.

Of course, I'm also not the Village type. What, exactly, am I then?

"Neither am I," Joe said. "But I could learn." He gently touched Dash's nose with his finger. "And so could ya."

They locked eyes.

"Well," Dash said, "you *would* look quite handsome chopping wood like a lumberjack."

Joe leaned his head back and barked a laugh in response.

That's when they could finally climb into bed, where Joe gripped Dash so hard in sleep, Dash wondered if he'd accidentally crack a rib or two.

They awoke to a blue-flame sky dotted with clouds and a frosty bite to the wind. Dash dressed in a light gray pinstriped suit with a light blue plaid shirt and a bright blue polka-dot tie. Fife's words echoed in his memory and he went to the chest of drawers, opened the top one, and retrieved the teacup drawing that fell from Rosalie's lifeless body. He tucked it into his inside coat pocket, vowing to always keep it with him, and turned to see Joe dressed in his usual work shirt, brown suspenders, and matching trousers. The man was nothing if not consistent.

"Ready?" Dash said.

By the time they made it to West Fourth, they were in need of Emmett's hot coffee to warm themselves.

Only they weren't to arrive at the Greenwich Village Inn. At the corner of Barrow and West Fourth, when Dash glanced to his right for oncoming traffic, he saw a familiar form a few buildings down standing in front of Hartford & Sons. The man was dressed in a muted gray suit and carried a large leather suitcase.

Dash touched Joe's shoulder and nodded towards the tailor shop. Confused, Joe followed him. The short, mystical-looking man looked up when they arrived.

A voice with a thick accent said, "Mr. Dashiell Parker? The owner of Pinstripes?"

Joe gave Dash a quizzical look.

Dash nodded assurances and said, "You guessed right. Good morning, Mr. Avogadro. It's nice to see you again."

And it *was* nice to see him again. Dash was struck once more by the otherworldly beauty of Fife's chemist. The thickest brown hair Dash had ever seen. Skin so smooth and glowing like a sunset. Mysterious eyes surrounded by dark smudges of ash. Could this man truly be a poisoner? A saboteur? A criminal mastermind? It was hard to figure.

The small Italian curtly nodded. "Likewise, *signore*."

Dash turned to Joe. "This is Angelo Avogadro, Fife's lead chemist. He tests all the liquor supply."

"Nice to meet ya," Joe said. "Here to explain how a wee lass died in our club?"

Joe's lack of tact didn't ruffle Angelo. He simply stood there, his body relaxed, his beautiful oval face serene. "Mr. Fife sent me to give you peace of mind."

"Oh ya? And how ya gonna do that?"

"Joe," Dash said.

Angelo replied, "I am going to test all of your liquor for methyl alcohol."

That must've been what was in the suitcase: his testing equipment.

Joe remained skeptical. "How do we know this isn't some kind o' trick?"

Joe's suspicion was contagious. Dash regarded the small chemist. "How can we trust the results you give us?"

Angelo was puzzled. "Why would he, or I, trick you, *signores*? What good would it be to him, to me? You'll find out the truth sooner or later, yes? Mr. Fife would certainly have me killed, and you'd certainly confront Mr. Fife."

The casual way he referenced his own possible murder chilled Dash. Was this what being in the speak world meant? Being so comfortable with violence?

Then the larger implications took shape. This was a test. If Angelo cleared Dash's liquor and someone else died from it, then Fife would have his proof.

But then one of my patrons would be dead!

Yet, did Dash have a choice? He could hire his own chemist but where would he go to find such a person? And who would agree to engage in an illegal activity? Dash supposed he could keep Pinstripes shut down, but then they'd lose all of their money until Fife's poison problem was resolved.

Talk about being trapped between a rock and a hard place.

"Mr. Parker?"

Dash looked up and saw both Angelo and Joe staring at him.

Angelo looked at him expectantly. "Shall I proceed?"

Dash glanced at Joe, who begrudgingly relented. "We shall."

"Excellent." Angelo gestured to the tailor shop. "Lead the way, *signores*."

Dash unlocked the tailor shop and the three men stepped inside. They walked over to the changing area. Joe pulled the hunter-green curtain around them so passersby couldn't peer inside and see the changing area mirror embedded into the back wall swing open like a door.

When Dash pushed open the mirror, Angelo raised his brows appreciatively. "Clever."

Once inside Pinstripes proper, he opened his suitcase and began setting various beakers, test tubes, and droppers onto the bar. Everything was set with deliberate precision.

"Tell me somethin'," Joe said. "How does one get into something like this?"

"Like what, *signore?*"

"Being a chemist for a gangster."

Angelo considered the question. "Necessity. I came over to America from southern Italy. The War was not kind to my village, and work was not to be found anywhere, especially for a scientist such as myself. I tried to get work here, but . . . you Americans, you are not fans of immigrants or of darker pigments. I am not sure what was worse, my being Italian and Catholic, or my being considered brown-skinned."

Joe grunted in agreement. The Irish, though a bit more accepted due to their paler complexions, still had to contend with the Protestant fears of their Pope.

"And then, I hear there could be a job for someone like me. A man I could talk to. I did. He said I could practice my profession and protect people."

"From who?" Joe asked.

"The American government."

"What is the American government doing?"

"Poisoning people."

This wasn't news to Dash, who learned it from Fife a month ago, but it was a big, bold headline to Joe.

"What?!" he said.

Angelo nodded. "I learned the history so I could know what I was looking for. You see, at the start of the century, the American government wanted to deter industrial manufacturers from selling alcohol on the side to avoid paying taxes on potable spirits. This was when the manufacturing and selling of liquor was still legal. In 1906, the government began requiring all manufacturers to *denature* their grain alcohol."

"Remind me again what that means," Dash said.

"Adding chemicals to make it less consumable due to taste and smell. When the Volstead Act passed in 1919, bootleggers began stealing this industrial-grade alcohol by the millions of barrels."

"All those holdups," Joe muttered, referring to the common news articles of trucks and train yards being robbed at gunpoint.

"In an effort to enforce the Volstead Act, the American government increased their denaturing efforts of industrial alcohol. Under President Coolidge, the government has created over *seventy* denaturing formulas."

Dash was staggered at the sheer scale of Uncle Sam's poisoning campaign. "Testing for all of that must be an immense job."

Angelo shrugged. "They are all variations on a theme. Most are compounds to make the liquid taste and smell bitter. Unfortunately, some of them are deadly."

Sudden fear cooled the back of Dash's neck. "What are the compounds?"

Angelo then ticked them off—in alphabetical order, Dash later noted.

"Acetone, benzene, brucine, cadmium, camphor, carbolic acid, chloroform, ether, formaldehyde, gasoline, iodine, kerosene, methyl alcohol, mercury salts, nicotine, quinine, and zinc."

Dash felt nauseous.

Even Joe turned a little green. "And . . . the U.S. government willfully and knowingly is putting in all that garbage to—to—"

Dash finished the thought. "Stop Americans from drinking."

"Yes," replied Angelo. "It is intensifying, as of late. I'm finding higher percentages of these compounds in our alcohol supply."

Dash approached his next question with care. "Is it possible, Angelo, that it's making Fife's liquor more . . . dangerous than it once was?"

A fierce shake of the head. "Impossible. My lab is well equipped to handle such things. I was the best of my field in my village. I *am* the best of my field in this country."

Joe was skeptical. "Cleaning up booze?"

"Si, *signore*, especially, as you say, cleaning up booze."

Dash replied, "I don't know if any of this has made me feel safer."

Joe agreed. "Aye, lad, ya just terrified us outta our wits."

"Knowledge can be frightening," Angelo said, "but that is why it's so powerful. Of all the compounds I listed, *signores*, methyl alcohol is the deadliest, so that is what we will test for today. Where would you like to begin?"

"The gin," Dash automatically answered. "Rickeys are one of our top sellers."

Joe gave a friendly smirk. "Coincidence that it's one of your favorites."

Dash smiled in return. "Pure coincidence." He handed Angelo the opened bottle of gin.

Angelo took it and began narrating his movements. He started with two separate containers. One was filled with a liquid, the other a powder. "First, we add drops of sulfuric acid to sodium dichromate. Then we swirl gently. Very good. Now let's start to add in the gin."

They watched as Angelo carefully extracted the liquid from the gin bottle using his dropper. He swung the dropper over to the beaker holding the acid-sodium dichromate mixture and squeezed the rubber top. A droplet hovered in the air for an agonizing few seconds before falling into the beaker. Several more drops followed. Once he had added enough to satisfy, he swirled the mixture in the beaker.

"And now, we waft and smell. If it is pungent and irritating, then we have significant traces of methyl alcohol. If it is dominating and fruity, then only ethanol is present."

All three men watched with bated breath as Angelo wafted and smelled. He smiled. "Try for yourselves."

Dash and Joe gave each other weary looks, but Angelo assured them it was safe. They mimicked his wafting movements, breathing in tentatively at first, then more deeply.

Dash looked at Angelo. "Sweet." He then turned to Joe. "It's very sweet."

"Si. That is ethanol, not methyl."

He repeated the process for every single bottle, opened and unopened. All the gins, whiskeys, beers. All cleared the test.

Angelo then packed up the suitcase, closing it with a snap. "You see, *signores*? Nothing for you to fear." He looked at Dash. "A pleasure seeing you again." He glanced at Joe. "A pleasure meeting you."

And with that, he left their club.

Dash and Joe looked at each other.

"Do you trust him?" Joe asked.

"Can a man trust anyone in this business?" Dash countered.

Joe feigned agreement. "We can't stay closed forever. At some point, lassie, we got to take a leap o' faith." He reached over and held Dash's hand. "Even if it's a risk."

Dash took a deep breath. If Angelo was indeed Fife's saboteur, he must be smart enough to know this situation was a trap, of sorts. He had to be. Otherwise—

"Lassie," Joe said. "What say ye?"

Dash swallowed the lump in his throat. "I say . . . I guess we're back in business."

Joe patted, then rubbed Dash's hand. He grinned. "Aye, that we are, lassie, that we are. What is it ya say? Time to return to good jazz, good gin, and good men."

Joe's attitude was infectious. Dash found himself grinning as well. "Come on," he said. "Let's see if I can charm Emmett into using his telephone again."

"Today seems to be the day fer miracles!"

Locking up Hartford & Sons, they practically ran down West Fourth to the Inn. Inside, the bohemians had moved on from Rosalie Frazier to discussing other matters of great importance.

"—it's like that bushwa happening in Saratoga!" an excitable young man said. "The district attorney, the sheriff, and the Commissioner of Public Safety *knew* the gambling laws were being broken and they did nothing!"

"Bet they got a cut," muttered his friend.

"Of course, they did! And I wouldn't doubt it one bit if

they laud morality and family values too. I swear, the hypocrisy—"

"—did ya see that the Klan marched on Washington again?" a booming female voice said.

A gruff male voice replied, "Second year in a row, though by all accounts, their marching was sloppy and unimpressive."

"Ay, but I heard they had more trains comin' from up north than from down south. Pennsylvania, New York, New Jersey. The Invisible Empire is growing and if we don't do something about it—"

"—they put off the cafe curfew, did ya see that?" a high-pitched female voice said.

"Shows they have *some* sense," replied an older man. "What business of theirs when we go home? Goddamn nannies—"

"—five cents! Five cents to ride the bus?!" a tight male voice exclaimed. "It's expensive enough in this city and now they wanna raise it to five cents?"

"Don't forget the two-cent transfer," replied a raspy female voice. "Did you see some fool wanted to raise it to ten?"

"It's criminal, is what it is—"

Dash and Joe settled themselves at the bar, barely able to contain their excitement.

Emmett flicked them a look. "What's got you dandies so gay?"

Dash replied, "We just heard some good news," at the same time Joe said, "I'm not no dandy."

Dash laid some money on the bar. "Any chance I can use your telephone again, Emmett?"

"What? Three times in one week? I'm not running a switchboard here." Despite the gruff words, he still took the money. "Though I need all the sugar I can get."

"Oh? Why's that?"

"Look around."

As Emmett filled their mugs, Dash swiveled his head and noticed that, despite the gusto of the conversations around them, the tavern was emptier than usual.

When Dash turned back around, Emmett said, "It's that damn Pirate's Den again. They're starting to take my customers. They tell me they like the atmosphere there more, whatever the hell that means."

"I can't believe they think yer place doesn't have—whaddaya call it?—atmosphere," Joe said. "It's got loads!"

He gestured to the roughhewn tables, uneven chairs, dirty baseboards, knee and elbow patches of the bohemians, and, of course, The Ex-Pats, haunted, silent, and sipping in the back.

"It's certainly . . . a distinct atmosphere," Dash offered.

Emmett waved them off with a scowl. Something caught his attention and he glanced towards the front door, the scowl turning into a deep frown. "Shit."

The few bohemians present quieted their chatter. The reason why hit Dash like a fist in the chest.

It's Thursday.

A day he tried to avoid the Inn, but he had lost track of time, what with Rosalie and Fife. Because on this day, a man Dash used to bribe came in to collect Emmett's "donation." A man who did not appreciate being cut out of Dash's business. A man who could cause trouble.

Officer Cullen McElroy.

10

"Morning, old man," said the familiar voice.

Joe cursed under his breath.

My sentiments exactly, Dash thought.

Dash and Joe turned to see the odious globe of the policeman standing in the doorway, his straw-like blond hair peeking out from underneath the brim of his hat. The full round face flushed pink, the eyes small and beady, the smile tobacco-stained.

Emmett ignored the greeting. Instead, he picked up the newspaper in front of him and rattled the pages until he found a story he liked. He began to read.

McElroy cleared his throat. "I *said,* morning, old man."

With his eyes still on the *Times,* Emmett reached into his pocket and withdrew the weekly bribe. He placed the stack of bills on the bar and turned the page of the newspaper.

McElroy's tiny eyes looked to the sides, taking in the bohemians staring at him. "Remember when I said you needed to learn respect, grandpa," he growled.

Emmett remained calm. "Remember how I told you respect was earned?"

McElroy barked a laugh. He sauntered towards the bar. "You mean letting your den of iniquity prosper and flourish instead of shutting you down? Seems to *me*, old man, you owe me a touch more politeness than you've been giving these days."

Emmett yawned and turned another page of the *Times*.

McElroy's face turned a darker shade of red. He was losing face in front of the villagers. He looked around the room again, no doubt wondering how he could get Emmett to respect his authority.

His beady eyes first passed over Dash and Joe sitting at the bar, then came right back to them. Those yellow and brown teeth flashed as his flesh-colored lips stretched into a snarling grin.

"Ah, Mr. Parker." McElroy walked towards him. "And Mr. O'Shaughnessy, is it? So nice to see you both again."

Dash forced a smile and replied, "Good morning, Officer McElroy."

Joe remained silent and stoic.

McElroy gestured to the two of them. "Former supporters of mine," he said to the room. He then stood in front of Dash and Joe, his body blocking the room's view of them. "Yes, former supporters," he said in a lower voice. "How goes it with your new protector?"

When Dash agreed to be one of Fife's speaks, Fife and his men told McElroy in no uncertain terms to back off. The lecherous man did not take kindly to his demotion and reminded Dash of it every time they had an unfortunate meeting.

Like this morning.

"It goes well," Dash replied. "How goes the money you're paid by him?"

"Oh fine, fine. Though I must confess, I do miss our weekly visits."

Dash tried to make his voice stern. "My *donations* are handled by another now, and there's no room for argument."

McElroy chuckled, releasing breath rotten with stale cigarettes and the sickly-sweetness of tooth decay. He looked at Joe. "He's cute, isn't he? Trying to sound all tough dressed in the *dandiest* outfit I've ever seen."

Dash looked down at his suit. It wasn't *that* dandy, was it?

Emmett looked up from his paper. "Are you going to harass every customer of mine?"

McElroy faced him. "When I'm ha-*rass*-ing anyone, you'll know it, old man." He looked back down at Dash, that tobacco-stained grin still in place. "Mr. Parker, Mr. O'Shaughnessy, and I were just having a conversation."

"Uh huh. Seems you're doing most of the talking." Emmett grabbed the stack of bills that he had placed on the bar—and that McElroy had dutifully ignored—and held them up. "You want this or not?" he gruffly asked.

McElroy's stare never wavered. Keeping his eyes on Dash, he reached his hand out. Emmett deposited the bribe into the slimy, meaty palm.

"Thank you, old man," McElroy said, pocketing the money. His eyes finally broke away from Dash. "Well, gentlemen, as always, it's been a pleasure." He reached up and touched the brim of his hat. He then looked around to the bohemians watching them. "The NYPD greatly appreciates your contributions. Your generosity helps keep this city safe."

Someone muttered, "For criminals."

Dash thought McElroy's temper would flare, but instead, he chuckled. "Carry on." He turned and sauntered out of the Inn.

Dash waited a few moments before breathing a sigh of relief. He reached for his coffee mug and caught Emmett pouring from an unmarked bottle into it.

"Thought you might need this."

Dash tried to object but realized Emmett was right. He watched as Emmett poured the same elixir into Joe's cup before adding to his own.

Joe said, "Ya doing the Lord's work, lad."

Emmett smirked a smile before placing the unmarked bottle back underneath the counter. He held up his mug. Dash and Joe did the same.

"To one day being free of crooks like him," Emmett said.

Dash and Joe replied, "Amen."

Fortified with coffee and breakfast, Dash and Joe were standing out front of Hartford & Sons. They had placed a sign in the window saying they were closed for a family emergency and smoked while they waited for Fife's motorcar to arrive. Dash's watch claimed it was a half hour past eleven. Fife's man was late.

Joe blew out a long string of smoke, tapping the ash onto the ground. "Yer sure he's comin'?"

"Without a doubt."

Despite the recent bout of good news about their liquor supply, the broad, ruddy man's body was wound tight like a wire spring. He shifted his weight and bounced on his heels, nervous energy in need of escape.

"What are you worried about?" Dash asked. "Angelo cleared us. The band's agreed to play tomorrow night and Boris was awake before noon for once and agreed to pick them up." He gestured for Joe's cigarette.

"Yer gonna go broke paying Emmett for all those calls."

"A necessary business expense."

Handing the cigarette to Dash, Joe replied, "I'm worried, lassie, because we're seeing more of Fife's operation than we need to. To these men, that could make us dangerous."

Dash placed the cigarette between his lips, inhaled deeply, then puffed out two thick clouds of nicotine. "We're just watching deliveries."

"That's my point! We're going to know Fife's map of the city. They're either going to expect more from us or . . . or consider us a threat." Joe nodded to the cigarette held between Dash's fingers.

Dash passed it over to him. "You think Fife will have us killed after this? I doubt that. He'd lose a speak, which is income. Besides, I think he likes us."

"He likes *you*. I don't think he gives a limey's ass 'bout me." Joe puffed greedily on the cigarette.

"But Joe, only Fife and this trusted driver of his know what we're doing. No one else in his organization will be the wiser."

"Says he."

"You don't trust him."

Joe barked a laugh. "Of course not! I can't believe ya do." Another puff on the cigarette before exhaling frustration. "Where *is* this lad? We ain't got all day."

"Actually," Dash said, "we do."

Joe muttered an obscenity.

There was a purr of an unseen motorcar gradually

getting louder. Somehow, Dash knew it was for them. He reached for Joe's cigarette, taking a long puff. "That'll be him."

"How do ya know?"

Dash exhaled a long stream of smoke. "I just do."

Sure enough, a black motorcar pulled up in front of the tailor shop. Dash dropped the cigarette, grinding it out with his heel. He stepped forward, looking into the open passenger window. At the steering wheel was Wim, the young barber who shaved Nicholas Fife.

"Is that you, Dash Parker?" The voice was light, even a bit playful.

"It is."

White teeth grinned at him. "Hot dog! Climb inside."

Dash opened the front passenger door at the same time Joe opened the rear passenger door.

Wim looked behind him. "Excuse me, sir, but who are you?"

The two motorcar doors closed, sounding like the pops of two gunshots. The engine idled while Dash turned to look at their driver. "He's my muscle." Dash expected a fight, like with Pinpoint Eyes who moved Rosalie's body, but what he got instead was a friendly chuckle.

"Muscle?" Wim said. "Oh my, you are a serious individual, aren't you?" He looked over his shoulder at Joe. "If you wouldn't mind please sitting behind your friend here and not behind me. We wouldn't want me to be a nervous wreck. A nervous driver is a dangerous driver, after all."

"Just keep yer hands where I can see 'em," Joe growled.

Another laugh. "Yes sir."

Fife's warehouse stood in the distance. The three men watched as the warehouse men finished loading a DANZIGER PAPER truck. They sat with the windows opened, parked on the riverfront road two blocks away by an abandoned tire factory.

"How are we gonna follow them without bein' seen?" Joe asked Wim. "We're the only motorcar around."

"For now. Once we get into the city, we'll blend right in."

Wim's jovial tone irritated Joe. "Ya daft? What if they *spot us* before we get to the bleedin' city?"

Wim leaned towards Dash, another smile on his face, displaying his long, narrow dimples. "He's not very trusting, is he?"

"He asks a good question though," Dash replied.

Wim sat back in his seat. "Well, my worrywart friends, I plan on staying at least one to two blocks away. I know the route they're supposed to use, so I know what streets and what blocks we'll be on and what alleyways to pull off into."

"What if they don't take their usual route?" Joe asked.

"Then we've found what we're looking for and I get a bonus." Another toothy grin. "We shall have cocktails to celebrate. I myself am thirsty for some authentic Caribbean rum. I know a rumrunner or two—they'll make us an honorable deal."

Joe muttered a response, but neither Wim nor Dash could make it out.

A minute of silence crawled by.

At the loading dock, the men were still carrying pallets of bottles. Wim nodded towards them. "Fife is now re-testing all the liquor right before it goes into the truck." He handed Dash a pair of old army binoculars and pointed. "See that table right there?"

Dash squinted as he raised the binoculars to his face, his eyes focusing and re-focusing until the table sitting in between the warehouse and the truck came into full view.

"Yes," he replied.

"And see the beautiful Italian standing behind it?"

Angelo Avogadro. "I see him."

"Good! Angelo is opening every bottle and withdrawing a little bit of the booze with his dropper to test for methyl alcohol."

Dash was impressed. "Every single bottle?"

Just like he did with my booze.

"Every single one. It now takes twice as long to load the trucks and believe you me, the men are *not* happy about it. But Mr. Fife was adamant. Any man who refused to let Angelo test the bottles would be shot on sight."

The threat, while not a surprise, still unnerved Dash. He concentrated on watching Angelo.

Joe asked, "Has there been any bottles that tested positive for the methyl stuff?"

"Angelo's cleared all of them."

Just like my booze.

Dash offered up a hasty prayer that Angelo wasn't Fife's saboteur. He looked over at Wim. Could *he* be in on the scheme? Fife said his trust in him was absolute, but if there was ever a fellow to fool a man like Fife, it would be the object of his affections. Dash had no doubt the two were involved—or about to be—and Fife wouldn't be the first man to be blinded by passion. He also wouldn't be the first man to underestimate an effeminate man.

Wim, sensing his scrutiny, gazed over at him. "Penny for your thoughts?"

"Not even worth that."

"Somehow, I doubt it very much, Mr. Parker."

A minute of silence passed.

"Do you mind if I ask what you do for him?" Dash asked. "Mr. Fife, I mean."

Another dimpled smile. "I'm a secretary . . . of sorts. I manage his schedule—"

Joe piped up. "Schedule?"

Wim gazed back at him. "Oh yes, Mr. Fife is quite the busy man. Meetings upon meetings upon meetings."

Dash asked, "With whom?"

Wim turned his head and smiled. "Now, now. I wouldn't be a very good secretary if I spilled his secrets."

Joe sniffed behind them. "Ya most likely would be a dead secretary if ya did."

A chuckle. "That goes without saying. Although I must confess, I don't know why so many men fear Mr. Fife. He's quite the pussycat."

"Ah, but cats have claws," Dash countered.

"Oh yes, yes they do. And Mr. Fife has his. But as long as you read his body, you'll know exactly when the claws come out."

Read his body? Did that mean what it was intended to mean?

As if reading his mind, Wim looked over at Dash and bounced his eyebrows, but said nothing more on the subject. Such a playful young man in such a deadly world.

It took another half an hour before the truck was finally loaded. Once the truck was in motion, Wim started the car.

"Alright, Mr. Detective and Mr. Muscle. Let's see if we have some backstabbers on our hands."

11

Dash didn't expect the first delivery to be the crooked one, but nonetheless, he was still disappointed when there were no sudden detours, no unscheduled stops, and no mysterious men intercepting the truck at any point in its journey.

Nor with the second delivery.

Or the third.

Or the fourth.

Not even the fifth.

Every loop around the city followed the same pattern. Angelo tested every bottle at the loading dock and saw no bad reactions. The bottles were loaded onto the truck and the truck crossed the bridge, sat in Manhattan traffic, and double-parked to unload its crates.

Through Wim's binoculars, Dash saw the crates themselves labeled as STATIONARY, ENVELOPES, LETTERHEADS. The only change in the routine were the cars Wim drove. Fife apparently had several, and each loop, they found themselves in a different one. They had started off in a black Ford, but then transferred to a dark green Chrysler, a maroon Chevrolet coupe, a cream colored Packard, and a blue Kissel Speedster.

After the fifth truck, Dash's body was stiff and sore. He tried to stretch in the confines of the front seat but was too tall to even raise his arms halfway up.

Close to five o'clock in the afternoon, Wim dropped Dash and Joe off at the Cherry Lane Playhouse. As they were exiting the car, Wim said, "Get yourselves a bite to eat. I'll be back tonight at eleven for the next batch of deliveries."

Joe, crabby and cross, growled, "We have to do this shite *again?*"

Wim was unfazed. "Boss's orders. Toodles!"

The car motored away.

That night, nothing happened.

Friday morning and afternoon, nothing happened.

All Dash, Joe, and Wim saw were the same variations on the same theme. Angelo testing and approving the bottles. The bottles being loaded into the trucks. The bottles being delivered. The trucks returning to the warehouse empty.

After the afternoon surveillance and before the nighttime rounds, Dash managed to convince Joe to let him go it alone. He argued that Wim was a careful driver and there hadn't been a hint of danger. Besides, they had the band returning to the club tonight, and they both knew Finn couldn't bartend alone—especially on a Friday night shift.

Joe wasn't convinced, but he could see Dash was determined. He could also see Dash was exhausted. "Yer sure ya can do another night of this?"

Dash was seated at the bar with his usual newspaper opened in front of him. To the side, a thermos of coffee sat next to a teacup, which Dash replenished at regular intervals. Joe counted the bottles in front of him while behind him Finn swept the floors.

"Emmett's going to prop me up with coffee," Dash replied, quickly scanning the pages for any reference to his tailor shop or to his club. "Finn offered cocaine, but I don't think that's wise, do you?"

"Anything Finn offers is probably best to avoid."

"I heard that, by the way, O'*Shaugh*nessy," Finn called from the dance floor. "And I choose *not* to be offended by it."

"Good for ya, Finney," Joe called back.

Finn came over and leaned the broom against the bar. "Did you see?" He tapped Dash's newspaper. "Rosalie still on the front page."

Dash nodded. "Everyone is trying to figure out where she got the poisonous booze."

Joe looked concerned. "They haven't said anythin' 'bout us, have they?"

Dash shook his head. "A whole lot of theories, nothing concrete. Apparently her former Times Square roommates couldn't provide anything specific."

Finn looked over his shoulder. "Hmm. It says right here that her former roommates at the Hotel Sutton claimed they weren't with her the weekend before she died and had no idea where she went. A Marty Grice, a master of ceremonies at the Siamese Cat Club, and a Tillie White, a fan-dancer at the same club."

Joe's concern refused to be abated. "I don't know, boys. Someone may still come forward and drop our name."

Finn leaned on the bar. "The only people who may

have seen her here were bell bottoms, Joe. They're probably back on the ship as we speak. Out to sea and onto the next port."

Joe grunted. "Thank the Lord fer small favors."

"You mean, thank the *goddesses*. Now if you'll excuse me, I need to go get myself ready for the night." Finn walked off to the water closet.

Dash continued perusing the newspaper, searching for any mention of a tearoom to explain that drawing of Rosalie's. Nothing. He closed the newspaper just as the club's secret door opened. Dash turned to see the first two members of his three-man band walk in, carrying their instruments.

Calvin, the drummer, led the way said, "Evening, Mr. Parker." The Black man was short and round and neatly clad in a spotless tuxedo. A circular bag holding cymbals was slung over his shoulders. "Good to see ya after all this time," he said. "I was afraid this place closed down for good."

Dash forced a smile. "Over my dead body, Calvin. I hope you didn't lose too much sugar this week."

He shook his head. "Nope. We found ourselves subbing for a band at the Watkins Hotel. Man, it was a hummer! That crowd 'bout blew my wig off."

A second Black man named Julius followed him, holding his cornet loosely by his side. "Yeah, and that dance floor was *ready*. Everyone came correct."

He and Calvin were opposites in the looks department: whereas Calvin was all wide curves, Julius was all thin, straight lines, towering over Calvin's modest frame by a good half a foot. Like Calvin, his tuxedo was well-fitting and spotless.

Dash said, "That sounds excellent! I'd love to check it out one night."

Calvin and Julius gave each other a nervous glance before Calvin situated himself behind the drum kit and started screwing on his cymbals.

Julius stepped forward, cornet still in hand. "Well, uh, Mr. Parker, normally we'd love to take ya, but you see, this club is in the Watkins Hotel, and the Watkins is, uh, well—"

Calvin got impatient and completed his thought. "It's for Blacks only."

Julius nodded. "That's right. Blacks only."

"Ah," Dash said.

"We don't mean no offense, it's just that they're advertised in the Green Book as a safe place with Black tenants, Black staff, and so on, and, well, if they see you, or someone like you there—"

"Not to worry, Jules. It's all jake. Truly." Dash looked around and asked, "Where's Vernon?"

"Vern?" Julius nodded towards the secret door while he sat at the bar, laying his cornet on the polished wood surface. "He outside flirting with the driver. Never seen a woman driver before, and he about lost his mind."

Joe's brow wrinkled. "A woman driver?"

Calvin called from the stage, "Yeah, man. Boris, our usual cat? He's out sick tonight, so his little cousin is filling in."

Julius added, "She's no-nonsense, drives fast, but doesn't get in a wreck, which is more than I can say for most of the hacks in this town."

Joe leaned his hip against the bar. "Aye, so now ol' Vern's tryin' to impress a young lass, eh?"

Calvin said to Julius, "What was his opening line again, Jules?"

"Something about *'how is a million-dollar girl stuck driving a ten-cent box?'*"

Joe barked a laugh. "Did she fall for it?"

"I doubt it. She said back *'those are some clever words from a man in a two-cent suit.'*"

"Boris was never one to suffer fools," Dash said. "Looks like it runs in the family. Which cousin is it? Lisa?"

Both men nodded.

Just then, a loud voice called from the club's secret door: "That's alright, Vern, we're sure you've got this giant bass by yourself. No need to hold the door open or anything like that."

Julius rolled his eyes and said, "Here comes Romeo now."

Dash heard Atty's voice reply, "I got it, mister."

Within a few moments, the large wooden body of the bass entered the club, followed by none other than Vernon, the lone white man in the band. If Calvin was all curves and Julius all straight lines, then Vernon was something in between: straight neck and shoulders, round middle, straight legs.

He called over his shoulder, "Thank you, Atty. You're a real pal, unlike some *others* I could name." It was said without malice and with a well-meaning grin.

Dash said, "How'd it go with Lisa?"

"They ratted me out, eh?" Vernon passed the bar and went towards the stage. He laid the bass carefully on the ground. "Not my fault you hired a real beauty."

"Purely coincidental, I assure you."

Vernon turned around. "Hey, I'm not complaining. My nights here, pretty ladies are quite rare."

Calvin added, "And even then, sometimes they're not real ladies."

Julius swiveled around on his barstool to look at his bandmates. "Speaking of ladies, did y'all read about that society girl who got dropped off at Bellevue earlier this week? That is some strange stuff."

Dash and Joe snuck worried glances at each other. The band, thankfully, didn't notice.

Vernon nodded, walking towards the bar. "Yeah, Rosalie Frazier. Now that's a new one on me, an anonymous donation to the cutting factory of Necro Norris."

Calvin stood up from behind his drum kit. "Wasn't she here a few nights ago?"

Julius spun around to face Dash and Joe. "I *thought* that picture in the paper looked familiar. Sunday night, wasn't it?" His eyes widened as he put the pieces together. "Oh shit. She died here, didn't she?"

Dash felt everyone's eyes on him.

Damn me for hiring intelligent men, he thought.

Vernon, standing between the bar and the stage, pointed at him. "Hey, now. So *that's* why you gave us the bum's rush that night."

Dash blushed. "It wasn't the bum's rush."

"Uh huh. It was polite, don't get me wrong, but you certainly wanted us out of dodge."

Calvin said, "Yeah, man, you all wanted us *gone*." His eyes narrowed. "What happened here, Mr. Parker?"

All three band members stopped and stared at Dash.

Dash took a big swallow of his coffee, wishing like hell it was gin. He had a choice to make. He could either lie to his band—and hope they never find out the truth—or he could be honest.

He gave what he hoped was a confident smile. "It appears that she did. Die here, that is."

The three men erupted in anxious exclamations. A stunned look froze Joe's face.

Dash held up his hands in a placating manner. "Gentlemen, gentlemen, please. It is all right. We've had all our booze re-tested for methyl alcohol. Joe and I saw it with our very eyes. Our booze is clean."

"What about Rosalie?" Julius said, his eyes bouncing back and forth between Dash and Joe. "You mean to tell me you two carried her body all the way to *Bellevue*?"

Calvin whistled. "That place gives me the willies. All those barber surgeons? And I heard they've been using some mysterious elixir to kill the city's poor folks. Hand to God!"

"Why would they do tha', lad?" Joe asked.

"To clean up the streets! If ya can't house 'em, might as well kill 'em. Hey, now! Maybe that methyl stuff is what they're using."

Joe's voice was full of skepticism. "And they announced that to the whole world?"

"The truth hides in plain sight, Mr. O'Shaughnessy. Makes it harder to believe."

Julius rolled his eyes. "Will you stop telling stories, Cal? Our bosses just dragged a dead body to Bellevue in the dead of night!"

"No, we didn't," Dash replied. "Someone else did. Someone who will not turn us in or blackmail us, that I can assure you."

This did not, however, assure them.

Calvin tossed one of his drumsticks to the floor. "We're all going to jail."

Vernon added, "I guess I should close the deal with Lisa. I might not see a woman for a long time, since I'll be up at Sing Sing."

Just then, the WC door opened and in walked Finn, dressed in an outfit that would stop any conversation: black pinstripe trousers and shoes, black suspenders, no shirt, and a bright pink bow tie. Black lines traced his eyes, and heavy lavender was smeared onto his upper lids. His lips were painted dark and arched in the popular "Cupid's Kiss" shape.

All five men turned to look at him.

Finn placed a hand over his heart. "My, my, good to know I can still turn a few heads."

Vernon said, "Finney, what the hell is going on? Why did a rich girl die here, and why'd you take her to Norris?"

"Goodness, Vern, there is such a thing as conversational tact."

"Yeah, well, we need to know if we're all going to go to jail as—what do they call it?—accessories after the fact."

"Dearies, will you three calm down? Our fearless leader has *everything* under control."

Julius snorted. "Don't seem like it."

Dash replied, "The cops and her father have no idea she was here, and we haven't had a newshawk come anywhere near our club."

"Yeah," Vernon said, "but all it takes is one person here to recall Miss Tabloid Sensation and then we're in the soup."

Finn waved him off with a flick of the wrist. "Vern, don't be such a worrywart; we will be protected by the goddesses."

"No offense, Finn, but I don't believe in any of that pagan stuff."

"Then believe plain old common sense. Rosalie was known to visit all kinds of speaks. Even if someone could remember her being here, it wouldn't be odd or strange. Certainly not out of the ordinary."

"And given our clientele, lads," Joe added, "no one is going to volunteer tha' information to anyone, *especially* the police."

Dash jumped in. "One more important point. The coroner stated very clearly the bad liquor she ingested would've taken thirty hours or more to kill her. If anyone is trying to figure out where she'd been when she consumed the lethal liquor, then they'll be looking at her whereabouts Friday or Saturday night, not Sunday."

"Which means," Calvin slowly said, "that nobody is looking at us."

"That's right." Dash looked at his band members. "You're safe. We're all safe here."

And please, please let that be the truth.

"Alright," Vernon said, "I'll buy it. For now."

Julius wasn't completely convinced, but a resigned sigh escaped his lips. "In the meantime, if anyone asks about Rosalie, none of us knows nothing."

Dash forced a smile. "Goes without saying."

The band, finally mollified, nodded to him and then returned to setting up for the night's show.

Finn came over to the bar and, with a graying towel, wiped down the surface. Joe was back to counting bottles.

"That was a close one," Finn murmured.

"Ya," Joe muttered, "I can't believe ya told 'em, lassie."

Dash replied, "It's actually better for them to know. That way, if they see something strange, they can protect themselves. Besides . . . I didn't want to lie to them."

A throat cleared behind him. He turned around to see Calvin. Behind him, Julius and Vernon were chatting up a storm, ignoring the rest of them.

"Mr. Parker?" Calvin said.

"Yes?"

"You said that wherever Rosalie was last Friday or Saturday was most likely where she drank something bad, right?"

"According to Charles Norris."

"Well. Ever since they reported about that Rosalie girl, everyone's been talking about her. And in our neighborhood, everyone's been saying they've seen her around."

"In Harlem?"

That wasn't a surprise. Harlem was one of the hottest places for speakeasies and music. A girl like Rosalie would've certainly made her rounds there.

"Yes, sir," Calvin replied. "And someone said she made a big scene at the Oyster House recently."

"The Oyster House. Recently." An anxious hum began to buzz Dash's chest. "How recent?"

"Last Friday."

It was at the farthest end of Charles Norris's timeline, but the implications weren't good.

"Does she know?" Dash asked, referencing a woman they both knew who performed there.

"I don't know. Maybe, maybe not. It's El. She pays attention to herself and any girl who strikes her fancy."

"She's like Vern in that regard." Dash stood quietly for a moment, thinking. Vernon and Julius were still laughing and carrying on, none the wiser. "Thanks for telling me, Calvin."

"You're welcome." He paused, then asked, "What do you think it means? Was she poisoned there?"

"I don't know, Cal. I honestly don't know."

"What do we do?"

Dash nodded to himself. "Simple. We warn her."

12

The Oyster House line was already down the block of 133rd and Seventh Avenue. A steady row of men and women, mostly Black, with a few white downtowners sticking out like bleach stains. All were dressed in their finest threads, men in their colorful cake-eater suits and felt hats, women in their peacock feathers and cloche caps.

And why shouldn't they show off their glad rags? They were in the heart of Harlem's nightclub district, which was pumping full of music, rattling motorcars, whistling traffic cops, men strolling and laughing, vendors yelling *hot peanuts!*, and women shouting for taxicabs. Every opened doorway spilled out the pounding of piano keys and the squeal of cornets. Every opened window the moan of the blues on Victrolas. And every person Dash saw was beaming with happiness—himself included, despite the bad news he had to deliver.

And he had to deliver it fast. Wim was to pick Dash up within the hour.

In the Oyster House line, cigarettes were constantly lit, their glowing embers bobbing up and down while conversations buzzed with anticipation of seeing Harlem's biggest cabaret sensation: El Train.

Dash couldn't wait either, so he walked up to the doorman, a man he knew well by the name of Horace. A giant Black man with a square-shaped head and a mean expression. His build threatened to rip the shoulders of his shiny black suit. Most men avoided his temper, which was slow to build, but once it did, heaven help who caused the fuse to blow. A few men, duped by alcohol, tried testing Horace's limits—and lost. Badly.

Despite the intimidating physique, Dash always found the man to be sweet and kind, with a gentle voice to match. The rough doorman was just a part he played—granted, one he played very well.

"Hello, Horace," Dash said.

Horace's face lit up in a grin. "Mr. Parker! I haven't seen you in almost a month!" Then he looked around, concerned. "Les doesn't know you're here, does he?"

He meant Leslie Charles, the owner of the Oyster House. Leslie and Dash had some words a while back, which resulted in Dash getting banned indefinitely from the Oyster House. Dash was hoping all could be forgiven.

Fat chance of that. You accused the man of murder.

Dash forced a smile. "He doesn't. I know, I know," he said before Horace could, "I'm not allowed inside. But I need to talk with El."

"El's on stage right now. Her first set should be wrapping up soon." Horace glanced behind him, looking through the opened door of the club. "Not sure if you'll be able to reach her though. Les is sitting in the middle of the bar watching the show."

Dash furrowed his brow. "Why's he doing that? He's

never watched her show before. Nor cared to, now that I think about it."

Horace grimaced. "He got some complaints from patrons that she was being too rough with them. You know how she does. Calling them out, putting them in the spotlight, getting the crowd to laugh along at their expense. One night, I guess she went too far."

"I bet she's thrilled with being babysat."

"Mr. Parker, the fuss she kicked up? I thought she was going to start throwing dishes like them Italians do."

"I think it's the Greeks, but Mediterranean all the same." Dash looked back at Horace. "Any chance you can give her a message from me?"

Horace said he'd try once her set ended. "What's this all about, Mr. Parker?"

"It's about a girl, a downtowner who was here last Friday night. Caused a big scene."

"Oh. *Her.*"

"You know about it?"

"I saw it. Ugly thing. She's sitting in the front row, minding her business. Then her father decides to drag her out of there. Les was on my back big time about that. Said how could I let that downtowner through? I said he paid, didn't seem to be trouble, didn't even cut the line. Not sure what Les wanted me to do in that case. Why you asking after her?"

"It's a long story, Horace. Think you can get to El for me?"

Horace glanced back inside the club, calculating the risk. He turned around to Dash. "I'll see what I can do."

Dash thanked him and stood to the side, killing time smoking a cigarette, then another.

Soon he heard the raving ovation El often earned. He saw Horace turn, nod at him, and then leave the line to go inside. A crowd of patrons exited the club, heading off to their next stop of the night. Several minutes passed. Dash was thinking about lighting another cigarette when he saw Horace return to his post. Dash walked up to him, and Horace handed him a piece of paper. Dash opened it and saw El's familiar handwriting.

GO TO THE BACK ALLEY, THIRD WINDOW ON YOUR LEFT.

Dash tapped the piece of paper. "Thank you, Horace."

"Any time, Mr. Parker. I hope Les forgives you soon."

"From your mouth to heaven's ears."

Dash turned on the corner and headed south until he came to the alley that ran behind the club's dark brick building. A narrow, darkened space. Gravel and dirt crunched underneath his heels. Trashcans with their askew lids allowed the rotting aromas to drift upward. Conversations and laughter from the tenants above the club floated down around him.

When he arrived at the third window on his left, he was surprised to find it higher up than usual. Just a rectangular opening half a foot above his head. Faint light escaped it.

He craned his neck upward. "El?"

Her moon-shaped face appeared in the rectangle, which was so small, it hid her usual top hat. "Dashiell High Hat Parker, *what* are you doing here? Les is gonna pitch a royal fit if he sees you. And if I had to deal with another one of his *this is my club, this is my office, you do what I say* nonsense, I might commit murder."

A knock thundered behind her.

She called over her shoulder, "It's occupied! That's why

the goddamn door is locked!" She faced Dash again. "People can be so dense these days."

Dash squinted. "Are you in the water closet?"

"Well, where did you *think* I was gonna go? Les's office? He says I'm on probation, whatever the hell that means, and I can't just use his office whenever I feel like it." She sputtered out an exasperated sigh. "Honest to God, I'm looking forward to the day when us women rule the roost and we hens get to order these ungrateful cocks around."

"Horace tells me you've been a bit too unruly with some of the guests."

"Shoot, they can't take a joke no more? All I said to the man was that his pencil dick couldn't push a single sheet of paper across a desk, much less—"

"I don't need to hear the rest."

El grinned, flashing bright white teeth with a snaggletooth in the center. "You should. It was damn funny."

"I take it the man didn't find it so humorous."

"Can you believe that? And Les normally doesn't take to downtowners complaining in his club. But I guess this man had some serious sugar. That's the only way to get to a man like Les." El shrugged, the shoulders of her usual men's tuxedo momentarily flashing into view. "Alright, enough chin music. What's so damn urgent I gotta yell out a WC window?"

Dash told her the situation as quickly as he could, asking at the end, "Do you remember seeing her last Friday night?"

"Oh yeah, and only because of the scene she made with her father. Otherwise, I wouldn't have noticed—all them white girls look the same to me."

"You saw the fight?"

"Uh huh, and I don't take kindly to interruptions in my

set, and they stopped my show *cold*. Yelling back and forth. Him saying she broke her promise to him, and her saying she made it under duress and he couldn't expect to hold her to it. Horace had to intervene and get them out. Les was *furious*. Almost banned downtowners from ever stepping foot in his club again."

"I don't think I've ever heard of Les getting that angry."

Except when I accused him of murder.

"Hell, I was angry too," El replied. "We had a special guest that night and we wanted to make a good impression."

"Who was the guest of honor?"

"Madam J. A. Watkins of the Watkins Hotel."

"I just heard about that place tonight. My band subbed there this week. Said it was a swanky joint."

"Get a bunch of Black folks together, we always take things to the moon and back. That hotel has earned her *millions*, Dash. *Mil-lions*. She's a bona fide millionaire."

He knew, of course, that there were rich people in Black Harlem, but still, he'd never heard of a *female* millionaire in this neighborhood.

"That's incredible," he said.

"It's rare we get a celebrity of that status in this joint, so for two downtowners to bring their worst behavior? Shit. And I could use a gig at her place too. Maybe I can finally get outta this dump."

Behind her, that was another loud knock and an impatient rattling of the door handle. Then a muffled female voice said, "What the hell you doing in there? Laying an egg?"

El turned. "As a matter of fact, I'm laying your husband. He was about to finish, but you interrupted us and now we gotta start all over."

"Don't talk to me like that, you jezebel bearcat! I'll give you a what-for—"

"Unless your gospel pipe is as big as mine, girlie, you're not going to do diddly! Now quietly wait your turn or I'll be in here *all* night." She returned her gaze to Dash. "What else you want to know?"

"Was there anyone with her that night?"

El looked upwards as she thought. "I believe so. Yeah, there was. A man and a woman. Girl, really."

"Did you get a good look at them?"

"The girl, I can't recall because—"

Dash joined her in saying, "All white girls look alike."

"But the man?" El scrunched up her round face. "He was the size of a Frigidaire—big and square-shaped—and had the whitest blond hair I'd ever seen. Almost like an old man's, you know?"

Dash wondered if those were Rosalie's former roommates Marty Grice and Tillie White. If it was, interesting they were with her two nights before she died—and interesting they lied to the press about it.

"Hey, Dash," El said. "You finished day dreaming, cause I've got to get back to work."

Dash shook himself. "Apologies, El. One last question: any chance that Leslie got a bad batch?"

"Of booze? You thinking she got sick here?"

"Timing is just about right. And we both know Leslie does things on the cheap."

"Shit, I know that's right. Door handles fall off, stairs splintered and cracked, barstools with uneven legs." She shook her head. "But I don't see him getting a bunch of poisonous brew to sell. That don't serve his purpose. Doors and chairs are one thing—liquor that makes you ill is another."

"Do you know who his supplier is?"

"No, I don't, and I don't wanna know. The less I'm familiar with his shit, the better."

"Ever heard the name Nicholas Fife?"

"Ever hear the phrase *I don't know*? Let me repeat it for ya—"

Dash waved her off. "No need, El, I got it."

Another pounding of the WC door behind El and then a man's voice—Leslie Charles's voice—shouted, "Whoever's in here, we got a line halfway to the Heights. You've got to the count of ten to get your ass out here."

El replied over her shoulder, "Les, is that any way to talk to your star talent?"

"El? Goddammit, woman, get your he-she self outta there. We got guests!"

"I'll come out when I'm damn good and ready."

"El, remember what we talked about and what I would do if you did not behave?"

Dash gave a quizzical look to El.

She half-turned her head to him and said, "He threatened to fire me."

"You should go. I don't want to get you into more trouble."

"Oh, please. He's all bark and no bite."

"But still—"

Leslie yelled, "Like I said, I'm gonna give ya to the count of ten."

Dash said, "Go on, El. Keep this gig so you can earn enough sugar to run your own place."

"Alright, alright, I'll go. You take care."

"You as well."

El's face disappeared from the rectangular window. Then Dash heard the squeal of an opening door, and her voice rang out, "Les, I'm so glad you learned to count. Are you still using your fingers and toes? You know there's numbers higher than ten. Well, eleven, if you count that pinky between your—"

"El, you better hush—"

The rest of the conversation was silenced by the slamming of the WC door and a frustrated female voice saying, "God Almighty."

13

"Which crew are we following tonight?" Dash asked.

He was once again sitting in the front seat of one of Fife's cars, this one a dark green, stamping his feet against the floorboards to keep them warm. Dash's breath came out like steam from a train. Same for Wim, his gloved hands idly tapping the steering wheel. A cold snap tonight. The windows had kept fogging up, so they'd resorted to rolling them all down. A thin mist hugged the ground around them with a charcoal sky overhead. Fife's Queens warehouse twinkled in the distance, the loading dock lit by large lights.

Wim glanced over at Dash. "Tonight's suspects are Val Russo and Louis Snyder, also known as The Blockheads."

"Why do you call them that?"

"Because they have big square-shaped heads and they're quite a few nickels short of a dollar. Not very original but overwhelmingly accurate."

Dash looked through the army binoculars. "Which one is which?"

Wim squinted his eyes. "Val Russo is on the right side of the truck, that short, squatty man with dark greasy hair and a sweaty, slimy face, like a toad's. And the one on the left side of the truck is Louis Snyder; dark, hooded eyes, thin lips, and a mustache that looks like a French *accent aigu*." Wim turned to Dash, mischievous grin wide and sparkling. "I know that because of the one French class I took."

"Where did Fife find them?"

Wim gave him a curious look. "Why do you ask?"

Dash shrugged. "Maybe their origins might give us a clue to motive."

"That won't help you there. Val and Louis came over from Europe. Val from Italy, Louis from Holland. Nobody would give them a room or a job."

"Why? Because they're Europeans?"

"Because they're Jewish. Mr. Fife likes to collect misfit toys, he told me once. Those people who are unwanted. He feels a kinship with them, he says. Also, they'll be the ones most loyal to you. In theory," he added with a trace of irony.

"Are you a misfit toy as well?"

"Oh, my yes. My parents threw me out onto the street after catching me with another boy. Spent several years learning how to cause distractions and pick pockets. I was picking the pocket of this one gentleman and to my absolute surprise and delight, he caught me."

"Was that man Fife?"

Wim grinned. "He's right. You are clever."

"Occasionally. And Lowell? How is he a misfit?"

"Mr. Henley? He keeps things real quiet about him. I had to do some snooping, but I found out he's an orphan. Spent his whole childhood in an orphanage. No recollection of his parents. No one taking him on neither. Truly unwanted."

"Might explain his disposition."

"Hmm, surly, at best. Doesn't help he can't stand our kind. Hates the fact Fife is taking on pansy speaks."

"Think he might be our saboteur?"

Wim smirked. "If he is, he's been damned lucky. He's more of the impulsive type. Can't imagine he'd have thought this one out."

They turned their attention to the warehouse loading dock. The minutes dragged by.

"What about Makowski?" Dash asked. "What's his story?"

"He's a fixer. He cleans up messes—which sometimes means taking care of living, breathing men. Mr. Fife says he's so sneaky, no one hears him approach before they've been killed. He keeps to the shadows and is one of the most feared men in our troupe. To have someone defy him, push him around like you did, well, he was, as they say, fit to be tied. But Mr. Fife was most adamant that you were not to be touched. If anything happened to you, he said, he'd kill Makowski and throw his family, parents and all, into the gutter."

"And that worked?"

"You're alive, aren't you? Makowksi has special reason to protect his family. Polish people rank about where Jews, the Irish, and Blacks are in this city. That hideous scar on his neck? From a bar fight. A few of the patrons didn't want a Pol sitting amongst them. Fife was the only one who'd employ him after that. Without Makowski as breadwinner, his family would starve. I daresay, I've never seen Mr. Fife be *so* protective of a speak owner before you. Makes me wonder if you, yourself, are a misfit toy."

Dash felt himself blush. He cleared his throat. "I suppose I am. I . . . " He cleared his throat again. " . . . my family was wealthy."

"I *knew* that. You seem so well refined, and your suits? Takes some sugar to look that good."

An awkward smile. "Yes, well. The Parkers are a wealthy bunch, and my parents raised me to follow in their footsteps. Work for my father's company, date the daughters of my mother's friends, go into complementary business ventures with my brother to expand the family influence throughout the city. My life was all planned out to the smallest detail. It would've been so easy to follow the plan. After all, it would've kept me rich, kept me in high standing in society. I never would've had to worry about making a mistake or doing something incorrectly, because my parents accounted for every possibility and mitigated every wrong turn."

"Why would they do that?"

"To ensure nothing but success, of course." Dash looked out the car window. "But I didn't belong there. I knew it from a young age, just like I knew gravity or the sky was blue. I never understood the things they believed were so important. Money. Reputation. Class. They all felt so *meaningless* to me. I tried, I swear to heaven, I did, but I just couldn't make myself . . . care about any of it. Don't misunderstand me, I know perfectly well what wealth, reputation, and class gets you in this world, and how hard life is without them. But being smack dab in the middle of those three realities, it just seemed such a narrow way of living."

Wim nodded, humming to himself. "What happened?"

Dash's cheeks burned even more. "My younger sister died. From that damnable flu years back. She was only twelve. It was then I realized how superfluous our world was in the grand scheme of things."

"Su—come again?"

"Oh. Silly, I mean. Such stress and effort over what was

nothing more than imaginary importance." Dash paused. "And . . . I fell in love. With someone I wasn't supposed to love. Someone who, in turn, loved *me*, not who I was supposed to be. He was our family tailor. Victor Agramonte, although professionally, he went by Victor Hartford." He turned to Wim. "The original Hartford of Hartford & Sons."

Wim gasped. "Scandalous!"

Dash couldn't help but chuckle. "Oh yes, that is the word to use."

"Did he approach you? Or was it the other way around?"

"I approached him. The first time I ever acted on my own, it seemed. I still remember the butterflies in my stomach, my knees buckling, hands shaking. I don't know how I got the words out, but I did. He didn't respond. Not then. I was so afraid I had intuited the situation incorrectly, that he would tell my father. But a few days later, he gave me a slip of paper with his tailor shop's address."

"The tailor shop you now own?"

Dash nodded. "My father found out about us. How could he not? I was never good at subterfuge for high society, so I was ill-suited for this kind of double life. I was given a choice. Wealth, reputation, and class, or, as he put it, a *'life of poverty and degeneracy.'*"

"You chose the latter."

"I chose freedom."

Wim nodded to himself. "If I had been given that choice, I'd have chosen the same thing." He waited a beat. "And what happened between you and the tailor? I assume he's not around any more, given your Irish Setter."

"Victor had to leave. He was trying to get his family

over to the States, but that new Immigration Act stopped him. In the end, he chose family over . . . over me."

A sympathetic glance. "That must've hurt."

"It did. It does. But I understand it. His culture—he was Catalan, by the way—family is everything."

"And what about in your culture?"

"Mine? You mean high society?" A bitter chuckle. "Family is a weapon. A name to beat others into submission —even those who have it. *Especially* those who have it."

"I assume this Victor character left you his shop and you turned it into a speakeasy."

"Yes to both. You see, I couldn't sew or cut worth a damn, though Lord knows, Victor tried to teach me. I wasn't good at a trade, but, thanks to my social climbing family, I was impeccably good at hosting. Seemed to me at the time, owning a club would be a natural fit. And an honest tribute to Victor."

"How was that?"

"He loved music, in particular jazz. He introduced me to it just as it was coming out of New Orleans."

"Sounds like he introduced you to a lot of things." Wim winked.

Dash smiled, remembering those calloused but gentle hands unbuttoning his shirt, those dark eyes reflecting the flickers of the candle on the nightstand, those lips touching the base of his throat . . .

"That he did," he said, his voice thick and heavy.

"And the name? Pinstripes? Was that just a tailor pun?"

Dash shook himself awake from the languid pull of his past. "Not exactly," he said. "Pinstripes was Victor's favorite pattern. He always wore them." Dash gazed out his window. "And looked marvelous in them . . . "

Suddenly, Wim sat up in his seat. "They're ready to go." He started the car and placed it into gear. "And so are we."

Like the days and nights before, they crossed over the East River into Manhattan. Val Russo and Louis Snyder apparently had the Money Route: high-end restaurants on Madison and Park, a few of the upscale hotels near Fifth Avenue, a few luxury places near Columbus Circle.

It was after the Dakota, a ritzy apartment building next to Central Park West, that things began to change.

"What's this?" Wim said, a peculiar note in his voice.

Val and Louis's truck turned onto Riverside Drive, heading north.

"I take it this isn't their normal route?" Dash said, stating the obvious.

"No, siree."

Wim turned onto Riverside Drive as well.

The road curved and snaked around the uneven landscape bordering the Hudson. They passed the Eighties and the Nineties. Apartment buildings gave way to mansions of the nouveau riche, immigrants who managed to make fortunes despite their place of birth.

"Where are you going, boys?" Wim muttered.

Once they reached the Hundreds, the truck began to slow down, as if they were looking for an unfamiliar location. At 107th Street, they turned, pulling to a stop in front of a white mansion.

Wim, who was three blocks down, turned onto 106th Street and gently braked the car. He opened the door. "Follow me, and whatever you do, don't make a sound."

That was when Dash saw the gun in his hand. Dash raised his hands, indicating cooperation.

Wim was confused for a second, then annoyed. "Oh, for goodness sakes!" he hissed. "I'm not holding you up. It's insurance against the blockheads. We're wasting valuable time. Let's *go*, Mr. Parker."

Wim stepped out into the street and took off like a shot, running towards the corner of 106th and Riverside. He barely made a sound as he did so. Dash hesitated for a moment, then followed after him. Once he joined Wim on the corner, they stood wordlessly, peering around the stone wall of the neighboring house.

Riverside was clear. Fife's truck was parked by the white mansion one house down from Dash and Wim. The truck's cab looked empty.

Wim looked up at Dash and nodded. Together, they quickly traversed the distance between houses. A three-foot high stone wall surrounded the lot of the white mansion, and they crouched underneath it to keep from being seen. They crept along Riverside, their heads down, their shoulders hunched.

At the corner of 107th and Riverside, they paused. Wim peered around the corner but jerked back when he heard voices. He turned to Dash and put a finger to his lips.

The voices were male but muffled.

A snarky laugh followed. No humor in it, just barely disguised contempt.

An unintelligible reply, the voice hard and tight.

Finally, a clear set of words in the response: "Right, bub. Whatever you say."

Wim whispered to Dash, "That's Val."

Another voice, older, replied, "Watch your mouth, boy."

"Watch *yours*, Old Timer. Or I'll—"

"Don't you threaten me. You're in no position to make such demands. *You* are breaking the law."

"Hey, Pops, I hate to break it to ya, but so are you."

A pause.

"Mr. Frazier, I sympathize with ya, I do. Ya gotta bury your daughter tomorrow, so I'll give you what you want, but it's gotta be for the right price. I'm not running a charity here. I'm already catching hell for missing Yom Kippur tonight."

Frazier! The name caused a surge of adrenaline to flow through Dash's veins. What were Val and Louis doing here with Rosalie's father?

Wim noticed the change in Dash's body and gave him a questioning glance. Dash shook his head, indicating he'd tell him later.

Leonard Frazier's voice was filled with fury. "You'll get the right price when you bring back what I've asked of you."

Another pause.

"I'll see ya Sunday night. Good evening, Old Timer."

The click of shoes on concrete.

Dash and Wim flattened themselves against the property's outer wall—as much as they could flatten themselves in a crouching position. Wim brought the gun up, his thumb on the hammer, his finger lightly touching the trigger.

"You get the money?" a third male voice asked. This must've been Louis.

"Not yet," replied Val.

"What's he want it for?"

"The less we know, the better, Louis."

The truck doors slammed, the engine turned over and rattled. A squeal of gears. Dash poked his head up over the stone wall and saw the truck driving away.

He felt a tap on his shoulder. Wim motioned for them to return the way they came. Still crouching, they made their way over to the neighboring house, where they stood upright and ran back to their car.

As soon as they got in, Wim placed the pistol in a

holster sewn into his door. Strange how Dash had never noticed it before.

"What was that back there?" Wim looked at Dash. "Are you all right?"

Dash couldn't slow down his racing thoughts. Leonard Frazier and Fife's men. What was going on?

Wim repeated his question.

Dash told him whose house that was and why it was significant.

Wim's expression darkened, an odd look on such a playful man. "How on earth did this Frazier fellow figure out who was supplying you liquor?"

"I don't know. I didn't think a man like Leonard would have any idea how to contact anyone in Manhattan's underworld." Dash tried to calm himself for a moment. "It might not even be about me and my speak. Fife's been having lots of poisonings lately in his supplied clubs. Perhaps Leonard got wind of it?"

"And how did he do that? Fife's problems are not in the free press. He made sure of that." They stared at one another for a moment. Then Wim faced forward again, starting up the car. "We need to go to Mr. Fife."

14

Where Wim drove Dash next, he didn't know. He was instructed to wear a blindfold, which initially didn't sit well with him.

"I know, it's disconcerting," Wim said when Dash objected to the request, "but those are the boss's orders. There should be one under your seat. Kindly place it around your eyes."

Dash's alarmed expression caused Wim to laugh.

"Nothing is going to happen to you. I told you, Fife has ordered you to be kept safe above all else. He just wants *his* secrets to be kept secret."

Reluctant, Dash rooted around under his seat and eventually found the strip of fabric. It felt like silk. Dash brought it up. It *was* silk. He held it up to Wim, who read his mind.

"He likes the finer things in life."

"Better than wool over the eyes, I suppose."

But still, Dash hesitated.

"Please, Mr. Parker. One more block and I'll unfortunately have to put the blindfold on you myself."

Dash watched Wim's eyes. Still playful. Still whimsical.

Yet Dash had no doubt if pushed, Wim would do whatever was necessary to keep his boss happy. He nodded once to Wim, then tied the black silk around his head.

Darkness.

Everything was reduced to its core elements. The vibrations of the motorcar. The push backward with its acceleration, the pull forward with its braking. The tug to the right and left during turns. Car horns blaring. People yelling. The smell of exhaust and cigarettes coming through the windows.

A jolt and then several bumps. Cobblestones? Bricks? There were still a few of those ancient roadways around the city, but usually at the edges of the island—the far south, the far west. Were they near So-Ho? Wall Street?

A few more turns, then they skidded to a stop.

"Alright, Mr. Parker. Someone will be opening the doors for you. Please don't be alarmed, but please follow their instructions. And the walkways are a little uneven, so keep light on your feet."

Immediately Dash's door was opened and a set of hands grabbed him, pulling him by the lapels out of the car. He was roughly jerked to his feet.

"Careful!" Wim called from behind Dash. "This is precious cargo."

"Whatever you say, Wim," a tough voice replied.

"It's not what I say, it's what Mr. Fife says. Would you like to explain to him why you're disobeying his orders?"

The tough voice grunted but relented. A gentler hand grabbed Dash's bicep and began leading him forward. True to Wim's word, the walkways were a minefield of trips and stumbles. The firm hand on Dash's bicep thankfully kept him steady.

A door squealed opened.

The tough voice said, "We got stairs, fella."

Downward, they went.

Damp earth and dust filled the air, tickling Dash's nose. He tasted something gritty and grainy through his teeth. At the bottom of the stairs, he was directed left, tripping over a doorway.

"Oops. Sorry," the tough voice said, though he didn't sound very apologetic.

Another left turn and then the smells changed.

Incense. Cigarettes laced with dope. Musky sweet-tinged sweat.

The sounds changed too.

Heavy breathing. Wet whispers. Soft moaning.

Dash's hairs on the back of his neck stood up. He knew those sounds, but why were they *here?*

The blindfold was removed, and the darkness disappeared.

Dash blinked, the light much brighter than he expected, causing black splotches in his vision. Eventually those dark circles disappeared and his vision cleared.

First he saw the naked flesh of men on top of men, bodies ranging from thin and hairless to thick and hairy. Then he saw Corinthian columns placed on either side of the mass of men, white curtains hanging in the background. The rest of the room was a typical Manhattan basement: brick walls, uneven floors, lightbulbs on chains. Which didn't explain the brightness of the room. Dash looked around. Ah, a giant spotlight was aimed at the writhing men. A large camera was next to the light, a bored man turning the hand crank on the side, the flick of the rotating film sounding like playing cards pinned to bicycle spokes. Lastly, he saw Fife sitting dressed in his usual tuxedo, elbows on the arms of his chair, hands together, his fingers forming a triangle with the finger tips touching his lips. His eyes watched intently the action before him.

Fife didn't notice their arrival, just kept watch over what looked like six men on top of a long dinner table in various positions, none of which, in Dash's opinion, looked particularly comfortable.

When one of the thinner, hairless men at the far end of the table leaned his head back and prepared to give a long, drawn-out cry, a booming voice suddenly filled the room.

"No, no, *no.* That's not right at all. Cut!"

All of the men stopped their movements and looked up.

Fife leapt from his chair and walked over to the man who had offended him. "Aiden, Aiden, my dear sweet Aiden. It looks like you're in absolute pain, not pleasure."

"I'm sorry, Mr. Fife," the small man replied, "it's just that this table is cutting into my lower back."

"I know, dear heart, I know. But that's the point. We're supposed to be in one of Caligula's famous orgies and Caligula was known to mix both pain and pleasure."

"But how do I make it hurt less?"

Fife gazed down at the young man. "You focus on the *pleasure,* Aiden. You work through the pain to get to the pleasure. Like in life, eh? Everyone, clean yourselves up and we'll start again in half an hour. And Aiden? I want you to think of nothing else but what our head centurion Wyatt is doing to you. I don't care if a knife is cutting into your back. Focus on that soldier and his impeccable . . . attributes. Got it?"

"Yes, sir."

The men began to climb off the table, grabbing robes that laid off to the side before exiting out another door. The realization of what this was stunned Dash. Fife was making a stag film . . . but with inverted men! Dash knew such films with so-called normal men and women existed, but to see his fellow kind in the same ludicrous sets? The same ridiculous poses? He was shocked.

Fife turned around and saw Dash standing there. "Mr. Parker! And Wim! A wonderful surprise!"

Dash managed to rouse himself. "Good evening, Mr. Fife."

Fife held out his hands, indicating the set. "What do you think of my new business venture?"

Dash struggled to find the words. "It's . . . quite . . . unexpected?"

Fife cocked his head to the side. "Why should it be unexpected?"

"I just thought you were only in . . . well, you know . . ."

"Booze? My dear naive Dash, don't you know a man has to diversify? One can't rely on one stream of income alone." Fife pointed at him. "You yourself have the speak in the back and the alterations out front, do you not?"

"I—I suppose."

"You suppose," Fife murmured. A throaty chuckle followed. "You do intrigue me, sir." The gangster looked over at Wim. "I'm assuming since you're here you have news for me."

"Yes, sir."

A slow, seductive smile. "Excellent. Would you both like a drink? I say, I am *parched*. Mr. Henley!"

Lowell Henley suddenly emerged from the shadows. "Yeah, Boss?"

Dash jumped at the sight of him. How could a man that big move so stealthily?

Fife was amused at Dash's reaction. "We need refreshment."

Lowell jerked his thumb at Wim. "Why can't he do it?"

"Because, Mr. Henley, he's here to give me vital information. He is a guest, not a servant tonight."

"Respectfully, it ain't my job, sir."

Fife's eyes flickered. His smile dimmed a bit. "Your job, Mr. Henley, is whatever I say it is. Now. Gin rickeys all around. And get the good stuff."

Dash held his breath. He'd never before seen anyone be insolent with Fife, and he was terrified of what would happen next.

The two men stared at one another. Lowell finally relented and stormed out of the room, taking the same door the actors had taken.

Wim said, "You okay, Mr. Fife?"

Fife frowned. "He's being more difficult lately. Says I'm not giving him enough challenges." He turned back to Wim and Dash. "Who needs challenges when you can have good times, am I right, gentlemen?"

Suddenly he clapped his hands together with a loud *pop!*

"Now! What have you learned, my dear Watsons?"

Wim went first, describing everything they saw, including the conversation with Leonard Frazier and Val Russo. Dash then confirmed the story, adding a little color with what he knew of the Fraziers, thanks to Finn's incessant tabloid reading.

Fife's face darkened. "And the Fraziers are the family of that girl who died in your club, Mr. Parker?"

Dash nodded.

"Why is her father doing business with my men? Is it information he's after? And if so, is it information about me?"

Fife's eyes stared off into the distance, those warm brown eyes going black.

"Val and Louis, what are you two up to?" he murmured to himself. His expression cleared and he stared hard at Dash. "I want you to look into this family. Keep a very close eye on them. And tell me everything you've learned."

"What about Val and Louis?" Dash asked.

"I'll deal with them later. You and Wim follow them Sunday night. Let's see what the old man asked for—and if my men give it to him."

15

Seeing it in the daylight, Dash could see just how impressive the Frazier mansion truly was, situated on a picturesque corner of Riverside Drive and West 107th Street. A four-story wonder done up in stunning white marble in the French Renaissance style. Bay windows, archways, and Juliet balconies abounded. The roof was made up of blue-green terra cotta and ceramic tile, brilliant splashes of color against the white stone.

The line of mourners waited patiently on the sidewalk circling the house to be admitted inside.

Joe growled, "What in Christ's name are we doin' here again?"

It wasn't easy convincing him they needed to attend Rosalie's funeral reception. Trying to fit him into his funeral suit he hadn't worn in years did nothing to improve his mood. He could button everything, but sitting down was uncomfortable.

Dash replied, "Fife said to keep an eye on the Fraziers. And an open funeral is one way to get inside the house and hear and see things."

"Ya, but what does that *mean*?"

Finn sighed, exasperated. "It means, you big oaf, that we're to find out just what old man Leonard wanted with Fife's men. What's eating you?"

"He didn't sleep well," Dash said. Truth be told, neither did he. "Our resident Don Juan Reggie had another run-in with another girl."

"Oh, I missed the next chapter!" Finn lamented. "You *must* tell me what happened. You must, you must!"

"Finney," Joe groused, "for cryin' out loud—"

"Oh, what's the harm, Joe?" Dash said. "It was the lead actress, the one the chorus girl despised. Our Reggie isn't too discreet, for said lead actress found out about said chorus girl."

Finn gasped. "Oh, the *scandal*. What did she do?"

"Gave him a what-for, then locked him out of the dressing room."

Joe grumbled, "Aye, and that daft lad kept scratching and pawing at the door all night." He glanced uneasily at the line of people. "Are ya sure they're gonna let us in?"

Dash looked up at the entryway, where the butler was greeting the visitors at the top of a gentle incline of steps.

"Positive," he said. "When I was growing up, the bigger the turnout to a family member's funeral, the better their social standing. If Mr. Frazier wants to retain any societal power in this town, he needs a crowd to justify the press coverage of Rosalie."

"Which," Finn cut in, "she made the front page yet again. This time about the funeral."

Thankfully, the papers made no more mentions of specific speaks. Now their columns were devoted to the Volstead Act and whether or not it should be repealed.

Joe looked around at the sheer number of people

waiting to get inside. "Seems he's gettin' his wish." He glanced over at Dash. "Do ya have a plan at least?"

"We'll walk around and eavesdrop on all the sidebar conversations. See if someone lets loose a secret or two."

Finn added, "And you *know* at a funeral like this, there's bound to be some juicy gossip."

They eventually made it up the short stone steps to the rounded archway of the front door. The butler conveyed his master's thanks for their attendance and detailed where they could find food, drink (no liquor, of course), and where Mr. Frazier and his family were receiving (the parlor).

They went through the grand entryway, itself an impressive display of woodwork, then stepped up into the gallery.

Joe muttered, "Fuck me."

Finn whispered, "Oh my goddesses, look at *this!*"

The impressive woodwork continued, with intricate designs cut deep into the dark, heavy wood ceiling that vaulted a good twelve feet above them. The chandelier hanging in the center acted like a prism, creating miniature rainbows in seemingly every corner. A grand staircase surrounded by gleaming wood archways was to their left, and to their right, two long rectangular windows that overlooked a lush evergreen garden dotted with freshly planted winter kale for the upcoming season. Between the windows sat a grand piano, polished and black, with nary a spot nor a fingerprint to be found upon its ebony surface. A grandfather clock ticked by minutes against the far wall.

The entryway, Dash's mother used to say, *should let people know* exactly *who they're dealing with.*

Up ahead through a grand archway was the dining room. The chairs had been removed from the long table so guests could wander around and pick from the piles of breads, cheese, and fruits.

Joe started in the direction of the food.

Dash caught his shoulder. "Not yet, growing boy."

He pulled Joe in the opposite direction towards the receiving line in the parlor. Finn followed.

When they entered, the full scale of the house began to take shape. A frescoed ceiling of a rabbit and a fox floated above them, marble paneled walls with thick drapes and wall hangings surrounded them, and a deep Oriental rug laid beneath them. Heavy, ornately carved furniture held court in the far corners where a few of the closer friends sat.

"Remember our story if anyone asks how we knew Rosalie?" Dash murmured.

Joe and Finn nodded.

Dash gestured towards the receiving line. "Let's meet the infamous Leonard Frazier."

Given the grandness of the house and the sharpness of his words to Fife's men last night, Leonard Frazier himself was quite a surprise. Unprepossessing, even bland. Modest height, maybe five foot six. Balding, and what hair was left was a dishwater gray. Round glasses dominated a round face on top of an egg-shaped body. Somehow, even the expensive, well-cut black suit seemed apologetic.

"Blessed are the meek," Finn murmured.

"Indeed," Dash replied. Perhaps Leonard played a good game when he needed. Wouldn't be the first time a shy man put on a brave persona.

Leonard stood at the far end of the room between the two windows overlooking the front of the house. Next to him was a woman who did not project the same air of humility. She wore a severe but expensive silk black dress, complete with a lace collar, black stones decorating the bodice, and a long coat. A felt, wide-brim black hat with veil sat squarely on her head, not to the side, as most young women did these days. This must be Rosalie's Aunt Beverly, Leonard's sister.

When Dash and his friends got to the head of the line, Leonard looked at them without seeing them and extended his hand. "Thank you for coming," he said in a quiet voice. His formal manner couldn't disguise his grief, which rolled over Dash in waves.

Sadness was contagious and Dash fought it off the best he could. "Rosalie was a lovely girl. We are so sorry for your loss."

"Thank you. How do you know—" A painful swallow. "Excuse me, how *did* you know Rosalie?"

Dash hoped Finn's recounting of Rosalie's history was accurate. "We worked together in the department store. When she worked, that is."

At first confusion, then recognition. "Ah, yes. Best and Company. And you all sold ladies' hats?"

Finn said, "Oh my yes. Very lucrative if you do it right. Of course, it helps to have superior inventory and I don't mind telling you, Mr. Frazier, that the new Fortmason Saunterer is the *best* felt hat a woman can get in New York City right now. And only at Best!"

Both Dash and Joe turned their heads to gaze at the little man in wonder. Where on *earth* did he pull that from? (Later, they would discover Finn had researched the place where Rosalie worked, including memorizing its advertisements in Dash's own *New Yorker*. "You can't expect me to play a part with nothing to go on, dearies!")

Leonard was also surprised by Finn's fervor. "I see. Well, young man, your enthusiasm is contagious. Or would be, under better circumstances. I'm . . . happy to hear she had friends in the working world."

Beverly finally spoke up, saying in an icy voice, "I'm surprised to find friends of hers from the daylight hours."

Leonard winced. "Beverly, there is no reason to be rude."

"Of course. How forgetful of me. One should always be polite while grieving."

A long-suffering sigh. "Gentlemen," Leonard said, "I'd like you to meet my sister, Beverly Stevens. Rosalie's aunt."

Dash, Joe, and Finn murmured greetings. Underneath the veil, Dash made out a heart-shaped face and pale hair that could've been blond or white.

"Tell me," Beverly said, "was Rosalie on time? Punctual? Respectful? Reliable?"

"Beverly—"

"I'm just curious to see what kind of girl she was outside of this house . . . and outside of a gin mill."

The verbal dagger hit Leonard between the shoulder blades. He bent forward a bit, his shoulders twitching upward.

She went on. "Though God knows I warned her about the cheap stuff. Smoke, I believe it's called."

Joe spoke up. "She was always nice to us, madame. And nice to the customers."

"Oh yes," Finn said, "and she knew her onions too."

The youthful slang confused the Fraziers.

Dash stepped in. "She was quite knowledgeable about the items we sold. As for being on time, she was no more late than the rest of us who have to deal with the unpredictable and quite *unreliable* trains."

"That's right, Bev," Leonard said. "Not everyone has a private car." He gave her a pointed look before returning to the three of them. "Thank you for coming to pay your respects. My family and I sincerely appreciate it."

They murmured their goodbyes and moved down the line. As Dash passed by Beverly, he thought he saw her eyes intently watching his every move. He fought off a shudder. Beverly Stevens was *not* a woman to be trifled with, nor was she someone he wanted interested in him.

Returning to the gallery, Dash, Joe, and Finn collected themselves.

"That woman," Finn said.

Joe replied, "We know, lad. We know."

"The father wasn't the least bit what I expected. From the tabloid reports, they made him sound like . . . well . . . his sister."

Dash needed them to re-focus on the task at hand. "Alright, gents. Let's spread out. Listen in on all conversations." He looked to the grandfather clock against the far wall. He nodded to it. "See the time? Let's meet here at a quarter past the hour."

"You know," Finn said, "if we had wristwatches like you—"

"Finney," Joe growled.

They dispersed. Joe, unsurprisingly, went to the dining room. Finn went to the right into what looked like a sitting room. And Dash, for his part, wandered around the gallery.

Guests had settled into thick clumps, with voices muted to respectful levels. The furtive glances over their shoulders told Dash gossip was being bandied about like a tennis ball. He slowly walked through the gallery, taking in the various murmured conversations.

First an older, married couple:

"What that girl put her poor father through."

"He's holding up well, I think. Not as strong as his

sister, but then again, she was always the tougher built of the two—"

Then two middle-aged men with mustaches:

"—how much do you think this mansion will go for?"

"Oh, I'd say a few easy million. Why? Do you think he'd sell?"

"Not sure what else would keep him here. Wife gone, daughter gone. If I got his commission, it would put me over the top—"

Two spinster-looking sisters:

"—why do you think he never remarried? He's not *un*attractive. A bit plain, perhaps, but nothing a good woman couldn't fix."

"Wanting to throw your hat into the ring, dear?"

"Well, I'm just saying no man should live alone, especially in a house as big as this."

"He doesn't live alone, dear heart, his sister lives with him."

"Oh, that's queer. I couldn't *imagine* living with my sister. Why the very thought of it makes me want to commit murder—"

Two younger-looking bachelors:

"—that sister of his is one cool customer. Absolutely frigid, she is."

"Well, she *did* marry Robert Stevens, and if she's cold, then he was the Arctic."

"What did he do again?"

"Something with railroads, what else? According to his victims—excuse me, former business associates—he was ruthless and pitiless. If he couldn't buy out his competition, he found out ways to destroy them. Didn't care if he ruined your life, as long as he got his share. And his share, from what I hear, was rather large."

"If he was so rich, what is *she* doing living here? I thought he'd have left everything to her in his will."

"The scuttlebutt is, he didn't. Highly scandalous. Gave her a pitiful allowance and gave rest to his mistresses."

"Makes you wonder what she did to deserve that punishment."

"Perhaps not giving him an heir before he kicked the bucket—"

Dash finished his loop around the gallery. What next?

He glanced upwards to the staircase. He and his younger sister Sarah loved sliding down the stairs after they'd just been shined. With a folded blanket underneath them, the freshly polished wood was as slick as ice. The two would scream with laughter as they flew down into the gallery. Every time they'd get to the bottom, they would race up the stairs to do it once more.

He wondered what kind of woman she'd have become. He shook his head at himself. No use missing what could never be.

He started climbing the staircase. A few guests had gathered at the edges, murmuring softly. No one paid him much attention. He kept climbing up until he came to a long hallway where guests waited for the two bathrooms. A crowd this size, the one available water closet on the first floor wouldn't be enough.

At the end of the hallway nearest the stairs were unlocked doors. Either someone forgot, or the Fraziers thought, by virtue of wealth, that no one would go where they weren't supposed to go.

Dash flicked a look over his shoulder and saw that no one was watching him. With a deft, swift movement, he opened one of the doors and stepped inside, closing the door behind him. A guest bedroom, from the looks of it. He rifled through furniture drawers and wardrobes finding nothing of interest before slipping out and sneaking into the adjourning room. Another guest room. Another disappointment.

He waited until the coast was clear, then left the second guest room and walked across the hall. Here, were two other closed doors side by side. He opened the door on the right and stepped inside, closing the door behind him.

Rosalie's bedroom. He was absolutely sure of it.

Unlike the rest of the mansion, this room was filled top-to-bottom with the latest styles. Black and gold bedspread in an eye-catching design of geometric shapes. An ivory lamp with a large base and a very narrow shade on the bedside table. Gold feathers resting in a vase on top of a dresser. Asymmetrical bookshelves with pulps, novels, and manuals on code-cracking. Curious choice, those. Water closet. Regular closet. Doors opening to one of the Juliet balconies. Fireplace for warmth.

Everything a girl could want—except freedom. How closely she must've been watched, especially those last few days. Insolent or not, a human being wasn't meant to be caged, no matter how gilded the bars.

Dash searched under the bed first. Lying on its side was an empty clear glass bottle with no label. Not large, about three inches high, perhaps three-to-four inches in diameter. Reminded Dash of medicine bottles in his mother's cabinet. He sniffed. The tell-tale signs of gin's juniper.

He returned it to its hiding place. He ran his hand under the mattress and searched the bedside table to no avail. The dresser was also a disappointment, with a few of the drawers locked and Dash without the means to pick them open. The dressing table was filled with the usual items for a girl: perfume, makeup, brushes. He did find several flasks of different shapes and sizes, one of which Dash recognized as a "garter flask," where if she were searched, it wouldn't be found. Unless, of course, they looked up her dress.

"Clever girl," he muttered to himself.

He turned his attention to the bookcase and, holding up the books by their spines, let the pages hang loose. Nothing. A frustrated sigh.

He was looking at the dresser again when an idea occurred to him. The dresser was standing on its four legs, a good four inches above the floor. He went over to it and knelt, his hands exploring its underside. Down the center, then the sides, and lastly the corners.

A sharp point of hard paper caused him to wince. With more caution, his fingers managed to extract it from its hiding place, and he brought it out.

A matchbook.

Black, like much of the furnishings and stylings here. The words NEW YORK CITY were printed on the back in gold. He turned it over. A gold etching of a multistory building rising upward. At the base of it was the name WATKINS HOTEL.

Dash glanced up. Where had he heard that name before?

His band. They subbed there while Pinstripes was closed. And El, who said the owner was a special guest the night Rosalie and her father fought at the Oyster House. Dash squinted. But it was a Blacks-only establishment. How on earth did Rosalie get this? Was she given the matchbook that Friday night at the Oyster House? If so, who gave it to her? Madame Watkins herself? But why? Or was she secretly dating a Black man? That would fit with the wildness of Rosalie.

He stood up, pocketing the matchbook. He'd been snooping long enough. It was time to get back with Joe and Finn.

He gently opened the bedroom door and peered out into the hallway. A young woman in black stood with her back to him, waiting for the bathroom. A few moments later, the bathroom door opened, an older woman exiting. The younger woman took her place, closing the door behind her. The older woman paused for a moment to adjust her hat and dress collar. Then she moved off down the hall to the staircase.

Dash waited until she was out of sight before opening the bedroom door wider and stepping through it. He had just closed the door, planning to return to the first floor, when the telephone rang in the neighboring room and a voice responded.

Except the telephone kept ringing.

He stopped.

He tuned his ears like radio dials, trying to find the signal. It was a voice, no doubts about that—but also an odd voice.

He waited.

The telephone continued its shrill warning.

Then, "hello hello, nobody home."

An odd thing to say. The slightly muffled voice was nasal, mid-pitched. It could've been a man or a woman.

Dash didn't move. He waited to see if anyone responded to the voice.

No one did.

The telephone kept ringing, followed by another "hello hello, nobody home."

Dash looked over at the door next to Rosalie's bedroom.

The voice and the telephone seemed to be coming from behind there.

"Hello hello, nobody home."

Then the ringing stopped.

Silence.

What was *that* all about? Curiosity itched at his collar. Dash turned the knob and entered a darkened room.

The voice, much louder now, suddenly changed its words. It said, "Hello, Rosie. How's tricks?"

16

Unfamiliar with the shape of the room, Dash's foot caught the corner of a side table, giving the piece of furniture quite a jolt. Something heavy fell to the floor with a sickening crunch.

"Oh bother," Dash said.

"Uh oh," said the strange voice. "Bev will yell, Bev will yell."

Dammit to hell.

The room was pitch black, which didn't make any sense given that it was nearly noon.

"Bev will yell, Bev will yell," continued the voice.

What the devil *was* this?

Dash paused by the side table and carefully extended his hands until his fingers found a roughened brass surface. His fingers gingerly traced it, around, then up, discovering it to be a circular shape that narrowed as it went upward. Praise be, a lamp!

He fumbled for the switch but was soon able to turn it on. With the hard-won illumination came the realization he had knocked over a vase. It lay on the hardwood floor, broken cleanly into two pieces.

"Oh no," he moaned.

He reached down to pick it up.

The voice said, "Bev will yell, Bev will yell."

Dash looked up.

Sitting diagonally across the room from him in a large brass birdcage was a blue parrot. The bird cocked its head to the right, then left, then right again.

"Well, I'll be," he breathed. "Hello there."

"Hello, Rosie. How's tricks?" the parrot replied.

Dash grabbed the two pieces of the vase and returned them to the side table against the wall. The papers had made no mention of the Fraziers having a pet, much less a talking parrot. Newshawks loved to put those kinds of details into their stories—the eccentricities of the wealthy.

Dash saw he was in a large office. Dark burgundy drapes, like the ones in the drawing room, had been drawn across all the windows, effectively blocking out any light. Odd. Why would they keep this room so dark in the middle of the day?

He looked around him. Nearby on his left was a fireplace, the mantle covered in photographs of a younger Rosalie and an older woman Dash supposed to be her deceased mother. Dash saw the resemblance immediately; same round face, same crinkle around the eyes, same smile, same hair, though the mother's was much longer and more traditionally kept. Dash felt a pang of pity for Leonard. After today, he would have to sit at that desk across from here and stare at the two girls Death had taken from him.

Dash closed the door behind him and explored the rest of the room, turning on more lamps as he went. Two floor-to-ceiling bookshelves met in the corner, filled with leather-bound volumes squeezed in side by side. Leather chairs were dotted here and there; one set in front of the fireplace, the other against the left side wall. A large mahogany wood desk dominated the far end of the room, stacked high with papers, folders, and books, a pair of reading glasses left on top of one pile like a paperweight.

The parrot made a trilling sound, catching Dash's attention. He walked over to the parrot, whose cage was situated in a corner of bay windows.

"Hello," he said, "what's your name?"

The parrot kept tilting its head from side to side. "Hello, Rosie. How's tricks?"

"You and Rosie must've been friends."

He placed his fingers through the bars of the cage to stroke the parrot's feathers. It sidestepped away and then, in a flash, tried to nip Dash's fingers with its beak.

"Hey, watch it," he said, pulling his hand back.

"A bitch. A bitch. Goddamn bitch."

Dash was taken aback. "Where did you learn *that* language, sir? Or is it madame?" Really, who could tell with birds?

The parrot looked at Dash. "She'll ruin us, she'll ruin us."

"I see someone's been having conversations about Rosalie in here."

"Hello, Rosie. How's tricks?"

"Not so good, I'm afraid," Dash replied.

He looked over at the desk. Curious, he sauntered over, pushing the chair ever so slightly back so he could scan over the surface covered in papers. Some documents seemed related to business—railroad-related. Others looked more political in nature. Memos, addendums, words redacted, legalese galore. A different language Dash didn't understand. Handwritten notes in neat, blocky text on official documents and stationary. Dash took out Rosalie's teacup drawing and held it next to some of the papers. The ink might've matched, although black ink was black ink. The paper, however, didn't.

Dash returned the drawing to his interior pocket. A phrase caught his attention: KLAN-SUPPORTED OPPOSITION. He read further. Someone was asking Leonard to financially and publicly support a candidate running against a Ku Klux Klan opponent in Colorado's state primary. The date of the letter was from June. The state primaries were held just a few days ago on September 15th. Dash wondered who won.

On impulse, he opened the center top drawer of the desk. A heart-fluttering thrill tickled his chest. He glanced down. Pens. Stationary. Matches. A tin that turned out to be full of tobacco.

He closed the drawer, then went to the side drawer and quickly pulled it open. A large *bang!* caused Dash to jump and the parrot to call out "Uh oh uh oh, Bev will yell, Bev will yell."

Dash inexplicably put his fingers to his lips and shushed the bird. The bird ruffled its feathers, unrepentant.

What had caused that damnable sound?

He looked down into the side drawer. A queer-looking metal comb lay on top of the collection of papers and letters. It must've been on the far side of the drawer and had slid down from the force of Dash opening it.

Dash more carefully closed the side drawer and, not wanting to press his luck, stepped out from behind the desk. He walked over to the parrot again, fascinated by it.

"Hello again."

"Hello, Rosie. How's tricks?" replied the parrot.

Suddenly, the office door opened behind him, startling Dash. A woman's voice filled the room. "Mac, you're not supposed to talk to the guests."

Dash turned around and saw a maid dressed in uniform enter the room. Dark brown hair piled high on top of itself was secured with butterfly combs and pins. It was so rare to see a woman with long hair these days, what with more and more women adopting the bob. He noticed she had a broom in her hand.

The parrot looked at the maid and replied, "Go chase yourself."

The maid rolled her eyes as she strode across the room, shaking the broom as she went. "You watch your language, you." Her accent elongated her vowels, creating a lovely sing-song lilt. Italian, Dash guessed.

The maid flashed a suspicious glance at Dash. "What are you doing in here? Guests are not allowed upstairs unless it is to visit the bathrooms."

Dash put on what he hoped was an innocent smile. "I apologize. I was sitting on the stairs for a moment when I heard this little guy making a ruckus. I didn't know what it was, truth be told, but I am gobsmacked by watching this wondrous bird."

"A bitch, a bitch, a goddamn bitch," the parrot replied.

The maid arched a rueful eyebrow. "Wondrous, eh? I think it's profane and a sin against God."

"Well . . . God made the bird, did He not?"

"Yes, but the sailors made his tongue. Mac lived right on the docks before Mr. Frazier adopted him."

As if cued, Mac launched into a tangent of: "Move your bloody arses, you lazy lollygaggers."

The maid went on. "He finds Mac amusing. I do not. I

find him vile." The bird puffed out its chest at the woman. She held up a warning finger. "Watch it, mister."

"A bitch. A bitch. A goddamn bitch."

The maid muttered something in her home language, then said to the parrot, "Mac, it's time to go to sleep. If he thinks it's night, he'll stop talking. Mr. Frazier doesn't want guests such as yourself to hear him. We tried to fool him by keeping this room completely dark." She looked at Dash. "That didn't work. So now I take him all the way upstairs, as far away from guests as possible. Come on, Mac."

"Hello, Rosie. How's tricks?"

The maid stopped. A line creased in her forehead. Her mouth slightly trembled. "Of all the—" Tears sprang to her eyes.

Dash watched her with concern. "Miss, are you all right?"

She sniffed. "I apologize, sir. It's just—" Tears fell down her cheeks. She glared at Mac. "Devil bird," she growled. She looked back at Dash. "My sincerest apologies. I have forgotten myself."

"There's no reason to apologize. It is a sad day."

"Yes. I feel so badly for Mr. Frazier. To lose a daughter? I wouldn't wish that on anyone."

Dash kept his voice gentle. "Were you close with her?"

She sniffed again, keeping the broom in one hand while reaching into the pockets of her uniform with the other to get a handkerchief. She dabbed at the tear-stains on her cheeks.

"We would talk some. Being an only child, she didn't have anyone besides us staff to talk to sometimes. Especially when her father would take his trips upstate, like he's been doing the last several months or so. Once a month, she'd be here all by herself. It was lonely for her. She'd talk to me and Mingus the most."

"Mingus?"

"Jack Mingus. He's in charge of the house. Poor man. He's never been lucky. One heartbreak after another, one bounced check after a good one. Anyway, we've been with Mr. Frazier ever since she was little. Before her mother . . . passed." She returned the handkerchief to her pockets. "I didn't approve of how she lived her life, and she knew that. Sometimes she would taunt me and I would tell her, I would say, '*Rosie, you keep dancing with the Devil, he's going to take your soul.*' She would just laugh and go off to God knows where."

"She never told anyone here where she went?"

"I asked once, trying to see what filthy places she was going to, thinking I could warn her father. She shook her head at me and said '*no can do, Sophie. If I don't tell you, then you have plausible deniability.*' I don't even know what that means."

"Sounds like she was trying to protect you."

"Ay, well, she can—could be a sweet girl. And she was clever, like her mother. Loved puzzles and riddles. Whenever she'd solve one, she'd get this, this light in her eyes. Her mother was the same. They would trade little codes as secret messages, something her mother did as a child. Oh, the games they'd play!"

In a mental flash, Dash saw the piece of paper falling from Rosalie's lifeless body as it was carried out by Fife's men. He reached into his inside coat pocket and pulled out the folded piece of paper. "Like this?"

Sophie unfolded it. "Yes. Exactly like this. How did you get it?"

"She left it by accident. I saw it flutter to the ground and

I picked it up. Meant to give it back to her, only I . . . never got the chance. Do you know what it means?"

"It's a meeting place. A form of hide-and-seek. Her mother would leave her something like this and Rosie—I mean, Miss Frazier—would try to work out where her mother was hiding." Sophie looked at the teacup drawing again. "Perhaps this meant meeting where the tea sets were stored, or where they often had tea."

"I see. Of great sentimental value."

"Were you good friends with her?"

"We hadn't known each other long, but I definitely felt a strong kinship with her." Which was, more or less, the truth.

Sophie nodded to herself, then returned the drawing to Dash. "You should keep this then."

Dash nodded, returning the piece of paper to his inside pocket.

Sophie seemed to gather herself and went towards the bird cage. She opened the door and held up the broom perpendicular to it. The broom handle slowly went inside the cage and towards the parrot.

"Now I must deal with this profane, blasphemous bird. And I mean it, Mac, watch it."

On cue, Mac replied, "A bitch! A bitch! A goddamn bitch!"

Dash pointed to the broom. "Why use that?"

The parrot gingerly stepped from his perch onto the broom handle. Sophie carefully removed the broomstick from the cage, bringing the blue bird out into the library.

"Because I refuse to touch it," she replied.

She stepped carefully across the room, working hard to keep the broom handle steady. Dash followed her. His heart gave a little lurch as he caught sight of the broken vase on the side table at the front of the room. Luckily for him, Sophie was too focused on Mac.

"When I've put him to bed," she said over her shoulder, "I'll come back for you and make sure you've found your way downstairs."

He nodded. "Right."

She paused at the door and turned sideways, allowing Mac to go out into the hallway first. As she walked through the door, the broomstick dipped down a bit.

Mac fluttered his wings. "I'm falling, Sophie, I'm falling!"

"Devil bird," she muttered.

They disappeared from Dash's sight. He waited a beat and then left the room, returning downstairs. Stepping down into the gallery, Dash didn't catch sight of Joe or Finn. He sidestepped a few gossiping clusters in the receiving hall of the sitting room. No sign of them there.

Perhaps he should find this Jack Mingus. As head of the house, he might know something about these midnight rendezvous between Leonard Frazier and Fife's men.

Dash beckoned one of the male staff members, who came over, and asked where he could find Mr. Mingus. He was told in the parlor. He then asked for a description and was told to look for a thick gentleman with slicked-back brown hair and a slightly reddish face who was always standing with his hands behind his back.

Dash entered the parlor, his eyes scanning for such a man. And he found him. Standing near the fireplace with his hands clasped behind him, as promised. Full face. Wide nose. Eyes watchful and always moving. Wide shoulders, substantial chest. His build reminded Dash of Atty, compact men with compounded strength. They might not be the tallest in the room, but they certainly commanded the most attention.

Dash slowly walked over, aware of Beverly Stevens and her evil glare. He stopped in front of Jack Mingus and introduced himself, using his brother's name ("Maximillian Bennett, sir, please to meet you") and offered his condolences to all the people of the house.

"Thank you, sir," Mingus replied, a slight brogue touching his vowels. "It has been a dark week for this household."

"I can't imagine. Life can be so cruel. If only they would test it."

"Eh?"

"The liquor. I know, I know, it's illegal to make it now, but it seems to me that if people are going to continue to imbibe, why not make it safe? Wasn't that why we went Dry in the first place? Now we've got all these bootleggers and gangsters around. Have you ever seen one? A bootlegger?"

Mingus wouldn't take the bait. "I haven't, sir. This is a Dry household. Is there anything I can help you with, sir?"

The chin music part of the conversation was clearly over. Dash needed to find a reason for chatting up Mingus and quick.

As he was furiously thinking, he noticed Mingus suddenly disengage from their exchange. Confusion wrinkled his forehead. His lips remained parted, the start of saying a word before completely abandoning it. He was staring at a place just above Dash's shoulder. Dash turned to see who had captured Mingus's attention.

An attractive man—a *very* attractive man—stood against the far wall across from them. Blond hair, fair brows, twinkling blue eyes despite the somber cast of his face. His suit was expertly cut, showing off a slim, athletic body. He was murmuring to another man with half his height and hair and twice his width.

Dash turned back to Mingus. "Who's that?"

"No one," Jack hurriedly replied. "I thought he was gesturing to me, but I was wrong. You were saying, sir?"

The request.

"Ah. Yes. Well." Dash cleared his throat again. "Where can I find the WC?"

Mingus was a little perturbed such a small ask was made of him, but he graciously gave Dash directions. Dash thanked the man and turned, keeping the mysterious blond man in Dash's peripheral.

The blond man looked up from his bald fat companion and stared right at Beverly Stevens. There was a hitch in Dash's step, but he continued on, hoping nobody saw it. He faced forward again, waited a beat, and turned his head, looking over his own shoulder. No mistaking it. The blond man was looking at Beverly, and for a split second, she returned his gaze and . . . was that a half-smile?

Some primal, animal instinct must've alerted Beverly to being watched, for she brought her gaze forward, towards Dash.

Dash smoothly faced the door again, not daring to look back as he exited the parlor.

17

Comparing notes on the cab ride home, Dash, Joe, and Finn learned the following:

1. Leonard Frazier was as upright and Dry as they come. Not a hint of impropriety whispered by anyone.
2. Non-coincidentally, Leonard Frazier was likely to remain a bachelor for the rest of his life. His wife Cynthia died over five years ago from illness, and he hadn't even *looked* at another woman since.
3. Everyone thought the Fraziers were cursed— both siblings the only surviving two of five, both widowers, and now the only child in the Frazier bloodline was dead.
4. Vast disappointment from the attendees that none of her Broadway friends arrived. It would've been the showdown of the year had they done so.

Finn spoke more on this last point. "The younger set in attendance was feverishly bored and *desperate* for some form of entertainment. An argument. A fainting. *Some*thing."

Joe scoffed, "It's a funeral, fer chrissakes!"

"Funeral or not, it was still a party and a dreadfully boring one at that."

Dash intervened. "Did you hear anything else?"

"Only that Rosalie—with the strength of the goddesses, I might add—seemed to defy the laws of nature and physics. Her father went out of town the weekend she died and apparently had locked her in her room and instructed his staff to always keep her in sight. No one was to let her out under any circumstances. And somehow—"

Dash finished the thought. "She still escaped."

Joe raised his brow. "A regular Houdini, this one."

"Truer statement than you think," Dash said. "Houdini is known to hide his keys. I suspect Rosalie did something similar."

Finn continued on. "I did find myself wandering around the basement to see if perhaps our Leonard was running a speak down there."

Dash perked up with anticipation. "And . . . ?"

"Sadly, no signs of anything. I looked for secret doors and panels, but all I saw were the servants' quarters, kitchen, food pantry, and the like."

"It was a good idea, Finn. Nice work." Dash turned to Joe. "What about you? What did you hear?"

"More of the family stuff. Leonard and his sister Beverly are fighting with one another, and by all accounts, it isn't pretty. It seems that taking Rosalie to court was *her* idea. The two are hardly speaking anymore. Some folks think he'll kick her out of his home."

"Which would be bad news for Beverly. I heard how her husband left her with nothing. It sounded like a strange marriage altogether."

"Their father arranged it back in the day. Wanted to bring the two railroad families together in a partnership. It worked, at first. The Fraziers' railcars and the Stevens' switchback signals."

Finn squinted. "Switchback signals? You mean there's a company that makes only signals?"

"Aye. Damn good money in it. And the plan was for the Fraziers and the Stevens to develop a railcar that minimized the jostling and bumping whenever they passed over the switches."

"For luxury trains, that would be a boon," Dash said. "No more spilled coffee on white linen or dropped trays in the aisle ways."

"Unfortunately, Mr. Stevens, cold-hearted son o' bitch was he, took the plans and filed his own patent."

Didn't care if he ruined your life, as long as he got his share.

"What a brute," Finn said.

"How did Beverly feel about all this?" Dash asked.

Joe crossed his arms over his chest. "Since he got his patent, he had no use for her. He wouldn't get a divorce— too unseemly, even for the likes o' him—but he didn't recognize their marriage bed anymore. Then, saints be praised, the devilish rogue died."

"What about you, Bossman?" Finn asked. "What did you learn today?"

Dash told them about the parrot and the queer things it said, the Watkins Hotel matchbook, Rosalie and her secret codes with her mother, and Mingus's odd staring at the blond man.

Finn said, "You think this blond billboard and Beverly are having an affair? Now *that's* some naughty behavior in such a high-minded household."

"If her marriage was as bloodless as they say," Joe gruffly replied, "can't say I blame her."

Even though the comment wasn't directed at Dash, his cheeks still burned. How long had it been since he and Joe last touched? And was Joe getting impatient, looking elsewhere for something Dash wasn't giving him?

Joe shifted, his motions agitated. "But what, lads, does any of this have to do with Fife's booze?"

"I'm not sure," Dash admitted. "Maybe nothing." He tapped his chin. "Perhaps her former roommates might have an idea."

Joe eyed him warily. "Oh no. It's one thing to be bossed around by this Fife fella, but to go off on our own?"

Finn cut in. "I think it's a wonderful idea! But . . . how are we going to get to them? We're not police or reporters."

"They're performers, yes? We may be able to use that to our advantage. Finn, do you think you can sneak into the Playhouse office?"

"Does a stevedore have grease on his hands?"

"Wait a moment, lads," Joe said. "What cockamamie scheme are ya cookin' up?"

"Don't worry, Joe," Dash replied. "We just need to borrow a few items from the Playhouse office they surely won't miss."

───

Less than two hours later, the three men had changed out of their funeral suits and found themselves standing in front of the Hotel Sutton on West Forty-Sixth Street between

Seventh and Eighth Avenues. The sign in the front window boasted rooms to rent ranging in price from sixty cents to two dollars. No amenities listed. Most likely, there weren't any.

Finn wiggled in place. "I can't believe I'm about to see for myself the apartment Miss Rosalie was in. Oh! Maybe she left behind a memento or two I can see . . ."

"Finney," Joe sighed, "I know what this lass represents to ya, but isn't spying on her things a bit *ghoulish,* even for ya?"

"Remember our story?" Dash asked.

Finn nodded with a grin, Joe with a roll of his eyes.

Dash then gestured to the hotel. "Let's get to it, gents."

The lobby, Finn was quick to note, was a depressing affair. A dark red rug dotted with stains laid in the center, the edges worn down to loose threads. Heavy wood made up the walls and the blocky columns surrounded the seating area, which was only two austere chairs with dingy cushions. Above them hung a faded painting of an older woman, her brow furrowed with disapproval, judging all who stood before her. The low ceiling trapped past and present cigarette smoke in a hazy cloud which, combined with the gas lamps, instead of electric, caused Dash to squint as he haggled with the front desk man.

The wiry man with tortoiseshell glasses wanted to know who he was and what he wanted and why he couldn't wait for his friends to come down and get him. Eventually, three dollars slipped from Dash's hand to the front desk man, who said, "Fifth floor. No elevator, I'm afraid."

"Fifth floor walkup?" Finn muttered.

Joe murmured back, "A Frazier wouldn't be used to that."

By the time they reached the fifth floor, Dash was

breathing hard. He took out his handkerchief and wiped his brow. "Apparently, a Parker isn't either." He pocketed the handkerchief and knocked on the door. A few moments went by, then he knocked again.

The door was opened by a large rectangle of a man with wide hips clad in white shorts and meaty arms and shoulders in a white sleeveless shirt. He had shockingly bright blond hair, almost white. A square face, thick lips, and a wide nose.

What had El said about the man sitting with Rosalie in the Oyster House? A white-blond man built like a Frigidaire?

Finn said out loud, "Oh my."

Joe silenced him with a quick *shh!*

The blond man leaned against the doorframe, one hand on his hip, the other holding a lit cigarette. "What do *you* want?" The voice was deep, but softened by the slight lisp at the edges.

Dash said, "Are you Marty Grice?"

"Who wants to know?"

"Were you friends with the late Rosalie Frazier?"

An exasperated sigh. "We've told you all we know. Christ, can't I get some sleep around here?"

"Mr. Grice, I know this is not an easy time—"

"An easy time?! Do you know what's been happening ever since the story about Rosalie hit the papers? We've had newshawk after newshawk try to get in here for an exclusive on her *Broadway lifestyle.* We told the front desk man to keep everyone away." Marty glared at the three of them. "I see he didn't follow our instructions."

Dash put on his friendliest smile. "Marty, I hate to be the one to tell you this, but it only cost us three dollars to get up here. You might need to slip the man a little more than twos and fews."

"Goddammit." Marty inhaled a long drag of his cigarette and blew the smoke straight at Dash. "Not all of us were born with silver spoons in our mouths. Nice suit, by the way. Now. You know who I am, which under normal circumstances I would *love,* but under *these* circumstances, I find it quite distressing. Forgive me if this seems rude, but just *who* the hell are you?"

Dash thought, *here goes nothing.*

"Hugo Boldt," Dash said. He gestured to Joe and Finn. "And these are my associates Kenneth Walsh and Cornelius Hunt. We are from William Morris, and we'd love to talk with you and your roommate, Tillie White."

On cue, all three of them produced cards, real cards from real agents of William Morris that Finn swiped from the desks of the Playhouse office. They held them up for Marty, who eyed them with suspicion. Dash sincerely hoped Marty had never dealt with these agents before, nor would feel the need to call the agency for verification. At least, not right away.

Marty studied the cards for a moment longer before saying, "What do you want?"

Dash feigned surprise. "Well, obviously, we'd love to represent you and Miss White."

He, Joe, and Finn then pocketed the cards, not wanting to leave them behind.

Marty worked his jaw as he thought. He pointed with his cigarette at the three of them. "Are we talking the stage? Or are we talking the cinema?"

"The cinema, of course," Finn replied. "The future is the silver screen. Why would we waste your time, and ours, bumping gums about the rotting boards?"

Marty considered that. "For both of us?"

Dash nodded. "If we like what we see, that is," he quickly clarified.

More working the jaw. Marty then threw a glance at Joe. "You don't talk much, do you?"

Joe cleared his throat. "I'm the money man. I'll speak when we start talkin' dollars and cents."

"I see." Another long drag of the cigarette. "My mother told me never to open the door to strange men."

Dash replied, "Your mother taught you well."

"She also taught me to pray every day. All I learned was how to spend a long time on my knees." He immediately turned around, leaving the door open behind him. "Close it on your way in, please," he called over his shoulder.

The three of them walked into the front room of the apartment, which was crammed full of furniture. A loveseat, a sofa, two chairs, a writing desk, and three end tables on top of a rug. The fabrics of the furniture were all mismatched, what with the loveseat upholstered in black and gold diamonds, the sofa a deep ruby red, the chair cushions tan, and the rug jade. Even the end tables were of three different sizes and shapes: an ivory iron rectangle, a boxy gold square, and a silver triangle. None of the pieces matched the seafoam-colored wallpaper surrounding the room, which was covered in gold lines intersecting at square-based pyramids. Truth be told, Dash liked the color and the pattern, but unfortunately the effect was marred by the curling edges at the baseboards. Cheap glue on cheap paper.

Marty saw Dash observing the front room and commented, "The décor is called eclectic, which is a fancy word for none of the damn things go together. Would you like a drink? All I have is whiskey, which is probably panther piss, and godawful champagne."

"Well, when you put it like that . . ." Finn said.

Joe nodded, saying he'd take a whiskey. "Wha?" he said to Dash's look. "I ain't picky."

Dash declined Marty's offer, not enticed by any of the options. "It's a little early for me."

Marty shrugged. "It's a little late for me. I'll be right back."

He turned towards the back wall, which had two dingy doors cut into it, separated by a flickering gas lamp. The bedrooms, Dash surmised. Marty opened the left-hand side door and disappeared into the darkness, leaving the door open behind him. There was a murmured conversation in the dark, then a singular "What?" before more murmurings.

Marty emerged from the shadows of the room, closing the door behind him. In his hands were a dark bottle with no label and two glasses. He set the glasses on the short, square-shaped side table and poured from the bottle. The liquid was a cloudy bronze, the smell so strong, it wafted over to Dash in no time. He held up one of the glasses and Joe walked towards him to get it.

With the cigarette in one hand, his whiskey glass in the other, Marty clinked his glass to Joe's and said, "Cheers," before sipping the whiskey. He grimaced. "Definitely more on the panther piss side. Well, beggars can't be choosers, I suppose."

Joe eyed the whiskey uneasily and decided, much to Dash's relief, not to take a sip. Who knew from where Marty got it and if it was renatured or denatured.

Marty took another drag of the cigarette, which was burned down to less than half an inch from his thick fingers.

He came around to the sofa, gesturing for them to take a seat while he sat.

Joe perched on the loveseat while Finn took one of the two chairs. Dash took the other one, finding the cushions to be unshapely and flat. His tailbone sent up a disgruntled cry that mirrored the groan of the chair's joints. He crossed his legs, wondering how he was going to lead this conversation.

Then the words came pouring out of him.

18

"Before we begin, let me first offer our deepest condolences for poor, unfortunate Rosalie."

Marty snorted smoke out of his nose. "Poor is not a word I'd use to describe her. That's why you're here, isn't it? Because she has, or rather, had piles upon piles of sugar."

Dash forced a smile. "Unfortunate, then."

"Well, that's true. She always did have unfortunate timing."

"What do you mean?" asked Finn.

Marty gestured with his cigarette. "Her dying is a case in point. She left us to go running back to her marble mansion, all contrite and compliant. A week later, whoops! Old Rosie's back . . . just now in the morgue."

"Ya sound a little bitter about it," Joe remarked.

"She promised us rent. Now we're twisting in the wind." He glanced back at the bedroom doors. "Tillie should be up in a moment. Are you sure you don't want a drink?" He crossed his legs, showing off his big, meaty thighs.

Dash saw the flash in Finn's eyes.

Down, boy, down.

"Was that the last time you saw Rosalie?"

"When she recanted and moved her stuff out." The lie was said so casually without any hint of hesitation. Marty inhaled another puff of smoke. "Now what's the angle here? How are you going to play up Miss Rosalie choking to death on booze to get me—I mean, us—onto the silver screen?"

"Angle?"

"Yeah, how we're going to use this—tragedy, for lack of a better word—to introduce me and Tillie to the world?"

Before Dash could respond, the left-hand side bedroom door suddenly opened and out stepped a young woman Dash took to be Tillie White.

She swept into the front room. "Good morning, gentlemen—"

"It's the afternoon, Till," Marty sighed.

"—Apologies for my tardiness. I had to spruce myself up a bit after the night we had."

Tillie White had to be twenty, if a day. Black hair cut into a bob, framing her delicate face like a bathing cap. Green painted eyes outlined in dark black. Blood red lips curled into a smile. Her dress was an olive green, sleeveless and straight, nary a ripple as it hung from Tillie's shoulders and flowed to just above her knee. The only ornamentation were the dark blue peacock feathers lining the hemline.

She looked at Marty. "Where did we put that champagne?"

"The icebox, dear." Marty rolled his eyes at Dash. "Where else would it be?"

"Don't be like that. I'm quite fragile at the moment. Last night, we went to this *amazing* little place in the Lower East Side. We were having the most glorious time when the raid light came on, and we all had to jump out of water closet windows and the like to keep from spending the night in jail."

"Sounds exciting," Finn said.

Tillie pursed her lips. "Exciting for some, I suppose. I tore my best frock, which is *most* distressing."

"That frock," Marty said, "was torn by that bartender you spent the night with and don't you dare deny it."

Tillie stuck her tongue out at him and then disappeared from Dash's vision, presumably to an alcove just off to the side. "What were we talking about?" she called.

Marty called back, "How William Morris plans to introduce us to the world in light of poor, dear Rosalie's tragic demise."

"Oh, for goodness sakes, Marty. Can't you have a little more tact?"

There was a monumental wrenching sound, then an exclamation of triumph. She returned with an opened bottle of champagne and filled an empty glass to the brim. Everyone noticed the distinct lack of effervescence.

Tillie shrugged. "I suppose now it's a white wine."

"More like vinegar."

"It'll do, my love." She held up her glass. "Cheers, boys!"

Marty automatically raised his glass. They both sipped and they both scowled.

"Horse liniment," Tillie said.

"Still panther piss for me."

Tillie sat down next to Marty. "Now what does William Morris want to do with a fan dancer and a master of ceremonies for gender illusionists? You know, some of them really do pass off as women. Sometimes I'm even fooled!"

"Dearest Till," Marty said, "perhaps William Morris doesn't want to represent someone in the pansy world."

"That's where you're wrong," Dash said, latching onto this new piece of information. "We want to produce a film that shows this fantastical world of . . . of gender illusionists. In fact, one of the big scenes of a film we're looking to produce has such a scene as the show you do in the—the—"

"Siamese Cat Club," Tillie said.

"Exactly. It's a comedy. The script is very light on its feet. Sure to be a crowd pleaser in the big cities." Dash looked to Joe and Finn, who nodded vigorously. "Of course, it has a moral," he went on, making it up as he went. "Those who pretend to be upstanding in public but are full of vice in private are led into social and financial ruin."

"Of course," Marty scoffed.

"And that's where the—the—the angle, you were asking about, comes in. We know Rosalie was the wild child of Leonard Frazier. We were wondering if you both heard of any details that could help . . . sell the plot of the film."

Tillie furrowed her brow. "What do you mean?"

"Well. Did she like going to pansy clubs, for instance?"

Tillie nodded fervently. "Oh yes, loved them! Thought it was the most extraordinary thing. She said the men there —or do we call them women? I never know!—are so irreverent and *funny*. They send up the upper crust in their acts, which she *adored*, for obvious reasons."

"Did she have a favorite club?" Finn asked. "We might want to check it out and perhaps replicate it on set."

Tillie scrunched up her face in thought. "Dear me, I can't seem to recall a name. There were quite a few. Marty, dearest, can you help my addled memory?"

Marty took another drag of the cigarette. "Unfortunately, they've slipped my mind as well."

"I *do* remember where they were. One was in West Harlem, the other two or three were in the Village, I think."

"Greenwich?" Dash said. "Do you remember their names?"

Tillie shook her head.

"The one in Harlem, was it called the Oyster House?" Dash thought he saw Marty's eyes flash a warning to Tillie.

She kept her eyes averted and replied garrulously, "I've never been good with names. Never. I could have the greatest night of my life and couldn't tell you where I was or who I was with."

"It's that cheap champagne that does you in, love," Marty said.

"Don't be beastly. And we were talking about Rosie, weren't we? Oh yes, the pansy places. One of the things she loved about them was the secret setups. She loved those secret knocks or secret codes, hidden doorways and hallways. She was a big fan of—oh, what's the word?—*spycraft*! Absolutely mad about it."

Dash leaned forward. "What kind of secret codes? Written on paper? Words, drawings?"

"Mostly drawings, I think. I could never puzzle them out, but Rosie could in a flash."

"Do you remember what clubs used those drawings?"

"This is all well and good," Marty interrupted, "but let's keep to the topic at hand. This film. When would it start shooting?"

Dash made up a few dates several months from now.

"And I suppose," Marty said, "you'd want to see our acts?"

"Very much so."

"Wonderful. We're rehearsing a new show for this coming Wednesday. It's going to be dynamite. You'll have plenty to work with for the film."

"Oh yes," Tillie gushed. "The pansies do such

extraordinary things, and then I, of course, am debuting a whole new dance. I'm absolutely in *love* with it—as I'm sure you all will be, as well."

Dash smiled. "Put us on the list. We'll be there."

"You know," Finn suddenly said, "I'm wondering if there are any other scandals in Rosalie's life. Perhaps within her family."

Tillie furrowed her brow. "What do you mean?"

"Well, dearie, she got her wild side from *somewhere*. It doesn't sound like her father—"

"Oh my, no," Tillie laughed. "He's a flat tire if there ever was one. No drinking, no partying. Gawd, he's such a bore."

"I don't suppose her mother . . . ?"

Another negative. "She wasn't as oppressed as dear Leonard, but she wasn't permissive. Clever, yes, but not permissive."

"What about an aunt?"

This sparked a laugh from Tillie. "Aunt Bev? Oh no. I can't imagine her doing *anything* remotely scandalous. Unless it's being left with nothing after a loveless marriage, but that's more embarrassment than scandal."

Finn cocked his head. "Really? She wasn't unfaithful during her, as you called it, 'loveless marriage'?"

"If she had any sense, she was."

Dash cut in with a question. "Is she seeing anyone these days?"

Marty growled, "Who cares about that old biddy? And what does it have to do with us and this picture?"

Dash nodded. "Apologies. Curiosity gets the best of us. Although anything in the Frazier family history might be useful for publicity."

"You're wasting your time with that one. Nothing Bev does is remotely interesting."

"I'm afraid Marty's right," Tillie said. "Aunt Bev the Boring."

"Ah." Dash couldn't see a way to directly ask them about the blond stranger—not without tipping his hand that the three of them weren't who they claimed to be. He thanked Marty and Tillie for their time and stood. Joe and Finn followed suit. "And again," he said, "our condolences for Rosalie. Such a tragedy."

"Yes," Tillie replied, "isn't it? Those damnable Drys. If they would just leave well enough alone."

"I heartily agree." Dash turned to go but paused. "One last question: do either of you know where she went that weekend?"

Tillie and Marty looked at one another before replying they didn't.

"As I said earlier," Marty said, "the last time we saw her was a week ago, when she disavowed her lifestyle —and us."

Tillie nodded. "Yes, that's right. We hadn't seen her since."

"Did she have any other friends? Other people with whom she explored Manhattan's night life?"

Marty eyed him suspiciously. "Why do you want to know?"

Finn jumped in. "Her other friends might give us more ideas for sets, dear Marty. Especially the last few places she went. Our heroine in the script visits swarthy speaks selling bad booze in the end, and we'd love to make it as real as possible."

Tillie tried to reply with "In that case, there's—"

But Marty jumped in. "If you're really interested, come to a rehearsal. That way, we know you're serious about the two of us, and not just Rosalie."

Dash flashed him a polite smile. "When is the rehearsal?"

"Tomorrow at noon. If you dare, that is."

"Why did they lie?"

This was asked by Finn as the three of them prepared Pinstripes for the night's opening.

"I don't know, Finn," replied Dash, as he set up the table and chairs. "But there's got to be a reason."

"Maybe they don't want to be any more involved in Rosalie's death than we do," offered Joe, placing bottles on the bar and noting how much liquor was left in each.

"At least we know how Rosalie got to Pinstripes," Finn said, sweeping the dance floor. "If she loved Village pansy clubs, she was sure to hear of ours." He paused. "That Tillie, though. She knows more than what Marty would let her say."

"Aye, makes ya wonder what."

"Makes you wonder a lot of things," Dash said, finishing with the last set of table and chairs. "Such as, was Rosalie's death intentional?"

Joe almost dropped a bottle in response. "Wha' the bloody hell are ya talkin' about?"

"No," Finn said, stopping his sweeping and coming to Dash's defense. "I think our resident high hat has a point. It's obvious there's tension galore with her father and aunt. And those roommates weren't the least bit friendly about her."

"That's cuz she stiffed 'em with the rent!" Joe countered.

"Maybe she stiffed them with her trust." Finn arched an

eyebrow. "Ten million dollars is worth killing over, don't you think?"

"Finney, how were they gonna get her trust when it's in her name?"

"Steal it or spend it," Dash replied. "I bet you *my* former family trust that when the three of them went out, she paid. As long as she kept paying for things, they wouldn't have—what did they call it?—panther piss and horse liniment to drink."

Finn leaned against the broom handle. "Real champagne and real whiskey."

"A palatial apartment. Maybe in the Dakota—"

"—or the Parkview!—"

"Face it, with Rosalie's money, Marty and Tillie would've lived the life of Riley."

Joe just shook his head.

Dash was adamant. "There's something off about the whole situation."

"Lassie, yer makin' somethin' outta nothin' again. Look, I know this girl—"

The secret door opened, interrupting them, and the voices of the Pinstripes band reverberated throughout the club.

"I'm tellin' ya," Vernon said, walking in and carrying his bass, "she's gonna come around."

Calvin and Julius, carrying their cymbals and cornet respectively, swatted his remarks away, laughing as they did so. They greeted Dash and continued on their way to the stage.

Dash said, "Vern, are you still going after Boris's cousin? He's not going to like that."

"Yeah, Vern," Calvin called, "he may not let you back in the car!"

Vern set his bass onto the ground, then stood up straight and hooked his thumbs behind his tuxedo lapels.

"All it's going to take, gentlemen, is a little bit of the Vern Charm."

Calvin rolled his eyes as he sat behind his drum set, screwing on the cymbals. "The Vern Charm. Might as well be skunk spray for all the good it does ya."

"Don't let them beat you down, Vern," Finn said. "I believe in you."

Julius replied, "Oh come on now, Finn, you believe in fairies!"

"Why wouldn't I? I am one, dearie, and I flutter around you every night." With his hands raised up to his shoulders, he waved them as if they were wings.

The band laughed him off.

At that moment, Dash had a sudden thought. He walked over to Calvin, who had just finished screwing on the cymbals. "Cal, you said the Watkins Hotel is a Blacks-only hotel, yes?"

"That's right."

"Could there be *any* situation in which a white person —a white girl—could be allowed in?"

Calvin looked at Dash as if he'd lost his mind. "Impossible! Every entrance, front, back, and sides, is guarded. All the staff are Black and there's no way a white girl could make it inside and not be noticed. And if she did somehow managed to get in there, she wouldn't be allowed to stay very long. Uh huh. No way could a white girl do that."

"I see," Dash said.

Then that matchbook was taken by someone other than Rosalie. But who? And why would she hide it? He, again, had the thought she could've been seeing a Black man in secret. Maybe that's why her father was so irate. Scandal on top of scandal. Granted, Finn said Leonard was more on the modern side, but a daughter having sexual relations with a member of another race tends to change opinions quick. Dash wondered if that was the real reason he caused a scene at the Oyster House—and why Marty and Tillie kept lying.

The Oyster House line was as long as it ever was. Dash walked up to the big, intimidating doorman. "Evening, Horace. How's the old lady?"

Horace's face lit up. "Mr. Parker!" They shook hands. "Are you here about that Rosalie girl again?"

"El told you, huh?"

"You know El. Secrets are not her strong suit."

"True. I'm trying to figure out who was with Rosalie that night. El said a white man and a white woman."

"Sounds about right. Man was big, like a freight car with white blond hair. Woman was a teeny tiny little thing. Young too."

"Did they go by Marty and Tillie?"

"Didn't catch their names."

"Was anybody else with them?"

"Don't think so."

Perhaps Rosalie's Black lover was already inside the club. "Rosalie didn't come by the next night, did she? Saturday, September the eleventh?"

Horace shook his head. "No, sir, just that Friday the

tenth. She couldn't have come back the next night if she wanted to. Les banned her from his club. You know, kinda like, uh . . ."

"Like yours truly. And that was the only night you saw her?"

"I can't swear to it, but I believe that Friday night was her first and only night here."

Dash looked through the doorway of the club. "Is Les in tonight?"

A pained look flashed across Horace's face. "He just left for a stroll—with his new girl, you understand—but now, Mr. Parker, I don't want to get into any trouble. And no offense, but helping *you* out leads to trouble."

"I promise, Horace, I'll be in and out. I just need to talk with El real quick."

"But if Les catches you—"

"How long do his 'strolls' usually take?"

"About an hour or so." Horace smirked. "Unless he gets lazy with her."

Dash cocked his head to the side. "Come on, Horace. I can hear the first chords of '*Cecilia.*' That's El's closing number."

Horace sighed. He held out his palm and Dash slid in some sugar. "In and out."

Dash nodded and ducked into the bordello-red speak. A tin ceiling stretched over the long, narrow room. A bar hugged one side; tables and chairs scattered on the other. The stage was down at the other end, opposite the front door. The audience was mostly Black with a few down-towners dotted here and there. Cigarettes, pungent gin and whiskey, and a spice of dope created a most intoxicating cologne.

The room was jubilant. Everyone clapped along to El's

playing. She looked larger than life behind that beat-up brown piano. Her white tuxedo shone bright underneath the stage lights, face slick with sweat, big hands pounding those piano keys within an inch of their lives. Her voice was as big and wide as the ocean as she sang:

Does your mother know you're out, Cecilia?
Does she know that I'm about to steal ya?
Oh, my, when I look in your eyes,
Something tells me you and I should get togetha!

"Should we get together?!" El called to the audience. The room shouted back "Hell, yes!!!" El laughed and kept on singing:

How about a little kiss, Cecilia?
Just a kiss you'll never miss, Cecilia
Why do we two keep on wasting time?
Oh, Cecilia say that you'll be mine!
Oh, Cecilia saaaaaaaaaayyyyyy you'll be miiiiiiinnnnne!

El slid her hands up and down the piano keys to tremendous applause. She ended the song with such force, she knocked her piano bench backwards. She stood up and grinned, taking in all the cheers, whistles, and foot stomps. Like she always did, she put her hands on her hips and surveyed the crowd, as if she were judging them.

Finally, she held up her hands to calm the crowd down a bit and said, "Well *shee-it!*"

"Well *shee-it!*" responded the crowd.

"Not bad for a Saturday night. Not bad at all." She pointed to the back left corner of the room. "Give it up for

Madam J. A. Watkins! For watching out for us colored folks!"

Dash turned to see the famous woman. He caught glimpses of her through the standing crowd. Big smile. Blue eyes. Black hair piled on top of her head. Butterfly earrings. Plum-colored dress. Hands applauding El, the movements creating a flash of jewel tones. Must've been the light from her rings.

El took in the applause a moment longer before sauntering off the stage. Dash made his way towards her. She shook some hands and signed a few autographs. When she got to Leslie Charles's office door right next to the stage, she saw Dash. Confusion creased her face, then exasperation. For the same reasons as Horace. She frowned and mouthed through clenched teeth *get your ass in here!*

She opened the office door and ushered Dash in. She slammed it shut behind them and locked it, cutting the noise of the cheering crowd in half.

Dash crossed the office and took a seat on what used to be his usual place, the windowsill overlooking the back alleyway.

Normally El sat at Les's desk, feet propped up, not a care in the world. Not tonight. She leaned against it with one hand while the other found her wide hip. "What in Sam Hill are you doing here?"

"Apparently, taking advantage of Les's romance call."

"I can *see* that. If Les catches you, he's bound to make a scene, and goddammit, Madam Watkins is here and I am *not* gonna let you futz this up. And all it's gonna take is one of those bartenders to rat you out and—"

"El, you're worrying for nothing. Those bartenders can't stand Les any more than you can."

That took the steam out of her anger. "You're not wrong

there. I've seen one of 'em spit in his drink. He deserved it, though. Wouldn't give him a night off to visit his sick mother."

There was a knock on the door. Both Dash and El froze.

"No, no, no, it can't be," El said. She called through the door, "Who is it?"

"Madam J. A. Watkins. Can I speak with you a moment?"

El looked at Dash. "Don't say a word or I will end your life."

Dash held up his hands as a promise.

El opened the door. "Madam Watkins." She invited the famous woman into the office.

J. A. Watkins was even more stunning in full view. She paused when she saw Dash sitting there. "I hope I'm not interrupting anything." She eyed Dash with suspicion.

"Not at all," El replied quickly, shutting the door. "This is—this is—this is Dash Parker, my secretary."

Both Dash's and J. A. Watkins's eyebrows shot up.

Watkins said, "A man secretary? A—forgive me, sir—a *white* man secretary?"

El nodded her head. "Hmmhmm. And he was just about to take down a message for me, but we can hold off on that. Mr. Parker, you're excused."

"That won't be necessary, El. I just wanted to come back here and say that was one of the *best* shows I've seen in a long time."

Dash had never seen El grin wider than in that moment. "Oh, thank you, Madam Watkins! I can't tell you what that means to me coming from somebody like you."

"It's an unconventional show, to be sure, but . . . you made me *feel* so many things. I laughed, I cried." She leaned in close to El and murmured, "I got horny as hell."

El hooted a laugh in response and together, the two women shared a good, long chuckle.

"Oh, me." J. A. Watkins slowly composed herself. "Anyway," she said, reaching into her purse, which matched her stunning plum dress, "I would like for you to think about doing a show at my hotel." From the depths of her purse, she pulled out a business card. "Come by sometime next week. I may have an opening for you." She glanced at Dash. "You can take down the press release, Mr. Secretary."

Dash replied, "Yes, Madam."

"Excuse me," she said, "I prefer *yes, sir*." She looked at El. "I like being talked to as a man. Makes life so much easier than being talked to like a woman, don't you find?" She touched El's forearm. "A really wonderful show."

And with that, she sailed out of Leslie Charles's office.

The moment the door closed, El made a high-pitched hum that became "Hell, *yes!*"

Dash couldn't help but laugh with joy at his friend's good fortune. "You did it, El," he said.

"You damn right, I did it. God. Can you imagine? The Watkins Hotel." She looked back at the office door, as if she could still see J. A. Watkins standing there. She shook her finger at it. "This could be it. This could be *it*. Get me outta these dives and into the big rooms." She turned to Dash. "And you really can be my secretary!"

"I'd take messages for you anytime, El."

"God-*damn!* What a good night this is." She looked at Dash. Her smile faltered some. "I suspect you're gonna ruin some of it. Why are you here?"

"I promise I'm not gonna ruin anything. I just need to know two things and then I'm gone."

"Talk fast. You're cutting into my Watkins whiskey celebration time."

"The Friday night when Rosalie Frazier was here, was she with anyone other than that white man with the white blond hair and the white woman?"

"You mean, anyone else at their table? No, just the three of them."

"Did it seem she was looking around for anybody?"

Another no.

"Any chance you overheard them?" he asked.

She shook her head. "All I can hear is my own voice or catcalls from the audience. Those three weren't brave enough to do that—" She stopped.

Dash said, "What is it, El?"

She pursed her lips. "One thing I did hear, though. Only one word. Washington."

"Washington? Like the Square?"

"Or the President. Or the capitol. She didn't clarify."

"Why would she be talking about Washington?"

"No clue."

Suddenly the door handle jiggled and a pounding fist hit the wood. "El? You in there? Why'd you lock my office?"

Dash looked at his watch. Les was back early.

El's eyes widened. "You gotta get outta here," she hissed. "The window. Go, go, go!"

Dash turned and opened the sash, which, of course, went up with a mighty wrench and squeal.

"El?" Les called. "What the hell are you doing in there? You better not have broken anything."

"Oh, pipe down, Les," El said, gesturing for Dash to hurry. "I just opened the window for some air."

Dash threw one leg over the windowsill, then the other, dropping down onto the crunchy gravel of the alleyway.

"Goddammit, El, open this—"

Dash heard the door open and El say, "Oh good grief, Les. You're scaring the customers."

"I wouldn't have to . . ."

Their voices trailed off as Dash scampered towards the end of the alleyway. He cut over on Seventh, then turned back onto 133rd. He quickly passed Horace, saying, "Don't worry, he didn't see me."

He then grabbed the first cab and slammed the door shut.

Sunday morning, Joe went off to be with his family in Sunnyside, Queens, attending mass and the subsequent meal. Finn was God-knew-where, so Dash was left to his own devices. Mostly, he sat and brooded. *Washington.* What the devil did Rosalie mean by *Washington*? The obvious answer was Washington Square Park, a mere block away from his tailor shop and club.

A block away from where she ultimately died.

Was this the location of another speak? A meeting place, like when Rosalie and her mother played their spy games? The name of the blond gentleman who stared at Rosalie's aunt Beverly?

Tried as he might, he couldn't make sense of the utterance. The voices coming through the wall didn't help. Apparently one of the producers of the show was giving Reggie, the Playhouse Don Juan, a talking to, saying how the cast morale was at an all-time low.

Reggie was incredulous. "And *I'm* to blame for that?"

"Yes!" replied both Dash and the producer.

The producer went on. "Frankly, it's disrupting the show, and we are officially asking you to stop."

A pause, then a scornful laugh. "Officially. Asking *me*, Reginald Thurgood Wadsworth III, to *stop?*"

"First of all, Reggie, that's not your real name and we both know it. Second of all, you don't have to stop *indefinitely*, just until the end of the show. Then you can schtup all the women you want."

"Now see here—"

"And I don't have to remind you that if we're forced to fire you, you will not be paid for the rest of the run. I'm sure your understudy will be thrilled at the prospect."

"You bastard," Reggie said.

"She ended up marrying my father in the end. At any rate, keep it in your pants, big fella."

For the sake of all of us, Dash thought.

He shuffled to the hallway WC. Splashing cold water on his face, his mind kept coming back to Rosalie and her mention of *Washington*. He dressed in an all wool cashmere suit in light gray with stripes, a green plaid vest, and a red striped tie, and headed towards Washington Square Park. Perhaps Rosalie was mentioning a new club. He strolled up and down the surrounding streets on all four sides of the Park looking for a tearoom, a China shop, a hat shop (she had asked Atty to see a hat . . .). No such businesses.

He stopped and sat on a park bench, twiddling his thumbs. If he couldn't guess what she meant by *Washington*, then maybe her two roommates could enlighten him. *If* they would finally tell the truth about being with her at the Oyster House the Friday before she died.

He checked his wristwatch. Almost one o'clock—according to Marty, they should be neck deep in rehearsals right about now. Time for William Morris's agent Hugo Boldt to make an appearance.

20

SUN AFTERNOON, SEPT 19, 1926

The Siamese Cat Club was awash with bamboo, sparkling jade, and gold. As Dash walked into the main room, he saw the curtained stage to his far left, the bar to his far right. In the corner creases of the ceiling, cutouts made to look like cat eyes peered down at patrons below. Hanging lanterns whose shades were made of multicolored silk glowed overhead.

There was a slight murmuring in the background, but the place seemed deserted. Suddenly he heard a voice call from the right side of the room. "Are we ready for the opening number?"

Marty's voice replied from off stage to Dash's left. "Yes, we are!"

The sound of a large gong filled the air, and the lights in the main room dimmed. The stage became aglow, lighting the ruby, jade, and blue silk curtains.

As more stage lights popped on, the curtains became translucent, illuminating a chorus of ten pansies dressed in silk pajamas. Just like the curtains and the lanterns, it was a rainbow of color from the darkest of reds and purples to the brightest of blues and greens. Fierce eyes stared at the pretend audience.

Somewhere off stage, a piano began playing. Marty's voice called out: "Dearly beloved, if this love only exists in my dreams . . . don't wake me up!"

And then the pansies began to sing:

> *So much life in the city*
> *You won't believe*
> *Been awake for some days now*
> *No time to sleep*

> *If your heart is a pillow, this love's the bed*
> *Tell me what is the music inside my head*

They began moving about the stage in choreographed wonder, a kaleidoscope of color as the music played faster.

> *Don't wake me up, up, up, up, up, up*
> *Don't wake me up*
> *Don't wake me*

> *I don't wanna fall, fall, fall, fall asleep, no!*
> *I don't wanna fall unless I'm falling for you*

A curtain at the back of the stage dropped, exposing a giant mirror held at an angle. In the reflection, Dash could see the pansies making patterns on the stage, including a giant heart and a pair of winking eyes. The spectacle seemed to grow in stature until the raised hands, and voices, of the finale.

The main curtain closed and walking onto the stage was none other than Marty Grice, his white-blond hair striking against the shiny black of his tuxedo. He stood center stage, his painted red lips wide in smile.

"Welcome, welcome, welcome to the Siamese Cat!" He paused, then looked uncertain. "Peter? Peter, the spotlight is in the wrong place."

"It is?" said a voice from somewhere in the main room.

"It's about four inches off."

"We'll fix it, Marty."

"Thank you. Okay, now, where was I? Yes. Patter, patter, patter, blah blah blah blah, and then the first act. Peter? Do we know who's opening now that Glenda is ill?"

"Still working on that."

"Well, let's figure that out before Wednesday, shall we?"

"Yes, Mr. Grice."

"Isn't he something?" a female voice said right behind Dash's ear.

He turned and saw Tillie White grinning. "He certainly is. Has perfect control of the stage."

"That's what I tell him! No nerves at all. Nothing phases him."

She wore a silk bathrobe and slippers, a cigarette held lazily in one hand. She looked admiringly at Marty, who was now conversing with another man onstage. They were both looking at a large piece of paper.

"I wish I could be as fearless as he," she said.

"Well, you are, in your own way," Dash replied. "I couldn't imagine getting on stage and . . . err—"

"Taking off your clothes."

Dash cleared his throat. "Yes, that."

Tillie's grin widened. "It becomes as natural as breathing, Mr. . . . ?"

"Boldt. But please, can call me Hugo."

"Certainly, Hugo. Shall I get you a drink? These

rehearsals get so tedious, I find a little libation is completely and totally necessary."

Dash figured she might be less suspicious and more forthcoming if she were imbibing. He gestured towards the bar. "Lead the way."

Soon, they were settled on barstools with champagne fizzing in front of them while Marty still worked through details on stage. He was chatting with a few of the pansies from the opening number, giving what sounded like performance notes.

Dash gestured to him. "I didn't realize he also directed."

"Oh yes. This is his show, no question about it. The lighting, the costumes, the music, the dancing. All comes from his brain." Tillie took a healthy swig, sighing with approval. "Much better than what we have at home. So! Hugo. What brings you by?"

What brought me here, indeed.

He couldn't just launch into the fact that she and Marty had lied to him. Not only was it confrontational, but it would expose him as being anything *but* a talent agent. He needed an oblique way in. He then remembered Tillie was interrupted before she could say anything about Rosalie and seedy places that served bad booze.

"We're still working on the backstory for the two of you," he said. "The press releases and the like. And you were about to say something when we first met about swarthy, seedy places. Did Rosalie ever attend establishments like that?"

Tillie scrunched up her nose. "I was? Oh! We were talking about her love of spycraft and why she loved pansy speaks and the like, weren't we?" Another sip of champagne. "Yes, now I remember. I was saying how she loved the elaborate disguises of the places. The more elaborate, the better. And no offense to the pansy club owners, but you simply can*not* get more elaborate than a blind tiger."

"A . . . blind tiger?"

"Imagine walking into some place ordinary, like a hat store or a place that sells radios. That's where we went, a radio shop."

"Where?" Dash asked, interrupting her flow.

"I told you I'm so terrible with names! Let me see . . . "

"On Washington?"

"No, that's not it . . . I *know* it wasn't the Village. Radio Row, I think it was? Cortlandt Street and something. Anyway, you walk in and browse around the store, all casual. You wait until all the other customers are gone, or at least preoccupied, and then you go to the man behind the register. You ask the man if they have a giggle radio. Silly, I know, but according to Rosie, the phrases have to be a little ridiculous and very much on the hep side, so undercover cops can't catch wise to it. Anyway, so we did as instructed, asked this young man for a giggle radio, and he pointed to one in the back corner of the shop. He told us to turn the dial, pay the five-cent toll, wait for the light, and then turn the dial again. We did exactly as he said and—"

She stopped to sip more of her champagne.

"—and then the most extraordinarily simple thing I've ever encountered. The—oh what do they call it? The thing where the sound normally comes out?—the speaker! Yes, the speaker swung open, like a door at the first turn of the dial. Rosie placed our money inside, one nickel, just like the man says, and closed the door. We waited. Suddenly we saw the glassed-in panel above us light up, as if the radio was actually turned on. Rosie turned the dial again, the door popped open, and inside . . . our money was gone! And in its place was a bottle. Rosie quickly took it and shoved it into her purse. We closed the door and we left."

Dash asked, "And the bottle was filled with . . . ?"

"Gin! Not the greatest gin in the world, mind you, but certainly serviceable."

"I get it. It's called a blind tiger because neither party sees one another. The booze seller or the booze drinker."

"Right-o!" replied Tillie. "Rosie was absolutely *mad* about them. She wanted to find as many in the city as she could. She was hoping at least one of them would be a Catholic Church confessional. Highly blasphemous, I said. Highly amusing, is what she thought."

"And when was this?"

"I want to say it was right before she recanted in front of that judge . . . yes, yes, it was! The day before—or was it the day of?—she goes to the judge to admit her father was right and disavow all imbibing, all the while buying gin from a blind tiger. We thought that was proof she was just saying what her father and the judge wanted to hear. But then—then she moved out without a single word to us."

"The week before she died," Dash said.

Tillie nodded.

"That must've hurt, when she decided to completely cut ties."

Tillie momentarily turned sentimental, helped along by the champagne. "It did. I thought we were friends. Marty's a bit of a bruiser, but he's always been rough around the edges. He liked her fame and money, but I—"

"What are you two going on about?" Marty's voice asked them.

Dash and Tillie turned in their chairs to see the large man standing close by.

Tillie quickly composed herself and said, "Marty! The new number looks extraordinary!"

"Thank you, love. Yours is coming along nicely too. And Mr. . . . Boldt, is it?"

Dash offered his hand for a shake. "Please, call me Hugo. I have to agree with Miss White here, the opening number looks breathtaking. It would make an extravagant scene for the film."

They shook hands, Marty eyeing him with suspicion. "Thank you. If we can get the timing right, it'll be much better. Are you still coming to the show this Wednesday night?"

"I wouldn't miss it for the world."

"Wonderful. Now," Marty drawled, "what chin music has Tillie been laying on you? I saw you from the stage. You were having quite the conversation."

Dash nodded towards Tillie. "She was just telling me about blind tigers and how much Rosalie loved them."

"Why would William Morris be interested in that?"

"Background, of course," Tillie replied. "I think it'll make a great addition to the script!"

"The script we haven't seen yet." Marty narrowed his eyes at Dash. "When *will* we see this script?"

"After we see the show." Dash stood. "Thank you for the champagne, Miss White, but I should be going." He paused, as if suddenly remembering something. "Speaking of backgrounds, for our press releases, the last time you saw Rosalie was the Friday night before she was dropped off at Bellevue, correct? At the Oyster House?"

Marty and Tillie froze, flicking panicked glances at one another.

"No," Marty said slowly, "the last we saw her was when she packed up and left."

Dash slightly tilted his head. "Are you sure? I could've sworn it was the Oyster House."

Tillie looked up at Marty, fear flashing on her face. "I never said that." She tilted her head towards Dash. "We never said that. Where did you hear such bunk?"

Dash just smiled. "Must be getting my wires crossed. Good luck with the rehearsals. And I'll see you this coming Wednesday night!"

21

In the darkness of Queens, Dash squirmed in the front seat of Fife's car, this one another black Ford. He tried to get comfortable as they waited for the delivery truck in the distance to be filled. Wim was, once again, at the wheel, amused grin firmly in place. And Joe, who was adamant that he be here tonight, was behind them in the backseat. ("Val and Louis are dangerous," he'd said. "Yer not goin' it alone this time. Finney can handle the bar and if he can't, well there are worse things.")

Atty even offered his gun for the occasion, noting the sights were off and to aim far right—which explained how, despite his bravado, the man couldn't hit the broad side of a barn. To Dash's surprise, Joe took it. ("This ain't yer world. It's mine.")

While waiting for Wim to arrive, Dash filled Joe in about the blind tiger. Joe didn't say much in response, which puzzled Dash. Why wasn't he more intrigued? He seemed downright hostile to any mention of Rosalie.

"Tell me about the two of you," Wim said suddenly,

shaking Dash out of his thoughts. "How long have you been together?"

The question took both Dash and Joe by surprise.

Wim was amused by their stunned reactions. "Oh, come now, no reason to be shy. I know what kind of club you own, and I can read bodies other than Mr. Fife's, you know." He turned in his seat and looked back at Joe. "I certainly read yours, Mr. Muscle. Making sure I don't cause Mr. Parker any harm."

"Aye, and ya better not."

"Oh my, you *are* protective." Wim glanced at Dash. "You've got yourself a regular guard dog. Does he attack on command?"

Dash nodded.

"Hmm. I bet he does tricks too."

Joe growled, "Stop bein' cute, lad."

"I can't help it," Wim replied. "My mother used to say to me, '*I should've named you Whimsical instead of William. You're as light as a feather and mischievous as a fairy.*'"

"Is that why you go by Wim?" Dash asked.

"Indeedy-do. Now don't be shy. Tell me your love story."

Joe barked, "What business is it of yers?"

"I'm a sucker for romance. Casual glances, furtive smiles, shy eyes. I love it all. Besides, it'll take our minds off the fact we're about to watch two men betray Mr. Fife."

Dash kept his eyes forward, unsure of how to further dodge the question.

Joe surprised them all by answering. "It was a speak."

Wim lifted his head. "Excuse me?"

Joe sighed. "Where we met. A place called the Golden Goose."

"I know that place!" Wim nudged Dash with his elbow. "Like the bruisers, I see."

"He was the only one wearin' a flashy suit at the bar," Joe said. "Poor lad was about to get his cuff links and pocket watch nicked, so I stayed close by."

"I see." Wim looked over at Dash. "And did you? Get nicked, I mean."

"Almost," Dash said. "I felt someone's fingers slip into my jacket pocket, and the next thing I know, this man grabs the thief's wrist and says—"

Joe supplied the words. "'*If you want your hand to polish off your knob later tonight, you'll drop whatever is in it and put it back in your pocket.*'" He chuckled. "It was some dumb kid, no more than twelve, and he ran outta there like a banshee from an exorcism."

Wim could barely contain his exuberance. "I absolutely a-*dore* that! A knight coming to the rescue." A throaty laugh followed. "And did you repay your knight's kindness, Mr. Parker?"

Dash felt his cheeks burn, both at the question and at the memory. "Well . . . it seemed to be the polite thing to do." He couldn't help himself; his burning cheeks stretched into a grin. He looked back. "Joe, do you remember the building super walking in on us?"

Joe roared with laughter. "Fuckin' hell! I almost forgot about that! What kind o' super makes an unexpected visit on a Sunday afternoon?"

"A crooked one." Dash turned to Wim. "Apparently, he would sneak into apartments when his tenants were at work or church and steal from them."

Wim clicked his tongue. "*Tsk, tsk, tsk.* And his reward was to find you two *in flagrante delicto?*"

Now Dash was laughing along with Joe. "I heard the

apartment's front door open and whispered it to Joe, but he did not believe me."

Joe cleared this throat. "In my defense, I was a wee bit distracted."

"Then the floorboard right outside the bedroom door creaked and I was up like a shot! The door was just beginning to open, and I slid across the floor slamming it shut and locking it. And then—"

"—the super was banging on the door, wantin' to know what in Christ's holy name was goin' on in there—"

"—and I'm whispering to Joe, '*we've got to get dressed!*' Only—"

"—we couldn't find our bloody clothes! We're scramblin' in the dark cause the shades were drawn, bumpin' into one another. I think we even knocked heads."

Dash nodded. "We certainly did. Almost knocked each other out too. Finally, we find some garments on the floor, but the super had gotten out his keys and started undoing the lock. We pull on whatever was in our hands. And it would've been jake, except—"

"—we had each other's clothes in hand. Dash here is lookin' like a kid wearin' his dad's clothes and I am—"

"—splitting seams and spilling out all over the place. My shirt he couldn't even button, and my trousers—" Dash and Joe's laughter was uncontrollable now, with Dash's eyes tearing up from the effort. "—stopped just below his knee, but—"

"—*but* I couldn't fasten 'em! I tried to cover myself with the shirttails—"

"—unsuccessfully, I might add—"

"—and the bloody super walks in and has a conniption—"

"—full-on tirade—"

"—and kicked our arses out right then and there." Joe took a breath, trying to get himself under control. "I lost a good apartment cuz a' you."

Dash wiped away the tears from his eyes. "No, you didn't. It was a regular dump. The roaches didn't even bother to scatter away when you walked in the room."

Wim said, "My, my, my. Romance, sex, *and* a daring escape—sort of. Where did you two go after the super kicked you out?"

Dash replied, "My place."

"The playhouse apartment?"

Joe corrected him. "The tailor shop. Where the club is now. That was the bedroom."

"Ahh, Victor's old place," Wim said. "What a *lovely* story. And you two have been together ever since?"

"In one capacity or the other," Dash replied.

It was after that night when Joe introduced Dash to Finn. Dash learned they had been bouncing from speak to speak in search of somewhat steady employment. Either the clientele didn't take to them—there was still some anti-Irish sentiment staining the city—or the speaks were raided and closed. Dash was new to the Village himself and had just inherited Hartford & Sons from Victor. He was lonely, untethered, and completely lost. It was Joe and Finn who turned his life around. Together, they came up with the idea for Pinstripes.

Dash turned in his seat so he could face Joe behind him. The two men locked eyes.

An intake of breath from Wim. "They're on the move. Alright, lovebirds, let's see what old man Frazier and The Blockheads are up to."

He yanked the car into gear, and they surged forward. This time, Val and Louis weren't making any of their usual stops. They crossed the East River and headed west until Riverside Drive.

"A beeline to the Fraziers," Dash said.

Wim nodded. "Seems that way."

They passed the Sixties, Seventies, Eighties.

By the time they got to the Nineties, Wim said, "Duck your heads." He surged the car forward and passed the truck.

"What are ya doin', lad?" Joe called from the backseat.

"We already know where they're going," Wim replied. "We might as well get into position early."

Soon they pulled onto 106th street, one block away from the Frazier's house. The three men got out of the car.

Wim motioned to Dash and Joe. "I snuck up this afternoon. There's a mini alleyway that cuts behind both houses," he said, meaning the neighboring house and the Fraziers'. "Follow me!"

Dash looked at Joe and shrugged. Joe nodded, and together, the two of them followed the flighty young man. They had just left the street when Dash saw out of the corner of his eye Val and Louis cruise by on Riverside.

True to Wim's word, the dirt path ran behind both houses, parallel to Riverside. The neighboring house was completely dark, like the night before, but the Frazier household had quite a few lights on. They followed the pathway until it ended at the other side of the house's entrance facing 107th.

They crouched down by a three-foot high marble wall that was a reasonable distance from the front door. Far enough to be shielded from view, but close enough to hear. Wim and Joe had their guns drawn.

A few more months of this, Dash thought, *and I'll need to learn how to shoot one of those damnable things.*

Footsteps on concrete. Someone was walking up the entry steps. A click of a lock, the opening of a door, a gruff greeting.

Joe whispered, "Damn brazen of them to use the main walk."

"Or maybe Leonard doesn't care who sees," offered Dash. He peered over the side of the wall.

Val stood a few steps down from the front door. Behind him was Louis, the man with the *accent aigu* mustache, carrying a wooden crate.

"Evening, Mr. Frazier," Val said.

"You have what I want?" Leonard stayed just out of Dash's sight.

Val snorted. "Yeah, yeah, I got what you want. More importantly, do *you* have what *I* want?"

A rustling of paper and a hand extending a thick envelope. Val took it, opened it, thumbing through its contents. Counting the money, no doubt.

Val looked up, satisfied it was all there. "Thank you, Mr. Frazier. A pleasure doing business with you."

Val turned on his heel and walked away. Louis stepped forward and dropped off the crate. The telltale clinks of bottles echoed in the night. Dash and Joe gazed at one another. Leonard was supposed to be Dry. Dash looked up to see Louis give the unseen Leonard a smirk and followed after Val. They stepped into the truck without a backward glance, started it up, and drove off.

Dash assumed they would continue to follow them and made moves to go back down the dirt path, but another man's voice stopped him.

"Are you ready to go, Mr. Frazier?" the new male voice asked.

"I am," Leonard said. "Mingus, if you'd be so kind."

Mingus.

Dash peered over the wall. A darkened figure bent down and picked up the create of bottles, the glass tinkling more prominently now. Dash thought he'd turn around and bring them into the house, but he had made the second wrong assumption of the night.

Instead, Mingus went to a fancy motorcar parked across the street, facing Riverside. Dash heard a door close, and a straight-backed figure followed Mingus. Leonard Frazier.

Mingus placed the crate into the trunk of the car and opened the passenger door for his employer.

Wim and Joe turned to face Dash. He nodded. They backed away from the front of the house, and once they were clear of it, ran down the dirt pathway until they reached 106th. As soon as they reached the car and jumped in—Dash and Wim in the front, Joe in the back—Leonard Frazier's motorcar crossed in front of them on Riverside heading south.

Wim started up the car, yanked it into gear, and pulled out. He left his headlights off.

Dash turned and looked at Joe, who asked, "Was tha' what I thought tha' was?"

"A rich Dry man buying booze from a gangster's truck? Yes, I believe that was." He looked at Wim. "I take it selling directly to private households isn't normally what Fife does?"

"Sometimes, but I can tell you this man, Leonard Frazier? He's not on the list."

"You mean to tell me Val and Louis just sold off a crate of booze they shouldn't have?"

Joe muttered, "Fife is not gonna be happy about that."

"No," Wim said grimly, "no, he will not."

Dash shook his head. "This doesn't make any sense at

all. If Leonard was buying it for himself, why not take it into the house?"

"Maybe he's takin' it to the police," Joe offered.

"That doesn't fit either. It's the buying and selling of liquor that's illegal. If the cops didn't witness what we witnessed, then a crate of booze by itself means nothing."

Dash faced the front again. The Frazier car was a good two Manhattan blocks in front. They cruised towards the heart of Manhattan, with nary a stop or interruption along the way. When traffic started to pick up the closer they got to the main part of the city, Wim flipped his headlights on. Dash held his breath, hoping the move wouldn't cause the driver Mingus to look in his rearview mirrors.

If he noticed them, his driving didn't show.

They continued steady on downtown, avoiding the tangle that was Times Square before cutting over onto Twenty-Sixth Street, heading east.

"Where is he going?" Dash muttered.

The answer would come soon enough, but it was just as perplexing as everything else that had occurred tonight.

Leonard Frazier was driven to Bellevue Hospital.

More perplexing was that Mr. Frazier didn't go inside the intimidating Gothic building, but Mingus did—with the crate of Fife's bottles.

"What the bloody hell is *this* about?" Joe sputtered.

Wim replied, "Ya got me. I feel like a Dumb Dora watching all of this."

"I think I know." Dash twisted his torso so he could look back at Joe. "Charles Norris works here. I think Leonard is having the booze tested by him."

Joe wrinkled his brow. "Why would he do that?"

"I'm not entirely sure, but it's the only thing that makes sense."

"Unless the bottles caught a fever," Wim said. When he saw the death glares of Dash and Joe, he replied, "Apologies. Bad joke."

Dash and Joe returned their attentions to one another.

"The bigger question, Joe, is how Leonard got in touch with Val and Louis. How does a Dry know who to call?"

"Aye, and was Fife the only gangster he called?"

"And if Fife was the only one, *why?*"

Wim looked from Dash to Joe and back again. "Whatever you say, boys. It's all Greek to me."

After a good half hour, Mingus returned to the car and drove Leonard Frazier home. Wim followed, taking the long, winding Riverside Drive back uptown again.

Wim passed them, just like he did with Val and Louis a few hours before, and parked on 106th. They snuck down the same pathway between the homes, noting this time that the Frazier mansion was as dark as its neighbor. Crouched down, they waited for Leonard to arrive.

Twenty minutes later, they heard the approaching motor car. They hunched down even further, making sure the headlights didn't illuminate them. The car braked to a stop and Leonard Frazier stepped out into the night.

The two men walked up the entryway steps. A door opened.

Mingus said, "Mr. Norris said the results would be ready by tomorrow morning."

"Excellent. Remember, Mingus," Leonard said, "not a word to anyone."

"Yes, sir."

The two men entered the house. The front door shut, the deadbolt slamming into place.

22

In the mid-morning light, Bellevue Hospital looked straight out of Dickens with its brick and stone Victorian buildings surrounded by wrought iron gates. Through the black bars, Dash could see the arched windows and Corinthian columns. The property sprawled across four blocks along the East River. Browning ivy, wounded by the previous August heat and the present September chill, clung to the stone walls—brittle veins no longer capable of pumping life.

Joe had been fast asleep when Dash had dressed himself in a simple navy suit and crept out of the apartment. Charles Norris would have the results this morning. Perhaps Dash could intercept them, so he could know what kind of danger he and Fife were in. After all, a man with Leonard's influence could cause all sorts of troubles for them both.

For the next half hour, he felt he repeated the name *Charles Norris* about a hundred times. Dash first approached a guard at the gate, who then directed him to the main front desk, who then directed him to the pathology building where a series of individuals pointed him down numerous hallways. Eventually someone was able to give him specifics.

"Norris is in the cutting room," Dash was told.

He swallowed. The cutting room?

He followed the directions until he came to a quiet and cool space. The reverent silence combined with the high ceilings, white plaster walls, and marbled surfaces reminded Dash of a church, not a morgue. This feeling was soon discarded when he saw a corpse lying on one of three long marble tables under a row of bright white lights at the far end of the room.

The young man was nude, his body hairless save for a tuft of pubic hair. His eyes and mouth were closed, his brown hair neatly brushed back. An odd blue color tinted the skin. The hands were relaxed at his side, feet turned outward. Dash stared at his chest, wanting it to rise and fall with breath. It remained impossibly still.

A clattering of metal turned Dash's head. A large man dressed in a three-button suit appeared in Dash's line of sight. Footballer build, square shoulders, much taller and wider than Joe. The man walked quickly, never slowing for a moment.

"Are you looking for me?" he asked briskly as he dragged a metal rolling cart behind him. His voice was booming and deep.

"I am if you're Charles Norris."

The man dismissed him with a wave of his hand. "I don't have time right now."

He sidled up to the marble table holding the dead young man. On the cart, Dash saw the tools of Norris's grotesque trade: knives with blades of various lengths and widths, what looked like cuticle scissors, serrated saws, forceps, scales that Dash had seen at butcher shops (*I may never eat meat again)*, tape measures, measuring glasses, and glass jars empty—thank God—of vital organs.

"But you don't even know what I want yet," Dash said.

"Doesn't matter. I'm backed up on autopsies, thanks to the holiday, and we keep having more bodies come in. I must find out what caused this poor boy's demise, though Alex seems to think he knows what did it."

Alex?

"Mr. Norris—"

"I apologize, but Alex has bet me dinner tonight he's right and I'm wrong, and I cannot delay another second." Norris finally turned around and faced Dash. "The only way I'm going to see you is if you died." A quick smile and a chuckle rumbled from his wide chest. "I tease, though I really am busy. Are you here about a relative?"

Dash regarded the infamous coroner, noting the reporters had, surprisingly, accurately described him. Slicked back salt-and-pepper hair revealed a large rectangle of a face. A bulbous nose. Nearly white eyebrows, which were bushy and thick and flew outwards in all directions. Intelligent eyes burned brightly underneath his brows' mayhem, and an unkempt gray and white goatee surrounded lips pressed together in a thin line.

"No," Dash replied. "I'm here about something else."

If Dash expected Norris to stop what he was doing, he greatly underestimated the man. Norris picked up a small knife and began slicing a few inches below the dead man's left shoulder down to just underneath the breastbone.

Dash felt his mouth immediately dry out. "Mr. Leonard Frazier gave you a crate of liquor to examine. He wants me to pick up the results."

Norris went to the other side of the marble table and replicated the cut from the man's right shoulder. Then he took the knife and made a straight line down to the man's abdomen. The incisions were deep, and Dash saw the skin separate, beginning to reveal its hoary contents. He immediately turned around so as not to face the autopsy.

"I see your employer is on the impatient side," Norris said behind him.

Dash heard the clatter of the knife being placed on the metal cart. Other than his breathing, which had intensified the moment Norris started, all he could hear was the sickening, smooth strokes of Norris's blade.

"Once I'm done with this poor fellow here, we can go to my office."

Another clatter. That knife sounded larger than the one Norris started with. Then Dash heard a pulling sound, reminiscent of peeling the tough outer skin away from an orange. Black spots dotted his peripheral vision.

"Is there a place I can sit down," Dash said, his voice thick and heavy.

Norris sounded concerned. "If you don't mind my saying so, my young friend, you don't seem all that well."

"Funny, I don't feel all that well."

Despite keeping his head still—and his back resolutely to Norris and the corpse—the room started spinning. The faint rushing sound in his ears had now turned into an intensifying roar. The black splotches were now crowding out his vision.

Dash thought, *is this what Rosalie experienced before she died?*

"Sir!" Norris said. "Steady yourself!"

But it was too late. Dash went down.

What Dash was aware of next was the sound of steam escaping and a faintly bitter smell. There was a bubbling sound as well, which didn't make much sense. Was he in a kitchen?

The smell became even more bitter. His eyes flew open as he coughed more. Norris was kneeling beside him, that bushy brow impossibly large.

"Ah, that's better," he said as he capped a small bottle and placed it in his jacket pocket.

Smelling salts.

Dash cautiously looked around. He was lying on the floor with his elevated feet placed on a chair, but it wasn't the same room he was in.

Norris anticipated his questions. "You're now in the toxicology lab. I surmised that if you were to awaken in the same room as our dead guest, you'd faint again."

Dash's mouth felt dry and full of cotton. "That would be a fair assessment," he said. He made a move to sit up, but Norris placed a large hand on his chest.

"Please, stay here for just a moment longer. Your body is still processing the shock."

Dash replied, "You're the expert." He then realized a cool, wet rag had been placed on his forehead. "I sincerely apologize for this."

"Don't be. You're not the first man to faint in my cutting room. And while you were out, I was able to complete that young boy's autopsy uninterrupted. I should thank you for the added efficiency."

"Glad I could help." Dash adjusted the cool rag to be more centered on his forehead. "Did you win the bet?"

"I'm afraid not. I voted for cyanide. Alex was correct in that it was thallium. For a man who's a constant gambler, he is surprisingly lucky." Norris stood up. "Isn't that where you met Frazier's man? Mingus? At the horse track, was it not?"

Another male voice, quieter and statelier, replied, "You'll have to excuse Charles. He believes no one is as clever as him. And yes. That's why Jack felt comfortable coming to us on Mr. Frazier's behalf."

Dash looked to the side. All he saw were a pair of black shoes and gray trousers underneath a white lab coat.

"I still think you cheat, Alex," Norris said. "I hope you don't mind, my young friend, but I took the liberty of looking through your personal affects. Mr. Dashiell Parker. I suppose you go by Dash?"

Dash almost nodded, but worried the room would spin again. "Yes, sir."

"And you're working for Leonard Frazier?"

"I . . . am. Yes. He wanted me to come down for the . . . results."

"Ah, yes, the impatient Mr. Frazier. Are you ready to get up?"

"I believe so."

Dash carefully lowered his feet from the chair and slowly sat up. As he did so, he felt large hands grip him from his underarms, pulling him upward to his feet.

From behind, Norris said, "How do you feel?"

Dash took stock. "A little woozy, but I can manage."

The hands left him, and Dash stood on his own. He looked over to the source of the other male voice and saw a stark contrast to the broad, bullish figure of Charles Norris —almost a half a foot shorter with a slight build and narrow shoulders. Short dark hair combed to the side and cropped close to his skull. Clean shaven with pencil-thin eyebrows. Compared to Norris's wilderness brush of a brow, Alex's looked drawn onto his oval face.

Complete opposites. A truly odd couple if there ever was one.

Just like Joe and I . . .

The man called Alex smiled. "Hello, there. I'm Alexander Gettler, Charles's partner."

He stood at a long rectangular table covered with beakers, jars, test tubes, and burners. Dash watched as Gettler raised with one hand an odd-shaped beaker—narrow at the mouth, wide at the bottom—that held a white powder. With his other hand, Gettler poured a red-tinted liquid from a test tube into the glass. Immediately there was the sound of hissing and bubbling. Gettler watched the chemical reaction with absolute concentration. The mixture bubbled upward, threatening to leak out the top. Gettler showed no sign of alarm; he simply watched as it oscillated up and down. It finally settled with the sound of the ocean spray after a wave has crashed against the beach.

Norris said from behind Dash, "Was I right?"

Dash turned to the side so he could see the two men.

Gettler gently placed the beaker down, keeping his eyes on it. "Yes," he said simply.

Norris laughed. "Ah ha! You owe me dessert tonight. Delmonico's, you think?"

"As long as you don't renege on paying for dinner."

Norris placed a hand over his heart. "You wound me, good sir! When have I *ever* reneged on a bet?"

Gettler nodded towards Dash. "I believe our visitor was here to get test results for his employer, not to listen to us bicker."

"Oh yes," Norris replied.

He went to a drawer embedded in one of the tables and searched through multiple pieces of paper. He found the one he was looking for and raised it up. He held his arm out, squinting as he read.

"Ah. Arsenic."

Dash didn't comprehend. "Excuse me? Arsenic?"

"Yes. Arsenic. Not what killed his poor daughter." He glared at Gettler. "And *yes,* you were right."

Gettler's smile was smug. "Charles here bet on methyl alcohol. It was a logical guess, Charles. Most of the bathtub gin in this city is rife with it."

"Arsenic," Dash repeated. "In the boo—in the liquor bottles? Could that be . . . a natural occurrence?"

Norris folded the test results, his wide fingers tapping the paper absent-mindedly. "My young friend, how much do you know about arsenic?"

Dash looked from Norris to Gettler and back again. "I know it's in rat poison."

"Rat poison, weed killer, insect killer, skin tonics, fabric dyes, even some wallpaper around the city. All have arsenic in them. Now it's possible that an insecticide or herbicide was used in whatever house or factory this liquor came from, infiltrating the water supply that was used to ferment this swill."

Dash saw the skepticism on Norris's face. "But you don't believe so."

Norris shook his head. "The traces of arsenic were in near equal amounts, as if measured. Accidental would be more slap-dash, inconsistent."

"How could someone poison the bottles?" Dash asked.

"Easily," Gettler replied. "Especially if they're using white arsenic, the powdered version of it. It mixes quite well with food and soups—"

"But especially well," interrupted Norris, "with alcohol. The surrounding flavors disguise the taste. Many people who have survived arsenic poisonings reported not tasting anything at all."

"Although a few," added Gettler, "mentioned an odd metallic taste or sensation in their mouths. However, it was not so overwhelming that it caused them to stop eating or drinking."

Dash scratched his head. "And how long does it take the poison to work?"

"Depends upon the amount," Norris answered. "If a poisoner wanted a person's death to appear natural, they would use small trace amounts over time. The symptoms would resemble failing health, and the autopsy would show failed organs. Most coroners would simply assume they died of old age or illness."

"But," Gettler said, "if in high amounts, then symptoms would start within hours. Convulsions, vomiting, gasping for breath. Arsenic wrecks particular havoc on the digestive system in acute cases."

"It's a blunt instrument of a poison. The stomach will show bloody lesions. The mucus membrane lining will be swollen, yellowish, and covered in scarlet patches. Intestines will present similarly. The heart will often contain blood clots. And if the dose is high enough, we will find arsenic crystals throughout the body, shining like diamond dust in a mine." He shook his head sadly. "An angry weapon. Like a bomb going off in the body."

Dash shuddered and fought off another round of queasiness. "From someone observing the victim, would it look like methyl alcohol poisoning?"

Norris and Gettler glanced at one another.

"Somewhat," Norris said slowly. "The only common symptom would be the gastric distress and possibly cardiac or respiratory failure, but the poisons attack different parts of the body. Methyl alcohol damages the nerves—victims will have trouble seeing and lose coordination of their limbs, become confused. Also, methyl alcohol takes much longer to be broken down by the body, so the time between a large dose and acute symptoms is longer."

Dash nodded, trying to process all the information Norris and Gettler gave him. It seemed that Fife had made a critical error. On the surface, it looked as if the victims from previous speaks resembled Rosalie—the vomiting, the heart and lung failures. But this liquor batch indicated a different poison was used. Which meant Rosalie wasn't connected to whomever was trying to sabotage Fife. She died by another's hand, another speak with tainted booze.

Gettler furrowed his brow. "Mr. Parker? Are you all right?"

Dash shook himself and forced a smile. "Just thinking. If I am hearing you two correctly, this crate of liquor was intentionally poisoned."

Norris's face was grave. "Yes. Whoever is selling this has a poisoner on their hands."

23

Arsenic.

The word kept reverberating inside Dash's aching skull. Someone in Fife's warehouse was dosing his liquor with arsenic. A dose high enough to make men and women seriously ill or dead. But who?

A sickening pit in his stomach. Were his patrons drinking this nasty poison? Oh God, he hoped not.

In any event, Leonard Frazier was sure to react badly to this set of news. True, it didn't explain his daughter's death, but poison was poison. Dash didn't expect a man as moral as Leonard to keep it quiet.

And what about Rosalie Frazier? She had ingested methyl alcohol and if not from Fife's liquor, then from where? The blind tiger she and Marty and Tillie attended on Radio Row?

The very setup as described by Tillie sounded perfect for cheap, dangerous booze. And though Tillie claimed she and Marty had the bathtub gin, she could've been lying, could've encouraged Rosalie to drink the whole bottle. Granted, they visited this tiger a week before Rosalie drank enough methyl alcohol to die (so Tillie said . . .), but a poison such as this didn't need the timelines to match up perfectly. If Rosalie took the bottle home with her, she would've eventually dosed herself properly.

The bottle.

Dash had found an empty, unlabeled bottle under her bed! He frantically tried to recall the details of this tiger's location. Tillie said it was in a radio shop on Cortlandt Street. "Radio Row," she had called it. Dash recalled the streets downtown weren't particularly long ones—not like those in midtown. It shouldn't take long to find it. He could be back at the Cherry Lane apartment before Joe woke up.

Joe. He wouldn't like what Dash was doing, though Dash couldn't fathom why. This adventure wasn't dangerous. He was in broad daylight! Besides, Dash had never experienced a blind tiger before—the prospect of it excited him, as did the possibility of closing the door on how Rosalie obtained the toxic booze. If Joe couldn't understand that, then forget him.

"Right," Dash murmured to himself, "Cortlandt Street. How many radio shops could there be?"

Dash learned that Cortlandt Street's moniker of "Radio Row" was no misnomer. A long line of shops dedicated to all things radio lined each side of the street. Dozens of them.

How many could there be, indeed.

With a dogged patience, he went into shop after shop, asking for a "giggle radio" and receiving many strange looks. A few told him to *get the hell outta my store, ya clown!* It wasn't until he got near Greenwich Street that his luck began to change.

Transworld Radio, like its neighbors, had large plate-glass windows for pedestrians to gawk at the multiple radios on display. Short ones, tall ones, square ones, round ones. Amazing how, just a few years ago, radio was new, and now, they were being built in all shapes and sizes. Seemingly faster than the automobile. Dash wondered if one day, things would move so fast that people could no longer keep up, much less catch up.

He entered the shop, which had a few visitors, a middle-aged married couple and two younger women. He walked to the clerk behind the register, putting on his best smile. "Good morning, sir."

The clerk was on the young side, reminding Dash of an old schoolmate. Short brown hair and smooth skin with a hint of blemish on the cheeks. Narrow face and nose, ears that stuck out in an endearing way. A long, square chin allowed for a deep and wide smile.

"Good morning, sir," the clerk replied.

Dash then leaned on the counter, dropping his head and hunching his shoulders. He said in a lowered his voice, "Now I have a request and it may seem a little strange."

The clerk mirrored Dash's movements. "Yeah? How strange?"

Dash glanced over his shoulder. The married folks and the two girls were paying them no mind. He turned his attention back to the clerk. "I'm looking for a . . . giggle radio."

"A what, sir?"

"A giggle radio. I don't know who makes it, admittedly."

Dash expected to be ordered out of the shop like in some of the others. But the clerk instead gave him a look of complete seriousness.

"Hmm," he said. "I think Edison makes one."

"Does he? I'm surprised he's into something like that."

The seriousness was replaced with a Cheshire grin. "You'd be surprised what Edison is into." His eyes darted over to a small radio in the back corner. "Check out that model over there. If you turn the dial, pay the five cent toll, and wait for the light, you might be surprised with what you find."

Dash pursed his lips and nodded. "I see. It's a popular model, that one?"

"One of our best sellers."

Dash looked into the clerk's amused eyes. They twinkled with mischief. "Thank you, sir."

"Don't mention it."

Dash straightened up and walked over to the back corner. The radio the clerk pointed to was an inconsequential thing. Hardly the item to catch a prospective buyer's eye —and he assumed that was the point. A wooden box with three dials drilled into the front. On the right side, a square with a needle inside pointed, like a clock's hands, to block-lettered numbers going up in increments of fives and tens. On the left side was the speaker, another square with a mesh-like inlay, crisscrossing over itself.

Behind Dash, he could hear the murmured gossip of the two girls while the married man discussed the merits of a Zenith versus an Edison versus an RCA. The woman would pipe up with a comment or two but was largely ignored.

Dash reached for one of the dials and turned. Nothing happened. He tried the second. Again, nothing happened. He began to wonder if the clerk was playing him for a fool. He glanced over his shoulder at him, but the clerk was busy notating something in his logbook.

Dash turned back around and tried the third dial. A

light click sounded. Dash's heart began beating fast. A slight tingling formed in his fingers and chest. He easily understood why Rosalie was fascinated by all this intrigue. It *was* exciting, to be breaking the law in plain sight. A different kind of thrill, and Dash felt his own body respond to it, just like Rosalie's would have.

He looked at the speaker, which had ever so slightly popped open. He snuck a peek at the married couple and the girls. No one was even looking this way. Fingers trembling with anticipation, he opened the door.

Just like Tillie said, an empty compartment was where the speaker should've been.

He reached into his trouser pocket and grabbed a nickel, quickly placing it inside the compartment and gently closing the door of the speaker.

He waited.

He strained to hear any kind of queer sounds. A rustling of the coin being spirited away. The click of another door opening. All he heard were the girls laughing and the pontifications of the married man. He was truly working himself up over wavelengths and frequencies.

The left-hand square with the needle and numbers suddenly illuminated. The light.

Dash turned the third dial again, the speaker once more popping open. Dash swung the little door open and inside the compartment, like magic, was an unlabeled bottle. It was small and slender, three inches tall and three inches circumference. Damned if it wasn't the same size and shape of the empty bottle of gin Dash found under Rosalie's bed.

He almost laughed.

He couldn't believe it!

He stared at the bottle for a second longer before coming to his senses and grabbing it and closing the speaker door. Once the door closed, the light behind the square of numbers extinguished. Dash wondered if the door was connected to an electrical source, or if his hidden bartender on the other side of this wall heard the click of the speaker door and simply flipped off the switch.

He quickly slipped the bottle into his trouser pocket and returned to the clerk.

The man looked up. "Find what you were looking for?"

"I did indeed. I have one question for you though."

"Yes?"

Dash reached into his inside coat pocket and removed Rosalie's teacup drawing. He placed it onto the counter.

The clerk glanced down at it. "What's that?"

"It's a teacup."

The clerk smirked. "I can see that. I meant, what's your question?"

Dash pointed to it. "Do you know where I can find a tea set that's, uh, similar in nature to the Edison I just looked at?"

The clerk brought his eyes upward. "Why are you interested?" The unspoken question *are you a cop?* laid between them like a held breath.

"I have a lady friend who is just *mad* about special types of tea, shall we say. And I was in a speak the other night, chatting up some fellas, and this one man hands me this piece of paper, saying this should keep my girl happy."

"Did he tell you where to go?"

"Well, now, I don't remember," Dash replied with a deprecating chuckle. "Had a little too much gin that night, you understand."

"Hmm. How much is it worth to ya?"

Of course. Nothing was free in this city.

"Depends on what you have to sell," Dash replied. "Do

you know where something like this is? For some reason, I remember the word *Washington* but I'll be damned if I know much more than that."

"Washington, eh? No, none of it rings a bell, but I can ask around. Come back here, say, Wednesday. I might have something for you."

"Excellent!"

"But I'll need some walking-around money to do that. You understand." The long, wide grin again.

Dash shook his head as he pulled out his dwindling pile of sugar. "Yes, unfortunately, I do."

———

Dash was buzzing all the way home to the Village. It was almost like he was following in Rosalie's footsteps.

Now if those footsteps would lead me to what happened to you . . .

It was now past lunch time and Dash was famished. He stopped in the Greenwich Village Inn. There he found Joe and Finn, sipping coffee and eating a late lunch. They looked up when he entered, Joe demanding where the hell he'd been all morning.

Before he could reply, Emmett appeared behind the bar, wiping a dish towel against his hands. "I see *all* the neighborhood dandies are here."

"Fer the last time," Joe said, "I'm not a dandy."

Finn lightly swatted Joe's shoulder. "Oh, don't be a flat tire. I, for one, *love* being called a dandy. Makes me feel like I have money."

Emmett scoffed, "Ya better have money with ya now." He gestured to the mostly empty place. "I'm gonna need all the sugar I can get."

Dash settled onto a barstool in between Joe and Finn. He looked around. Besides the three of them, there were only The Ex-Pats. "Pirate's Den?"

Emmett scowled. "Goddamn thieves. They're not gonna rest until they take all my customers."

"You know, Emmett, why don't you come up with some sort of theme for this place? Do The Pirate's Den one better."

Finn gasped. "That's a *marvelous* idea!" He glanced around the room, taking in the rough atmosphere. "I think you can make this place like the docks. Sea shanties playing in the background, rough ropes tied everywhere. Shirtless stevedores painted on the walls, and waiters dressed as bell-bottoms—"

"Finney," Joe warned.

"What? It's inspired, admit it." Finn turned to Emmett. "What do you think? I'm thinking we can name this place *Dockside* or *Dockers*. Or—oooo—the *Rusty Anchor!*"

An incredulous look on Emmett's face. "You must be joking! You all must be joking! I'd rather be damned. Be damned, I tell you!"

"It's just a first draft," Finn said.

"No, no, absolutely not. I will not *stoop* to such nonsense. This place is for food and drink, not theatre, and that's final!"

Dash held up his hands in a placating manner. "Apologies, our friend. We were only trying to help. Forget we mentioned it."

Still grumbling, Emmett poured Dash coffee and said he'd start his usual.

When Emmett went to the kitchen, Joe asked Dash again where he'd been. Dash was unnerved by the increasing gruffness in Joe's tone. Where was *this* coming from? He spoke fast, nerves accelerating his words.

Both Joe and Finn reacted with the same confusion when they were told about the arsenic being in Fife's booze.

"Do you think it's in all of his new bottles?" Finn asked. "Or just the crate Leonard bought?"

Dash sighed. "I don't know. We haven't heard of any of our boys getting sick?"

Finn considered the question. "Most of what we've had lately are bell bottoms, and word gets around on the ships. They wouldn't be coming in if we were making half the United States Navy ill."

"Aye, and the Village is the same," Joe added. "I haven't heard a peep from anyone."

"Nor have I," Finn replied.

Dash shook his head. "Nor have I." When he got to the part about the blind tiger, he produced the bottle of boot-legged gin. "This is the same type of bottle I found in Rosalie's room. Under her bed, completely empty."

Joe took the bottle first, examined it, then handed it over to Finn.

He opened the top and smelled. "Not complete lighter fluid, but not much better. What are you going to do with it?"

"I'm going to call Fife up and have Angelo test it. If it has enough methyl alcohol in it, then we may have a possible source of Rosalie's misfortune."

"Why Angelo?" Finn asked. "Isn't he still 'under suspicion' in your and Fife's investigation?"

"Who else could we call? Besides, if we say it's not from our speak, I'm not sure why he'd give a false negative or positive."

Joe crossed his arms, his voice impatient. "Lassie, why does any of this matter?"

Dash warily regarded the big, ruddy man. "Because if this is full of methyl alcohol, then we can somehow give it to Leonard Frazier."

"Ayuh. And *what* will tha' accomplish?"

Finn jumped in. "It will give Leonard someplace else to look, you grumpy bear. Away from Fife."

"And away from *us*."

Joe rubbed his jaw. "And *then* will ya stop playin' detective?"

Dash suddenly felt meek. "I . . . as soon as Fife releases me, then yes."

Joe raised his coffee mug and took a healthy swig. "Saints be praised."

Dash managed to charm Emmett into using his telephone for the fourth time in seven days, a fact Emmett made sure Dash knew. He called Fife's number and was assured someone would be there within the hour.

As promised, an hour later, Dash, Joe, and Finn were inside Pinstripes with Angelo Avogadro. Angelo was his usual meticulous and patient self, which was more than what could be said for the three of them. Joe paced the floor behind them, Finn hopped on his heels, and Dash lightly tapped the bar in front of him, a Morse code of anxiety. Anticipation beat his heart against his chest. He was trying not to get his hopes up, but he yearned for this to be it, for this to be the solution. Blind tiger booze killed Rosalie Frazier. End of story.

But what about Marty and Tillie's lies? The matchbook from a Blacks-only hotel? Beverly's possible secret liaison?

Joe had said they were the goings-on of a bunch of bored rich folks and to quit paying them any mind.

"Where did you find this?" Angelo asked.

"A blind tiger in lower Manhattan," Dash replied.

"And this girl, this Rosalie, she went there?"

"She did."

Angelo arched an eyebrow. "Blind tigers and pigs are known for selling low quality liquor. I know of several places like this."

"You do, Angelo?" He thought about Rosalie's teacup drawing. "Any of them tearooms or china shops?"

A half-smile. "Unfortunately, no. Clothing stores with a cutout door in the changing room. Like yours. Bakeries with a phone booth that has sliding panels. Really, you Americans are quite creative when it suits you." He looked at the three men. "Are we ready?"

Joe stopped pacing and stood beside Dash and Finn at the bar.

Angelo repeated process they'd witnessed with their own liquor supply and with the countless bottles during Dash's surveillance. All three men watched with bated breath as Angelo added the mixtures, paused, then wafted and smelled.

"Hmm," he said, closing his eyes.

"Wha?" Joe said. "Wha is it, lad?"

Angelo opened his eyes. "I am . . . surprised."

Dash leaned forward. "Why?"

Angelo set the beaker down. "Because for blind tiger gin, there is no methyl alcohol present."

Dash went to soak and steam away his disappointment at the Carmine Baths. It would've been such a neat solution to Rosalie's mystery. Death by blind tiger. An accident of Prohibition. An unintended consequence of the Volstead Act.

Now Dash was back to square one.

In the changing room, Dash placed his clothes in a locker, secured it with the key he'd been given, and returned to the main room with the bathing booths. He found one empty and entered. The room was dark with only streaks of light coming in from the high window covered in netting, illuminating the claw-foot tub and little else. Shadows hid the walls and corners.

Dash undid his robe and struggled to find the hook in the darkness. His feet chilled against the cool stone-tiled floor, but his bare body warmed in the surrounding heated air. The baths were the only places in the Village to find hot water, and the tenement dwellers reveled in the chance to bathe without chattering teeth.

He eventually found the hook and hung his robe, stepping towards the tub. With a wrench of the levers, hot water roared into the porcelain oval. It took a few moments to fill and then Dash shut off the faucet. Inviting steam hovered above the waterline like mist. Gripping the sides of the tub, he slowly lowered himself into the warm water. Once he settled back, he let forth a big sigh, closing his eyes.

"Satisfying, isn't it?" said a voice.

Dash jerked upward in the water, splashing the stone tiles. He searched the hazy darkness for the source of the voice.

A man in a robe sauntered forward. The sunlight slowly lit his frame, inch by inch, before lighting his face.

Nicholas Fife.

Dash stared at him.

"I apologize," he said. "I didn't realize this booth was occupied."

Fife pointed to the darkened corner. "I was standing behind the opened door. You wouldn't have seen me."

"H-h-how did you know I'd come in here?"

"I saw you walking this way. You were much too involved in your own thoughts to notice me slipping into the vacant booth." Fife continued walking towards the tub. "Pray tell, what *is* on your mind?"

He stopped right next to the edge of the tub. Fife's height plus Dash's lowered position forced Dash to stretch his neck upward to see Fife's face. A bemused smile on an otherwise bland expression.

Should I cover up?

Fife's chagrined smile seemed to say, *Why bother? I've already seen everything.*

Dash cleared his throat and replied, "Nothing of interest."

"Shy, are we? Well, I'll tell you what's on *my* mind.

Leonard Frazier buying my booze from my men." He placed his hands on the edge of the tub, drumming the porcelain with his fingers. "After your evening with Wim, I took it upon myself to speak with Val and Louis."

Dash didn't want to ask his next question, but he knew he must. "What did you find out?"

Fife knelt onto the tiled floor, his face now just above the tub's edge. "It took a moment for them to, shall we say, warm up to the conversation. But eventually, they confessed to finding a note on top of a crate saying to make this delivery to the Frazier address and that they would be well paid if they went off their usual route."

"It sounded to me like they tried to extort Mr. Frazier a little on their own. The first night they met with Leonard, they didn't have the booze with them."

"I wouldn't doubt that."

"Did they know who left the note?"

"They didn't know and they didn't ask." He began lazily dragging his fingertips across the surface of the water, making circular, intricate patterns. "Val and Louis are not the most curious creatures on the planet."

"Did they shortchange a customer of yours? Meaning, did they give away another speak's booze?"

Fife gave a tight smile. "No, it was some extra bottles."

"Someone pre-selected the booze and hoped The Block-heads—I mean, Val and Louis—wouldn't ask questions."

"It would appear." Fife looked Dash in the eyes. "What did you find out?"

Dash swallowed, dreading how the mercurial man would react. "It seems that Leonard Frazier bought the booze to have it tested by the city coroner Charles Norris. Leonard used his influence to have the results expedited. I snuck in and got them."

A twinkle in Fife's eyes. "Did you now? And were the results ready?"

"They were. The liquor in that crate had been . . . contaminated."

Fife stopped his movements. He kept perfectly still. "Methyl alcohol?" he asked in a quiet voice.

Dash shook his head. "Arsenic."

Suddenly, Fife reached out. Dash flinched, ready for the blow. Instead, Fife went for the bar of soap hanging from a rope on the other side of the tub. He unhooked it and dipped it into the bathwater. Raising it up again, the excess water sprinkling down, he rubbed the soap with his fingers.

Reflexively, Dash tried to stand, but his feet slid across the porcelain bottom of the tub. Fife placed a gentle but firm hand against his chest.

"Wait a moment, Mr. Parker. You haven't finished your bath."

Then inexplicably, Fife rubbed the soap against Dash's damp chest, working up a lather. The action stunned Dash into stillness. What kind of killer *bathes* another man?

One who's obsessed with being the powerful one.

Fife idly mused, "This arsenic is a curious development."

Watching the circular motions of Fife's hand, Dash replied, "Yes, it is. Does Angelo test for arsenic?"

His chest was now thoroughly covered in suds. Fife began making long, smooth, soapy strokes on Dash's left arm. Dash kept his eyes on the hand washing him.

"He will now," Fife replied. He lowered Dash's left arm. "Sit up, please."

Dash hesitated.

A sly grin twitched the corners of Fife's full mouth. "I

need to get your back, Mr. Parker. You paid good money to be here. We must be thorough."

Warily, Dash sat up, exposing more of himself.

Fife dipped the bar of soap into the bathwater and, with the sound of falling droplets, began those circular motions in between Dash's shoulder blades.

Dash kept watch of Fife's face. "Any idea who could've left that note and picked out that crate?"

"Someone who wants me ruined. Leonard Frazier won't sweep this arsenic business under the rug."

"Did Val and Louis give your name?"

"They had the wherewithal *not* to do that."

"So they claim." Dash's upper back and shoulders were covered in suds.

"Have you had any dead patrons since you opened?" Fife dipped his hand to Dash's lower back, dangerously close to his buttocks.

Momentarily distracted by where Fife's hand had gone, Dash eventually replied, "No, but then again, we're still using the supply we got from you a few weeks ago. And these poisonings started only recently, correct?"

"Correct." Fife finished Dash's back and gestured to Dash's lower extremities. "Shall I get the legs?"

"I can get them," Dash quickly answered.

Fife chuckled, then handed over the soap. Dash lifted his left leg and began scrubbing. The fallen soap suds clouded up the water, giving Dash a bit more privacy.

Thank heaven for that.

Dash asked, "Have *you* had any more people die in your speaks?"

Fife nodded. "The newest batch of corpses has been dropped off with good old Mr. Norris." He touched the tip of his soapy finger to the end of Dash's nose. "You started a trend, dear Dash."

"When will you know the answers?"

"Depends on how fast Mr. Norris can cut," Fife said. "In the meantime, if someone were deliberately adding arsenic to my booze, when and where do you think they're doing it?"

Dash thought for a moment. "It can't be in the trucks. Too many bottles to uncork, then reseal. Plus, we saw no one in the truck bed once they were loaded."

"I would agree with you, Mr. Parker. I've also had the trucks inspected. No false bottoms, no false doors."

"Then the sabotage is occurring in the warehouse. What is the process of when the denatured alcohol comes in until the renatured alcohol goes out?"

"Relatively simple. We get it into the warehouse, Mr. Avogadro and his team renature it in his lab. Another quick test to be sure all the additive toxins have been removed, then it's bottled and shipped."

"What containers are used for the denatured alcohol?"

"Metal drums. They're emptied and immediately cleaned for the next delivery. The liquor bottles are kept in a rack in the bottling room."

"How easy would it be to drop a few crystals of arsenic in the drums? Perhaps after Angelo's lab and before they're shipped."

"It would appear very easy. We try to keep it under lock and key, but obviously, in a warehouse full of men coming and going, it's not fool proof."

"As I see it, that's probably your best bet. Unless . . . " Dash hated to ask the question. " . . . unless it was Angelo."

"Impossible. He takes samples, not the whole drum."

"But he has access to them, doesn't he?"

Fife sighed. "Yes, yes he does."

A silence fell between them, broken up only by the gentle sloshing of the water as Dash scrubbed himself. He finished his left leg and concentrated on the right. A thought occurred to him. "Does everyone know what Angelo tests for?"

A curious look from Fife. "Some. Why?"

"Seems to me, if they knew what compounds Angelo was testing for, they could pick a compound not on the list."

Fife began dipping his hand into the bathwater, scooping up water and rinsing Dash's chest. "Thank you, Mr. Parker. You've given me . . . quite a lot to think about." He stood up. "If I could ask one more favor of you. Watch Mr. Fazier tonight. I wonder what his reaction will be when he learns about this arsenic business."

"Will Wim pick me up?"

A pause. "No. I think it best if you observe Mr. Frazier alone."

Dash tilted his head. "Do you suspect Wim now?"

Fife's expression was dark. "You're the only man I trust at the moment, Mr. Parker." He opened the bathing booth door. "I'll be in touch."

The cab dropped Dash off, as requested, on the corner of 106th and Riverside. Night had fully descended, giving Dash the cover he needed. As the taxi pulled away, Dash lit a cigarette, knowing it might be his last one for a while. He certainly needed one after the look Joe gave him when he said where he was going tonight. Joe didn't say anything— but he didn't have to.

Dash smoked two cigarettes for good measure and then

traversed the same dirt pathway that ran behind both houses until he came to the clearing by the Frazier's front door. He settled behind the marble wall and waited.

Without the intensity of Joe or the whimsy of, well, Wim, Dash was able to appreciate his new surroundings. The stillness. The utter stillness was astounding. No car horns, no rattles of trains, no shouts between people. Just a chilled darkness, as peaceful as the very first winter snow-fall. A midnight-blue sky above him was partially lit by the moon and covered in stars, like a dress with sparkling sequins. The air was crisp and clean. Dash drank it in deep.

He must've dozed off, for he felt his head falling to his chest and he jerked up, hitting the back of his head against the marble wall.

Damnable *hell,* that hurt!

Luckily, he didn't cry out because the next thing he became aware of—besides his soon-to-be-throbbing skull—were male voices. One of them was Leonard's; the other, he didn't recognize. Was that Val? No, not as mean and slimy. Louis? He hadn't heard Louis talk much. It could've been him.

Dash's body was stiff, having been in the sitting position for too long. His joints groaned as he moved. He winced as he rearranged his disagreeing body into a crouching position so he could see over the marble wall. He slowly turned his head and peered over the ledge.

It was Leonard alright. He was being let out of his car by Mingus. He fumbled with his inside coat pocket, muttering to himself. The only word Dash caught was *arsenic.* It appeared Leonard was late in getting the results. He wondered if Charles mentioned an "errand boy." Not good the man had Dash's real name. Dash hoped Leonard wasn't familiar with the Parker family—though he was fairly certain he'd been scrubbed out of the family portraits by now.

There was a *snick* of a lighter, followed quickly by the glow of the flame and a hasty but grateful exhale. A cloud of smoke circled around Leonard's hatted head, a nicotine embrace, before slowly rising upward into the night sky. A car motor whined in the near distance. He glanced to either side of the street and stood in the center of 107th, lost in thought.

Dash couldn't help but feel for the man. He had lost so much in so little time; first his wife, then his daughter.

The whining motor gradually got louder. An approaching car coming from Riverside on the southbound side, heading towards Manhattan.

Dash heard the *ping* of metal hitting something hard. Leonard had dropped his lighter. He bent down to pick it up.

That's when there was a mighty wrench of gears and the motor roared to life, sounding as urgent and furious as an airplane. The car was still nowhere to be found. Where was it?

Then Dash saw it. Barreling down the southbound side of Riverside, cutting over across the median.

Instinct caused Dash to cry out "Leonard!" and run towards the man, who looked up, his face confused, then terrified.

Dash cleared the side alleyway in a second flat and sprinted towards Leonard. In his periphery, Dash saw the approaching car, which had crossed over the northbound side of Riverside, heading, at an angle, straight for Leonard. Dash put it out of his mind. If he concentrated on that, he wouldn't make it. He hit the pavement of 107th Street, all eyes on Leonard who didn't move, couldn't move.

Just a few feet more.

The motor roared in Dash's ears. He lowered his shoulders and leapt, colliding with Leonard. The force of the impact caused them to fly out of the path of the approaching car, though its fender clipped Dash's foot, spinning him and Leonard around. They landed on the ground, rolling over each other several times before slamming into one of the walls circling the house across the street from the Frazier mansion.

Dash's heart pounded in his ears, his chest. His vision was slightly blurred from the adrenaline and the impact. There was a murmur of pain, but it kept at bay—for now. It would come roaring back like the damn car that almost killed Leonard.

Dash looked down the street. The car was nowhere to be found. The murderous machine must've turned off 107th. The sound of its roaring motor was quickly fading away.

Leonard was underneath Dash, his round glasses miraculously still on his face, though knocked seriously askew. A small cut on the side of his forehead caused a trickled line of blood down the side of his face.

Both men breathed heavily.

"Sir! Sir!" It was Mingus. "Are you all right?"

Eventually, Dash rolled off Leonard. He was lying on his back, noticing the parts of his body that had hit the concrete and the marble hard—his knees, his elbows, his hips and shoulders. He looked down and saw that the impact of the car's fender had taken his right shoe. He looked down the darkened road. Where the devil had it gone?

Mingus stepped around Dash and began tending to his employer. He lifted Leonard up onto his feet, assessing the damage and looking for other injuries besides the cut on his forehead.

Leonard waved him off. "Mingus, quit fussing over me. Check on my savior over there. He seems as bewildered as I am."

That's when Mingus started tending to Dash. Like Leonard, he waved the well-meaning man off, though he accepted his assistance in standing up.

"Good sir," he said, once he was upright, "could you see if a leather shoe is anywhere in sight? I seem to have lost it."

Mingus went off in search of it.

Dash turned and looked at Leonard, who said, "Thank you."

Dash nodded. "Are you hurt?"

"I . . . I don't know yet." He adjusted his glasses and reached for his handkerchief in his inside pocket. He began dabbing at the blood on his face. "How about yourself?"

"I don't know yet either."

Mingus returned to them and said he couldn't find Dash's shoe.

"Damn," Dash replied. "It was my favorite pair."

The front door of the Frazier mansion opened and a woman's voice called out. "Leonard? Leonard?"

"I'm right here, Bev."

A sharp intake of breath. "Where are you?"

Leonard gave a sideways glance to Dash, as if to say *here we go, get ready*. "Across the street, Bev."

Dash heard footsteps on the entryway steps and soon saw Aunt Beverly appear in a dark robe.

She gasped, "Leonard! Oh my god, what happened?!"

Leonard began to limp his way towards his own house. "A car tried to run me over," he said matter-of-factly.

"What? What are you talking about? A car? Around *here*? At this hour?" Her tone was incredulous, as if she thought Leonard was making it all up.

Dash followed Leonard, limping as well, though his was caused by only having one shoe on. "I can assure you, madam, that's indeed what happened."

Mingus stepped in line after Dash, a procession of confused men heading towards one exasperated woman.

Beverly was rapidly shaking her head. "I—I—I don't understand. Why would a car try to run you over?"

Why, indeed.

Leonard replied, "Perhaps they weren't paying attention? Drunk? This city has had no shortage of accidents from those imbibing who then get behind the wheel."

"It's possible, madam," Dash said. "It crossed over the median there and made a diagonal line onto this street. Could've been someone half-seas ov—I mean, someone intoxicated."

Though Dash didn't believe a word he said. It was deliberate. One look at Leonard told Dash he knew it too.

Beverly seemed to accept that. "Are you alright?" finally asking after her own brother.

"Banged up and probably bruised, but alive, thanks to this gentleman here."

"Yes, this mysterious gentleman who isn't one of our neighbors." Beverly set her sights on Dash. "Thank you for saving my brother's life, but I'd very much like to know who you are."

This was going to be tricky. They might recognize him from the funeral, as one of Rosalie's hat shop colleagues. The salary he'd make there would *definitely* make him a stranger in these parts. On the other hand, he couldn't tell the truth, could he? Not to a pair of Drys like Beverly and Leonard.

Beverly arched an eyebrow. "Hmm? Concocting a story? You're not thinking fast enough. Perhaps you're involved in this so-called accident."

"You're a very astute woman, Mrs. Stevens," Dash said. "I was indeed trying to concoct a story, as you say, but I believe you and your brother here deserve the truth." A lie suddenly leapt to his lips. "My name is Max Bennett, and I am an undercover agent working for the New York Police Department."

"An undercover *agent?*"

"That's right. I'm hired to infiltrate speakeasies, gather evidence, and help them get shut down."

Beverly crossed her arms over her chest. "Do you have any identification?"

"No, I don't. You see, it wouldn't be very smart to have that kind of thing on you when you're going into enemy territory."

Leonard said, "He's right, Bev. What if he were searched?"

Like when Charles Norris searched me, Dash ruefully thought.

"You're too trusting, Leonard." Beverly shook her head at the two men. "And what are you doing *here,* Mr. Agent?"

"Leonard's name has come up in an investigation of mine."

"That's patently ridiculous. My brother wouldn't *dream* of going to speaks."

"He may have information. I need to speak with him."

"At this hour?"

"It's dreadfully important."

Beverly was unmoved, but Leonard proved to be more magnanimous.

"Bev, we should at least invite the man in for some tea or cocoa. He did just save my life." Leonard clapped Dash on the shoulder, causing him to wince. "Come in, my boy, come in."

When they crossed through the front door, the vestibule, and the grand entryway, Dash expected Mingus to recognize him from the funeral. If Mingus did, he didn't let on. He nodded to Leonard's order to have Sophie bring them some hot tea. He looked at Dash.

"Don't worry, our head maid is a night owl."

Beverly breezed through the grand entry, slamming the doors behind her. "She's an insomniac. And a snoop to boot."

"Bev!"

"Shall we retire to the library? I for one can't wait to hear what's so urgent that it can't wait until a decent hour."

The library was adorned with carved teak panels ("from India," Leonard proudly said) and floor-to-ceiling bookshelves, like the ones Dash had seen in Leonard's office. A globe cocked at an angle was in one corner, a Victrola in the other. ("I like to listen to music while I read," Leonard said.)

They settled onto thick leather couches, Beverly and Leonard on one side, Dash on the other. Both looked at him expectantly.

Now what? Dash thought.

"Yes?" Beverly said to break the silence. "What's your story, Mr. Bennett?"

The look on her face said, *and it better be a good one.*

Dash cleared his throat. "Mr. Frazier, I need you to tell me why you're buying booze from known organized crime syndicates, and bringing them to Bellevue Hospital to have Charles Norris and Alexander Gettler run tests on them."

Beverly's mouth dropped open. "Leonard! What in heaven's name are you doing? If the press catches wind of it—"

"It's all right, Bev. It was only once and in the dead of night. No one is the wiser."

Beverly pointed to Dash. "Well, you're obviously not doing a good job. At least *one* person is onto you."

"Mr. Frazier." Dash gave what he hoped was a serious look. "I need you to tell me what you're doing."

Leonard let loose a long, sad sigh. "My daughter, as you

are probably aware, died from ingesting bootlegged alcohol. I am trying to determine from where she could've gotten it."

"How did you even know who to contact?"

"I didn't. Someone contacted me."

"Who?"

"He wouldn't give his name. Only that he worked for the crime boss Nicholas Fife and knew this man's liquor supply was deadly. That my daughter attended a speak supplied by Nicholas Fife and died there."

Dash mentally swore. Someone was truly trying to sabotage Fife—*and me, as well.*

"Did this man"—Dash cleared the tickle in his throat— "did he say where this speak was?"

"He didn't. He said I'd have to pay extra for that. I told him, '*no sir, first I need to corroborate what you say is true.*'"

"You needed to test the booze first."

"Right. And now that I have it confirmed, I need to decide what to do next. Arsenic wasn't how my daughter died but—if others are consuming this, then this speak and others supplied by Fife need to be shut down. Immediately."

"I see," Dash said. "Did this man give you a number to telephone?"

Leonard shook his head. "The man will call me later this week. We both didn't know how long Mr. Norris and Mr. Gettler would take."

Just a few days. That was all Dash had before the name and location of his speak were given to a man who could shut him down—and have him, Atty, Joe, and Finn arrested.

"Oh Leonard," Beverly said. "What an utterly preposterous idea you've had. Hadn't you thought it through? I swear, ever since Rosalie decided to thumb her nose at you, you've lost all sense of intellect. If your political detractors find out about your—your *mobster* source, they'll—"

Dash interrupted her tirade. "Mr. Frazier, while I can appreciate your intentions and completely sympathize with your reasonings, we simply cannot have an amateur like you running your own investigation."

Oh, the irony.

Dash sat forward. "That car tonight was most likely a drunk, but suppose it wasn't? Suppose it was sent by Nicholas Fife himself, who got wind of what you were doing and didn't like it?"

Leonard was nodding the entire time Dash spoke. "There was something odd tonight. Mr. Norris said a messenger boy I supposedly sent visited him for the test results. A Dash Parker, I believe the name was." He looked at Dash. "Maybe he worked for Nicholas Fife?"

Dash kept his face as bland as possible, despite the pounding of his heart. "We know most of Fife's associates and that's not a name we've heard of. Regardless, Mr. Frazier, I'm going to need you to stop communications with this anonymous source. For your own safety. For your household's safety."

"I . . . understand."

But he would still take that phone call. Dash had no illusions about that.

"And one other thing," Dash said. "We have it on good authority that the crate of liquor delivered to you was deliberately sabotaged by someone in Fife's organization. You were being used, Mr. Frazier."

So please, Dash thought, *don't go to the press about this.*

Beverly just shook her head. "Honestly. You men are prone to such ridiculous foolishness. As much as you hate to hear this, Leonard, Rosie made bad choices for most of her short adult life. What happened to her was nothing more than a foregone conclusion. You need to let it go."

"I cannot, Bev!" Leonard shouted, showing the first signs of strong emotion—inside the house, at least. He glared at her. "That was my daughter. I don't care if she was careless. I don't care that she made a mistake. I don't *care* if she broke the law. She didn't deserve to *die*, Beverly." He faced Dash again, his face red, his voice tight. "Nobody does."

Dash gave a slight nod to Leonard. "Do you have any ideas where she went that weekend before she—she was found at Bellevue? Specifically the nights of September tenth and eleventh."

"Is that the investigation you're working on?"

At that moment, the maid Sophie walked in carrying a silver tray stacked with teacups, saucers, and a tea pot.

As she set them out on the coffee table between them, Beverly said, "Well, I can tell you where she was Friday night. We both can. That horrid place on 133rd, where that unnatural woman plays piano. Leonard followed her there and just about had a fit. Dragged her home kicking and screaming, didn't you, Leonard?"

Leonard's hand shook as he rose the teacup to his lips. "I'm ashamed of that, really. Not sure what came over me."

"You had *every right* to do what you did. She told us she'd reform, that she wouldn't sneak out in the middle of the night and attend such blasphemous places. Thank you, Sophie."

The maid murmured "You're welcome" before turning and seeing Dash. Recognition flashed in her eyes.

"Nice to see you again," Dash said, hoping to head her off.

Beverly's eyes darted between them. "You two have met?"

"I attended Rosalie's funeral and reception."

"I thought you looked familiar. The hat salesman, weren't you? Though I suppose that was a lie." Beverly then said to Sophie, "He's apparently an undercover policeman looking into speakeasies, illegal clubs, and, the like."

Sophie nodded. "Nice to see you again, Mr. . . . ?"

"Bennett. Miss . . . ?"

"Esposito."

"Miss Esposito, we were just discussing where Rosalie might've gone the nights of September tenth and eleventh, that Friday and Saturday respectively. Did she mention any clubs or drop any hints?"

Sophie Esposito fervently shook her head. "No, sir. She kept quiet around me about things like that. I don't think she trusted me, sir."

Dash remembered Beverly's comment that Sophie was a snoop. "Perhaps something you overheard . . . "

Sophie fiddled with her apron, shifting her weight from foot to foot. "I did overhear her on the telephone once. She was talking with roommates—old roommates. She said she found a new speak that would greatly interest them."

Dash sat forward. "When was this?"

"The same week she went to that place in Harlem."

"That Friday? September tenth?"

She shook her head. "Earlier than that, but just by a few days. Maybe Tuesday or Wednesday."

Dash's heart pounded against his chest. "And did she say the name or the address of this speakeasy?"

Another shake of the head. "Perhaps Mr. Mingus knows more. I've heard her confiding in him once or twice before."

Beverly dismissed her and requested Mingus join them at once.

Jack Mingus, looking none-too-pleased by Sophie Esposito's loose lips, endured questioning by both Dash and Beverly.

"She didn't say where she was goin'," he said, his brogue thick with frustration. "If she had, I would've told ya, Mr. Frazier, as God is my witness, I would have."

"It's alright, Mingus," Leonard said, his voice tired but gentle. "We're just trying to get to the bottom of things and stop more people from being hurt."

"That's right," Dash said, nodding at Leonard to show his appreciation. "She didn't mention a new speak?"

Mingus took a deep breath. "She didn't tell me anything about that, but . . . she did ask me a question. She asked, '*Mingus, if you knew someone's secret, something that would change everything, what would you do?*'"

"Did she say what the secret was?"

"No, sir. I told her if the secret had nothing to do with her personally that she should let it lie. No one likes a gossiping girl."

Beverly gave what Dash assumed was a rare nod of approval. "Good for you. She should mind her business. There are enough gossiping girls around, like gnats."

Dash asked, "What did she say when you told her that?"

Mingus looked at him. "She said '*typical high hat reply*' and stormed off in a huff."

Dash looked at Leonard and Beverly. "Did Rosalie come to you with any secrets?"

She hadn't.

"Are there . . . any secrets law enforcement should know about? Anything worthy of . . . blackmail?"

Leonard dismissed Mingus. Once Mingus left, he said, "I'm not sure what you mean, Mr. Bennett."

"I don't mean to be indelicate but . . . any love affairs? Business deals? Things that could be harmful to the family name?"

Beverly cleared her throat. "I'm afraid, Mr. Bennett, we're both rather dull people."

"Have any of you seen a blond-haired gent hanging around? Tall, fit, blue eyes? He was here at Rosalie's funeral reception."

Leonard sat up. "Aubrey? You mean Aubrey Harrington?" He snapped his head towards his sister. "What is that rogue up to now?"

Beverly rolled her eyes. "He's not the *only* blond-haired man in New York, Leonard."

"Who's Aubrey Harrington?" Dash asked.

"Some friend of Bev's—"

"An acquaintance," Beverly corrected. "He used to run in Robert's circles. And you *were* aware, dear brother, that he came to pay his respects. Despite your opinion of the man, he is decent."

"He wanted to be my assistant," Leonard explained. "I interviewed him, and it became quite apparent his opinions and mine were incompatible."

"Brother, you have to accept that there are people who simply don't wish for Black men and women to be integrated into society. This is America. Everyone has the right to an opinion."

"It is a hateful one, sister—"

"I'm not having this argument again. You're just as intolerant as you claim the other side to be." She looked at Dash. "Why are you interested in Aubrey?"

Dash gave her a bland smile. "Where can I find him?"

"I haven't the slightest idea." She glanced at her watch. "It's late. Leonard, you should go to bed. We all should." She stood up. Dash had been dismissed.

Leonard said he would walk him out. When they were out of earshot, Leonard whispered in Dash's ear, "I have an extra pair I can give you." He pointed to Dash's shoeless right foot.

Dash nodded. "Yes, well. That would be extremely helpful."

"Who do ya think it was?" Joe asked.

They were in the bedroom getting undressed for sleep. When Dash told Joe what happened that night, Dash could see Joe rear up to chastise him for almost getting killed. But he stopped himself. Instead, he just asked questions. A palpable tension was humming just below the surface of his words, and Dash tried to tread carefully.

"Leonard's anonymous source? Could be Val or Louis. Maybe Makowski, the man who moved Rosalie's body."

"Maybe Wim."

"Do you think so?" Dash had developed a fondness for the playful man.

Joe was obviously not as taken with Wim. "Ya, I do. He knows too much."

"But he was there spying on Val and Louis—"

"Could've been there to make sure of the delivery. Make sure Leonard did what he was supposed to do by taking it to Bellevue."

"But why have us witness it?" Dash shook his head. "I'm not convinced."

"Not surprised," Joe said, roughly adjusting the pillow on the bed, "Yer clearly enamored with the fella."

Dash focused on hanging up his suit in their wardrobe. He was stung by Joe's words. Dash hadn't ever seen the man jealous before. But why be jealous of Wim?

Dash could, however, see Joe's point about Wim's possible involvement in the sabotage of Fife. After all, Fife didn't have Wim chauffeur Dash tonight. "He could've been the driver of the car tonight."

"The one that almost killed ya."

Still on shaky ground. "The one that almost killed Leonard."

"No offense, but I don't care one damned bit about Mr. Leonard Frazier."

Dash spent some time smoothing out the suit on the hanger before turning around to face Joe. "In any case, now we know a direct threat is being made against us. Whomever is going after Fife has thrown us into the soup with him. I know you think differently, but it was actually a *good* thing I was there tonight." He ran his fingers through his hair. "Now if I can just figure out where Rosalie got poisoned—"

"Goddammit." Joe stood on the opposite side of the room in his undershirt and shorts, hands on his hips. "Why are ya meddlin' in affairs that aren't yers?"

"I—because our liquor supplier asked me to."

"Christ on a cross, Nicholas *Fife* again. I curse the day that crooked arse came into our lives."

"We agreed we had to do business with him. You and I. We both did."

"Well, ya don't have to *fawn* over the man the way ya do."

Anger was filling the room. That was Joe's first shot. A battle would soon be under way.

Dash fired back. "Fawn? What are you *talking* about?"

"I'm talking about doing his bidding whenever he asks."

"He held a *blade* to my throat, Joe! A blade! Do you even know how terrifying that was? I thought I was going to die if I didn't agree to whatever he asked of me."

"Ya and ya've done it. No switcheroos bein' done. It's someone in his warehouse and I'll be *damned* if yer gonna go traipsing around it."

"What do you want me to do? Let whoever is sabotaging Fife call Leonard and tell him about Pinstripes? About us? Everything, Joe, *everything* we worked for will be gone with a snap of the fingers."

"And what, I ask again, does this have to do with goddamn *Rosalie*?"

Dash didn't see Joe's point. "She died in our club, Joe. Don't you feel some responsibility to find out how and why?"

Joe dropped his head, a bitter laugh escaping his clenched jaw. "Ya don't get it. Yer not bein' asked to figure out what happened to that damned girl." His voice was growing like a fire, the edges of his words charred. "For that matter, yer not bein' asked to visit El like ya did and see what she saw that Friday night. Yer not bein' *asked* to go talk to Rosalie's old roommates again and again."

"Joe—"

"*Don't* 'Joe' me with yer excuses and yer reasons. Ya could've been killed tonight. Ya lucky ya only lost a shoe instead of yer damned fool head and yer—" Joe stopped, shaking his head.

Dash reflexively reached up and touched his own

cheek. He felt as if he'd been slapped. "Why are you talking to me this way?"

"Because it's the last straw. I can't—I can't keep going off, playing detective, because ya've got an urge. What is it? Huh? Is it because she reminds ya of yer sister?"

The fire that been building from Joe suddenly changed directions. It surged from Dash, who roared, "Don't you *dare* use Sarah like that!"

"Yer one to talk! Yer the one using yer dead baby sister to justify lookin' into this lass's death, putting yerself in needless danger, for what, I can't for the *life* of me figure. Everyone can see it but *you*."

Dash felt his head start to shake now. "Is that right? Is that what you think I'm doing?"

"Yes! I do!"

"Well you have no right, O'Shaughnessy, no right at all to—to—"

"To what? Know you so well?"

"You *don't* know me!"

"God help me, yes I *do*! Ya don't think I've been watchin' ya? Ever since that goddamn Walter Müller, ya been runnin' 'round, always on the move, never stoppin', givin' a moment to me, or hell, even to yourself. Ya won't stop because if ya do, then—" He broke off.

"Then what? Come on, Joe. Say it. *Say it*."

A pained look. "Then ya'd realize yer afraid of the man ya love."

"I—" Dash choked up.

The two men glared one another, breathing hard.

Joe furrowed his brow, frustrated and confused. "*Why* are ya afraid of me, Dash? Huh? Look at ya. Look in the mirror. Look at ya face. Yer terrified. Not of Fife. Not from almost bein' *killed* tonight. Not even at the threat of our speak bein' shut down. Yer terrified that I, Joe O'Shaughnessy, yer dependable bartender and partner, actually know who *you* are. Bloody Mary of Scots, I can't explain *why* I've been taken with an—an *exasperatin'* high hat like ya . . . but I have. And yer terrified of me."

Dash tried to make a reply but couldn't. He felt hot. Angry. *Mortified.* Tears welled up in his eyes. Dammit, not now.

He turned away from Joe. He focused on his breathing, but his father's voice loomed large in his head. *Be a man, for chrissakes! Dammit, Dashiell, no woman is gonna want anything to do with a crybaby. And no businessman will make deals with you neither. I didn't raise no pansy, so stop acting like one!*

The floorboards creaked. The sound of Joe crossing the room. Dash felt Joe hesitate, then felt his large hands cup his shoulders, giving him a reassuring squeeze. Dash reached back with one hand and touched Joe's, giving it a squeeze of his own.

"I—I'm sorry, Joe."

Joe's voice had lost its fury. "Why are ya afraid of me?"

A tear escaped Dash's eyelid and rolled down his cheek. More would surely follow. And did. "Because," he said, not liking at all how thin and quiet his voice was, "because I'm afraid you'll dislike what you see."

"Why do ya think that?"

He could've named his father or his mother as the reason. Maybe even his older brother. But that wasn't the truth, at least not the whole truth. He said, "Because . . . because sometimes I don't."

Silence.

Dash wiped his damp face. "I still see him, Joe. Walter. Every time I close my eyes. Every time I try to go to sleep.

Every time you try to . . . to touch me. And I'm afraid—I'm afraid, because you'll see my weakness. That I can't handle it. Hell, I wasn't even the one who pulled the trigger, for crying out loud. Somebody else much stronger than me had to do it. A man who was threatening me, threatening you and Finn and Atty, a man who could *only* be dealt with in violence, and I couldn't do it. I couldn't do it, and I can't handle having seen it." Tears rolled off his chin. "I'm not tough like this world of yours, Joe. I'm a fraud, an imposter, a *dandy playing bohemian,* as Emmett would say." Dash sniffed, his nose now running. "And he's right. I don't belong here. I've tried to belong. Christ, I ran in front of a car trying to prove that. Can't believe I did that, actually, and even still, I did it badly." A bitter laugh. "Dash Parker plays hero. Ha. I'm anything but." He thought of his own childhood mansion, and that of Rosalie's. "But—but I don't belong where I come from either. I—I don't belong anywhere, I suppose."

More silence.

This is it, he thought. *The moment when he pulls away.*

Instead, he felt Joe's hands turn him around and lift his chin. "Look at me."

Dash shut his eyes and shook his head. "I can't."

"Lassie, look at me."

Dash shook his head again.

"Dashiell."

Dash opened his eyes and saw those emeralds, those heart-stopping emeralds, looking back at him.

Joe kept silent for a moment, letting his eyes say pages and pages of words before simply stating, "My sweet bonny boy . . . you belong with me."

Several hours later, Dash awoke in a panic. One look at his watch told him he overslept. Dammit. Joe was still sleeping soundly and Finn still hadn't come home yet, which left Dash by himself with his thoughts. The last few days had left him exhausted, fragile, and on edge. Hell, the last twenty-four hours. Too many flashes of adrenaline, too many crashes. Saving Leonard. Fighting with Joe.

He splashed his face with cold water in the hallway WC and dressed, putting on the pair of old shoes Leonard had gifted him. They were as beat up as he felt. He headed towards the Greenwich Village Inn for a much-needed cup of coffee.

The dismal, gray weather didn't help his exhaustion. When he stepped into the Inn, he saw with alarm that The Ex-Pats were the only customers.

Emmett standing behind the bar saw his concerned expression. "I know. Perhaps you and that Finney boy were right about me making a theme. Docks or some shit."

"I'm sorry, Emmett, really I am. Maybe this Pirate's Den is just a phase."

Emmett waved him off. "Ah, bellyaching isn't going to solve it no-how. The usual?"

Dash nodded while settling onto the barstool.

Emmett poured two mugs of coffee. "I can see you need it," he said, pushing them both towards him.

Halfway through his second cup, a thought finally made its way through Dash's thick, sludgy brain. "Emmett, have you heard of any blind tigers in our neighborhood?"

"Say again?"

Dash repeated his question along with a description of how they operated. "Perhaps around Washington Square?" That utterance of *Washington* by Rosalie at the Oyster House truly stuck in Dash's craw.

Emmett stroked his chin. "Can't say that I have. Sounds like another goddamned thing to take away my business."

"Yours and mine both, Emmett."

Dash laid two dollars on the bar and asked to use the telephone. For his part, Emmett kept quiet about how many calls Dash was making from his bar. Dash dialed the number Fife left him. The message he left with the neutral male voice who answered the call was simple: "Leonard has an inside source who's going to name Pinstripes as a dangerous place sometime this week."

God knew how Fife would react to this bit of news, but it was out of Dash's hands. Both of their feet were being put to the fire, and Dash hoped whatever Fife was doing on his end would lead to answers.

After leaving the Inn, Dash went to Hartford & Sons to open it up and do a little bit of legitimate business. The gods continued to conspire against him. Standing in front of the shop was none other than Officer Cullen McElroy.

"Damnable hell," Dash said aloud.

McElroy looked up and chuckled. "Mr. Parker! A lovely day, isn't it?" The globe of a man flashed his rotten teeth and gestured with a fat, sweaty hand to the dark, gray skies overhead.

"Officer McElroy. How may I help you?"

McElroy tapped a thick finger on the glass of Hartford & Sons's front door. "I've been seeing ya havin' some family problems."

Dash squinted in response, perplexed by the man's statement. Then he remembered. The sign he and Joe left in the window, so they could go off with Wim.

He replied, "I didn't realize you'd taken such an interest in my shop."

Or that you've been watching it.

"Once a member of the McElroy family, Mr. Parker, always a member."

"I told you—"

"I know, I know, you're with another family now." The smile dimmed a wattage or two. "But the family you're born into, it takes a lot more than a new marriage to leave that, my boy. Your shop was born into mine when that Victor fella owned it. I hate to see it go into the arms of another."

Dash ran his tongue over his teeth, trying to figure out what game McElroy was playing.

"Look, Officer, it's just business."

"To you, it is. To me . . ." His voice trailed off, but his eyes bored into Dash's. A tense moment passed before McElroy looked away. "I'll let you open up. But remember what I said now, Mr. Parker."

He sauntered away, whistling as he went.

Dash quickly got out his keys, opening the tailor shop front door before slamming it shut again, locking it on instinct. He shivered. Whatever McElroy was up to, he didn't want to know. He couldn't know. He frankly couldn't handle any more problems. He had Leonard Frazier and his anonymous source to worry about.

Dash half-heartedly took random measurements from real tailor shop customers and gave half-hearted secret knocks to those interested in Pinstripes. A few men gave him wary looks. One even asked if he was all right. Dash said he was fine, but he didn't sound convincing.

He decided to close early. As tired as he was, he was itching with energy and without being conscious of it, he found himself heading towards Times Square. Towards Rosalie's former roommates. Two times now, he'd met with Marty and Tillie, and two times they'd lied to him. This third time, he wasn't about to let them get away with it.

Tillie answered on the third knock.

"Oh," she said. "Mr. Boldt. What a surprise. I thought the next time we were seeing you was tomorrow."

"I know but something urgent has come up." Dash gestured to the room behind her. "May I come in?"

She thought to herself for a moment, then stepped away from the door. The silk of her robe rustled with the movements.

Inside on the floor were two large fans made of peacock feathers. They reminded Dash of Fife's lamps, when almost a week ago, he held a barber's razor to his throat.

Why am I always surrounded by peacocks? he wondered.

Marty was sitting on the couch, drinking his usual whiskey. "Mr. Boldt," he said, his voice flat. "What an unexpected pleasure."

"Thank you for seeing me on such short notice," Dash said. "I hope I'm not interrupting."

Tillie replied, "I was just working on my fan dance."

"Yes," Marty said, "we have to choreograph the feathers

just so. Otherwise, the whole club is going to see a lot more of Miss White than we're legally allowed to show."

Tillie touched Dash's arm. "Would you like to see it? It's quite a number!"

Dash shook his head. "I want to be surprised tomorrow night."

"So," Marty said. "What is this urgent matter?"

"I'm afraid I've heard some—well, I don't know if it's distressing news . . . perhaps it's just *new* news and we don't know yet if it'll be good or bad."

"I'm intrigued," Tillie said, sitting down beside Marty on the couch. "What is the *new* news?"

"We've got confirmation that Mrs. Beverly Stevens is having a secret love affair with a man named Aubrey Harrington."

Tillie stared at Dash for a full five seconds before laughing out loud. So loud, in fact, that Marty grimaced.

"Tillie? Will you quiet down?"

She waved her arms in front of her face, trying to control herself. "I'm sorry, I'm sorry. That was the *last* thing I expected you to say. Wherever did you hear such bunk?"

"A newshawk on our retainer saw her making eyes at him at the funeral. They later confirmed Aubrey interviewed for an assistant position with her brother Leonard. Unfortunately, Leonard and Aubrey had a disagreement, and Aubrey wasn't offered the job."

This interested both of them.

Tillie licked her lips. "My, my. Bev the Boring trying to get her secret lover a job. I didn't think she had it in her."

Marty sat forward. "Are they going to print the story?"

"We don't know," Dash replied. "This reporter intimated there was something nasty in Aubrey's past, though he wouldn't say what. Naturally, if it's going to be damaging to our artists, we'll try to bury it."

"And by your artists, you mean, us?"

"Potentially, yes."

"Potentially, of course."

Tillie looked to Marty. "I wonder if we've seen this Aubrey character before." She turned to Dash. "What does this Aubrey look like?"

"He's described as blond, fit, blue eyes. On the taller side. Well-dressed and well-groomed."

Tillie's eyes flashed. She was most definitely not a poker player.

Dash focused purely on her. "You've seen him?"

"Yes," she said, drawing out the word, then picking up her pace. "Yes, I believe so. And around the Frazier house, I should add."

"Tillie," growled Marty.

Dash ignored him. "When?"

Tillie kept darting her eyes from Dash to Marty. "Whenever we'd pick Rosalie up on our way uptown."

"Did you ever see him in the house?"

"He may have been inside, but we wouldn't know. We weren't allowed in, of course. We always saw him standing outside the house."

"Street corner? Alleyway?"

"Not exactly." Tillie chuckled, a strange sound that resembled a quiet sneeze. "This will make an excellent addition to your script for your film. There's an old smuggling tunnel in that house."

"Tillie, for godssakes," groused Marty.

Dash's surprised expression prompted Tillie to laugh even more. "Oh, yes. It's how we met up with Rosalie after her father tried locking her out. She said she found it while exploring the servant's quarters. Goes straight from the train tracks by the river under Riverside Drive and into the house. And that's where we saw this blond-haired man. Just outside that very tunnel. Marty and I were shocked—we thought we were the only ones who knew about it."

Dash rubbed his chin. "So Beverly has been sneaking him in and out of the house. Do you know how often?"

Tillie scrunched up her nose. "I couldn't say for certain, but we did notice him whenever Leonard went out of town for his monthly visit upstate."

"What were those about?"

"His trips? I suppose to get out of the city. That's what he told Rosie, at any rate. '*Fresh air to clear the mind*,' he'd say."

"And he'd go alone?"

A rueful arch of Marty's eyebrow. "Leonard did *everything* alone."

Tillie chuckled again. "Apparently, not his sister though. Marty, can you believe it?"

Dash asked, "Does Mr. Frazier know about this tunnel?"

"I suppose not. He'd have boarded it up otherwise, wouldn't he?"

"I thought the house was his?"

"Oh no, he didn't build that house. He bought it from an industry man in cigars and cigarettes. And a smuggling tunnel isn't something the owners would advertise to a stranger, especially a bluenose like old Leonard."

Marty took an angry sip of his whiskey. "Any *more* secrets you'd like to tell, Tillie?"

"Did Rosalie know about Aubrey?' Dash inquired. "Make any mentions of him, say, when you were with her Friday night September the tenth at the Oyster House?"

Silence.

Tillie froze while Marty stiffened. They glanced at each other, communicating with the slightest of looks.

Tillie squinted at Marty. "Was that really the last time we saw her?"

Marty began pulling at his lip. "I suppose, but I really don't remember." He turned to Dash. "I don't remember telling you that though."

"You didn't. You both lied to me about it—twice. Another client of ours saw you there. You're quite distinct looking, Marty."

Marty smirk. "My hair. Yes, it is eye-catching, isn't it? You know, I suppose it *was* the Oyster House."

Dash crossed his arms over his chest. "Why did you lie to me? I can't represent you successfully if you don't tell me everything."

"Because it's none of your business!"

"*You* are my business, Marty, which means anything that has to do with you also has to do with me. Again, I ask, why did you lie?" He glared at both Marty and Tillie.

A patch of red glowed from the bottom of Tillie's neck. "We were afraid."

"Afraid of what?"

"Look, Mr. Boldt, we didn't mean to deceive you, it's just that—that the last things Rosalie said to us where truly queer. And then she *died,* and it just seemed . . . too big a coincidence."

Dash kept his voice easy. "What did she say?"

"Tillie . . . " Marty shook his head.

"We can't keep lying forever!" Tillie's eyes pleaded with Dash. "She told us that she kept finding these codes all over the house. Little pieces of paper with a simple drawing on them. It was like her mother had come back from the dead. Only that's not possible, is it?"

Marty's hand was now covering his brow, shielding his eyes from Tillie's confession. "No, dear heart, the dead can't come back."

"That's what I said, and I know Rosie agreed, but she couldn't explain these codes."

Dash reached into his inside pocket and pulled out Rosalie's teacup. "You mean, something like this?" He held it up.

Tillie nodded fervently. "Yes, yes, exactly like that! She didn't know what they meant until that night, at the Oyster House, we sat down and she said, '*I figured them out! It's Washington.*'"

"Did she explain what she meant by that?"

"She didn't get the chance. All of a sudden, she got this look over her face and the next thing we know, her father comes up. Starts shouting and saying beastly things. He grabbed her by the arm and led her out of there. The whole club was staring at us. And the performer, something-Train, glared at us so hard, I thought we'd catch fire."

Marty lowered his hand from his brow. "Was that your client, by the way, Mr. Boldt?"

Dash ignored the question by asking one of his own. "That was the only time you were at the Oyster House?"

Tillie nodded. "First and only."

"Did Rosalie say anything else to you?"

"So that's what it is."

Dash looked at her. "Pardon?"

"What she said. '*So* that's *what it is.*'"

"Huh." Dash pursed his lips. "This is all very queer."

"I agree, it *is* all very queer," Marty said. His face darkened. "Too queer to be believed . . . "

Dash returned to the apartment above the Cherry Lane Playhouse to find Joe still in bed. The tousled redhead looked at Dash with tentative eyes.

"How are ya, lassie?"

The thread between them was so fragile, it could've snapped with the slightest movement of the wind.

Dash kept his voice as gentle as possible. "I'm not perfectly well . . . but I'm getting there."

Joe held out his hand, which Dash took. Joe pulled Dash down into a sitting position on the bed.

"Tha's a start," he said. "Better than an end."

The voices on the other side of their bedroom wall interrupted them.

Joe rolled his eyes. "Aye, Christ. They've been at it all day."

"Who? Reggie and one of his many, many women?"

"If only."

The voices came into focus.

"My love, you are *much* too sensitive," Reggie's voice said. "Don't you realize I must keep up appearances for the sake of the show?"

To Dash's surprise, a male voice replied, "Appearances are one thing, Reggie, but when you're out of the spotlight and you're spending more time with her than with me?" A scoff. "What kind of fool do you take me for, Regi-*nald*?"

Joe whispered to Dash, "This fella has been gettin' 'round."

Dash looked at him. "I thought you didn't care about these actor's lives?"

"When in Rome . . ."

"It's a shame Finn can't be here for this afternoon's drama. He'd love this latest development."

Reggie, the Don Juan, said, "She forced me to, dearest. If I refused, she would've kicked up a fuss."

"Nobody forces people to do anything. Please. Show me some respect and just tell me the truth. You prefer her over me. I can take it . . . I *can*. I just can't take being lied to."

"I am not lying to you. I promise. I *swear* it."

Joe whispered to Dash, "He's a lying arse."

A pause. Dash envisioned Reggie placing his hands on the other man's shoulders, perhaps even cupping his face.

Finn was right, he thought. *This* is *better than radio.*

Reggie's voice softened. "I've never known a feeling like the one I have with you. It's like . . . it's like flying. Soaring through the air. Defying gravity. Defying the world. And it's nothing short of exhilarating."

Joe rolled his eyes. "Oh, what *gob*shite."

A bitter laugh from Reggie's lover. "You're just feeding me lines now."

Dash and Joe both whispered, "Yes he is!"

"My love, my love," Reggie said. "Can't you see the hold you have on me? Feel my heartbeat. Isn't it racing?"

Another pause. Dash pictured the other man placing his hand on Reggie's chest.

"Touch my neck. Aren't I burning up? Like I'm consumed by fever?"

The other man replied, "You are . . . rather warm."

"Kiss my lips. They only want yours. Only yours."

Dash heard the gentle pop of the kiss followed by the rapid fire of more. Repeated murmurs of *don't stop, don't stop* followed. The bedroom wall seemed to pulsate with heavy breathing, heavy sighing. The bed's headboard suddenly rattled as the two men must've fallen against the wall on the other side.

Joe winked at Dash. "Aren't they bein' a bit naughty."

"Yes," Dash replied, "they can't seem—"

"My god, Reggie, I forgot how *big* you are!"

Dash cleared his throat. "—can't seem to keep their hands—"

"That's it, my love. Touch it like that. Just like that."

Dash swallowed. "Uh, their hands off . . . one another."

His smile faded. So did Joe's. They stared at one another, acutely aware of the passion occurring on the other side of their wall. The passion that had been missing between them.

Suddenly, Dash crossed over to the bed and grabbed Joe's neck, bringing him up for a kiss. He was overcome with the need to touch, to connect, to *feel*. Their kissing imitated what was happening on the other side of their wall —hungry, yearning, desperate.

"Is the door locked?" asked the other man.

"Yes, my love," replied Reggie.

"Then take me. Now. Do it before I come to my senses!"

Dash hastily undid his clothes, tossing them to the side. Their headboard shook again from Reggie and his lover. Dash ripped the covers off the bed and, naked as the day he was born, climbed on top of naked Joe. He settled onto him just at the moment there was a gasp of surprise and a guttural growl from the actors.

Time seemed to stop. Nothing else in life mattered— Rosalie, Fife, McElroy, the Fraziers—nothing, except what was occurring in this moment in this room. In *these* rooms.

Joe closed his eyes and breathed in deep. Dash ran his

hands over that broad, hairy chest, feeling Joe's throbbing pulse inside of him, their heartbeats in unison.

A murmured plea from Reggie.

A whispered encouragement from Joe.

Dash braced his palms against the headboard as Reggie and his man moaned together. For their part, Dash and Joe were silent, with only their uneven, quickening breathing and the squeak of their bedsprings betraying their actions.

Dash's fingers ran up Joe's neck to his face to his hair. Joe grabbed his hand and brought his palm to his lips, kissing it. Dash groaned in unison with Reggie's man as he rocked against Joe's hips.

Joe then pulled Dash down for a series of open-mouthed kisses. He took over and began to thrust his hips upward. Their movements escalated along with the sounds of the other men, the four of them simultaneously experiencing forbidden pleasure. All of Dash's senses were overwhelmed. The breathless voices. The pounding against the wall. The musky sweat. Joe's flashing eyes. The wet touch and whiskey taste of his mouth. No more fear. No more blood-drenched images. No more running for the sake of running. Just pure, electric sensation.

Reggie on the other side of the wall started crying out. His lover joined him.

Joe grabbed Dash's buttocks and squeezed his eyes tightly shut as an involuntary moan escaped his lips. Dash gripped the headboard and joined the three men in their release.

A large *thud!* sounded against the shared wall. Reggie and his lover must've collapsed against it.

Dash fell to the side, the bed squeaking and groaning a few more times until it, as well as Dash and Joe, settled.

Dash turned his head to look at Joe, who was still breathless, his entire body beet red, covered in sweat.

Exhausted but exhilarated, Dash thought to himself *that Reggie . . . he truly does make passion wherever he goes.*

With a spring to his step, Dash walked from Cherry Lane towards West Fourth Street again. It was close to dusk, and he was even more famished than he was earlier that day.

Good loving will do that to a man, he thought with a naughty smile.

After their initial burst of passion, the two of them went at it again. Slower this time. Gentler. Longer. Joe letting Dash take control. Afterwards, they napped and when they awoke, Dash promised Joe he'd go out and bring back some sustenance.

"I'd go with ya," Joe said, "but ya left me too weak to walk."

Damn right, I did.

The high didn't last for very long. As soon as Dash turned onto West Fourth, there was Lowell Henley, standing in front of Hartford & Sons.

"Your presence is requested," he wheezed.

Dash glared at the menacing torpedo. "You know, Lowell, you have the absolute *worst* timing."

"Mr. Parker!" boomed Fife. "So glad you can join us."

He was standing in the middle of his Queens warehouse. Crates were stacked on either side of him, stretching all the way to its four-story ceiling and making a large space feel strangely small and claustrophobic. A strange metallic smell permeated the air.

Dash's and Lowell's approaching footsteps echoed off the concrete floor, sounding like colliding bocce balls. Spotlights hung overhead, creating columns of light in the center while casting off shadows to the far corners.

Behind Fife, standing in those columns of light, were five men: Angelo Avogadro, Makowksi, Wim, Val Russo, and Louis Snyder.

Lowell stopped a few paces behind Dash. Dash looked over his shoulder and faced forward again.

"Come, come," Fife said, urging him closer.

Dash hesitated.

"No need to be shy. We *have* shared a bath together, after all."

Something flickered across Wim's face. Jealousy, perhaps?

Dash forced a smile and walked forward until he stood next to Fife, shoulder to shoulder.

Fife looked over at him. "Oh my, my, my. Someone has beard burn." He leaned in and whispered, "Mr. O'Shaughnessy?"

Dash blushed but didn't reply, which caused Fife to chuckle.

"Good news, gentlemen! Mr. Parker here is fresh from what I can only assume is a marathon of lovemaking. He will be the magnanimous judge." His voice hardened. "I, however, will not be."

Val, Louis, Makowski, and Angelo stood stoic. Only Wim seemed nervous. Dash was nervous as well. What exactly had Fife planned? And what role was Dash supposed to play?

Fife said, "Someone in my circle of trust is trying to ruin me. Contaminating my booze and killing my patrons. Our latest victims have been cut open by Mr. Norris, and do you know what he found?"

"Arsenic," Dash guessed.

"Correct, Mr. Parker! Arsenic! Just like in the crate that *you*, Mr. Russo and Mr. Snyder, delivered to Leonard Frazier."

Val spoke up. "Boss, we had nothing to do—"

"You took his money, did you not? And did you *share* it with me? Huh? How about with the rest of the class?"

It was then Dash noticed Val's frog face sported a deep, dark bruise on his right cheek. Louis had a lip that was scabbing over. The marks of Fife's first interrogation. Dash was terrified what the second interrogation would bring.

"Can you," Fife continued, "imagine my utter disappointment to learn I'm being betrayed? And it's not just me, oh no!" Fife suddenly put his arm around Dash's shoulders. "One of you is also betraying this gentleman here. A paying customer. A *loyal* customer. One of you wants to give his name and his speak to a man like Leonard Frazier. A man who would have our customer prosecuted." Fife stage whispered to Dash. "I got your message."

His arm left Dash's shoulders, and he began to pace in front of the five men. "Which one of you is behind this? Hmm? Which one of you has decided to double-cross me?"

The five stood silent. Dash was relieved to see Wim and Angelo sported no marks on them.

At least, none that I can see . . .

Annoyed with their silence, Fife said, "*W-e-l-l,* let's go through our list of suspects, shall we?"

He stopped in front of Angelo.

"Is it my chemist? Who would know all too well how to doctor my booze. No one would have a clue what he was doing, not even me!" He brought his face within an inch of Angelo's. "Is it you? Hiding behind your beakers and your test tubes?"

Angelo's face was still serene, even glowing. "No, sir," he replied, his voice steady. "I would never betray the one man who would hire me for my expertise in all of New York City."

Fife watched Angelo's face a moment more before coming to Makowksi. "Or what about my fixer? My man in the shadows? Seems to me poison would fit your bag of tricks."

Makowski stood stock-still, those pinpoint eyes glowing. "You've given me and my family a good life. Nobody wanted us Pols. Without you, we'd have nothing. I'd never betray you, sir."

Fife nodded before coming to Wim, whose face was blanched white, his bottom lip trembled.

"Wim," Fife said, his voice taking on a bittersweet warmth. "Wim, Wim, Wim. My Wim. Was it you? Had you blinded me with your smile? Your wit? Your puckish sensibility?" Fife reached out and caressed Wim's cheek. Wim's body was shaking now with fear. "Oh, Wim. The things you can do with that lithe body of yours. Tricks I thought only whores down in the Bowery could do, oh Wim. Tell me it isn't you?"

It took Wim several tries, but he gasped, "It's not, sir. You've . . . given me . . . so much. A home. A job. A purpose. I would never—never—" He whispered, "*Nick*," then said full-voiced, "Please, believe me."

Fife wiped away an errant tear that had fallen from Wim's face before moving on to Val and Louis. "And you two. You've already betrayed me once. The question, how *deep* does your betrayal go?"

Louis replied, "Like we said, boss, we don't know who left us the crate. We'd never seen it before."

"And the handwriting?"

Val shook his head. "Didn't recognize it."

"I see. And the money?"

Louis held up his hands. "We was gonna give it to you, we swear. It's just we never got the—"

In a flash, Fife had turned his hand into a fist and punched Louis in the stomach so hard, the man buckled to his knees. He leaned over towards Val and vomited.

Val leapt up. "Goddammit, Louis, not on my shoes!" He pulled out a handkerchief and began to wipe off Louis's sickness from the leather. "Jesus Christ, Boss, we made a dumb mistake, but we'd never try to get you shut down. We didn't know the damn crate was *poisoned!* If we did, we'd have never delivered it. Hand to God."

Louis was coughing and spitting now. "He's telling the truth. You're the only one who took us in when we got here."

Val nodded. "Nobody wanted us Jews in their neighborhoods, in their offices."

Dash thought back to what Wim said about Fife. *He collects misfits from around the world. Men nobody wants.*

Fife stepped away from Val and Louis and returned to Dash's side. "So! All of you are grateful for the opportunities I've given you. And all of you steadfastly deny taking part in this sabotage. Who am I to believe?" He looked to Dash. "It's a conundrum, isn't it, Mr. Parker. A conundrum I'd like you to solve."

Dash's heart stopped. "Me? Now? Based on what?"

"All that you've seen and heard. I know you, Mr. Parker. You are clever. You're perhaps the most clever man in this room. If anyone can figure out who is *lying* to me, it is you."

Those chocolate eyes stared into Dash's. This wasn't a request; this was a command. But how could Dash know the answer? And more terrifying than that, what if he was wrong? Fife would surely kill whoever was responsible. What if Dash sent an innocent man to his death?

He looked at Fife. "I don't know if I can, Mr. Fife."

Fife turned his head slightly to the side. "Oh, come now. I know you can. Besides! You've just been thoroughly . . . sated. I find that usually clears the head."

They continued to stare at one another for a moment more, before Dash turned his attention to the five men.

Like Fife, Dash began to pace in front of them. He started with Angelo.

"It is true," he said, his voice cracked and frayed at the edges. He cleared it and tried again. "It is true, Angelo has ample opportunity to introduce poison into the supply. He's there when it arrives, he's there when it goes out." A spark. "But arsenic? It's so . . . commonplace. Mr. Charles Norris told me it's in damn near everything. Easy to obtain, easy to identify. If Angelo were to contaminate the supply, he'd do so in a much subtler way. Perhaps a way that might even elude the great Charles Norris."

"What are you saying?" Fife asked.

Dash turned. "I'm saying arsenic is too pedestrian. A man with Angelo's knowledge would choose an untraceable poison. Or, at least, an unknown one."

He walked to Makowski, who scowled at the sight of him.

"Makowski wanted me killed, as you well know, Mr. Fife. And it is indeed probable that he would want to take me down for revenge. For daring to speak against him, I imagine."

"Yes," Fife said, "I know the feeling."

Dash adjusted his lapels and tie. "Right. Well." He regarded the tall, thin man with the angry, red scar across his throat. "Arsenic is an angry weapon. And Makowski here is prone to bouts of anger." He cocked his head to the side. "But it's also a blunt one. Wim described you as a man who could sneak up on someone and kill them before they could even hear the footsteps. You keep to the shadows. Arsenic is a Times Square billboard. Like Angelo, if you were to use poison, you'd find one undetectable."

He then walked down to Wim, who had managed to control himself somewhat.

Dash shook his finger. "Death is not Wim's nature. Mischief, yes. If he were the poisoner, he'd cause trouble—

blackouts, upset stomachs, the worst hangover of a person's life—but death? A man nicknamed for whimsy isn't interested in that, are you, Wim?"

Those downcast eyes raised up, filled with relief.

"It's possible you got the dose wrong, but again, arsenic is well known as dangerous, deadly, and unstable. Seems a wrong weapon of choice for a Wim."

Dash then turned to Val and Louis, who managed to get onto his feet again.

"These two acted impulsively. They saw a note, they saw an opportunity, and they took it, however ill-advised. But impulsiveness is not the characteristic of our poisoner. Look at the planning it would take to introduce it into the supply with no one suspecting. And how does one go about getting arsenic? Unless it was sitting right there on the table next to the bottles, I highly doubt these two would go to the same lengths as our poisoner."

Fife clapped his hands. "So! Mr. Parker. You have just cleared all of our suspects. Does this mean I don't have a saboteur?"

"Oh, you do," Dash said. "Those phone calls to Leonard Frazier are real enough."

"Then who could it be?"

Dash's eyes scanned the five men before coming back to Fife. Or rather, to the man standing behind Fife.

Somehow, Fife must've read Dash's mind, for he quickly turned, raising a gun that must've been concealed in his coat pocket.

Before Fife could take aim, a shot rang out.

Dash jolted, stunned by the suddenness of it all. The sound of shattering glass was followed by a plunge into immediate darkness.

Lowell Henley had shot out the light above them.

Footsteps sounded as the large man ran from the main warehouse floor.

"Get him!" Fife bellowed.

Val, Louis, and Makowksi sprinted after him, guns already drawn and raised. They shouted orders to one another—which hallways to cover, which doors to slam shut. The sounds of running men faded into the distance.

Wim came forward and brushed the glass that had fallen from the light to Fife's shoulders. "Are you cut, sir?"

Fife slowly shook his head. "I don't know. I don't think so, Wim."

"Let's get into some light."

They walked over to the side where another spotlight shone. Wim began inspecting Fife, looking into his hair, his collar, and his sleeves for errant shards of glass. Dash looked to the side. Angelo still stood stoic, unfazed by the violence.

Fife looked over at Dash. "How did you know?"

The sound of muffled gunshots caused Dash to jump. He fought to get his pounding heart under control. "How did I know. Well." He started to run his hand through his hair but thought better of it. There might be shards of broken glass in it.

"Mr. Parker?"

"Apologies, Mr. Fife. Catching my breath. Oh, yes. Arsenic is blunt and angry and common. It sounded like Lowell to me."

Wim gave him an incredulous look. "That's *it*?"

"Not all. Mr. Fife, you'd mentioned his attitude had changed. Been less patient, unsatisfied with the jobs you'd given him. Temper climbing, talking back. And Wim here said Lowell despised having pansies and bulldaggers as clients. And now with your new stag film business? I suspect he wanted your job, if for no other reason than to move away from inverts, and discrediting you was an effective way to do that."

Fife nodded. "And your speak?"

"Ah, that." Dash shrugged. "He never liked me anyway."

———

Dash later learned the chase ended just as quickly as it began. Lowell Henley had been cornered on the far side of the warehouse property. He got off a few shots but missed. Makowkski's aim was true, nicking him in the leg, then the knee, causing him to fall to the ground. In Makowksi's account to Fife, Lowell was crawling to a car, hoping to get away. Makowksi, Val, and Louis stood on either side of him, kicking his gun away.

What happened next, Dash didn't want to know. He quickly left the group huddle before hearing any gritty details.

After listening to the stories from his men—and seeing Lowell's lifeless body for himself—Fife returned to the main room and put an arm around Dash's shoulders.

"My dear Mr. Parker. Lowell Henley will not be a threat to you, or to me, any longer."

Dash awoke the next day, thrilled with the prospect that his name and his speak wouldn't be given to Leonard Frazier. Fife promised he would give them a new batch, so they wouldn't have to worry about arsenic in their booze supply.

He looked over at Joe, who was snoring deeply under the covers. The poor man. For the second time in a week, he had desperately searched the Village for Dash. When Wim dropped Dash off at their apartment, he and Joe collapsed in the tightest hug Dash had ever experienced.

"It's over," he had said. "The poisoned booze, Joe. It's over."

Except there was still the mystery of Rosalie.

Amazing, the hold she had on him. Having her father's old pair of shoes didn't help matters. So many unanswered questions, so many loose ends. That teacup drawing. The blind tiger. The Watkins Hotel matchbook. The attempt on Leonard Frazier's life. Beverly's blond-haired lover Aubrey Harrington. The queer utterances of *'Washington'* and *'so that's what it is.'* The smuggling tunnel.

Dash sat up. Was Tillie lying about the smuggling

tunnel? And if she wasn't, could there be some clues hidden away in there?

He silently crept out of bed and dressed in a blue all-wool worsted cheviot suit, red tie, and white shirt. A light brown trilby worn with the brim pinched down into a diagonal angle completed the outfit. He left Joe a note saying where he went and not to worry. Then he caught a cab and journeyed uptown.

Dash stood on the southeast corner of Riverside Drive and West 107th Street. He glanced back at the Frazier's mansion before heading towards the river. The land sloped downward and soon, the riverfront park appeared. A path was filled with couples strolling arm in arm, women pushing baby carriages, and several men walking dogs on leashes. People sat on benches, reading books or newspapers, sipping coffee, or having conversations. Picnic blankets dotted the grass overlooking the Hudson. A wayward kite had escaped its handler and was bouncing upwards into the sky.

Dash crossed over the path and meandered over the knolls before coming to the edge of the park, which was marked by a thigh-high concrete wall. Beyond here, the land sloped down even further, leading to where the train tracks traced the edges of the riverbank. A cool breeze with a bite blew through, ruffling Dash's hair and stinging his cheeks. The mostly cloudy skies above cast shadows onto the rippling Hudson, looking like dark bruises on the churning gray water.

He glanced back at the picnicking couples, the walkers, the readers. No one paid him any attention. With as much grace as he could muster, he swung his legs over the wall and officially left the park.

And my senses. What on earth am I doing?

He didn't have to spend much time wondering, for the slope was steeper than Dash anticipated, and gravity began pulling him downward. He tried to stay upright, but the soft earth and the old shoes Leonard gave him made it impossible to gain any traction. With alarm, he realized he was sliding towards the train tracks.

He reached out to see if he could grab a tree branch or a rock for purchase. No such luck. His feet slid out from under him and his behind hit the ground with a spine-rattling thud. He bounced upward and forward but managed somehow to stop himself from doing a somersault. He was slammed back down again before his feet skidded across the gravel rocks of the train bed. Friction finally stopped him, just a scant few feet away from the rails. A dust cloud formed from his journey wafted over him like cigarette smoke. He coughed.

He sat still for a moment, his heart pounding in his ears. Thank heaven no trains were coming at this moment. He slowly got to his feet, brushing away the dirt and grime from the seat of his trousers and the sleeves of his coat. He tasted gravel between his teeth, and he sputtered and spit, sincerely hoping no one saw his ill-advised adventure down the hill. With trepidation, he looked up. No one was peering over the concrete wall, nor calling to one another about a man who fell.

It was then he realized he'd lost his trilby somewhere in the brush. Well, damn it all. He was about to retrace his fall to retrieve it when he saw it had landed in front of a rounded concrete entryway embedded into the hillside. A large metal door laid just beyond the trilby.

"I'll be damned," he breathed.

Tillie was telling the truth.

He looked to his right, then to his left. Nobody there. He looked back to the river. A distant sailboat was inching along, struggling against the rough current, looking forlorn and lonely in such a vast body of water. Probably a straggler from the Columbia Yacht Club about twenty blocks south from here.

He turned back to the door and walked slowly towards it, picking up and dusting off his hat. The door had rusted from the moisture of the river and the exposure to the extreme elements that made a New York winter and summer. Cracks of rust, like spider's legs, fanned out across the surface. Paint peeled off in curious ribbons. The copper handle was turning an odd shade of green. Dash remembered reading somewhere about why all the copper in the city was changing into that color—something to do with the oxygen in the air interacting with the elemental makeup of the metal itself.

He prayed to Finn's goddesses the door wasn't locked. He placed the trilby back on his head and, with a steady hand, he grabbed the door handle and pushed it downward. There was a little resistance, but the handle gave way and the door swung inwards.

The darkness in the tunnel was absolute. Dash reached into his pocket and found a lighter. He flicked the wheel until a flame appeared with a forceful *snick!* With this meager light source, he cautiously entered the secret space.

The floor of the tunnel was soft earth, slightly squishy. An occasional drip of water splashed his shoulders. He traversed carefully, hoping the rats would hear his footsteps and scurry away. (Indeed, he heard the pitter-patter of fast-moving feet to his right and left.)

Good, keep to the edges, and I'll stay in the middle.

After what felt like an eternity, Dash finally came to another door. He paused. If Tillie was right, this would lead him into the Frazier family home. He stepped forward towards the door when the sound of crumpling paper underneath his shoe stopped him. He looked down at his feet, but couldn't see what he had stepped on. He knelt down with the lighter, scanning the floor.

Pieces of paper. Dozens of them. Some folded, others balled up, a few torn. Dash picked one up and studied it. What he saw chilled him. It was a drawing done by the same hand with the same black ink of the teacup drawing in Dash's pocket. A rounded capital A.

He dropped the piece of paper and picked up another. And another. And another. All were of that same rounded capital A. There had to be twelve pieces of paper here at the door. The clues Rosalie mentioned to Marty and Tillie. But a capital A couldn't stand for Washington. What was going on? And why would the letter A bring people here? It wasn't the first letter of the family name, nor even the names of the masters of the house. And *who* was coming here? Whomever they were, they did not want to be seen.

A dangerous thought occurred to Dash. Perhaps this wasn't a rounded capital A. Perhaps this was a symbol for a tunnel.

The secret door suddenly opened, and Jack Mingus, with his brown hair slicked back from his reddish wide face, flinched with surprise.

"Losh!" he exclaimed. "What the blazes are you doing here?" He stepped forward, his muscled body looking menacing backlit by the light behind him. His red face frowned with confusion. "Mr. Bennett?"

Dash almost corrected him but, in a flash, remembered

the alias he was using with the Fraziers versus the alias he was using with Marty and Tillie. "Mr. Mingus. How very nice to see you again."

"Why are you—"

Dash added authority to his voice. "Why am I here? Well now, I could ask you the same question. I thought nobody in the Frazier household knew about this tunnel."

"Where did ya hear tha'?" Mingus's Scottish brogue was coming in full force. The same thing happened to Joe whenever he was flummoxed.

"From sources."

"Sources?! What bloody sources?"

Dash just smiled. He pointed to Mingus. "Are you going to let me in? Or were you going out?"

"No, I'm not goin' to let ya in! I can't believe ya'd even think of it. Mr. Frazier is in a fragile state right now and —and—"

"And you don't want to explain how I snuck into the house. Understandable. But I think you're going to let me in."

"Oh? And why is tha'?"

"Other than me being an undercover policeman, in case you forgot," Dash said, repeating his lie from the other night, "I'm going to tell him his sister has been sneaking in a rakish man named Aubrey Harrington for, shall we say, torrid reasons."

Mingus glared at him. "What are ya scheming?"

"Not blackmail, if that's what you're worried about. I have an altogether different motive. I want to know where Rosalie got the booze that killed her."

"A speak. Who cares where?"

"Because I want to find the person responsible for her

drinking it. I think Mr. Frazier might want to know that, don't you?"

Mingus considered Dash's words. "Alright, come in."

Dash seriously hoped this wasn't a ruse to bash his head in. He stepped through the doorway, with Mingus closing the door behind them. Dash glanced back and saw the faint outline of the secret door in the wall. How did Finn miss this when he searched the downstairs during Rosalie's funeral?

They entered a storage closet. Stacks of canned goods filled the floor-to-ceiling shelves, everything from canned meats and fruits to salves and castor oil. Crates and boxes of cleaning supplies, mops, brooms, brushes. Spare candlesticks, polished and at the ready for any last-minute dinner engagement, were lined up in a row, like soldiers waiting for inspection.

They passed through another doorway, turned left, and entered an L-shaped hallway. They were now in the basement of the Frazier house, the servant's floor.

"Follow me," Mingus murmured. "And be quiet. I don't want Sophie to hear us."

As man of the house, Mingus had his own private space, whereas the rest of the staff had to share larger bedrooms, with beds stacked on top of one another. At least, that's how it was in Dash's household. He assumed the same for the Fraziers.

Mingus quietly closed the door and gestured for Dash to sit.

Dash found a chair and watched as Mingus composed himself and sat on the edge of his bed. "How long have you known about the tunnel?" he asked.

Mingus looked down at his fat fingers. "A year or so ago."

"How'd you find it?"

"I saw Rosalie coming through the wall paneling in the storage closet. Gave me such a fright. Last thing I expected to see."

"How long had she known about it?"

"Couldn't say. She wouldn't tell me. When she saw me, she giggled and put her finger to her lips. *'Please keep my secret,'* she said. *'It's the only way I'll ever stay sane in this household.'*"

"You didn't tell Mr. Frazier?"

Mingus struggled with that one. "I—I didn't see the harm. She was so lonely in this big house, and her father hardly let her have any friends. 'Specially the friends she wanted to have. It's hard enough for a girl to grow up without a mother, but to grow up in a museum? That's what she said to me once. Like she was a piece of art on display." He glanced up at Dash. "I don't know if that makes sense to ya." He stared at his fingers again and began to rub his knuckles. "I kept her secret. I kept her secret and now she's dead. It's my fault."

"Even if you had told Mr. Frazier, she still would've found a way out of the house. From what I know of her, she was clever and determined, and when she set her mind to something, she did it."

"Aye, that she was. And that she did."

"Did Sophie, the head housekeeper, did she know about the tunnel?"

Mingus shook his head. "I never told her. She would've gone to Mr. Frazier for sure."

"Yes, I got that sense as well." Dash waited a beat. "Did you know about Mrs. Beverly Stevens and this Aubrey Harrington?"

A weary sigh. "Ay. One of the late Robert Stevens's

friends. Worked in one of the factory offices, he did. Had a falling out with Mr. Stevens and was sacked."

"What did they fall out over?"

Mingus hesitated. "I don't know."

"Oh, come now, Mingus, I know you know. I grew up in a house like this. You know *everything*. The man of the house always does." Dash watched him intently.

Mingus stuttered under the gaze. "I heard a rumor that Aubrey and Mrs. Stevens had an affair. Mr. Stevens caught them, fired Aubrey, and cut Beverly out from his will."

"Ah. That's how it came about. And leaving money to his mistresses was the final insult to injury."

"Ay, Mr. Stevens was cold hearted. The final spiteful act of that man was stealing Mr. Frazier's patent. The money Mr. Frazier could've made from that? I don't think he's fully recovered from the betrayal."

"Tell me about Aubrey," Dash said.

"Wha' about him?"

"Who was he, besides tall and handsome? You're a good judge of character, Mingus. What kind of character did he have?"

A scowl darkened his thick face. "Something's missing from him. He's not quite human, if that makes sense. Oh sure, he can smile and laugh and joke with the best of them. Make ya feel like the most interesting person in the world. But if ya look closely, there's no twinkle to his eye, no warmth behind the smile. He's just . . . empty."

"I understand he tried to get a job with Mr. Frazier."

A bitter laugh. "Ha! Mr. Frazier saw right through him. Told him to get out and stay out. He'd be furious Mrs. Stevens was letting him inside his house."

Dash reached into his pockets and pulled out Rosalie's

teacup and the rounded capital A from the tunnel. He held them up. "Have you seen these before?"

Mingus squinted. "What are those?"

"Secret codes, or secret messages. I keep finding them wherever Rosalie goes."

"She did love that—that spy silliness. Got it from her mother."

"Is this by Rosalie's hand?" Dash pointed to the drawn lines.

"Possibly. I don't know."

"Leonard's? Beverly's?"

"Be hard to say. All their handwriting looks alike. Each one taught the other. Leonard taught Beverly and Rosie."

"Why didn't Rosalie's mother teach her?"

"She—she was ill by then."

"I see. Any idea what they mean?"

"Ya got me."

Dash pocketed the papers. "Do you have any idea where Rosalie went that Saturday night? The tenth?"

"She didn't go anywhere."

"You don't expect me to believe that?"

"It's true! After her father found her at the Oyster House that Friday before, he ordered her locked up. I even put the weekly supply crates in front of the secret door, blocking it. Even as strong as she was, there'd be no way she could lift those crates. And I gave the staff strict orders not to move them. She couldn't have left if she tried."

"Mingus, she had to have gone *somewhere*. She drank poisoned liquor!"

"Maybe at that Harlem club."

Dash frowned. "What about Sunday? How did she get out on Sunday?"

"I don't know, sir. I didn't move those crates until after

Mr. Frazier arrived home, which was at sunrise Monday morning."

"Were you here all of Sunday night?"

"No, but . . . Mrs. Stevens and Miss Esposito were, and they watched her like hawks."

"How did she get out then?"

"I don't know, Mr. Bennett, I swear to ya! One minute, she was here; the next, she was gone."

Dash stared at Mingus. The man certainly sounded sincere. Was it a performance? "Did she tell you what she found out?"

"Who?"

"Rosalie. The secret she knew. You mentioned it when I was here last."

"Just like I said to you and Mrs. Stevens and Mr. Frazier, she didn't tell me what it was."

"I remember, Mingus, but I think you're lying. I think she *did* tell you. And I think it was bad, Mingus. I think it was really, really bad."

There was a knock on the door. Both men turned to see the bedroom door being opened by Leonard Frazier.

"Oh hello," he said. He scrunched his forehead as he tried to recall Dash's fake name. "Mr. . . . Bennett, is it? I didn't hear you announced. Is everything all right? Am I interrupting something?"

"No, sir. I just had some follow-up questions about what Mingus here saw the other night. He's being very helpful."

Leonard looked from Mingus to Dash and back again. "Well, then. Carry on. Uh, Mingus, when you're finished with Mr. Bennett here, I'm wondering if you can see me in my office." He lowered his voice. "Miss Esposito is threatening to quit because of what the parrot is saying to her."

"What did the bird say now?"

"He keeps saying '*can't goddamn march.*' I don't understand it, Mingus. Every time I leave the house for any length of time, he says something new." He sighed, shaking his head. He looked at Dash. "How are the shoes holding up?"

"Just fine, sir."

"We haven't found the other one, the one you lost when you—well, you know. We'll keep looking."

"I appreciate that, sir."

Leonard nodded to himself. "Carry on, you two." He turned and left the bedroom.

Dash stood as soon as he exited. "Mingus, I'm going to give you one more chance. What was the secret Rosalie knew?"

"Mr. Bennett . . . I can't tell you."

"Why not?"

"I just can't."

Dash sighed. "You don't need to protect her anymore."

"It's not her I'm protecting."

"Then *who*?"

Mingus just shook his head.

"If this secret is truly as awful as I think it is, it's dangerous. You need to be careful, Mingus. You need to be real careful."

He left the downcast man and entered the main downstairs hallway. Sophie Esposito stepped through the doorway of the storage closet.

"Afternoon, Miss Esposito."

"Afternoon, Mr. . . . ?"

"Bennett."

She nodded, carrying two large cans of tomatoes. Her dark eyes watched him as she left the storage closet and went down the hall towards the stairs to the upper floors. Dash shivered. She didn't miss a thing, that one.

He retraced his steps in the storage closet until he found the outline of the door and pushed. Like his own secret door in the tailor shop, this door swung open on disguised hinges. Dash stepped into the tunnel, gathering up the rest of the pieces of paper. He didn't want Mingus or anyone else destroying this evidence.

———

If Joe was angry at Dash sneaking off, he was soon assuaged by Dash's discovery of the secret tunnel.

"A smuggler's tunnel? No wonder she could get in and out of there." Joe picked up one of the secret codes Dash brought back with him. "What do ya think this all means?"

"I haven't the foggiest idea, Joe. Some kind of meeting happened at the Frazier house, but I'll be damned if I know what it was about."

"Ya think this is the secret Rosalie told Mingus?"

"It has to be. And it has to affect someone else in the house. Leonard? Beverly?"

"What about Miss Esposito? The maid?"

"It could be any of them. All of them, even." Dash sat silent for a moment. He puzzled on it some more but couldn't come up with a plausible answer.

Joe turned over one of the secret codes, examining the paper. "What about that Radio Shop fella? On Cortlandt? What if he knows what this is?"

Dash looked up at the ruddy man. "What day is it again?"

"Err, Wednesday."

"Joe, you're a lifesaver." He grabbed Joe's hand. "Come on. We have an appointment with a radio man."

———

Radio Row on Cortlandt Street was less intimidating than it had been before, now that Dash knew where to go. He and Joe entered Transworld Radio. The same clerk who was there last week was behind the register. He was dealing with a customer—a real one, it looked like, not a blind tiger one. A stiff-looking gent with gray hair, straight back, perfect posture. He left with a small radio in his hands.

The clerk smiled when he saw Dash. "Teacup Man," he said. "How have you been? Did you like your purchase?"

"Delicious, thank you." Dash learned on the counter, dropping his voice to conspiratorial levels. "My girl is on my case about having tea, shall we say? Find out any places that could whet her appetite?"

The clerk with his long face and long smile hummed. "I might have, but I'll need some sugar to jog my memory."

Perhaps this was why the NYPD took bribes. Investigating was an expensive proposition.

Dash peeled off a few dollars and placed them on the counter.

The clerk slid them into his pocket and brought out two pieces of paper. He leaned forward on his elbow, holding them upward with his fingers. "You've got perfect timing. I hear there's an afternoon tea tomorrow at two at the White Rabbit. Or rather, the basement underneath the White Rabbit on MacDougal and Bleecker. Say you're there to meet the Mad Hatter."

He handed over the papers. Teacup drawings, just like the one Rosalie had.

"White Rabbit?" Joe said. "Wha' the bloody hell does that have to do with mad hatters?"

"Alice in Wonderland," Dash replied. "Down the rabbit hole."

The clerk smiled. "Always helps to be clever in this business."

After pocketing the teacups, Dash brought out the rounded capital A's, or the tunnel codes. "Have you seen these before?"

The clerk picked them up, regarding them with

bemused interest. He shook his head. "Never before in my life. Looks like the same ink as your cups."

Dash thanked the man and left the shop with Joe at his heels.

"Dash," he said, "that Rabbit place, that's in our neighborhood."

"I know. Things are coming together, Joe. They're *finally* coming together."

A concerned look. "We need to know what we're walkin' into. I don't like the thought of bein' ambushed."

"Good point." Dash tapped his chin. "Joe, I just had a flash. Remember what Atty said when Rosalie came through the door? She was asking to see a hat."

"Aye. Not hat. *Hatter.*"

Dash nodded. "And if she knew about the White Rabbit, then I'll bet my last pile of sugar Marty Grice and Tillie White did as well."

When they were opening Pinstripes, Dash managed to convince Joe to let him go see Marty Grice's show later that night. They were at the bar, Dash on a barstool sipping a Rickey while Joe was wiping the dust off the bottles.

"It's in a public place," Dash said. "There's no way I can be harmed."

"What is this cockamamie place called again?"

"The Siamese Cat Club."

"Hey, I know that place!" called a voice behind them.

They turned to see Vernon walk in with his bass.

"You've been, Vern?" Dash asked.

"I have indeed! Someone said they had a hep show that had to be seen to be believed." Vernon set his bass down on the floor of the stage. "And they weren't kidding! Never seen anything like it."

Dash nodded, taking a sip of his Rickey. "Glad you enjoyed it, Vern."

"That's not all I enjoyed. I met this blond there I am just *crazy* about. She wants me to see her after tonight's show. At her place, if ya know what I mean."

"Oh." Dash flicked a look to Joe, who caught his concern. "And this blond? Was she a patron?"

"Nah, she was one of the performers! Came up to me after the show and said hello."

"Was her name Tillie White by any chance?" Perhaps Tillie wore a wig.

"Nope, though I saw her act. Nice but this Mona, she's worlds better. In every way. Now I don't wanna jinx it, but maybe ol' Vern might cash some checks tonight."

Julius picked that moment to walk into Pinstripes. "You know, Vern, the day you cash a check when you say you gonna cash a check is the day Wall Street stops being greedy."

"Uh, Vernon?" Dash said. "Can I talk to you for a moment?"

He left the bar area and went over to his bass player. He wrapped an arm around Vernon's shoulder and slowly walked him towards the WC door. Dash kept his voice low.

"Listen, Vern, I'm thrilled to death you saw a new show and met a new girl."

"Thanks, Boss."

"But this club and that show . . . it's a pansy place." Dash watched Vernon's face, expecting to see confusion, panic, even outrage.

Instead, he saw bemusement.

"I know, Boss."

Now Dash felt the confusion he expected Vernon to feel. "And that's jake with you?"

Vernon grinned. "Sure it is."

Maybe he didn't understand. "If you cash that check, when the dress comes off, it . . . how do I explain this . . . ?"

"You don't have to. I know."

"You . . . do?"

Vernon nodded, his usual go-lucky smile still on his face. He leaned over and whispered in Dash's ear, "I like 'em both." He patted Dash on the shoulder and went back to the stage area where Julius continued to tease him.

Dash returned to the bar.

Joe came over and murmured, "Did ya tell him?"

Dash nodded.

"And?"

"He likes them both."

"Ain't tha' a wonder." Joe finished wiping down the bar and leaned forward. "I mean it, Dash. There better be no danger to ya in that place tonight. I've almost lost ya twice. I won't have it a third time." He gently touched Dash's cheek.

Dash reached up and clasped his hand. "I promise, Joe. There won't be any danger." He meant to keep his promise, he truly did. Only someone else had other ideas.

The Siamese Cat club was filled to capacity. The cat eyes, the silk lanterns, the sparking jade and gold were all here from before. But now there were a hundred people or more, cigarette smoke wrapping its tendrils around the room, creating a gauzy effect. It all felt like a surreal dream, a hallucination. Which was the point, of course. Tonight's show would be filled with nothing but illusions.

Dash found a booth in the very back corner. He idly sipped his Rickey while he smoked, his exhales adding to the room's fog of nicotine. By the time he finished his drink and asked for another, the sound of a large gong filled the air. Conversations quieted. The offstage male voice called out: "Dearly beloved, if this love only exists in my dreams, don't wake me up!"

And then the pansies began to sing the same song Dash heard at rehearsal:

Don't wake me up, up, up, up, up, up
Don't wake me up
Don't wake me

I don't wanna fall, fall, fall, fall asleep, no!
I don't wanna fall unless I'm falling for you

The dancing and the staging effects worked perfectly, earning the troupe momentous applause. When the number completed, the main curtain closed and onto the stage walked Marty Grice. He waited for the applause to die down before launching into his monologue.

"Welcome, welcome, welcome, my friends, to the Siamese Cat! Where we long to be petted, but we'll scratch your eyes out if you do it wrong. You're about to enter our dream world full of dream girls, the likes of which you've seen before."

A male voice called out "I've seen 'em!"

"Oh, you have?" Marty said. "A repeat customer. Were you here last week? You were? Did you get the clap? You didn't? Oh, I'm *so* glad! Last week was a particular stressful one, that. So many of us had the clap backstage, every time we dropped our trousers, it sounded like a standing ovation at the Palace!"

He grinned at the guffaws and whistles from the audience.

"Oh, my my. You can't *imagine* the worry I was under. But it's all about perspective, ladies and gentlemen, yes indeed, it's all in how you look at it. I simply took a look at my worry that I was under and by changing a letter or two, I found myself a *Rory* to be under and my world changed for the better!"

More laughter and applause.

"Yes, indeed. But if you can't find a Rory to replace your worry, there is still something you can do."

A trill of the piano keys and then Marty launched into a

frisky frolic of a tune, sung in a surprisingly strong, full voice:

How about a drink?
I wish I had a drink,
Just a little drink or two!

The crowd, apparently familiar with the jaunty song, yelled out: "Why stop at two?!"

Can't we have a drink?
Just a little drink,
Any little drink will do!

The crowed replied, "I'm with you!"

If I had a drink,
Just a little drink,
Then I wouldn't feel so blue!

"Oh, how dry I am!" shouted the crowd.

Don't you really think
We ought to have a drink?
Just a little drink with you!

As if cued, everyone raised their glasses at the end of the number in a collective toast. Marty, for himself, raised an imaginary glass. "May your glasses be full and your mouths fully wet, now swallow it down before Coolidge truly frets!"

Everyone took a large sip of their respective libations, even Dash.

Marty continued on. "Ladies and gentlemen, get ready for a shock. 'Cause we have a surprise fresh from the docks. Her tail is delicious, you'll truly want a bite. Put your hands together for our very own deep-sea delight. Miss Swell Bottoms!"

The curtains parted to reveal a set change. A cardboard cutout of the ocean surf was in the background along with a painted blue sky and circular yellow sun. On either side of the stage were two posts with rough ropes wrapped around them. Center stage, seated on a buoy was a blond-haired mermaid, complete with fish tail and a coconut brassiere. The illusion was note-perfect.

The show went on like that for over an hour. A female impersonator would perform solo on the stage—though there was one "sister" act—and Marty would cover the set and costume changes with ribald stage patter.

"And now, ladies and gentlemen, we have a special guest. Her sex isn't an illusion . . . but her clothes are. Please welcome to the stage, Missus Rock-My-Feller!"

And there she was, Tillie White, with a fan in front and a fan behind, those peacock feathers covering her middle and leaving for all eyes to see her flashing grin and her long, shapely legs.

The audience whistled and cheered with each tantalizing tease. A dip of the feathers. A movement of the fan. All precisely timed to prevent the audience from seeing her completely naked. A simple turn of the head or flick of a finger, an innocent gesture, and all would be exposed.

Exposed.

A waiter came over to Dash, alerting him this was last call as this was the second to last performance. As he paid his bill, he asked the waiter how to get backstage. It was said on impulse. It cost him a fiver, but the waiter eventually told him.

Tillie was halfway through her number when Dash left the booth and found a narrow hallway that ran alongside the main room towards the stage. There, as the waiter had promised, was a nondescript door. A man sat on a stool, working a toothpick in his mouth like a dentist scraping his vindictive metal hook. Another fiver changed hands before Dash was let through.

Pandemonium. While the scenes on stage were the epitome of clockwork precision, this side-stage hallway was nothing short of calamity. Pansies in half-dress were shouting at one another to get a move on. Half were in need of wigs, the other half in need of dresses. A long table with mirrors ran along the wall where pansies were hurriedly doing their makeup.

A deep voice kept demanding to know where Marty was. At the third instance, a nearby pansy, looking like a baby bird with yellow feathers, orange fringe, and a beak of a nose, yelled back, "Marty isn't here, goddammit! Now somebody figure out how to tell the band to stall so we're ready for the finale!"

Dash zeroed in on Baby Bird, who sat down in front of the set of mirrors closest to him. "You said Marty isn't here?"

"That's what I said, sweetie."

"You're talking about Marty Grice?"

"The one, the only. You a fan? Cause he skipped out, the rat. I know it's only a Wednesday show, but be a professional, for Pete's sake!" Baby Bird added false eyelashes and dabbed at the corners of her eyes.

Dash looked around the chaos of the backstage area. "Did anyone come for him?"

"Couldn't tell ya. If you want to nick a pair of shorts to smell later, his dressing room's over there," she said, pointing to a closed door at the other end of the narrow hall.

"I'm not interested in that."

Baby Bird shrugged. "Suit yourself. He usually sells 'em for two bucks a pop. It's a literal steal if you grab 'em now."

Dash muttered a thanks and pushed his way through the panicking pansies to get to Marty's dressing room door. He knocked once and tried the knob. Miracle of miracles, the door was unlocked.

He stepped inside the room, closing the door behind him. The noise and tension level dropped by half. The room was nothing to look at: a dressing table with a mirror on one wall, a floor-length mirror on the other. In between was a metal rod holding suit jackets, waistcoats, and trousers of different colors and styles. Leather shoes were lined in a row underneath.

Dash went to the dressing table, looking across the surface. Stage makeup and brushes. He opened each of the drawers and found more of the same, along with handkerchiefs to wipe away the sweat from performing. No notes, no cards, no photographs, no books. Nothing related to who Marty was. Were all dressing rooms this impersonal?

It was when Dash checked the wastebasket in the corner of the room that he hit pay dirt. Amidst the matted blond hair removed from a hairbrush was a note hastily torn in half. Dash picked up the two pieces and placed them together. An angular hand wrote:

MILTON HOTEL, 44TH & BROADWAY, ROOM 3B,
BRING CASH.

No signature. Dash didn't recognize the handwriting,

but he did recognize the hotel name. A fleabag if there ever was one.

He pocketed the torn pieces of paper, took one last look around, and then left the dressing room. He sidestepped several rushing pansies as they made their way to the stage. Muffled applause throbbed in the background. Must be the curtain call.

Dash muttered "excuse me, excuse me" what felt like a hundred times until he got to the stage door. He passed by Baby Bird who called out "did you find what you were looking for?"

"I did, thank you!" Dash replied over his shoulder before stepping into the alleyway behind the club. The narrow space was filled with trash, rotting food, and wet urine marks. He looked down towards either end to get his bearings. Forty-Fourth should be to his left, shouldn't it?

He ran down the alleyway, hitting the cross street. He had guessed right. Now where was Broadway? Ah, to his left again. A few steps forward and he was in the electric-lit, congested Times Square. The pedestrians were barely ambulatory, full of food and drink and awe at the sheer spectacle of the place. Electric signs and billboards. Theatres and cinemas. Radio towers and radio display windows. The modern world converging in one gaudy spot. He walked briskly, only mildly pushing the tourists out of his way, as he inched towards the flashing sign of the Milton.

He managed to cross over Broadway, narrowly escaping a speeding taxi, circled around a threesome of drunk men in suits, ties askew, breath foggy and sweet with hops, and ducked into the Milton's lobby.

He walked with purpose, as if he lived there, bypassing the front desk entirely. Luckily for him, whoever was manning the front desk was lost in his pulp novel and didn't see Dash charge through.

No elevator in this place, just a set of creaking stairs. Dash climbed up to the third floor. As soon as his feet hit the landing, a loud *pop! pop!* in quick procession reverberated throughout the hall.

32

Dash froze.

He'd heard that sound before—and he had hoped he would never hear it again. His hands started shaking. His eyes darted around. Where had it come from?

The lighting here was muted, from the cheap lamps hanging on the walls. Next to him on the landing was a short, square table with a vase of yellowing ferns. A red carpet stretched the entire length of the hallway, leading to a narrow rectangular window glowing from the electric signs of Times. There was a set of five doors on each side of the hall, the doors a flimsy wood, the doorknobs an unpolished brass.

All the doors were closed, with the exception of one at the far end. It was slightly ajar, a sliver of light peering out. He sincerely did not want to walk all the way down there.

"Marty?" he called.

The muffled sounds of Times Square was all he heard.

"Marty!" Dash hissed.

No reply.

He looked around once more. No one else seemed

disturbed by the sound he heard—or more likely, they've learned to ignore it.

He needed a weapon, something to defend himself with. He looked at the vase holding the sad ferns, a twin-handled piece of pottery with chipped edges. It didn't match the red decor at all, what with its ivory-white body and mint-green base. If it got destroyed, Dash figured he was doing the Milton and its guests a favor.

He dumped the ferns out and started creeping towards the open door. Without even seeing the letters on it, he knew it was 3B. He tried to make every step as light as possible, keeping to the long rug to avoid creaks and groans. His breathing was ragged and short. Any second now, he expected to see a killer with a smoking gun rushing out of the room towards him.

He'd just passed the third set of doors, with only two more sets to go, when he heard an angry crack and a squealing scrape. He jumped as if shocked by electricity. The muffled sounds of the Square got clearer and louder. What followed was the unmistakable *tink tink tink* of shoes on metal. Someone was climbing down the fire escape.

Dash picked up his pace, reaching Room 3B in no time. He paused at the doorway, momentarily unwilling to go inside, because he knew what he'd find. And he wasn't sure he could see such a sight again.

The *tinks* on metal faded.

They're getting away! Move, Dash!

He raised the vase in his left hand while his right hand, only slightly trembling, pushed open the door to Room 3B.

At first, he didn't see anything, just the knockoff Tiffany lamp in the corner on a round wood table. Red curtains fluttered in the breeze from the opened window.

Dash rushed over to it. Flattened against the wall, vase

still in hand, he peered around the window frame to see if anyone was waiting on the ledge of the fire escape.

Empty.

He gingerly stuck his head out and looked down. A darkened figure was one floor below him, trying to unhook the ladder to take them down to the street below.

"Hey! You!" Dash called. "Stop right there!"

The figure looked up. The nighttime obscured its features and Dash couldn't clearly see the face. What he did see clearly, though, was the pistol in its hand, rising up and aiming at Dash.

He dropped to the floor, the vase flying from his hands just as the bullet sailed through the opened window and hit the plaster ceiling with a *thwack!* Crumbs of plaster cackled to the floor. The sound of gunfire followed shortly after. A strange sequence of events, the bullet moving faster than the sound of it firing.

Or perhaps Dash's senses were all discombobulated.

His heart thundered in his ears.

He looked over and saw the ugly vase had fallen to the floor, but was still intact. A shame, really.

He left the vase where it was and crawled to the other side of the windowsill. Slowly rising up, he flattened himself once more against the wall, hoping he was out of sight of the shooter.

He paused.

No sound of feet climbing up towards him.

He waited, breathing hard. Sweat covered his face and neck. He felt nauseous and slightly dizzy.

Keep it together, old boy. You can do it now.

He slowly peered around the corner of the window frame and glanced down. The fire escape ladder had been dropped down to the side street. The shooter was gone.

A wet gasp behind him.

He spun around, discovering the rest of the room beyond the window and the imitation Tiffany lamp. A sofa with fringed pillows on one wall, two wingback chairs with a floor lamp in between them on the other. Cracked plaster moldings surrounded them. No framed pictures of any kind. That would be too high-class for a place like the Milton.

The coffee table had been knocked slightly askew. And Dash saw why. The sole of a leather shoe was resting against one of the table legs.

Dash walked forward, his eyes tracing the soles to the legs to the torso, which was stained heavily with blood. The chest moved haltingly up and down. The pale, thick neck was speckled with crimson, the face shiny with sweat.

A face Dash recognized.

Poor Jack Mingus's chest was ruined by two bullet holes, one on each side of his heart. Blood seeped out of them. It looked like those rare instances when Dash saw meat cooked, the bloody juices rising slowly to the surface, puddling, then draining off to the sides.

Dash put a hand to his mouth, willing any sick to stay down . . . at least long enough until he got out of there.

Mingus's eyes were opened but barely registering any of his surroundings, his breath as raggedy as Dash's own. A slight groan escaped his lips. Blood was pooling on either side of his torso. Dash stepped around the crimson carnage to avoid leaving bloody footprints all over the apartment. He knelt down by the dying man's head.

"Mingus," Dash said. "Mingus, who did this?"

The Frazier houseman's eyes slowly slid over to Dash. His lips moved but no sound came out.

"Come on, Mingus," Dash urged. "Come on. Tell me. Who shot you?"

The dying man tried but failed to form any consonants or vowels. He was bleeding out, his weakening heart pumping blood into his open wounds. He would be dead soon. That Dash could clearly see.

"Did Marty do this? Rosalie's old roommate? Big man with white-blond hair? Did he do this to you?"

Mingus, poor Mingus, he struggled to answer, to give a name, but his body was failing him.

Dash tried coaxing him once more for information but by that point, Mingus's eyes could no longer focus. They rolled up to stare at the ceiling. And there they remained. Dash actually saw the light go out of them. A shiver shook his spine, goosebumps chilled his scalp. He could've sworn something brushed against his cheek, a spirit leaving the bullet-torn body of Jack Mingus for places unknown.

Unbidden tears welled up in Dash's eyes (not *again,* dammit!) and he began saying "I'm sorry" over and over again. Not because he felt responsible for what happened to Mingus, but because any human suffering, any hastened death, was a tragedy.

The creak of the hotel stairs halted his apology.

Dash sniffed back his tears and looked to the door of the apartment and saw it was still open. He shot up and leapt over the pooled blood to shut the door, locking it in the process.

Determined steps charged down the hallway. Had someone called the police? Perhaps the tenants of this hotel didn't ignore the gunshots after all.

A forceful knock on the front door caused Dash to jump.

"Mr. Mingus," a muffled voice called. "Mr. Mingus. I

apologize for being late, but I needed to grab some, uh, cabbage for you."

Dash kept quiet. He tried to place the voice, but the frazzled nature of his nerves and the thickness of the door thoroughly disguised it.

Another loud series of knocks.

"Mr. Mingus!" Then a stage whisper. "I don't have time for this! Open the goddamn door!"

Dash concentrated on his breathing, keeping it quiet. Perhaps this man would figure Jack to be out and leave.

No such luck.

The man tried to turn the doorknob and push open the door, but the deadbolt held.

A queer silence followed.

Dash held his breath. What was the man doing? He hadn't left. Dash would've heard his thundering footsteps down the hall. A strange scraping sound drew Dash's attention to the deadbolt lock. Metal on metal.

He's picking the lock!

Whoever this was, he was getting inside this apartment. This apartment with a freshly shot corpse inside of it.

Dash went to the opened window. He lifted one leg out into the frigid night air, then the other.

The apartment door opened just as Dash disappeared from view and, for the third time in so many minutes, flattened himself against the wall. Only this time, it was the outside of the building. Wind whipped his hair and stung his cheeks. He looked down at the stomach-lurching three-story drop. Just thin strips of metal bolted into the brick were all that kept him up. Given the city's landlords' penchant for doing things on the cheap, Dash had exactly zero confidence in the safety of this contraption.

It was then he realized too late that he had flattened

himself on the wrong side of the window. While being on the left side of the fire escape shielded him from view, the right side was the side that led downwards to the street.

Dash cursed again. He had to get to the other side. Perhaps when this stranger found Mingus's body. His back would most certainly be turned.

He peered around the edge of the window frame. As he predicted, the stranger was kneeling down by Mingus's body, feeling for a pulse.

Dash began to cross in front of the window to the other side.

The stranger suddenly stood up and turned around.

Shock on the stranger's part; confusion on Dash's.

"Marty?" Dash said.

Marty Grice pointed at him. "What did you do?"

Dash held up his hands. "I didn't do this. I found him like this, I swear."

"Why would you *kill* him?"

"I *didn't*, Marty!"

A siren wailed nearby. Both Dash and Marty took note of it. Whatever differences of opinion they had over the situation, neither one of them wanted to deal with the coppers.

"Come on!" Dash said. "They'll be watching the front."

"Don't have to tell me twice," Marty replied, as he walked towards the window.

Dash started down the fire escape, wanting to keep a safe distance between him and Marty.

They made their way down the fire escape, the metal landings and stairs only *slightly* shaking as they went. With Marty's heft, Dash sincerely hoped the metal would stay bolted into the side of the building.

They got to the second floor and the ladder the actual

murderer had used to escape. Dash went down first and stood off to the side as Marty followed.

The moment Marty's shoes hit the ground, they both broke out into a run, getting to the other end of the alley in a few seconds flat. At the mouth of the alley, they stopped. Dash held a finger to his lips and peeked around the corner. A cop car was parked in front of the Milton with one cop standing out front, watching for anyone leaving the premises.

Dash turned around to Marty and mouthed *they're out front.*

Marty mouthed back, *what do we do?*

Dash looked at the other end of the alley. They could run there, but then they'd have to run right underneath Mingus's window. The coppers would surely be up there now.

Dash turned and concentrated on the sidewalk in front of them. A big crowd of bell bottoms, drunk with shore leave, were stumbling down the sidewalk. They crossed in front of the copper out front, blocking his vision.

"Now," Dash said. He stepped out of the alleyway with Marty as his heels.

"Don't look back," Marty murmured.

"I have no intention to."

They made for a leisurely stroll, hearing the copper yell at the bell bottoms to get a move on and the bell bottoms heckling the poor copper.

"They might end up spending the night in a cell, they keep acting like that," Marty said.

"Better them than us."

"Agreed."

They continued until they got to Seventh Avenue, then they turned uptown.

Once they were a decent distance away, Marty said, "You swear you didn't kill him?"

"What would be the reason?" Dash asked.

"Does anyone need a reason these days to pull a trigger?"

"One would hope so." Dash looked over and saw Marty's eye roll. "What about you, Marty? Did you pull the trigger?"

Marty scoffed. "Why would I do that, then turn around, and come back again?"

"Then who did?"

"How the hell should *I* know?"

"You knew him."

"I didn't know him."

Dash glared at him. "Right. You just went to his room, knew his name, and picked his lock. Why were you there in the first place?"

They walked half a block in silence, crossing over Forty-Fifth.

"Alright," Marty acquiesced. "I did know him. A bit. From Rosalie. He was her confidante, of sorts. As much as a mere houseman can be a confidante to the wealthy."

"What were you paying Mingus for?"

Marty was surprised by the question. "How did you know—?"

Dash held up the two pieces of paper. "I found his note in your dressing room."

"Damn. I'd forgotten I invited you. Of all the rotten luck."

"You're not answering my question."

Marty glanced around. "Look, let's go to my place and we can talk. I'll tell you everything you want to know."

Dash shook his head. "Let's find a bar instead."

"My place is safer."

"For *you*, maybe."

They crossed over Forty-Sixth.

Marty sighed. "Fine. There's a place near Eighth."

"Lead the way."

33

The speak was one of those that had been shoved into the side of a deli. One had to duck underneath the counter, go past the slicing machines to the freezer, sidestepping hanging meats, and push the false door in the back.

The space was narrow, no space for barstools or chairs. Standing room only. Cheap plywood wall on one side, exposed brick on the other. A tiny bar stood at the opposite end and only had two offerings: gin or whiskey.

Concoctions poured, Dash and Marty stood off to the side, taking well-deserved sips. Dash drank half of his in one gulp; Marty downed the whole thing and ordered another.

When he returned, Dash got down to business. "What was Mingus going to tell you? And don't give me the runaround, Marty. I just saw a man shot to death and almost got shot myself, so I am in *no* mood to deal with any chicanery."

Marty looked at him. "Before I do, let's start with your real name, because you're *not* Hugo Boldt from William Morris. I called, and the real Hugo has absolutely no interest in my act."

"When did you find me out?"

"Today."

"I'm surprised it took you this long to figure it."

An impatient gesture. "They wouldn't return my calls until now, the damnable pricks. If you're not somebody, William Morris is not interested."

"I'll level with you. My name is Dash Parker and I own a speak."

"Why is a speak owner running around playing detective?"

Dash took a chance. "Because she died in my club."

"Ah. Taking it personally, I see."

"I do, yes, I do. Having to deal with corpses is not my forte."

"You seem to be doing quite well, considering our, uh, current circumstance."

Dash took another sip of gin. Lord, the stuff was vile. "First question: What was Jack Mingus going to give you? And don't deny there wasn't some sort of extortion payoff happening. I know all too well how *those* appear."

Marty finished his second whiskey in as many minutes and stared at Dash. His eyes were becoming red, his forehead dotting with sweat. "I could blackmail you, you know."

Dash scoffed. "You could, Marty, but then you'd find out quickly I don't have much money. Not like the Fraziers. That family had sugar. Hell, their house looks like a pile of sugar. Marble walls, marble balconies, marble sconces. You wanted a piece of that, which is why you befriended Rosalie in the first place, didn't you?"

Marty's words became slightly slurred, and his self-control started to slip. "Alright, alright, I will admit that we liked Rosalie's family wealth more than her. That's not a crime in this city."

"No, but when she reformed, as it were, you and Tillie were left high and dry."

Marty swayed slightly on his feet. The cheap whiskey was hitting his system fast. "She had everything, that girl," he said, his words slurring. "Everything. Was going to piss it away to thumb her nose at her father and her aunt. You know, it was Tillie and I who convinced her to 'reform.' *Get the money*, we said, *and then we can live the life of Riley.* We didn't count on her completely abandoning us. We thought she'd play pretend, but she didn't need us anymore."

He raised his glass to his lips, not realizing it was completely empty of whiskey.

"But then when you dropped that little bomb about Aunt Beverly and the Aubrey Harrington fellow, well now, we had another course of action."

Dash nodded. "You paid a visit to the Frazier house."

Marty grinned, his lips sloppy and wet. "Yes, we did! We did indeed, Mr. Porter, we did indeed."

Dash didn't correct his last name. If Marty wanted to remember him as Mr. Porter, then that was just jake by him.

Marty kept going. "That man, what's his name? Mingus? Mingus. Yeah, Mingus answered the door and we told him all about Aunt Bev and her stallion Aubrey. He tried to deny it. Tried to protect his masters. I'll give him that. He was loyal to them . . . at first."

Marty leaned towards Dash, whispering wetly into his ear.

"But greed always wins out in the end, doesn't it, Mr. Porter?"

Marty straightened up—or tried to. More swaying on his part. "So, he told us he might have something even better to know. Trading, is what he called it. How much would *we* pay for that? Isn't that interesting? We got there to extort and here is the houseman doing the same thing to us. Tillie and I didn't buy it at first. But ole Mingus, he said there was something far greater than just a typical love affair. *Who would care*, he argued. *She was a widow.* The important thing was *who* Aubrey was. That was worth some sugar we could sell to the papers."

"So much for loyalty."

"Loyalty, Mr. Porter, is always bought and sold."

Hadn't Fife told me the same thing so many nights ago?

"Why would he need the money?" Dash asked himself. He felt a spark. "Gambling."

"Eh?"

"Alexander Gettler said he knew Mingus from the horse track. And Sophie said something odd, that Mingus has never been lucky." Dash tapped his chin. "I wonder if he had gambling debts."

"That would certainly make any man desperate for money." Marty took another sip from his empty glass. "Mingus said he'd be in touch. And was. Now he's dead. I wonder who killed him?"

"It would have to be someone who knew about the tunnel," Dash said. "He was about to use it when I surprised him yesterday."

"Where was he going?"

"My guess would be to rent the hotel room for your meeting."

"Well Aubrey sure knew about the tunnel. And I'll bet ya dollars to doughnuts, Mr. Porter, his lover Beverly does as well."

Dash thought for a moment. "There's also Sophie Esposito. She may know about the tunnel. She was certainly close by when I was chatting with Mingus in his bedroom. Maybe she overheard us and followed him."

Marty squinted his eyes. "Eh?"

"The maid."

"Oh, she was there too. When Tillie and I talked to Mingus."

"She was? Interesting." Dash thought for a moment. "Of course, Mr. Frazier walked in on us when Mingus was talking about Rosalie's secret ... "

"Maybe Leonard killed him to protect his sister."

Now there was a thought.

Marty hiccuped. "God, I wonder what Mingus knew. Too bad Mingus died before he could tell anyone." An accusatory look. "He didn't tell you, did he?"

Dash shook his head.

Marty ruefully nodded to himself. "Damn." He held up his empty whiskey glass. "I'm getting another." He staggered towards the bar.

Something was bothering Dash. Something about the weekend Rosalie died. Damn it all, what was it?

When Marty returned, he had two whiskey glasses in hand this time.

"Marty, did Rosalie always use the tunnel?"

"Yessir!"

"That Friday when you met her at the Oyster House?"

"Don't see why she wouldn't."

"And how did Mr. Frazier know where to go that Friday night when he found Rosalie missing?"

"Hmm?" Marty's eyes were as glassy as ice.

"How did he know? Was the Oyster House one of her haunts?"

"No, we'd never been there before. First time, actually."

"So how did he *know* she was there?"

"Saw her come out of the tunnel."

"That he doesn't know exists. Marty, I've been in that

tunnel. You can't see the entrance from Riverside or the park. Did you and Rosalie climb up from the tracks to be in front of the house?"

"Pfft! 'Course we didn't. We didn't want to be seen."

Excitement started building in Dash's chest. "So how could Leonard Frazier follow his daughter to the Oyster House?"

A flash.

Dash pictured the Oyster House. Rosalie with Marty and Tillie in the front row. El on stage. Suddenly, Rosalie sees her father, mutters *So that's what it is*, and then enter Leonard Frazier, angry, pulling his daughter out.

"Suppose," Dash said softly to himself, "just suppose it wasn't Rosalie who was caught that night. Suppose it was *Leonard*."

Marty, completely frazzled at this point, just furrowed his brow. "Hmm? What are you saying? You're making no sense. Have you had too much to drink, young man?"

Dash shook his head. "Make sure you don't fall down, Marty."

———

Dash didn't even bother with the line at the Oyster House. Instead, we went to the alleyway that ran in the back. Not only was the WC here but so was Leslie Charles's office. And before showtime, El was always in that office—much to the consternation of Leslie.

Dash picked his way down the alley, sidestepping overflowing trash, wayward rats, and potholes filled with old rainwater. A large rectangle of light lit one section of the alley. Dash slowly walked up to it and peered around the ledge. He immediately jerked his head back. Leslie was in there with El. A part of the window must've been opened for he could hear their voices.

"Now listen," Leslie Charles said, "I know we've had our differences, but you've got to admit, we're a good team together."

"Says you!" El retorted. "I'm the one who does all the work, brings in all the people, and you have the nerve not only to underpay me, but also to tell me how to do my own show. My own show that has packed your tin box for months now!"

"And without my tin box, as you said, you wouldn't *have* a show. Ya see? We need each other, El. I don't have a place and you don't have a stage without one another."

"You act like you're the only place with a stage. I got bad news for you, there are *hundreds* of stages I can play."

"Like what? That Watkins mess?"

"Don't trash talk her," El warned. "She's doing mighty well, and that hotel gets a lot of travelers from all over. Might be able to get my name outside of Harlem."

"And do what?! Ain't nobody gonna take your he-she ass outside of Harlem. You think St. Louis is gonna like you? Chicago? *Virginia*? Unless you put on a frilly dress and sing frilly songs, you ain't going anywhere."

Dash heard a loud *bang!* The sound of fist on wood.

"You know what, Les?" El said. "I'm gettin' tired of your *he-shes* and *listen heres* and all the other bushwa you've been spouting from that dandy mouth of yours."

"Who you callin' a dandy?"

"I can be loved wherever I go. I make people laugh. I make them cry. And by the time I'm done, they don't give two rats' asses whether I'm a he-she."

"You gotta get through your set without them shooting you first, El."

"Get out."

"What? This is *my* office."

There was the sounds of a scuffle. It ended with El shouting, "Get *out!*"

Dash jolted when the door slammed. Heavy breathing followed, then El muttering, "Goddamn fool. God-*damn* fool."

Dash peered around the window frame again and saw El, standing with her head hanging down, her hands on her hips. She was dressed in her usual white tuxedo. The top hat sat upright on top of the desk.

Her voice changed. "Or am I the fool?" Then a self-deprecating chuckle. "Shit . . ."

Dash tapped on the windowpane.

El brought her head up and squinted at him. "Dash?" She went over to the window and threw up the sash. "What in hell are you doing here?"

"El, I need some help."

Her eyes widened. "No. Uh huh. You have run out of favors." She went to lower the sash.

"Wait!" Dash called. "I promise, no trouble for you this time. I just need to know one thing you might've seen. Please, El. Please. It's important."

She glared at him. "Why are you always in a fix? Didn't they teach you anything at that High Hat Academy?"

"Just Latin and nepotism."

Her smirk almost gave way to a real smile. "Why do I like you?"

He shrugged. "Beats me."

"Beats the hell outta me too." She shook her head—at him, at her, maybe both. "You got five seconds. Make 'em count."

"The night Rosalie Frazier was here and her father fought with her in front of everyone."

"Uh huh."

"Did you see Rosalie's father walk in? Plain-looking man, balding, round glasses?"

"Gonna test my memory, huh? Shit. Hold on, let me visualize." She closed her eyes. "Alright. Boring white man, boring white man," she chanted. She cleared her throat. "I was in the middle of '*Cecilia*.' Audience was eating right out of the palm of my hand—except for those two sitting with your girl. They looking pouty and wrong. I no longer want to look at them. I'm looking out across the floor, trying to see Miss Watkins. She's in the back corner booth, smiling. I can see her teeth in the dark. I smile back. I look over to the bar, make sure my drinkers get their money's worth. A shadow comes through the main door. I look up."

Her brow darkens, then lightens. "It's your boring white man. I think. Balding, round glasses, completely nondescript. I remember thinking *I'm gonna eat this one alive once this number ends.*" She laughs. "He looks over to his left and waves, then he looks down front and stops. At first, I think it's because he saw me and didn't know what he was getting into. Now I'm really thinking I'm gonna lay into him once this number's over. He glances to his left again and then marches down front. That's when all hell breaks loose.

"He tries to be discreet. Firmly grasps the little girl's wrist, murmurs in her ear, and tries to get her to go with him quietly. But she's not gonna do that, oh no. She stands up and says '*I will not go with you! How dare you treat me like a child!*'"

She opened her eyes. "It goes downhill from there. I can't remember what they said next, because I forgot a verse and the chords, and my piano started going haywire like my hands lost their connection with my brain."

She sighed. "They ruined my favorite number, damn them. And in front of Madam Watkins too!" She licked her lips and looked Dash in the eye. "Did that help?"

Dash took a moment to process what she said. "You're sure he looked off to the side first before looking at Rosalie."

"Uh huh. He did it twice."

"Did you see who he was looking at?"

"Nope. I was too busy focused on him, then him and his flailing daughter. Now," she said, sitting at the desk and pulling out a mirror and a comb, "I've got to get ready for my show."

Dash tapped the windowsill. "Thank you, El. I mean it. From the bottom of my heart."

She waved off his sentimentality with her comb. "Oh shush." She started combing her way with a large metal comb with a tubular wooden handle.

Dash was about to move away from the window when he stopped. He could barely feel his heartbeat. Barely feel anything. He stared at the comb in El's hand.

She gave him a queer look. "What? It's just a comb. Well, really, it's a hot comb. By another Madam, Madam C. J. Walker. Made by Black, for Black. And thank goodness, cause white combs can't do diddly with Black hair."

He pointed to the comb. "I've seen that before."

"Oh really? Some WC up here?"

He shook his head. "In a white man's drawer."

She laughed. "Now that don't make any damn sense. Why would a Black woman's comb be in a white man's house?" She stopped and stared at the comb the way Dash was now. Then she slowly turned her head to stare at him.

"Well, I'll be damned," she said.

Dash and Joe walked briskly towards MacDougal and Bleecker. For once, Dash asked Joe to accompany him, admitting this could be dangerous and he needed his partner by his side. Before Joe could object, saying this wasn't their business anymore, Dash said someone else could be in danger. And if they had an opportunity to save another human life, shouldn't they take it?

"Who is it?" Joe asked. "Who's life is at stake?"

"I'm not entirely sure yet, but I think Leonard Frazier. He's already had one attempt on his life. I think there's going to be another. And I think . . . I think I know why."

Along the way, he told him about Mingus and Marty and El. Joe asked if Dash was all right after what he saw last night. Dash truthfully answered he didn't know yet, that he was running too fast to notice.

"Once we figure out what's going on, then I can deal with it," Dash said. Then he looked at Joe. "*We* will deal with it."

Joe nodded. "That we will. That we will."

The White Rabbit ended up being the kind of place for

proper ladies with proper manners in proper dresses. Which is why the appearance of Dash and Joe turned more than a few heads. Dash just smiled at the ladies while Joe gave them an awkward hand up as a greeting.

A hostess in long sleeves, a high collar, and a dress hitting her ankles (and not an inch higher, please note) walked up to them. "Gentlemen?" she said. "How may I help you?"

Her complexion was fair, a slight smattering of freckles high on her cheeks. Light eyes, light hair.

Dash handed over the two teacup drawings. "We're here to see the hatter. The . . . Mad Hatter?"

The woman looked down at the pieces of paper, then up at the two of them. "Empty your pockets, please, sirs."

Dash and Joe glanced at one another but did as they were told. Money clip. Apartment keys. Thank God they'd both left their flasks at home.

"You're late," she said. "Follow me." She led them to a water closet and opened the door. "It's through there."

A quizzical look from Joe, but Dash just nodded as he stepped into the room. Sink. Toilet. A blank wall. Dash gingerly pushed against it, and it swung open. He looked back at Joe, who raised his brows, and stepped into the darkness. Joe followed, closing the makeshift plywood door behind him.

Dash reached into his pocket and pulled out his lighter. The tiny flame exposed a set of stairs leading downwards. "Down the rabbit hole," he said.

They carefully navigated the wobbly wooden staircase. At the landing below, a rounded brick archway to their right introduced a square, dark room. A crowd of men stood with their backs to them. The darkness prevented Dash from making out any features beyond necks, shoulders, and backs. A male voice was speaking.

"My brothers. We have had a few setbacks recently. I don't deny that. Colorado. Louisiana. Those Congressional losses hurt. But we *will* have Kentucky, I assure you that! Indiana too! And yes, Washington wasn't quite the display we wanted, but we made our presence known! Isn't that right, New Jersey?!"

A few of the men in attendance cheered.

"Pennsylvania!" the man said to more applause. "And yes, even New York!" The biggest set of applause. "We are growing in numbers, my brothers. Our message is not only getting heard, it is getting accepted. *Believed.* We are marching towards a future where the Constitution of the United States will say that only *white* men were created equal."

"The bloody hell?" Joe murmured among the loud cheering of the room.

The applauding men turned to talk to one another. Once the heads moved, Dash could see who the speaker was up front. Lit by two lamps was the blond-haired, blue-eyed man Dash saw at Rosalie's funeral, the one who shared a look with Beverly Stevens.

Aubrey Harrington.

Dash nodded towards him and murmured to Joe, "That's the secret Rosalie wanted to tell."

They had to endure more pontifications upon the greatness of the White Man and how his place in the natural order of things was being threatened by the '*growing acceptance*' of Black men and women. Aubrey was counting on his "brothers" to contribute what they could to the cause.

"I know asking for money almost two weeks in a row

may be gauche. But those who gave the Sunday before last, we are grateful for your contributions again."

As the collection plate was being passed, Joe and Dash inched their way out of the club.

"Dash," Joe said once they were on the street and as far away as they could get from the White Rabbit. "Dash, was that the—the—"

"The Ku Klux Klan, yes, Joe, that was."

"Here?! In New York? In *Bohemia?!*"

They were walking down MacDougal towards West Fourth, occasionally glancing over their shoulders to see if they were being followed.

"And that Aubrey fella, he's one of their leaders?"

"I don't quite know where he sits in the leadership circles of the Invisible Empire, but I imagine he's got some power."

"But I thought the Fraziers were anti-Klan."

"They are. Or rather, one of them is." Dash looked at Joe. "That's why Leonard is in danger."

"Oh shite. And Rosalie found that out?"

"She must have to have told Mingus she had a secret that changed everything."

They reached West Fourth and made a sharp left.

"Aye," Joe said, "it would destroy Leonard's reputation. He could never be an influence in politics or government again."

Dash waffled his hand. "Somewhat. A house divided wouldn't be the most unheard-of thing in the world. But there's one other reason why Leonard's in danger."

"Wha?"

"Who he loves."

They decided to go to the Frazier mansion at nightfall, figuring Leonard would be working all day. It was dark when the cab dropped off Dash and Joe two blocks down. They waited until the cab was out of sight before cutting across Riverside and the neighboring park. Once they were through the trees, Dash flicked on the flashlight he got from Emmett. Joe took out the Smith & Wesson he got from Atty and nodded at him.

They carefully picked their way down the slope towards the riverside train tracks. A few slips and slides, but nothing like the fall Dash took the first time he was here.

Soon they heard the crunch of gravel. The train bed. They looked to either side for headlights from any oncoming trains. Nothing. Just darkness. The sky was even darker than usual, the clouds covering the moon and stars, and it made the air around them chilly and thick with shadow. The only sounds were the occasional distant rush of the motorcars on Riverside above them, the gentle lapping of the river next to them.

The two men glanced at one another again, nodded, and carefully went forward. Strange how two blocks on concrete felt shorter than two blocks in the foliage. They breathed in time to the crunch of their footsteps, Dash's beam of light seemingly bouncing in the air.

"Ya sure about this?" Joe whispered.

"Not entirely," Dash admitted, "but it's the only thing that makes sense to me."

"And the tunnel just . . . goes to the house?"

"It does. Empties into the storage closet."

"Clever."

"If you're a smuggler. And it seems old Aunt Bev was one."

Joe furrowed his brow. "What did she smuggle in?"

"Klansmen. And terrible, terrible ideas."

They walked a little bit farther in silence. Dash looked up to the hillside. It was hard to locate where he fell so he could determine the location of the tunnel's door. He let his flashlight illuminate the shoreline.

"There!" whispered Joe.

The rounded concrete archway. The rusted metal door.

They slowly walked towards it, Joe bringing the hammer back on Atty's gun. The hope was that no one was there, certainly not anyone from Aunt Beverly's circles.

Joe pointed to himself. He'd go in first. Dash nodded. He turned out the flashlight and waited, letting his eyes adjust to the darkness. Once they had, he gave another nod to Joe.

He was ready.

He stood on one side of the door, and Joe stood on the other. Joe reached over with his non-pistol carrying hand and pushed open the dilapidated door. The hinges squealed and groaned as the door swung inward. Dash held his breath.

No sounds coming from inside the tunnel.

No voices.

Most importantly, no bullets.

They waited a moment longer, to see if someone would come out and investigate the noise.

No one did.

Dash gazed over at Joe, who was watching him intently. An unspoken command. Forward they'd go.

Joe went in first. Dash waited a second, then followed. He closed the metal door, sealing them inside the tunnel. He turned on his flashlight and arched the beam over the walls, seeing the width of the tunnel for the first time. It was about six feet wide, the low ceiling seven feet tall, if that.

Dash looked to his right to see if Joe had to hunch down to keep from hitting his head.

That's when Dash heard the cocking of a pistol hammer. He was confused. It couldn't have been Joe's. He'd already cocked his.

Then a female voice said, "Get your hands *up*."

A flashlight to Dash's left clicked on.

Dash turned to face the beam of light. He could make out the shadowy outline of a woman, but he couldn't see the pistol. He raised his hands as instructed, his flashlight beam aimed at the ceiling.

Joe was not quite as compliant. "Who are ya, lass?"

"I'm not no lass, mister. I'm a Black woman with a gun and I swear to God, I will use it if I have to."

Dash squinted. "Madam Watkins?" He brought his flashlight down to see her face.

"Get that damn light outta my eyes," she said.

"Apologies, Madam."

"I told you *yes, sir* will do just fine." Then her voice changed. "Hey, I recognize you. You're El's secretary." Her voice went back to sharp and commanding. "What are you doing here? And you, Mister Ireland, you better put that gun away before I blow a hole through your pot of gold."

Joe slowly lowered the Smith & Wesson and, bending down, gently placed it on the ground. He slowly raised back up into a standing position, hands high.

Dash said, "Madam Watkins, it would take too long to explain but suffice it to say, Leonard Frazier is in grave danger and we're here to help him."

"What kind of danger?"

"His sister Beverly Stevens is involved with the Klan, as is her lover Aubrey Harrington. Leonard's daughter found out about them and later, she died. I don't believe it was an accident."

"Ya don't?" Joe said.

Dash shook his head. "It was murder, plain and simple, and the same thing almost happened to Leonard a few nights ago. I fear the killer will strike again."

"Why kill Leonard?"

"Because of you, Madam. Or partly because of you. Your affair got discovered. First by Rosalie, then by Beverly. When Leonard dragged Rosalie out of the Oyster House, it wasn't because he followed her there. The doorman said he waited in line. Now why would a man do that if he's just going to charge in, grab his daughter by the arm, and yank her out of there? Furthermore, he couldn't have known she left. She used this smuggling tunnel, a tunnel by all accounts, he didn't know about it. And lastly, how could he have known to go to the Oyster House once he found her missing? She'd never been there before. And he didn't see her leave."

Joe nodded, putting the pieces together himself. "Got it. He was there on his own." He looked at the millionaire. "To meet you, was it?"

"That's right, Joe," Dash said. "When Leonard walked in, first, he saw you. El told me he glanced to his left first. Stage right. Where *you* were sitting. *Then* he saw his daughter. And his daughter saw him. He couldn't very well expose your affair. He loved his daughter, but even he knew she was a loose cannon. So he played the part everyone would expect him to. The cranky bluenose trying to control a wild young woman."

Dash paused to catch his breath. So far, Madam Watkins hadn't said a word and he wasn't surprised by that.

She wasn't weak or drunk like Marty. She wasn't going to admit anything to two strange men in a darkened tunnel.

"A few other odd things," Dash said. "I found a matchbook in Rosalie's room from your hotel. A Blacks-only hotel. How did she get it? Did someone give it to her? Possibly, but then there's the comb I found in Leonard's office drawer. A C. J. Walker comb. Made by Black for Black? It's your comb, isn't it? You left it behind with Leonard. Perhaps on your rendezvous upstate? Sophie Esposito, the head maid, she told me how lonely Rosalie was when, once a month, Leonard would leave her behind. It was the only way the two of you could get together without public scrutiny. Two millionaires together would generate interest regardless of your race, but a white and a *Black* millionaire together? That would sell a huge chunk of newspapers."

Dash waited. "But it got too hard, didn't it? Especially with Rosalie acting out the way she did. So you tried meeting in the city. Just once. That night at the Oyster House. I have to say, Madam Watkins, you must have Leonard wrapped around your finger."

"Why do you say that?" The first time she spoke since Dash began laying his cards on the table.

"You got a Dry to go to a speak! With the most unusual act, to boot." Dash bowed his head in admiration. "He must . . . he must love you. To do things he'd never dare to do otherwise."

Madam Watkins watched him with a steely gaze. "What does a young man like you know about love?"

Dash flicked a look at Joe. "Not much, I'll admit. I can be quite the Dumb Dora about it, actually. But I'm learning. And I'm learning sometimes it hurts, other times it's lonely. Terrifying. Liberating. Devastating. It's never just one thing all the time, but those moments when all the doubt and fear fall away—"

"It's breathtaking in the best of ways," Madam Watkins cut in. "Alright, Mr. Secretary, you can wax poetic. And you're cleverer than a fox to put all this together from a matchbook, a hot comb, and a look across a room. But answer me this: if Leonard didn't know about this smuggling tunnel, then why did I get a note saying to meet him down here?"

At first, Dash didn't comprehend what she said.

She produced the note. "Here. Take a look at it yourself."

Dash took it and held it up to his flashlight. On the front side of the note was a message from Leonard, written in the same blocky script he saw on Leonard's papers the day he crashed Rosalie's funeral.

MEET ME IN THE TUNNEL BY THE TRAIN TRACKS JUST ACROSS FROM THE HOUSE. I NEED YOU. MINGUS IS DEAD AND I DON'T KNOW WHERE TO TURN. MY DAUGHTER AND MY FRIEND, BOTH TAKEN FROM ME. I DON'T KNOW, MY SWEET, IF LIFE IS WORTH LIVING ANYMORE. PLEASE COME. I KNOW IT'S RISKY BUT I NEED YOU. ~L

Dash turned the note over. On the back was a crudely drawn map showing how to get to the smuggler's tunnel.

"I normally wouldn't have come," Madame Watkins said, "but I never heard him like this. Losing a daughter and another friend almost at the same time? I was worried he'd— try something drastic. How could I refuse his cry for help?"

Dash nodded. His eyes went back to the paper.

Joe said behind him, "I thought Leonard didn't know about this tunnel."

"He doesn't."

Dash looked back at the crudely drawn map. It was done in the same black ink on the same cheap paper as the blind tiger codes. A terrifying rush of fear dizzied his head as he shoved the note into his trouser pocket.

"Turn out the flashlight!" He turned his off and looked at Madam Watkins, who still had hers aimed at him. "Now!" he hissed.

35

Something in his voice caused her to listen to him.

"I've still got my gun on you," she said, flicking her flashlight off.

"It doesn't need to be on us. It needs to be on who invited you here."

"Who? Leonard?"

Dash shook his head. A ludicrous gesture since in the dark, since she wouldn't be able to see it. "Not Leonard, I'm afraid."

A far-off distant creak silenced them.

They waited.

The creak turned into a groan. A door was closing.

The door to the storage closet.

How far away was it? Dash felt like he'd walked for miles when he traversed the tunnel the first time.

"Don't. Move," he muttered to Watkins and Joe.

They needed to get out of there.

A crunch of gravel.

Close by.

Dash turned his head to the tunnel's metal door.

Someone was outside the tunnel, waiting for them. Classic ambush. Whomever lured J. A. Watkins here wanted to make sure she stayed trapped.

"Did you hear that, Joe?" Dash whispered.

"Aye."

More crunches of gravel on the other side of the tunnel's metal door, then silence.

More footsteps way up ahead of them now. Someone was creeping down the tunnel from the Frazier house while a confederate—dear god, maybe *multiple* confederates— gathered outside of the tunnel.

How were they going to get out of this?

Dash whispered, "Everyone get against the walls." He then decided to put his whiteness to good use. "Hey brother," he said full-voiced. The approaching footsteps stopped. "Is she here yet?" A pause. "I didn't miss her, did I?"

A whispered male voice replied back, "Someone said they saw her come up the train tracks. Why are you in here? You're supposed to stay outside."

Dash hoped like any other organization on the planet, there would be incompetence in this one. "They told me to come in here and join you."

Another pause.

"Who did?" the voice demanded.

"Does it matter?"

"Yes, it does matter, goddammit, because someone isn't following my orders." The voice grew from a whisper to an irritated rasp. He was sounding more and more like Aubrey Harrington.

I'll bet he was the one behind the wheel of that car that almost ran over Leonard.

"Well, shit," Dash said, his rasp sounding bereaved and defensive. "How am I supposed to know if someone says to do something? They sounded like they knew what they was doing!"

"Jesus Christ, will you shut up? You'll tip her off. Look, did ya at least bring a flashlight?"

"I—I—meant to—"

"You know what, just stop. I'm gonna turn mine on so you can get your dumb ass over here. We're supposed to trap her in here."

Once he turned on that flashlight, he'd know who was truly in the tunnel with him. Dash sincerely hoped J.A. Watkins and Joe heard him and were flattened against the tunnel walls. He reached behind him, feeling for the metal door's handle.

"I'm truly sorry about this," Dash rasped, buying time. "My first time and all, and I so wanted to do this right."

"It's alright, just. Dammit, where's my light?"

Dash heard the sound of a gun being holstered, then the snap of a strap being undone. His hand found the door handle. The door would open inward, shielding him and J.A. Watkins from the confederates outside. All he'd have to do was pull at the exact right moment. Joe might be exposed — it all depended on where the men looked. He was counting on them focusing on the tunnel path ahead, not looking to the sides. His pulse pounded against his temples. They had one shot. He hoped to God this worked.

"Found it," Aubrey said.

Dash pulled the door open the moment Aubrey flicked his light on.

Dash yelled, "There she is, boys!!"

The resulting gunfire was deafening. Bullets zinged into the tunnel, bouncing off the walls. Dash stayed hidden behind the door, hoping the stray bullets wouldn't hit him.

A few bounced off the walls and plunged into the dirt just by his feet.

He looked to his left and saw Madam Watkins had flattened herself against the tunnel wall next to him. He couldn't see Joe. Aubrey was on the ground. He had been less than ten feet away from Dash.

Once the bullets ceased firing, Dash could hear excited murmurs outside. They didn't have much time. He flattened himself more against the wall, the opened door still shielding him from view.

I hope to God Joe is all right.

He also hoped Joe couldn't be seen.

Madam Watkins, still next to Dash, suddenly raised her arm, her pistol in hand. A few shuffling feet, then two shadowy forms crept into the tunnel through the doorway. Aubrey's flashlight had been thrown back, illuminating the other side of the tunnel leading towards the Frazier house.

The two men held pistols at their sides. They walked over to where Aubrey lay.

"Shit," one of them hissed. "It's Mr. Harrington!"

"What? How? Where's the—"

Madam Watkins's voice roared out. "Right here, boys."

They turned just as she fired her pistol. Two shots. They were all she needed. The two men went down, their bodies crisscrossing over Aubrey's.

The booms still echoed in Dash's ears. The acrid smell of gunpowder filled the air.

"Are there any more out there?" Watkins called out.

"If there were, they scattered," Joe shouted in return.

Dash finally closed the tunnel door so he could see, with his own eyes, that Joe was safe and sound. He turned on his flashlight and saw the sparkle of those emeralds.

Joe was unharmed. A nod of his head. "Nicely done."

"I can't believe that worked." Dash looked over to Watkins, whose gun was still in her hand, the barrel smoking. "Nice shot." He then frowned. "If you thought you were meeting Leonard here, why'd you bring a pistol?"

A baleful glare. "A Black woman going to a white part of town? Damn right, I packed it." She nodded over to Joe. "Can you make sure the coast is clear? I gotta get out of here."

Joe nodded. "Yes, sir."

With Atty's Smith & Wesson still in hand, he opened the door and went scouting in the brush and gravel.

Watkins said to Dash, "Keep my Leonard safe, all right?"

"I'll do my best."

She paused. "You're not El's secretary, are you? You do something else. Detective?"

"I own a speak down in Bohemia. El's a good friend of mine."

"And how did you get involved in this mess?"

"Leonard's daughter died in my club. I—I wanted to do right by her. See her home. See her grieved. See those responsible held accountable."

Watkins regarded him with an inscrutable look. "And are you? Going to hold those responsible accountable?"

"Oh yes," Dash said. "Yes, I will."

She nodded once to herself. "That note I gave you? Use it carefully now."

Joe came back through the door. "All clear. You need help, Madam?"

She waved him off. "I can take care of myself. I've got a driver a few blocks down who's going to take me home." She pointed her finger at Dash. "I was never here."

"And neither was I."

She nodded, turned and left the tunnel, her feet crunching gravel until they faded in the distance.

Joe looked at Dash. "Ya all right?"

He meant having seen three men get shot in one night. It was an excellent question. Three human lives lost—four, if he counted Mingus—in almost a single day. An extorter and three Klansmen. It might've sounded crass—maybe Dash's heart was beginning to callus over, he thought with alarm—but he was all right with that.

He replied to Joe, "We don't have much time. We need to get into the house."

He started off towards the other end of the tunnel, steadfastly refusing to see the crisscrossing bodies of the three men. Joe was on his heels all the way up to the secret door. He pulled it open and stepped into the storage closet. The house was shockingly quiet.

Dash crept forward in the closet, allowing Joe to step inside. They closed the door behind them. Dash led the way through the closet until they reached the hallway. He looked down the hall. No one. He and Joe tiptoed to the stairs that led up to the first floor. The gallery was empty. No sign of Beverly or Leonard or even Sophie.

They checked the sitting room, the parlor, and the library. Dash pointed upstairs. It made a strange bit of sense. If Beverly knew what Aubrey was about to do, she'd need Leonard as far away from the sounds of shots as possible.

Up the stairs, they went.

At the top of the stairs, Dash heard voices—a man's and a woman's—coming from Leonard's office.

Dash motioned to Joe with his finger. They kept silent as they traversed the hallway to the entryway of the office.

They paused at the doorway. They couldn't see either one of them, but they could hear them plain as day.

"Really, Leonard," Beverly said, "I really do think you should take some time away like Sophie. She was right to get out of this house and visit her family. First Rosalie, now Mingus. It's a horror! An absolute horror."

"Who would want to kill Mingus?" Leonard replied. "I don't understand it."

Dash strolled into the office. "I can answer that, Mr. Frazier."

36

Their mouths gaped open at the sight of them.

Leonard was seated behind his desk, whereas Beverly was in one of the leather chairs.

She demanded, "W-w-how did you get in here?"

"The tunnel," Joe replied. "Ya know about the tunnel, don't ya, Bev?"

"Would you like to tell your brother, or should we?" Dash looked hard at the murderous woman.

She faltered under his glare. "I don't have the *slightest* clue what you're talking about. Leonard, are you going to allow this?"

Leonard looked to be at his wit's end. "Mr., er, em, Bennett, was it? What have you found out with your investigation?"

"Oh, for goodness sakes, Leonard, he's not an undercover policeman! I can't believe you fell for that."

"Come now, Bev, why would he lie? Mr. Bennett? Do you and your—err—partner have any news?"

"Quite a bit, I'm afraid," Dash said, standing in between the two. "And none of it good."

"This is outrageous." Beverly made a move to stand, but Joe drew Atty's gun.

"Yer gonna stay right there," Joe growled.

Beverly blanched at the sight of the weapon. She may have given the orders to kill, but she wasn't there when it happened. Out of sight, out of mind, like getting someone else's maid fired. No frets, no mess, and certainly no confrontation.

Not like this.

"How—how *dare* you aim that wretched thing at me. Leonard!"

Dash went over to Leonard's desk. He noticed a full cup of tea on its corner. He blithely picked it up and placed it on an end table far away from Leonard.

"Did you make this for him, Mrs. Stevens? A special treat to calm him down? Cheer him up? Mr. Frazier, you might want to take that to Charles Norris's lab. He'll find traces of poison in it, I'm sure."

Leonard's eyes widened. "Poison?!"

"Yes, sir, poison," Joe said. He gestured to Beverly with the barrel of Atty's Smith & Wesson. "Seems our Bev here is quite the poisoner."

"What are you two talking about?"

"Rosalie," Dash said. "It all centers around Rosalie."

"Hello, Rosie, how's tricks," Mac the parrot responded.

Beverly muttered, "That damnable bird."

Dash smiled. "Exactly. It's this damnable bird that gave me the first clue. *She'll ruin us,* Mac said. *She'll ruin us.* I assumed—much like anyone else who might've heard him—that he was talking about Rosalie. Makes sense. Wild child constantly in the papers. In the courts even." Dash held up a finger. "But what if that's not the case? What if the *she* meant a different person?"

"Well, it's certainly not me," Beverly said.

"Quite right. But who else could it be?"

Beverly frantically searched for an answer. "Sophie perhaps?"

She really is a detestable human being, Dash thought. *Trying to cast suspicion on a maid.*

Dash shook his head. "No on that count as well. It's another woman." He looked at Leonard. "The woman you love."

Beverly frowned. "What woman, Leonard?"

"You know damn well who she is," Dash said. "It's why you tried to have her killed tonight."

Leonard stood up from his chair. "What's happened to her?"

"She is safe, sir. I promise you, she's safe. She never showed." He looked at Beverly. "Your trick with the note didn't work. She knew Mr. Frazier didn't write it. She called the police and gave it to us." He held the note out for Leonard to see first. Leonard's reaction was exactly what Dash predicted it would be.

"She was right. I didn't write this."

"However, it is your writing style. Didn't you teach your sister to write?" Wide eyes met his.

"And the tunnel?" Leonard said. "What tunnel is this note referring to?"

"Now we get back to the notorious tunnel," Dash said, taking the note back from Leonard and returning it to his pocket. "There's a smuggler's tunnel that leads from the house to the train tracks. Rosalie discovered it while exploring the house, most likely during those trips upstate you take once a month. It's how she always escaped, no matter how hard you tried to keep her safe in this house."

"The people we bought this house from never mentioned it."

"They wouldn't, sir," Joe said. "Not if they saw ya was a teetotaler. Ya'd have never bought the house otherwise if ya knew there was a smuggler's tunnel in it."

Leonard looked at Beverly. "Did you know about this?"

"Oh yes, she did," Dash answered for her. "She had several people meet in the house while you were gone, employing a technique she learned from her sister-in-law and her niece. Spycraft, isn't that the term? Secret codes, secret meanings. Rosalie loved the stuff, which was what, sadly, got her into trouble. She found your codes, didn't she, Mrs. Stevens? To be fair, your confederates weren't quite the bastions of discretion. I found their latest set of codes in the tunnel by the door." He brought one of the codes out to show both of them. "At first, I thought it was a rounded capital letter A, but it means a tunnel, doesn't it, Beverly?"

"This is preposterous," she replied.

Leonard began massaging his temples. "Who were these people? Why were they here?"

"To discuss, among other things, the Klan rally in Washington, D.C."

On cue, Mac said, "Can't goddamn march!"

Dash nodded towards the bird. "Interesting that Rosalie was overheard saying the Friday before she died, '*the answer is Washington.*'"

"Can't goddamn march!"

"The march on D.C. Apparently, they were less than impressive this year, unlike the last. You see, sir, your sister is part of the Invisible Empire."

Leonard looked from Dash to Joe to Beverly and back again. He stammered, "Y-y-you must be joking."

"I wish," he said, keeping his eyes on Beverly. "But I just

attended a speak that was filled with nothing but Klansmen, led by none other than Aubrey Harrington." He glanced back at Leonard. "We know Aubrey, don't we?"

Leonard glared at his sister. "What are you doing with him, Beverly?"

"Now this speak that held the Klan meeting, it needed a very specific code. More spycraft. This code was a teacup drawing to get into the White Rabbit." He held up the pieces of paper the Transworld Radio clerk had handed him. "The same drawing found on Rosalie's body when she was taken to Charles Norris. She found it, puzzled it, maybe even followed Mr. Harrington, and must've been horrified by what she found. Especially when—" Dash turned to face Leonard. "—she learned who you were in love with. She saw you come into the Oyster House that night. She saw you search for this woman, find her, wave to her, before you discovered your own daughter watching you. You had to act fast. This was the first time you were in public and already caught! In a speak, no less! The worst-case scenario, and you had to do something. So you pretended you followed Rosalie there and took her home. But Rosalie's smart. She knew you didn't know about the tunnel, so you couldn't have followed her. And then there was your face. Your face when you thought nobody was watching. Interesting how the truth is plain as day when we think no one we know is watching, when we're in between poses. That's why she said to herself 'so that's *what it is*.'"

"Why what is?" Beverly asked, impatient.

"Why the trips upstate."

Beverly scoffed. "That's a reach. Pure guesswork."

"I'll grant you that one. But you know what isn't guesswork? The fact that you and your confederates discussed Leonard's love affair in this room."

Leonard was rubbing his forehead now with his hands. Beverly's eyes were hot pokers.

Dash continued. "You plotted in this room to kill her. You hated this woman because of who she was. Because she was Black." He had their attention now. "Watch what happens when we say the name—"

Beverly squirmed in her seat. "No," she murmured.

"Madam—"

Mac, hearing the name for the first time since Dash walked in, automatically said, "She'll ruin us, she'll ruin us!"

"—J. A. Watkins."

"Bitch, bitch, goddamn bitch!"

Joe said in the wake of the stunned silence, "How on earth did you figure tha'?"

Dash replied, "Sophie and I kept saying words that sounded like her name." He looked at the parrot. "Watch it."

"Bitch, bitch, goddamn bitch!"

"Nice to see you, madam."

"She'll ruin us, she'll ruin us!"

Dash turned back to his captive audience. "Rosalie found out about it and she had to go, didn't she, Mrs. Stevens? And it was so easy to do. The girl drank. If she managed to drink a bad batch of booze, who would be the wiser? You knew good and well how methyl alcohol would affect her. My God, you even mentioned it at the funeral, that you tried to warn her about cheap booze, about Smoke. Now the question is, where did she drink it? Well, it wasn't at the Oyster House on Friday. It wasn't at"— Dash almost said *my club* but managed to catch himself in time—"a club on Sunday. That leaves Saturday. She was locked in on your orders, Mr. Frazier, and Mingus swore she never left the house, even by the tunnel, which he knew about and blocked with crates. So how did she drink the bad booze?"

He paused.

"Her flasks. She has quite a collection in her bedroom. And if she were to find one of her flasks with—surprise!— some booze in it, she's not going to complain or ask questions. Especially being trapped in on a Saturday night." Dash folded his arms across his chest. "That's how you did it, isn't it, Mrs. Stevens?"

"This is—how am I a multiple murderer?! All because of a talking parrot and—and—a bunch of conjecture by you."

"There's Aubrey Harrington. I'm certain if we find his garage, I'll be able to identify the car that almost killed your brother. We may even find the pistol used to shoot Mingus, who, because of gambling debts, decided to sell Aubrey's Klan secret to the highest bidder. Unlucky for him, Sophie overheard his conversation with his buyers and told you, didn't she, Mrs. Stevens? You always said she was a snoop, although this time it worked in your favor." Dash went over to the end table and picked up Leonard's hot tea. "And of course, we have this. Care to taste it, madam?"

Dash was making a blind guess that she was intending to poison Leonard that night. The worried look on her face told him he had guessed right.

"Oh? You don't want this? It smells delicious. Here," Dash said, crossing the room towards her, mug in hand. "Have a sip. You look like you could use it."

"Get that away from me, you, you *impertinent* young man."

Leonard said, "Go on, Bev."

All eyes turned towards him.

His face was gray, his eyes dark. "Take a sip."

Alarm widened her eyes. "I—I—I'm not thirsty, Leonard."

"I'll have it poured down your throat, then." His voice was getting closer to the commandeering tone he'd had the night he bought Fife's booze. He stood up.

She lunged for the mug, but Dash jerked it away from her, so she couldn't cause him to spill it. Wild eyes darted about, her hands clenched into fists. "Where's Aubrey?" she said.

Leonard gave a nasty smile. "Yes, where is that man? You said he's downstairs? Bring him up here. Let's settle this once and for all."

Dash looked at Joe. "Well, Mr. Frazier, he *is* downstairs but he's not necessarily in the chattiest of moods."

Beverly turned her head, her face whitening. "What—what's happened to him?"

EPILOGUE
ONE WEEK LATER

That damnable Pirate's Den, as Emmett would say, was just as impressive as his patrons and former waitstaff had said.

At least, Dash thought so.

It was on Christopher Street in an abandoned three-story stable. And just how Emmett described it, each floor represented a different part of the pirate ship: Main Deck, Gun Deck, and Hurricane Deck. "Jolly Roger" black flags abounded, complete with skull and crossbones. Riggings and caches covered the walls, and casks and kegs decorated corners. Only candles were used for light, which made it exceedingly hard to read the treasure maps that also functioned as menus.

Finn said, "Ooo, look at this! The Rules of the Deck!"

Joe sighed. "Finney, me boy, are ya gonna be as insufferable as our waiter?"

"Why is he insufferable? I thought he was quite polite."

"He tried to sell us his book of poetry while wearing an eyepatch and a fake gold tooth."

A week had passed since the horrible events at the Frazier mansion, and Dash decided he and his partners needed a night out. He asked where they'd like to go, and Finn insisted—no, begged, was more like it—to visit The Pirate's Den.

"Emmett will kill us if he finds out," Joe said.

"We'll tell him we're doing reconnaissance for his own theme," Dash said. "Staking out the competition." He leaned forward across the table. "What are the rules of the deck, Finn?"

"'*Any attempt to locate the hidden vaults or seize any personal property of the Pirates will be punished by loss of eyesight or imprisonment in the Black Dungeon.*'" Finn looked up from his menu. "My, my, that is quite a steep punishment. And speaking of punishment, whatever happened to that Beverly Stevens?"

"Ah!" Joe scoffed. "She folded like a napkin tha' one, once she found out her precious Aubrey Harrington was dead. Damn near confessed everything."

"Did Leonard force her to drink the tea?"

Dash shook his head. "As neat of a solution as that would be, he didn't. Leonard, unlike his sibling, isn't a murderer. He called the police and had her arrested. He did take that tea to Charles Norris, who confirmed the presence of cyanide, so at the very least, she'll be charged with attempted murder."

"How did she expect to get away with it?"

"Claim suicide. Leonard found the forged suicide note in her desk drawer. Couldn't stand the loss of his dear Rosalie after losing his wife, so he wished to join them in heaven. Since their handwriting is the same, it would look genuine."

"The one thing I still don't understand," Joe said, "is how Rosalie ended up in our club to begin with?"

"Simple," Dash replied. "The symptoms of methyl

alcohol poisoning resembles being very drunk. Difficulty thinking, walking, seeing. In her state, she mismatched the Rabbit place with ours when she got into her cab. That's why once she gave the secret knock on our door, she tried to hand the teacup drawing to Atty. And when she asked to see the mad hatter, she only got the 'hat' part out."

"And why was she going to go to The White Rabbit? To confirm her suspicions of Beverly and Aubrey?"

"Exactly. Remember when Aubrey thanked his 'brothers' for their contributions the Sunday before last? That would've been the Sunday Rosalie came to our club."

"Ah ha!"

"After they dosed her that Saturday night, ol' Bev was supposed to keep an eye on her. I'm sure she saw Rosalie's state and purposefully let the girl slip by her, who likely went out the front door because of the blocked tunnel."

"Seems awfully risky," Finn remarked.

"It was, but anyone who knew Rosalie's consumption habits would guess she'd eventually dose herself properly. And if she had the option to escape, she'd take it. Dying out in the city was preferable to her dying inside the house."

Finn buttered a piece of bread. "What was the plan for J. A. Watkins?"

"It's distasteful. They were planning to just throw her in the Hudson. *Black Millionaire Disappears*. But she'd never be tied to the Fraziers. That was of the utmost importance to Aunt Beverly."

Finn shook his head at the cruelty of it all. "But what happened to all the dead bodies in the tunnel?"

Dash furrowed his brow. "You know, I have no idea. It never hit the papers."

"Me thinks Mr. Frazier quietly got rid o' them," Joe said.

"Or paid the NYPD off. Especially when he found out there was no Max Bennett working for them."

Finn leaned forward. "You never told him your real names?"

Joe scoffed, "Are ya daft, lad?"

"But doesn't Madam Watkins know? What if she tells Leonard?"

"She won't," Dash said. "I visited El at the Oyster House to see if she got the Watkins Hotel gig. She did, by the way. And El gave me a message from Madam Watkins. Leonard indeed asked her who I was and she replied, '*a man who saved your life and that's all that matters.*' Since I kept my promise to her, she kept her promise to me."

"And all this because, what? Beverly was Klan?" Finn was being forced to yell now that the orchestra, on a freight elevator in the back of the place, had risen to their floor— excuse them, *deck.*

"Not all of it." Joe nodded to Dash. "Ya tell 'em."

"Remember how we heard at the funeral Mr. Stevens swindled the Fraziers out of the railroad deal?"

Finn gasped. "Of course! And then when the little rat died, he denied her his fortune."

"With Rosalie and Leonard gone, she'd have the entire Frazier estate all to herself. Or rather, she and Aubrey. The other Klansmen had no idea what they were up to."

Finn shook his head. "The lengths people go to for money."

"Yes," Dash said, looking at the fishnets around them. "What lengths indeed."

Dash returned to Hartford & Sons to pick up a few items before heading to the Carmine Baths. Joe said he'd meet him there. ("In the steam room," he added with a wink).

Despite the violence he'd witnessed, Dash found he was handling it quite well. Whenever he had a nightmare, whenever he felt a flash of fear, he told Joe. Without embarrassment or shame. He didn't have anything to prove. Simply being Dash Parker was enough. A strange feeling, that. Still took some getting used to.

In any event, the air was back to crackling between them, to the point that Finn was starting to complain about all the noise they were making.

"My goddess, *some* of us are barely getting by. It's been so long, I think I've forgotten how to do it."

"Don't be so overdramatic, Finn," Dash said. "Besides, I have a possible date for you."

"You do?"

"Yes. I have it on good authority that our Cherry Lane Don Juan Reggie is, uh, open to male flirtations."

Finn licked his lips. "Really?"

Now while Dash and Joe were going to the bathhouse, Finn and Reggie were locking the dressing room door.

All's well that ends well.

Even Vernon was having the time of his life with his Siamese Cat pansy. "I'm tellin' ya," he said, "she's changing my whole world, Mr. Parker!"

Calvin and Julius, of course, weren't letting him off the hook.

"Don't worry, Vern," Calvin said, "you've got plenty of time to futz it up."

Julius added, "She's gonna see you dance and know she made the wrong decision."

Dash was smiling as he walked into Hartford & Sons.

He went through the secret door to grab some cash for the baths and stepped back into the shop. He had just pulled the mirror shut when he heard his front door open. Luckily, he had closed the hunter-green curtain around the changing area, so no one could see the secret door.

"We're closed," Dash called as he opened the curtain. His smile instantly faded. "Officer McElroy."

The odious globe of a man graced Dash with his gray, humorless smile. "Mr. Parker."

"Looking for a suit? I'm afraid we've closed for the night."

"Uh huh. Seems to me you've been closed a lot lately. Family emergencies, is it? I've been watching you a lot, Mr. Parker."

"Whatever for?"

"Because I have a *very* inquisitive mind and I must say, you intrigue me. Uptown, downtown, out of town. It's almost like you're anything *but* a tailor."

"I'm late for an appointment, McElroy, so if you can just get to the point—"

"Over a month ago, you paid me to not give your address to that blond kraut fella. Remember him?"

Walter Müller. How could he forget?

"You never did tell me why."

Dash cleared his throat. "If I recall, you gave my address to him anyway, despite the fact I paid you."

"I didn't mean no offense by it. He just paid me more."

"I gave you what I could."

"I know. And it makes me wonder what you were so afraid of? Why didn't you want that man to know where you lived?"

Dash attempted a nonchalant shrug. "I don't like strangers asking questions like that."

"Ya didn't know him?"

Dash shook his head. "All I heard was a strange man wanting to know where I lived. Wouldn't *you* be unnerved if that happened?"

"Uh huh. What if I were to say I *know* you knew him?"

"Then I'd think you were drinking on the job."

"I've got witnesses. I've got proof."

Dash glanced at his watch. "I really am late—"

"I think you should cancel."

"Why?

McElroy leaned forward. "Because you and I are gonna have a little chat about that kraut fella, Walter Müller, and where he ended up . . . "

AFTERWORD

Much thanks to the many people who supported me in the developing, writing, and producing of this book: David Bishop, who patiently and lovingly endured many Author Crises of Faith and provided multiple plot suggestions; Michler Bishop for read throughs; Mary Louise Mooney for editorial suggestions; Robin Vuchnich for yet another fabulous cover; Brad Shreve and Justene Adamec of *Queer Writers of Crime* for their support of the first book and interest in the series; John Mainieri, who stopped me everyday on the street while he walked his pugs to ask how the book was coming; and our fantastic apartment neighbors for cheering me on and for providing plenty of food and libation.

This work was built from the thorough research efforts of Deborah Blum (*The Poisoner's Handbook*), George Chauncey (*Gay New York: Gender, Urban Culture, and the Making of the Gay Male World, 1880-1940*), James F. Wilson (*Bulldaggers, Pansies, and Chocolate Babies: Performance, Race, and Sexuality in the Harlem Renaissance*), and Joshua Zietz (*Flapper*). Additional thanks to the archives of the *New York Times* and *The New Yorker,* as well as to *Vintage Dancer* for info on 1920s fashion.

The referenced events in this novel—Mussolini's attempted assassination, and the KKK's two marches on Washington, their presence in NY, NJ, and PA as well as their funded Congressional candidates—are all true.

The Rosalie Frazier court case was inspired by the Eugenia Kelly case in 1915, and yes, the trust *then* was $10 million. The Frazier Mansion is loosely based on the Schinasi Mansion, and the real life house does indeed have a smuggling tunnel leading to the Hudson. The Watkins Hotel is based on the Olga Hotel, the first Blacks-only luxury hotel owned by Ed Wilson on the corner of 145th and Lenox. Mr. Wilson purchased the property with the help of his sister-in-law A'Leia Walker, the heiress of one of the first Black woman millionaires Madam C.J. Walker.

The Frazier family parrot is based on a real bird in my husband's family. The original Mac was owned by my husband's great-great-grandmother. Mac was raised on the docks and cursed like a sailor. He also truly said "Hello hello, nobody home" every time the phone rang, "Hello, Larry. How's tricks?" to the great-great-grandmother's son, and "I'm falling, Gertie, I'm falling" to the family maid, who did indeed carry the bird on the end of a broomstick. After the great-great-grandmother's death, Mac was donated to the Central Park Zoo, where he lived out his days with the canaries, because the other parrots at the Zoo were too mean to him.

The first "stag" film on record is *A Free Ride* from 1915, which currently resides in the Kinsey Institute. Heterosexual, or "straight," stag films were produced throughout the 1920s. The first homosexual "stag" film on record is *The Surprise of the Knight* from 1929. Granted that is a few years after the events of our story, but I figure a man like Nicholas Fife would be ahead of the curve.

The Pirate's Den was a real themed restaurant in the Village, right down to the fishing nets, costumed waiters, and elevator orchestra. The Village has a long history of themed, or gimmicky, restaurants. Personally, I think we need to bring this one back. Arr, ye maties!

And lastly, it is true that the U.S. government intentionally poisoned its citizens for the sake of upholding the Volstead Act. What a time, huh?

—Chris Holcombe

ABOUT THE AUTHOR

Chris Holcombe is an author of LGBTQ+ historical crime fiction. *The Blind Tiger* is the second novel in his *Hidden Gotham* series, which showcases New York's lively but criminally under-represented queer world of the 1920s.

He is also an award-winning songwriter, winning "Best Folk Song" at the 2009 Hollywood Music in Media Awards, as well as an accomplished brand strategist in marketing and advertising.

He lives with his husband in New York City, where he is hard at work on the next *Hidden Gotham* novel.

facebook.com/thechrisholcombeauthor

instagram.com/thechrisholcombe

Printed in Great Britain
by Amazon

34995984R00212